D1231499

THE RUNAWAY

THE RUNAWAY

BY
KATHLEEN NORRIS

PALO ALTO EDITION

New York
P. F. COLLIER & SON CORPORATION

BY SPECIAL ARRANGEMENT WITH
DOUBLEDAY, DORAN & COMPANY, INC.

NEW YORK

MANUFACTURED IN U. S. A.

One more book that old friendship brings to you,
One more line that will try to say
Love and thanks and all happy things to you:
Ellen and Nelson Doubleday.

THE RUNAWAY

THE FARAWAY

SARAH GIBSON was one of the fortunate women to whom life never becomes tiresome. She could be cross, she could be doubtful and disappointed and worried, and she was often tired. But hers was a heart that awakened every fresh day to a sense of excitement and satisfaction. Her alarm clock always rang too soon, arousing her from deep dreamless slumber, but the moment she was on her feet life seized upon her with a thousand plans and prospects, and she welcomed them all.

The creak of the old back stairs as she somewhat heavily descended them to the kitchen, the thunder of the children's voices and feet above her, the feel of the dew-wet newspaper when she picked it up from the side porch, the good scent of coffee and fresh toast, the cat yawning and stretching with a cat's invariable morning cry of reproach and self-pity, all these things satisfied some need of Sarah's, deep in her soul, and never grew stale or uninteresting to her.

Sometimes there was snow on tops of the mountains a few miles away from her windows, and she looked at it with appreciation. "I declare, I do love snow, now and then!" she would say to herself. Sometimes it was only frost, with the cold winds of a California mountain winter blowing the children's shabby toys about the yard, rattling branches, fluffing up the feathers of the offended and uncomfortable poultry. Sometimes summer brought blazing days to her seven o'clock kitchen, and she and Anita drew shades and watered down the porches and the yard. But loveliest of all, and lingering longest of all, were spring and autumn; the thrilling clear season when lilacs rustled and grass spurted in emerald everywhere, when larks swooped down and pear trees lifted pale green turrets against blue skies, or the mellower, softer days when the air thinned to crystal, and the trees were red, when apples and persimmons and pumpkins were ripe, and through the hazy blue mountains drifted the smell of brush fires.

And these were the times when Sarah's heart sang within her, and her round healthy face wore a look of complete felicity from morning until night. She liked the part in which life had cast her; she played it to the full. No Hollywood actress ever enjoyed an exquisite wardrobe more than Sarah enjoyed her crisp ginghams, her old velvet for winter evening wear, and the new flowered georgette gown, in a comfortable size forty-four, that, with a wide, flower-wreathed hat, she bought every spring for church and club wear.

Her world was a world of small incessant services eagerly, enthusiastically, incessantly rendered. It was not a wide world, but she would not have exchanged it for any other known to man. She planned meals, she cooked meals, she did ingenious things with leftovers; she fussed with lamps and bathtub faucets and boys' shirts; she fed chickens, watching them sharply as they pecked and gabbled and jumped senselessly into the air over the battered old pan; she mothered all the dogs and cats that the boys brought home.

The pivotal point in her scheme of life was of course Spencer Gibson. A gray, quiet, kindly man of fifty, whose entire business life was spent in the oil-scented, coffee-scented, wheat-scented atmosphere of the town's big hardware, grocery and general store, the Middle Valley Exchange. Spencer was to her everything that a husband and father should be. He settled her problems, listened to her daily tales of affairs domestic, read her important items from the paper at night, adored his children, paid his bills and thought "Mom" the most important and admirable person alive.

They had five children. Rebecca, the one daughter, was nineteen. The boys followed at some distance; Robert was fourteen, Spin twelve, Andy nine, and Gary just short of six. They had come to the San Joachim Valley when Becky was a baby; all the children's remembered lives had been spent here in the little town that perched at the foot of the great mountains.

Salletts had been a mining town seventy years earlier; the great shafts and the blackened buildings of the mine, and enormous heaps of stones dredged out of the Plumitas, still fenced off the eastern boundary of the town. Now it was a rich agricultural center with olive, grape and orchard interests, and enough pasturage for occasional cows and plow horses. Like every other California town it had a handsome grammar school and a beautiful new Union High, the latter built like an enormous hacienda, with arcades and cloisters and tiled roofs to set off the adobe walls and the drooping eucalyptus trees and widespread oaks of its great yard.

Spencer Gibson had come to Salletts to buy a farm. He and his wife with the bright-headed little girl had looked the place over with an intent to criticize and compare it with other possible locations. But their instant capitulation had furnished them with an inexhaustible family joke. They had criticized nothing; from the moment of their descent from the train, their first look at the sleepy beauty, the peace and prosperity and comfort of Salletts, they had been reduced to a trembling fear only that they might not be able to live there, that money could not buy what they saw with their own eyes before them. The eastern line of blue, high mountains, trembling in gauzy faintness against the sky, the fruit trees wheeling away from the town in every direction like lines of soldiers—as indeed they were in a hungry world—the oak-shadowed plain farmhouses with their windmills and barns and fences, the wide pool where the Plumitas joined the Sacramento, and where children happened to be splashing and shouting on the day the Gibsons arrived, all were so many arguments against every other place, every other climate, every other consideration.

Hardy Summers, real estate agent, had thought they might like to see the old Foster place. Real pretty place; kinder run down. They had liked it—dubiously. Four hundred acres was a good big place, especially as practically none of it was under cultivation.

On the way home they had chanced to pass the Walldrew ranch and its big sign: "Desirable Home Property. Self-supporting. Inquire Hardy Summers, Main Street, Salletts."

"Oh, Spence!" Sarah Gibson had said. And she had repeated it breathlessly for the next hour and seventeen minutes, and by that time they had owned the Walldrew place. Hardy said surprisedly that he hadn't known they wanted to go as high as seven thousand; he could shave that, he thought, to six thousand seven hundred and fifty, but the Foster place was a better buy, if a feller wanted to work it, for three thousand.

The Walldrew ranch, to be known as the Gibson ranch from now on, boasted a comfortable old white house with electricity and bathroom already installed; it had a garden, neglected but quite capable of being saved; it had barns and chicken houses and a pig pen and a home orchard, and it had forty acres in apples and pears. There was a spring on the place, a rare advantage in California, and a windmill; sixty Plymouth Rocks and two Jerseys were actually there, and to be included in the price of sale. Spencer, who knew nothing of farming, had looked wisely at the machinery that was nicely stored in one of the barns; Sarah, who knew everything about chickens, had gone to the Exchange that very afternoon to buy wheat and bone meal.

She had been happy all her life; she would always be happy. But this afternoon stood out in her memory as one of ecstasy. In the big store, with its hundred-foot frontage on Main Street, women had been marketing for bread and sausages and sunbonnets and needles; awkward big men, down from the lumber camps and packing plants, had been buying high oiled boots with long leather thongs for laces, and blue jeans, and canned salmon. A neighborly, a friendly atmosphere had prevailed in the big dim place. Sarah had come straight from a cramped flat in Brooklyn; she had dreamed of high mountains and cowboys, and chickens of her own to feed. They were all here, at Salletts. She had looked at egg beaters and blue-striped ticking bungalow aprons and thought that she must buy them all; she must go back to the Walldrew place and see what was needed in her kitchen. She had stooped in the shadowy store and laid her face against Rebecca's little cheek. "Oh, Becky, we're going to have such fun!" she had exulted.

And it had been fun—the exciting fun of a woman's fulfilled life, of her satisfied heart, ever since.

Sarah was country bred; she took naturally to farmyard and farm-kitchen activities. On the two hundred acres of the Gibson ranch there was a little tenant house, and when Spencer's qualifications proved to be clerical rather than agricultural, he had seized the chance to buy in at the Exchange, and Sarah had capably established a good Swedish farmer and his rosy-cheeked wife, Anita, there. They managed the ranch; Spencer did well with the store, and Sarah supervised them all.

Her sons had come along in regular order; big, tumble-headed, noisy boys who grew broad as they grew tall, and delighted and a little scared her with their violence, their strength, their independence, their achievements. They had guns in their hands at five; they were somehow on top of the farm horses at six; and at nine Bob could leap into the tin-can open green car that was always spattered with mud when it was not inch deep in dust, and rattle into town for mail or for baking powder with all the confidence in the world. They went hunting, fishing, hiking; they dug caves and stifled tnemselves with smoke, and built tree houses and broke their arms and legs falling out of them. They had poison oak over scratches, and sunburn under both; they killed rattlers and brought them home dead yet mysteriously wriggling, to horrify their mother and cause gentle blonde Anita to lock herself in the pantry.

Rebecca was different. Where her brothers' black hair and red cheeks and blue eyes made them striking, she was a creature of one color: honey-colored hair with gold lights, brown eyes that could look gold in shadow, brown soft skin all one delicate tan shade. Her lashes were dark gold; her wide mouth the only line of contrast anywhere.

She was tall, strongly and broadly built, with beautifully modeled chin and shoulders and line of young breasts, with narrow hips and fine ankles and wrists. Her forehead was low and broad, her eyes and cheekbones set well apart, and her mouth, if too large, full of humor and sensitiveness. There was a healthy down on her cheeks, so that a light fuzz could be detected when one saw them against a strong light. At nineteen she was health, vigor, high spirits, restless youth itself personified; clumsy, fastidious, moody, amusing, dull, keen in rapidly alternating moods. Sometimes she knew despairs that bewildered her mother; sometimes through a whole hot Saturday morning, when she had washed dishes and washed dish towels, washed her soft tawny hair, hosed the side porch, Sarah would hear her singing like a lark under the oaks and maples of the back yard, her brothers shouting and whistling as they pursued a hundred holiday chores around and about her.

She had fads, this Rebecca Gibson, and pursued them with energy, if only briefly. When younger she had gone in heavily for Persian kittens, and a modest sign on the gate had advertised that they were for sale. Then she had raised berries, writing the government bureaus in Washington for directions, working hard throughout summer vacations between the long fierce trailers of the vines. Rebecca had almost two hundred dollars in the bank as a result of this fifteen-year-old venture. The squab experiment had followed the berries, but that had not been a success. The noise of the pigeons and the inevitable dirt had discouraged even cheerful Sarah. Later poetry had engrossed Rebecca, and she would have bored the family with Patmore and Emily Dickinson if her own sparkling enthusiasm had not made it extremely difficult for her to bore anyone.

She collected bowls and frequently made her supper fastidiously from a blue bowl filled with crisp crackers and creamy milk. She liked certain small eccentricities in dress, rarely wearing a hat; affected certain niceties of pronunciation. For a time she would arise early for a two-mile walk before breakfast, or try a diet of scraped raw carrots and hard brown bread. Rebecca found dishes, games, ideas in the backs of magazines and tried them on the family; she read up on plays and spoke of them as familiarly as if she had attended their opening nights on Broadway.

Full of youthful affectations, yet she admitted their absurdity so frankly and entertained the family so enormously with her eager pursuit of them that she was not only forgiven but adored by everyone at home. Sometimes she was the model daughter, helping Robert, Spin and Andy with their homework, helping to spoil Gary, the latest born, helping everywhere, her mother's delight. Sometimes she appeared to transfer her interests and affections to some zone to which the others could not follow her, becoming abstracted, mournful, vague, talking mysteriously of "plans."

Whatever they were, she never explained them if indeed they had form at all. She would presently emerge from the vapors and begin to laugh and sing, to practice scales passionately, to pack picnic baskets again. For like most Californians who live outside of the immediate cities, the Gibsons liked to have many of their meals in the open air. The children of the family need go no further than the windmill, a hundred yards from the house, to enjoy the full pleasure of a basket lunch or supper.

CHAPTER II

IT WAS on a languid, heavily sweet March afternoon that Rebecca and her mother had a certain talk in the kitchen. It began casually enough, like many of their talks, but the girl was to remember it many months later with strangely mixed emotions.

Rebecca taught a kindergarten group in the public school. Her share of teaching, as Miss Patton's chief assistant, consisted principally of superintending games and walking back and forth keeping order in the schoolroom as the children perspired and panted over cut-out tulips, cardboard ships, tissue-paper tassels and odorous putty. When there was a display for the Mothers-Teachers group Rebecca helped the children arrange the exhibitions in the auditorium passage; when there was a cut or a bruise she painted it rose-red; when there was nosebleed or nausea she was the one to telephone the sufferer's mother and sit stanching the blood or sponging the pale little face until maternal succor arrived.

Her pay was fifty-five dollars a month; she had Saturdays and Sundays at home, and by her associates, who worked in the bank or the post office or filled secretarial posts, she was considered fortunate. But Rebecca did not always consider herself fortunate.

"Mother," she said on this particular afternoon, "would you like me to marry Joe Feratta?"

Sarah Gibson was scraping cold artichokes for a salad. The soft, breeze-filled, scent-filled day had been unseasonably hot. Now at five o'clock the sun was at last close to the sum-

mit of the faraway western hills; shadows were falling over
the flowering orchards; the great oak dropped a round disc
of cool shade. Mother and daughter were at a table on the
side porch, Rebecca frankly idle and panting with heat,
Sarah's face finely beaded with perspiration as she worked.

Surprised at the question, the older woman looked up with
a little change of color. Rebecca saw that her mother paled,
and laughed in a little confusion.

"That came right out of a clear sky, didn't it?" she said.
"But I've been thinking of Joe all afternoon. He came to
school today at the two o'clock recess."

"And asked you to marry him?"

"Well—in a way, yes. He was all agog because Judge
Miller's taken him into the firm and put him on the Miglia
case. Joe speaks beautiful Italian, you know."

Mrs Gibson was interested and pleased.

"Well, for pity's sake!" she said. "I think that's very
much to Joe's credit, I really do. He's a smart boy. He isn't
but twenty-four, is he, Becky? I think that's very much to
his credit. I'll see his mother at the club tomorrow and con-
gratulate her. And he speaks Italian, does he?"

"Well, Mother, why wouldn't he, with his father and
grandfather right from—wherever it was? Italy, anyway."

"That ought to help him a lot with his law practice, Beck;
there are so many of them around here. Italians, I mean."

"Well, exactly," Rebecca said in an odd, abstracted tone.

"If he's going to practice here, that is?" her mother added,
looking up. The girl roused herself from dreams with a start.

"Oh, he's going to practice here," she said in a faintly
ironical tone. "His father's giving him a slice of the ranch,
just as he did Gory and Lucy when they married. Lucy and
Buck Williams are going to build an awfully pretty Spanish
place there. I told you I saw the plans when I was in the
library the other day? Holman did them; they're beautiful.
And Joe gets the canyon strip with the redwoods, because

Lucy wanted to be where she wouldn't have to drive up hills; she hates hills."

"Well, the Ferattas are awfully nice people, Becky. They've been here from the beginning, and I don't know any citizen of Salletts that's more respected than Gregorio Feratta. And a little money doesn't hurt, dear, when you're getting started."

"You don't sound very enthusiastic, Mother."

"Well, I would be, Beck, if *you* were! But somehow I don't feel you're in love with Joe, for all he's so handsome and nice," Mrs Gibson said, a little troubled.

Rebecca was silent for a moment while her mother's busy knife steadily scraped the soft green pulp and the hot day died slowly in a glory of fragrance. The yard was big and irregularly shaped, rising toward the barns on the east, beaten flat under the trees between the paddock fence opposite and the orchards that stretched away to the north, and bounded by the house and the berry bushes and the garden on the south. The last lances of light were falling across the lilacs and the new sprays of banksia roses now, and laying trim shadows under the white-painted trunks of the fruit trees. Chickens were sauntering toward the shed; Robert Gibson, tall, black of hair and eyes, ungainly, young, attractive in old jeans, a blue shirt open at his dark throat, came down from the barns with two pails of milk. Little Gary, also dark, clad in faded jeans, like a small edition of his brother, admiringly accompanied him. Gary adored Bob; Rebecca called him the big boy's "pilot fish."

When the boys had disappeared into the springhouse, where the milk pans were ranged on long shelves, Sarah returned to the conversation.

"And Joe wants you to marry him, does he? You seem so young, Becky."

"He always has," Becky said simply. It was true. Big dark clever Joe Feratta had not looked at another girl since that night, now six years ago, when Rebecca Gibson had taken the part of "California" in the grammar-school pageant. Surrounded by her satellite counties, seeming to float in her diaphanous robes of varicolored pale chiffons, her browned young face very earnest, her aureole of soft tan hair standing out in a cloud under her gold crown, her great blue train sweeping the floor in a wide circle, Becky had walked straight into ardent Joe's heart, and through years of study, through the strain of bar examinations and the loneliness of exile from home, he had dreamed of no one else than "the little Gibson kid."

Now she was grown, graduated, teaching kindergarten, very busy with that bunch of fresh kids, very serious when she told Joe about her work and her ambitions, completely charming in her own home circle, with her brothers teasing and spoiling her, and always beautiful. The pale browns of her, the red wide line of her gipsyish, enchanting, laughing mouth were always before his eyes.

"He always has wanted to marry me," she told her mother now simply. "And that would mean," Becky went on slowly, "living up on the Feratta place. May and Gory 'll have children, and Lucy and Buck 'll have children, and I'll have children. Nice little black-eyed children with curls, whose grandpa is one of the big vineyardists of the state. Every Sunday we'll have a big two o'clock dinner of chicken and red wine and macaroni——"

"Well," her mother said mildly as she paused, "there are harder lives than that, Beck. You'd have to search the world over to find a lovelier place than Salletts. And if old man Feratta built for Joe, as he has for the others, you'd have an awfully nice house, with two baths—at least Lucy's going to have two baths, her mother was telling me, and a refrigerator and an electric automatic hot water heater and everything. Holman's going to build Lucy's place, and he'd probably do yours. You could have a lovely Spanish house up there with patios and fountains and everything." She stopped on a wistful note.

Becky spoke reluctantly, thoughtfully. "You'd like me to, wouldn't you, Mother?"

"Well, I don't think there's a nicer boy in town than Joe," Sarah Gibson said hesitatingly. "There isn't a girl here that wouldn't jump at him. And of course Daddy and I would love to have you near us. It seems better than teaching on and on for years like Miss Beattie and Miss Pierce, I should think."

"It certainly does," Becky agreed with fine irony.

"Certainly Alan Ridley . . . or Cyril . . ." her mother offered dubiously.

"Ha!" Becky ejaculated, and was still.

"But you just don't feel that you could love Joe?" Sarah ventured after a pause.

"Mother," Becky began decidedly, bringing her attention back from some faraway consideration that had abstracted it for a moment, "here it is: Joe is a darling, he'd always be good to me, and work hard, and eat and drink a little too much, and like to sleep Sunday afternoons with his collar off, and want all his children to be boys—I know Joe, I know all that about him! If I happened to displease his mother, or if his father thought I was too slight for the job— I hear he likes big fat girls like Minnie—then Joe 'd always stand up for me and be kind to me. If we couldn't have children he'd feel he was a martyr, and his mother 'd feel that it was a judgment for marrying a girl of another faith, but he'd go right on buying me what I wanted—a new car, a trip to San Francisco with him to hear *Rigoletto* and *Trovatore*—his father says that Germans can't write music. I'd have a position in the club; I'd be one of the Ferattas—very important. And so what—and so what—and so *what?*"

She put her tawny head down on the table for a moment,

and her mother, troubled and surprised, imagined that she was crying. But when Becky raised her head her eyes were bright and dry.

"Now I'll tell you," she went on, speaking with a sort of angry desperation that was yet quiet and controlled. "I want to live *my* life, not Joe Feratta's life or old Gregorio Feratta's life. I want to go to cities, and run around them in the rain, and see the lights of big opera houses and hotels, and work and worry, and fall in love and make mistakes and *live*—not *vegetate!* I want to do—dangerous things, in villas on the Mediterranean and hotels in London—— What's the matter?"

She interrupted her rhapsody with the sharp inquiry. Sarah was staring at her with an odd frightened expression on a face that had suddenly grown pale.

"What is it, Mother?" Becky repeated, alarmed.

"Just . . ." Sarah's voice had dried in her throat. She spoke with difficulty. "Just that that's a silly way to talk, Becky," she said.

"Mother, why it is silly to want something better than Salletts?" the girl demanded passionately.

"Because it—it makes me nervous," her mother answered with what for her was an unwontedly agitated and reproachful manner.

"I could take care of myself," Becky stated simply. She looked away with narrowed eyes.

"It isn't that. It's that there's nothing but disappointment and—and trouble for you out in the world. Here you have peace and sunshine and fruit and friends and the river—everything, everything. And if you married—I don't say Joe, but anyone, anyone, someone you loved, of course—you might have children, you might have as happy a life as any girl in the world! Think of the Eastern climate, Becky, and the slums, and the poor little children in the slums——"

"I do," said Becky in the pause, "and I want to see them.

I want to be one of them! And I want to be rich, to go to those shops that advertise in the smart magazines, and have a fur coat, and have some stunning man with tons of money——"

She stopped short again, amazed. For Sarah had risen to her feet and was speaking with colorless lips. She spoke breathlessly, sternly.

"I don't want you ever to talk that way again, Becky. It's wicked. You don't know what you're talking about, you don't know what misery—what utter misery might be waiting for you out there, or how—how helpless you would be if once you got into it! For God's *sake*——"

The last words were a prayer. Sarah, her back turned now as she carried her pans and bowls into the kitchen, said them half to herself. Becky sat on at the table, staring bewildered after her. What on earth was the matter?

When she presently went in to the kitchen her mother was quietly busy with the usual dinner preparations. But she was not yet herself. She was nervous and pale, continually returning to the present, to answer the boys or continue her operations, with an air of awakening herself from some painful dream.

Except for this, however, dinner proceeded as usual, and it was only after dinner that a phrase or two, seemingly meaningless at the time, was overheard by Becky as she straightened spice boxes and cereal jars in the big dim ranch-house pantry. Her second brother, Spin, was outside in the dusky yard under the window, feeding the dogs; Becky heard her mother speak to him.

"Spin, what made you ask that at dinner tonight?" Sarah's tone was sharp with anxiety.

"Ask what?" Spin's big rough voice asked in return.

"About where Daddy got his money."

"I don't remember. Oh yes!" Spin's tone was surprised. "Well, I—gee, I don't know," he answered bewilderedly;

"some of the fellers at school were talkin' about Salletts real estate, and they asked what Dad paid for this place. I said I didn't know. But I was rememberin' what you said about you and Dad startin' in on twenty dollars a week———"

"Beck didn't suggest it?" Sarah asked swiftly, in an undertone.

Becky, unseen in the pantry, heard her own name at this point and rattled some tins, drowning out further eavesdropping. Though a little puzzled, she thought no more of the matter at the time.

But later, when she was in bed, the little episode came back to her and connected itself with unerring instinct with her earlier conversation with her mother in the afternoon. She had said she wanted to go away, to live dangerously, independently, to taste riches and poverty and love, and her mother had looked ready to faint, and had assumed a most unusual tone of sharpness and anxiety in answering her. And afterward her mother had interrogated Spin as to an innocent question at dinner . . .

Well, what had Spin asked? His father had been suggesting to Andrew, the third son, that he content himself with the cheaper seats at the movies; he and his wife, Dad had said, hadn't had much money for loge seats when they had married. Twenty dollars a week didn't leave any room for luxuries . . .

"But then how'd you ever come out here and buy this place?" Spin had asked, interrupting his father's mild complacent moralizing. What had Dad answered? Becky tried to think. Had he glanced swiftly and apprehensively at Mother as he did so? She distinctly remembered that he had. They hadn't enlarged on the matter, but how had the subject been changed? Dad had said: "Oh, I had a streak of luck," and Mother had said instantly: "Mrs Bates came over today with Margie's baby."

And then later Mother had asked Spin if Becky had put

him up to asking that question. Why should Becky do anything of the sort? To want to go away for adventures, and the point of Dad's having somehow been able, on an income of a thousand a year, to buy a seven-thousand-dollar piece of property and improve it—what was the connection between them?

Well, what? It came out nowhere. Becky was still puzzling over it when she dropped off to sleep.

CHAPTER III

SALLETTS' Main Street ran for five blocks from northeast to southwest, and contained all the important stores in town. There were small negligible shops on the side streets, straggling up toward the hospital and library and churches; pale little bakeries, exhausted embroidery shops with curling cards announcing fiestas and concerts in their windows; second-hand furniture stores with stained, dusty davenports and old iceboxes on the sidewalk; second-class groceries whose jumbled windows of cans and potatoes and cigarettes were in startling contrast to Main Street's beautifully banked displays of ranged brilliant fruits and vegetables.

The motor agencies were on back streets too, and the big corner lots where secondhand cars were sold, and many of the gas stations. But Salletts' shopping district, the dignified stores with plate-glass windows and attractive displays that were changed every Thursday night, were all on Main.

Rebecca Gibson knew them all by heart. A new shop starting up was an object of deep interest to her and her friends, and before the merchant and his stock had time to move in they were completely aware of what he had to sell and what he meant to ask for it.

The girls loitered on winter and autumn afternoons at Cunningham's, whose simple window announcement was "Frocks." They liked it better than the A La Mode, which had gone rather cheap, gone in for bungalow aprons at one ninety-eight, and windows full of hats, "Your Choice, One Dollar." Long hours of their lives, bored, amused, escorted

17

by beaus or linked arm in arm with each other, were spent on Main Street.

They were interested in Dobney's shoe shop, where some of the nice boys worked for a while before finding more dignified jobs, and Agnes O'Donnell's Le Parisien hat store. Old Miss Agnes was always nice to them, and let them try on her stock as much as they liked. Puckers', which was frankly a slop shop, with blue jeans waving like a fringe at the doorway and great smelly unvarnished shoes jumbled into tubs along the sidewalk, sold hats upstairs too, but the girls only went to Puckers' for barn-dance costumes, or great straw hats for picnics, or such odd things as bandanas, or flannels for old men in the poorhouse, or coon traps, or old-fashioned slates bound in red cloth. Everything that was not sold at the five-and-ten or the hardware store could be found at Puckers': cotton stockings to be dyed red for the pageant every May, wigs, long iron chains, secondhand blue-flame stoves.

Then there were a bakery, two or three chain stores, two banks, a movie house, a haberdashery, the new post office, brave in granite columns and wide shallow steps; the furniture store, with "Undertaker" modestly lettered under "Everything for the Home Beautiful" on the window; the delicatessen store whose strong pickled odors and foreign wares supplied a pleasantly exotic note to the block; the tailor, with uninteresting strips of woolen material pasted to cards in his window; the telegraph office, always necessarily so bare and dull; the State Commission Bureau, with mammoth preserved pears in glass jars on display between chunks of quartz and smooth slabs of polished redwood.

Also two real estate agents and three drugstores. Three of them, for every woman among Salletts' more than two thousand women had to buy powder and cold cream regularly. And, well placed on the town's most important corner, the two-hundred-foot-square building of the Middle Valley Exchange, the pioneer shop of them all, beloved by everyone and trusted by all the ranchers and country folk to give them a fair deal, supply them with the boots, guns, canned beans, raw beans, oil cake, seed, potatoes, lanterns, chicken feed, guns, fishing poles, baby bottles, arnica, root beer, tents, household stoves, currycombs they wanted at an honest price.

On the second floors along Main Street—and few buildings boasted more—doctors, dentists, quacks, dressmakers, photographers, agents of all sorts flourished and expanded, or languished and disappeared, as their fates decreed. Rebecca Gibson watched them; she had watched them all her life long.

She knew the three hotels intimately, to the point of screaming boredom. The new Sierra Grande, the old Imperial, the quite disreputable Cosmopolitan, where there had once been a murder. It was all typically small-town; it was all Salletts; she was sick of it all.

Sick, sick, sick of it all! Sick of meeting the people she knew in the Exchange; grinning tall men from the mountain mines, smug townswomen who asked: "How's Mamma?" and clucked: "That's good" in a breath, who wanted to recall their tiresome offspring to one: "You remember Jean and Peggy? Weren't they the little tads when you had them —dear me, it seems such a short time ago!"

❧ CHAPTER IV ❧

On a certain spring afternoon she went to the Exchange on an errand for her mother, to wander with her basket along the shelves; opening the big icebox to take out a box of butter, looking at her list: cinnamon, crackers, ice-cream salt, coffee. And after the ice-cream salt Mother had thoughtfully written: "Tell Daddy to bring home."

Oh, God, with everything going on in the world—girls signing movie contracts, girls and men meeting at restaurant tables in scintillating cities, women buying steamship tickets, riding on the tops of London omnibuses, looking at pictures in the Louvre—she must be here in the Middle Valley Exchange at Salletts listening to the idiot Fessey boy explain that a blue cup or saucer went with every pound of Toxman's coffee!

"What good's the cup without the saucer, Leo?"

"Well, two pounds for forty-four, and you get both. Plain, but it makes a swell little souvenir," said Leo, sounding, as he always had sounded at school, as if he ought to blow his nose.

Perhaps Gemma O'Donnell, Agnes' niece, would call to her from the collar counter:

"Listen, Beck, Aunt Agnes has just got in some swell Easter models. One looks just like your blue linen. New York copies, you know."

Of course, of course. New York copies. Everything was a New York copy. Agnes O'Donnell's copies would undoubtedly startle New York more than New York would

startle Agnes. Copies, to Agnes, were just as smart as the
originals. "Dressy" was Agnes' word. It's real dressy on
you.

Rebecca Gibson Feratta would never see New York. Or if
she did she would be a stout, macaroni-nourished woman of
forty with three big black-browed children at home: Maria,
Gregory, Joseph. New York would mean nothing to her
then. She would not thread its crowded streets, hungry perhaps, certainly shabby and anxious, but thrilling to great pos-
sibilities. The job, the money, the new chance, the potentiali-
ties of tomorrow and the day after tomorrow! These would
not stir her blood then. No; she would be complaining to Joe
that none of the pretty dress models came in size forty-four,
and telephoning to California after nine o'clock at night,
when rates were reduced, to ask about Grandpa's stroke.

All right, if that were one's fate. But it was dull. Dull and
hard to shut one's dreams and hopes and ambitions into some
little airless chamber of the soul where they must starve for
want of light and food. Perhaps, if young Mrs Joseph Harrison Feratta hammered them down hard enough and long
enough, they would die, and she become the happy and con-
tented wife and mother she ought to be. Joe would have as
much of a career as Salletts could afford. He would never go
away because he shared with his Italian-born father and
American mother a firm conviction that everyone who did
not live in this rich valley below the California Sierras was
unfortunate or a fool. In four hours you could be in San
Francisco, if you wanted to see a surgeon or a play or a ship,
but Joe's philosophy had little to do with any of the three.
He loved the open vineyards and the woods that rose up to
the mountains where he hunted deer, and the smell of brush
fires and ripening prunes and pepper trees, and Mamita's
house with its pervading odors of musk and of garlic and
onions frying in good olive oil, and the kitchen and the closed
parlor where there were bunches of sweet grass and trembling

grass, and enlarged photographs on tasseled easels of Joe's dead brother and sister, Benito and Teresa.

Joe was a smart lawyer; he might go in for politics sometime, especially if he had a wife to spur him on. District attorney or state senator. "Keep in Office Joseph Feratta, Incumbent!" She could see the cloth sign swaying over Main Street before some future election. But even that—even that wouldn't be *her* life! She'd be just Joe's wife, sitting beside him on the platform at rallies, saying, "I'm proud of you, Joe," when the returns came in.

But of course it all came back to this: she did like Joe. She didn't love him because she never felt for him that rush of sheer adoration that she had felt for Claire de St Lorier. Claire's mother, hoping to cure some lung ailment, had lived near Salletts when Claire had been seventeen and Becky fourteen. They were Eastern people, the De St Loriers, and Claire had played the violin at a church concert.

Oh, what a moment when the slender girl, half smiling, glancing from the expectant audience to the strings of the instrument she had been tuning, had first come to the platform! Mrs Forest, fat and nervous and turning down the corners of sheets of music anxiously, had been at the piano in her ruffled organdy; Claire had looked a very lily beside her. There had been no printed programs. Chuck Leonard, announcing, had mumbled the name: "A newcomer to Salletts. Miss Dersannlerear." Afterward Becky learned that Claire had whispered the name to poor Chuck, and he had done his best with it.

She had met Claire, had gone into a trance of floating ecstasy, had lived for three dizzied, chilled, fevered, intoxicating months on Claire. Claire had been staying at the King place, eight miles away, and quite out of Salletts' familiar zone. The Kings had affiliations with social San Francisco and Burlingame; they had little to do with the country round about. Yet Claire more than once had asked Becky to come out and have tea with her, and Becky had gone out on the bus and been driven back to town by one of the Kings' hands. Claire had been lonely; there had been no other young person staying at the house, and the two girls had formed a friendship unbalanced by Claire's cool, sweet superiority and seniority and Becky's uncontrollable adoration. Becky on these occasions had hardly been able to speak for her eagerness to listen to Claire, to make great eyes of helpless love at everything Claire said.

She had bored her mother mercilessly about Claire.

"And, Mother, she has the sweetest way of looking at you when you say anything funny; she thinks about half the things I say are funny, and she looks at me—honestly, Mother, with the *sweetest* look! Oh, Mother, I wish I could play the piano; I could accompany her! She speaks German— she's lived in Germany. Imagine. And two men want to marry her, but she doesn't want to marry anyone because she says all she cares about is for her mother to get well!"

And then one day it had been:

"Mother, why am I so utterly miserable when I'm away from Claire, and why does it make me just tremble if I hear her voice or see her?"

"Well, you're a little bit in love with her," Sarah had explained it simply.

"Oh, but, Mother, no! Not with a *girl!*"

"Well, it's something of the same feeling, Becky. Being in love is an uncomfortable sort of thing—not like love. Love is the most wonderful thing in the world. But being in love —yes, that's the sort of feeling."

It had been a relief to Sarah when Claire disappeared from the scene, and Rebecca had returned rapidly to normal.

But Rebecca still remembered the keen emotions of the Claire episode, the exquisite excitement of dressing herself in her best and taking the bus ride out to Kings' ranch, the tremendous moment of meeting Claire, the trembling joy of talking to her and seeing her pale gold hair and blue eyes, her delicate hand on a perfumed handkerchief, the expressions of her face as she said: "I'm getting so lazy about practicing. Rebecca, you're so pretty in that blue. Ça va sans dire—— You don't understand that! Forgive me."

And she knew today, so many years later, that such a thrill as she had felt in Claire's company, augmented by her increased age, her knowledge of manhood and womanhood, might have made her engagement to the right man a thing intoxicating, bewildering, all-absorbing. What she felt for Joe was not that. She felt liking and admiration and confidence and a certain girlish pride in his passion.

Nevertheless she was shyly pleased at the loyal and affectionate interest that both families felt when the great secret of her engagement to Joe was somehow made known a few weeks later. There was no announcement, yet in a hundred ways the little town gave a favorite son and daughter its hearty congratulations upon the suspected state of affairs; on all sides Rebecca heard praises of Joe, and among her intimates expressions of satisfaction that he was so fortunate, and she doing so well for herself.

On a certain Sunday Rebecca went with Joe to dinner at his father's house. She had been there before, but not often, not easily. There was an indefinable atmosphere of strain at the Feratta dinner table when she was there. A Gibson wasn't an Italian, wasn't a Catholic, she didn't belong.

Gregorio Feratta was enormously heavy, hearty and hospitable enough, but suspicious with the suspicion of the simple, absorbed in his own thoughts, which were centered entirely in the great winery, and inclined to feel that an American upbringing was demoralizing for "keeds." He himself had been only a child when brought to America, but he retained much of the old-world prejudice against the pampering of the young, and was abetted in his attitude by his aged father, a bald, toothless, beaming man of eighty, whose efforts to

speak English were marked by an invariable singularizing
of the plural and pluralizing of the singular.

Mrs Feratta was of Irish descent, with pale eyes and gray
hair. A silent, anxious woman, she was concerned principally
with things spiritual. The money that might have brought
ease and pleasure to her was a trust, a responsibility only, and
she worried constantly over her fitness for that trust. Wasted
food to her—and her household was one of phenomenal
appetites—was a sin. Idle talk of movies or comic strips, or
anything approaching gossip, was wrong. And especially
wrong was any criticism of churches, priests, tenets of the
faith, or any sluggishness about attendance at mass, or fasts
or regulations generally. These considerations kept her
fretting and apprehensive; she consulted authorities constantly; she gave timidly to charity with admonitions and
warnings; she distrusted women whose beliefs differed from
her own. When she bought a handsome coat or a new chair
or a set of pink-and-gold dishes she wondered miserably
for hours whether such an outlay was "right."

Annie Feratta feared those who did not fear God. She
knew that the tall, vivid, eager girl who was to be her new
daughter-in-law had been brought up with no religious training at all. The Gibsons were affiliated with no church. And
this seemed to his mother a great danger for her wonderful
Joe—her only child. The others, Gregory and Lucia, were
her husband's by an earlier marriage; she had been nursery
governess to them, had married their father a few months
after their mother's death, and taken the crying babies to
her heart. They were small and dark, typically Latin. But her
own boy, although black of hair and eyes, had her fair skin
and was tall and lightly built, and might have come from
Mayo itself.

She handled Becky cautiously, nervously. Joe's father
slept in his chair before the midday meal and immediately
after it. May O'Connor, who had married Gory Feratta some

five years earlier, was at the meal, trying to control the table conduct of two lively little boys and pantingly awaiting the advent of a third child. May came from a family as religious as the Ferattas, and was complacently confidential with Mrs Feratta on the subject of Lenten devotions at St Rose's. Lucy, Joe's half sister, was there with her new husband, Buck Williams.

Becky talked, her cheeks crimsoning with nervous effort; she tried to eat what Mr and Mrs Feratta expected her to eat. But at two o'clock on a very hot spring afternoon the good minestrone, the roast goose, the onions and spaghetti and asparagus and biscuits and crab salad and chocolate layer cake constituted a pretty hearty meal.

"Papa likes a real good dinner, Sundays," Mrs Feratta said mildly; "at supper we just have a pickup."

"A pickup that would knock a horse through a barbed-wire fence," Joe commented dryly.

"Drink the wines," said old man Feratta suddenly to Becky. "Good for you. It make bloods."

"Oh, thank you. It's delicious." But Becky had been raised not to drink at all; both her father and mother had been definite about that. Girls must never drink. She sipped the red wine smilingly but cautiously and with no pleasure. She thought the Feratta dining room simply hideous with its walls of red brocaded paper and its sideboard ornate with little railed porches and beveled diamonds of mirror, crowded with silver cake plates, pitchers in glistered blue glass, colored china steins. At the windows heavy curtains of tapestry were drawn back to show under-curtains looped and frilled and lacy as underwear. Below the windows the vineyards stretched away in wheels and lines, and beyond them were the blue Sierras, but nobody could see anything of this from the Feratta dining room.

After dinner they sat uncomfortably in the straw chairs

and canvas hammocks of the square porch, a porch stoutly railed with fat banisters painted pale gray and speckled and mottled to look like granite. Lucy brought down her house plans again, and after a while Mrs Feratta excused herself and went inside, and Rebecca and Joe walked up to the canyon and looked at the piece of property his father had promised him upon his marriage, and talked of a quite different house, a low spreading place with cool blue shadows on adobe walls, and plants in tiny pots set around a fountain whose blowing waters would keep them fresh all the year around.

"Gory didn't want this hundred," Joe said, his arm about her as they wandered and talked, stood still and wandered on again. "It's not grape property. He could always sell his hundred for grapes. But I like this."

"Ah, with the redwoods, and the spring! Lucy's house will be right down in the hot vineyards; I wouldn't have it for a gift."

"She's got a couple of oaks, and they'll put in peppers and things."

"But not like ours! We'll have a wonderful place, Joe." At such moments as this she felt happy and confident. It was going to be all right, her marriage. Sometimes when she was not with Joe she felt misgivings. Or if not misgivings, she felt at least a little unresponsive to the excitement and joy that he felt, and that to a lesser extent everyone who knew of it seemed to feel where her marriage was concerned. But when she saw how he glowed about it, and how lovely the site of the new home was to be, and when she thought of herself as established up here, fussing happily about her eight rooms and two baths, telephoning Mother to ask how much gelatine went into an aspic, setting her hair and assuming her prettiest hostess gown to welcome Joe home in the evening, presently the proud mother of a girl baby called Sally, a baby with gold hair and Joe's dark eyes, interest and satisfaction stirred in her, and she was willing to agree with her mother, and with everyone else who mentioned her engagement, that she was a lucky girl.

"We'll have view, Joe," she said.

"Pop was saying yesterday that we'll have to have everything screened. Grapes bring flies," Joe answered. "Hello!" he said in a changed tone. Becky looked up quickly from her study of the spring that rose damply under a heavy covering of matted leaves and tight-tangled twigs. A man had come out of the woods and was standing looking at them.

"Hello. Any water round here?" the man asked.

He was a stranger, a handsome, well-groomed fellow of perhaps thirty, with a half smile on an attractive face. His clothes were not new, not showy at all, but Becky instantly knew that they were right: the faintly checked brown tweed suit, the brown sweater, the brown cap he lifted from brown hair.

"We've got a hot engine here," he said. "Fan belt broken." He jerked his head toward the ranch road that here came within half a mile of the canyon. "McSwayne said there was a pipe here," he added. Joe was instantly all interest.

"McSwayne came up to look at the vines?" he surmised. "He's from San José; he buys grapes from Pop every year," Joe explained in an aside to Rebecca. "You got stuck, hey? Sure there's a pipe here. But the best thing would be to run her down the grade on gravity to the garage. My sister's husband runs a garage; he'll tell you what's the matter."

They walked down between the vines together and out onto the dirt road, and presently saw McSwayne, a fat, perspiring man who sat on the shadiest running board of the car and mopped his brow.

"My name's Flood," the strange man explained as they went. "Gavin Flood. That's a Scotch name, Gavin, but my people were Irish. North Irish. You're certainly kind to bother."

"No bother," Joe said. "Pop 'll certainly be glad to see Mr McSwayne. How's it happen you came in the back way?"

"Driving down from Eureka; we've been a couple of days on the way," the other man explained. "McSwayne's mother lives up there, and Ned had to go up anyway to see a man in Gerber about some alfalfa. He was sure he could find your place without going into Salletts, and we did find it. But I guess we came in the wrong gate."

"His sister's living up here, isn't she?" Becky said, speaking for the first time. "I know her. She married Willy White."

"That's right," Gavin Flood said with a nod and a glance. "We're going to stay with her a few days while Ned scouts round here for olives and grapes and so on."

"San José man yourself?" Joe asked.

"No; Hollywood just now. Born in New York."

They had reached Ned McSwayne now, and presently they all got into the car, and on loosened brakes it slid down the grade to the garage that stood behind the Feratta mansion. Becky's part was merely a watching and listening one from this point; she and Joe and Gory and Lucy and the two strange men made a respectful audience for Buck Williams, and presently the car was in shape again.

Just before they left, Gavin Flood had an opportunity for a word alone with Becky.

"You live in Salletts, Miss Gibson?"

"I teach in the kindergarten. Yes; my people live there. Dad's ranch is about three miles out of town."

"Any chance of seeing you—say, tomorrow?"

The warm clear tan of her cheeks colored. There was no mistaking the look in his eyes.

"I don't—believe so." And unexpectedly even to herself she added: "I'm engaged to Joe, you know, and we have so much to do . . ."

"Oh?" Gavin said with a glance for Joe. "That's it, is it?

That's Joe? Well, lucky Joe. And unlucky me. I've fallen in love with you."

He said it regretfully, but with an air of casualness, of philosophic carelessness especially his own. Immediately he had left her side and joined the group; he was talking to Lucy. Lucy, holding tight to her boys, who were evincing a passionate determination to get under the car, smiled up at him appreciatively. The woman did not live whose heart beat normally when Gavin turned the battery of his quiet, his secure and sophisticated charm upon her.

Becky moved in a dream of him for the rest of the day and lay awake thinking about him at night. She did not want to do it; she felt it silly, reprehensible, disloyal. But there was no help for it. There he was in her thoughts, a dark-haired tall man in tweeds, with something in his eye, in his glance, in his manner . . .

The few words he had said to her all came back. And especially she was haunted, as she lay quietly, electrically wakeful by those simple words: "Unlucky me. I've fallen in love with you."

It meant nothing. It meant everything. It kept her awake all night. She breakfasted in a dream, went to the kindergarten in a dream.

The little White boy was there; Royal White, a spunky little fellow of five.

"You've got company at your house, haven't you, Royal?"

"Yes ma'am, my yunkle Ned."

"And another man with him?"

"The one what swallowed a match, an' he lightud it too?" Royal inquired. Miss Rebecca laughed.

"I imagine so. You tell him that your teacher told him not to get burned," she said. But she knew that Royal would not remember.

Monday always dragged. This Monday was a strange day of dreams and emotions, and sudden awakening from dreams to more ordered and rational emotions. It dragged more than ever. Rebecca felt languid and vague.

She was to meet Joe in his office at five for supper downtown and a movie. They always did this now on Monday nights. As usual, today Rebecca went home at half-past two and had a bath and a nap and dressed herself afresh. When she went into the office Joe was deep in consultation of great yellow lawbooks; she sat on the wide window sill of Judge Miller's office above Main Street and read about mayhem cases, and looked down at the street through which home-going throngs were moving. A May sunset blazed against western-facing windows; Feratta and Baldocchi, cousins of Joe's father, who had come from Italy to share in the family prosperity, were watering with little hoses the vegetables in their banked display in the market across the street. The world was moving toward summer again.

Joe spoke suddenly out of the leather-scented shadows of the room, looking up under a cone of gold light.

"Becky, the judge has just telephoned; I'll have to run out to his house."

"But it's six o'clock, Joe!"

"I know. But he wants to see me."

"Oh, bother," said Becky amiably.

"Listen, you don't want to come," Joe said. "I'll drop you at home. If you go, it 'll mean that the old judge wastes a lot of time in compliments and all that, and we'll miss the seven-thirty show. I'll eat something out there—his housekeeper always brings in sandwiches with the sherry—and you— you——"

"I'll go across the street to the Saddle Rock, Joe, and have a club sandwich, and you meet me there. If I go home I'll get into dishwashing and all that, and it's out of your way anyway. You go along, and I'll dawdle over my supper and expect you about seven."

"That 'll do it! What a partner you turned out to be!"

They descended to the street together, Joe to leap into his waiting car, Becky to saunter across to Salletts' one good restaurant and to study a menu card that, if somewhat spattered with catchup and marred by running wet blue pencil, still offered an amazing variety of good food.

"Loch Levin Trout." They had probably been swimming around in the Basin, forty miles up in the mountains, a few hours earlier. The Saddle Rock was famous for them. Becky said that she would have trout.

"Me too," said Gavin Flood, seating himself opposite her. "You aren't alone?" he asked, almost with awe. "It couldn't be that we're to have our dinner together? I've been thinking about you, and you've been thinking about me too, haven't you? This is fate. This is our fate."

"This is fate," she conceded with a little laugh. Joe would come for her in an hour. But this hour was hers.

✥ CHAPTER V ✥

WHEN JOE FERATTA came back at a quarter past seven they were talking earnestly, Gavin leaning forward, arms laid upon the table, Becky sitting back, her linked fingers resting on the edge of the cloth, her head bent a little, her brimmed hat shadowing her eyes.

Immediately the three left the restaurant together and separated, Gavin saying only: "I'll see you both again. I'm going to be here until Friday!" and Becky merely raising her eyes to his with an odd look that had something of bewilderment and something of expectation in it.

She and Joe went to the movie. Gavin did too, for that matter, for she saw him when they were coming out at ten o'clock. But he did not join them, and she told herself that despite his farewell remark she probably would not see him again. She knew it was wiser, safer so, and he had said so.

At the table in the Saddle Rock he had said: "It's very funny, this. I never saw you until yesterday. But after all, you don't see an earthquake until it comes along. But it changes everything; it changes your whole life. I think I've been dreaming all my boyhood, manhood, of a tall honey-colored girl with a face like yours! I don't say anything's going to come of it because I don't see what *can* come of it. You belong here; you're going to marry one of the Ferattas. And I'm simply—nobody. I've tried more things and failed at more things than any other white man in America."

She had listened, saying very little. Of course nothing could "come of it"! It had never crossed her mind that anything could come of these whirlwind emotions that were

shaking and possessing her. They were definite and breath-
taking; how could anything more devastating result from
them, when they themselves were so utterly, so strangely
complete? Becky was like a person in a high fever. All life
had retreated from her, was heard and felt and seen but
vaguely; there existed in her consciousness only the one
thought—the thought of this tall man with his rather white
face and dark eyes and thick, dark brown hair, with his
strange sophisticated air of knowing the world and yet caring so little for the world, despising the easy surface suc-
cesses of many of the famous persons in that world, and yet
so honestly admitting that he himself had tried many
avenues of work without success.

On the Wednesday of this week Joe went with Judge
Miller to Sacramento, to be gone overnight. Becky's mother
always went to the club on second Wednesdays; Becky herself usually joined her there. But on this particular day,
a windless day of soft rain, Becky said she had work to do
at home, and came back to the house from school to find
the place deserted and quiet at three o'clock. She fussed a
few minutes with her hair, changed her gown, picked up a
book and walked up to the hay barn.

The great doors at each end were wide open; the soft air
poured through, wet and fragrant from alfalfa and plowed
fields. Hay was packed to the rafters, which were softly
draped with powdered cobwebs; all along one wall were the
grain bins and the stacked sacks of grain. Chickens had
taken shelter here; a dozen hens and a cock were nestled in
the loose hay of the floor; a laying hen fluttered heavily
down from a manger, and Becky went to get the egg, still
warm, with a Plymouth Rock's gray feather curled softly
about it.

There were no horses in the stalls; Knut Pedersen was
plowing the prune orchard today; the ground had been
packed hard and dry this year and needed loosening. But

the place was still scented from cattle. Becky turned in the doorway and looked down the slope of the hill past the farmhouse to the village. Rain was sweeping across it in a silver veil. Perhaps Gavin would not keep his appointment. It was awful to start out into a rain.

But even while she watched, the clouds broke and the sun burst out in blazing afternoon brightness. Everything glistened and twinkled now, and steam rose from the fence posts and smoked softly above the town. The black oilcloth hood of the little car that turned in at the gate shone like the rest.

Gavin and Becky sat on the grain boxes and dangled their legs and talked. They would have barely two hours together, they grudgingly estimated in the very beginning, for Gavin had to pick up Ned McSwayne and Willy White in town at half-past five. To both Becky and Gavin it seemed but a stingy allowance of time. They sat with hands linked, in the sweet dimness of the barn, and watched the silver bayonets of a fresh onslaught of rain march across the orchards and vanish and give way to the flashing spears of the sun again.

They talked hungrily, eagerly, with the knowledge that they would not have many more hours together, perhaps never another one. But what they said was important only because their eyes and voices made it so.

"And you've lived here all your life?"

"Since I was about three."

"And before that?"

"Brooklyn. But I don't remember it, of course, as Brooklyn. I remember having crayons, and my rubbers coming off in snow. And I remember cooking in a little saucepan; helping Mother, she called it. And the train of course, and seeing fruit blossoms as we came down from Truckee. There was a man on the train who asked me where I came from, and I said, 'Drawing Room D,' and I remember how they laughed."

"Drawing Room D? Traveling very Ritzy, eh?"

"Well, we did. It seems funny now that they'd spend money for that, Mother and Dad, for they hadn't very much. But I suppose . . . with a small child . . ." Becky left the sentence in the air and turned the conversation to him. "You know New York, don't you? And Hollywood? I'd love so to see Hollywood."

"Good Lord, why don't you go down there, then? Six hundred miles. You can make it in a day."

"Ah, but what 'd I do when I got there?" Becky asked. For answer Gavin squinted at her thoughtfully.

"You might get a break," he said. "You've got the right sort of nose. But what I did down there wasn't so much fun. There's a feller down there named Pete Orchard; I've known him off and on for years. He's a cameraman and makes pretty hot money. I was three years in Mexico on a cattle rancho, and when I came out I had a little dough and I went to see what was going on at Agua Caliente. Pete was there with a girl, and he told me to report to his company and they'd use me. I was with them six months and then they merged—which is Hollywood for going bust—and I was out. I could get back in, I guess."

"Was the cattle ranch fun, Gavin?"

"Tough," Gavin said.

"But then in New York, what 'd you do there?"

"I was born there. Born in Far Rockaway as a matter of fact, just about half an hour away from where you were born! But they sent me to my grandfather in Michigan when I was about eight. My mother divorced my father and married again. I went to high in Detroit. Then I went back to New York and sailed on a cattle boat with a feller named Underwood. The first hour out he took one look at the quarters and gave me his watch and money and jumped overboard, and they put me in irons."

"Put you in irons!"

"Yep; thought I'd murdered him for his money. They

held me in Liverpool, pending action on the part of the United States, but the consul there was swell; I didn't have any trouble."

"And then what?"

"Oh, Underwood turned up in Buffalo. He hadn't heard anything about it."

"He swam home?"

"Yep; it seems he was a good swimmer—it was only about three miles. But he hadn't reported to the company because he'd jumped his contract."

"And suppose he hadn't turned up, Gavin?"

"Well, men have been tried for murder for less than that."

"And how'd you come to know Ned McSwayne?"

"I was working for an oil company out here in Kern, and he used to come down. He was in the oil business then. Funny thing happened there once. . . ."

There was no end to his stories, to the adventures which he had either shared or experienced himself. Adventures in theatricals and movies and radio, adventures on cattle ranches or Canadian hunting trips, adventures with ships and cars and planes. He told them all marvelously well, not exaggerating, not sensationally, but with a real sense of their humor and their values.

"And now what? What will you do next?"

"Now," he answered this question seriously, "for the first time in my life I want to settle down; I want to get married. You've changed everything. I know how silly that sounds. I know I've nothing to offer you. But—well, there you are! I'll be gone Friday, and I hope you'll not forget me too soon, and I know I'll never forget you. And that's all there is to it."

"I'll never forget you." Rebecca spoke slowly, her amber eyes full upon him. Gavin answered her lightly, with a little laugh that showed he was touched and shaken.

"I hope you won't, my dear. I hope these days will seem

to you what they do to me, a little interval in our lives that's been"—his eyes watered, although he was smiling—"that's been darned sweet!" he finished it youthfully.

And quite suddenly they were in each other's arms, their lips together, Becky's ribs all but cracking under the force of his hold. For a long time the embrace held, and when they drew apart the girl was breathless, with a stinging mouth and fast-moving breast. Neither spoke. They looked at each other for a full minute in complete silence.

Around them were the sweet-scented shadows of the barn; outside the open door warm rain rapped down upon the packed earth of the yard, shook the crisp leaves of the oaks. Cows slumped across the side paddock; Knut Pedersen shouted at them, clanked the bar of a gate somewhere unseen. From the village far away the shrill high pipe of the five o'clock mill whistle faintly sounded. With great staccato puffs of white smoke that rose into the whitening rain the afternoon train came along the embankment and vanished behind the trees and roofs of Salletts.

"I'm sorry," Gavin said in the silence.

Becky turned upon him a radiant face flushed with unwonted color. The damp weather had curled her honey-colored hair into tight rings above her dark brows, her dark lashes. Her eyes shone.

"But why?" she demanded, frightened, ecstatic, laughing. "We—we can't help it. It's no *harm*."

Gavin got down from the feed box.

"I have to go," he said in a cooled, quiet voice. "I told Willy a little after five."

Chilled in her turn, Becky walked beside him. In a streak of sudden sunset light they crossed the yard to his car, and he got in.

"Why couldn't I be Joe Feratta?" he said, his fine hand playing on the wheel. "Why couldn't I have a good job, a rich father? Wouldn't it be easy? Well, we're going up to

Jack's place tomorrow to buy pears. And we leave Friday at six in the morning. So I'll not see you again."

He drove away, and Becky went in to the kitchen with her head spinning, joy and despair and doubt and utter confusion in her soul. But the joy predominated; the world sang about her; it was with difficulty that she could keep her feet on the ground.

Oh, oh, oh, what a thing it was to feel this way! This was being in love, of course; having a man's arms hard and big about you, feeling his hard cheek crushing your own, his lips pressing yours! Oh, Gavin, Gavin! Every word he said must be treasured; put away in the sweet spices and fine linens in her memory, to be taken out and touched reverently and held precious forever.

CHAPTER VI

SHE WENT dizzily through dinner. Where was Joe tonight? Joe was in Sacramento, Dad. What had she done after school? Oh, worked a little, and gone up to the barn. Everything had looked so lovely in the rain.

At eight o'clock the telephone bell rang, and she knew Spin, who was always hopeful of having interminable telephone conversation with Hube Harrison, would take it and say disappointedly, "Aw, gosh, it's for Beck!"

And she knew it would be Gavin's voice.

"Rebecca," Gavin said, "just say yes or no. Don't say my name! Say it's the school superintendent or something. Is there any chance in the world of my seeing you tonight?"

"No," she said, trembling.

"Could you come to the movie with the Whites and me? They're going. New bill tonight."

"No. They're holding it over. Joe and I went Monday night, you know."

"That's right, too."

"Beck, it's pouring. Don't you go out tonight!" Sarah called.

"I won't, Mother. Thank Mrs White for me, will you?" Rebecca came back to the kitchen. "The Whites were going to the show," she explained.

"But you didn't feel like it, dear?"

"No." Becky's voice was flat. Home was flat with an awful new flatness. She moved restlessly about, not knowing what to do with herself.

"You miss Joe," Sarah said in motherly satisfaction. Becky could do no more bring her mind, her thoughts to Joe than to the pyramids.

Twenty minutes later Gavin Flood came into the Gibson kitchen. He was spattered and breathless and laughing. He said that Willy White had had to go on up to the Ferattas', and since Joe was away, he, Gavin, had thought he might as well stop in and say hello to Miss Gibson.

He stayed only about twenty minutes, and he and Rebecca were not alone for any moment of that time. He was introduced to her mother and father and brothers, chatted with them agreeably and easily, and interrupted Sarah's hospitable murmurs as to the parlor with the assurance that he loved the kitchen and could not stay but a moment anyway. They all were completely won by him, Becky saw, but then everyone capitulated to Gavin.

The thought that his need to see her was as keen as hers to see him, that he had not been able to resist the impulse to rush out to the ranch and talk to her, even for a moment only, even before them all, was as wine to her spirit. She forgot Joe; she could not think of Joe. And again she lay wakeful all through the night, dreaming and remembering.

Every instant of the hours in the barn—they had indeed been hours although they had flown so fast!—was relived again. Again his hand was warm over hers, his dark eyes drinking in her face, his voice in her ears. The barn was a sacred place now; just to glance at it shook her heart. The barn doors open, the mingled scents of hay and of wet earth and early summer, the silver rain warmly, swiftly falling— ah, it had been an enchanted time, such as she never before had known in her life!

The next day Gavin came to the kindergarten, and she telephoned her mother that she could not be home for luncheon, and Gavin and she went to the cafeteria and had something to eat. Rebecca knew that they laughed as they filed along the counters, but what she chose, and whether she ate it or not, she could not say. Jean Bailey was there, of course, ladling soup. She gave a sharp look at Gavin.

"I hear Joe's gone to Sacramento?" Jean hazarded.

"Yes. He and Judge Miller—driving. They'll be back this afternoon sometime."

Becky and Gavin chose a remote corner, half hidden behind a post, and for an hour and twenty-two minutes had the world to themselves. The cafeteria gradually emptied; the tin trays were crashed together; Jean Bailey had long gone home. And the jealous minutes flew.

Becky was late in returning to the kindergarten for the second time in three years. Miss Patton, who was often late, was the last to make comment. And after thirty-eight minutes with the children Rebecca was free to walk home. Her mother asked her about the man who had stood at the gate with her chatting.

"Gavin. Gavin Flood. He walked home with me."

"H'mph!" said Sarah.

"He goes tomorrow at five in the morning," Rebecca volunteered with a casual air. She could almost hear her mother's "Thank the Lord!" Nothing more was said on the subject. After dinner Rebecca said she was going over to the Eldridges' for a minute. The Eldridges were a pale little man and a pale little wife with two pallid babies who some years earlier had taken possession of a languishing little ranch across the road. Becky often went over to the Eldridges' in the early evening to help wash dishes and get the babies into bed.

Gavin was at the gate in the strengthening moonlight. There had been no appointment, but she had known he would be. She saw him move from the shadows into the stream of silver as she went down under the elms and maples. They linked hands. They went a little way down the road to where there was a fence rail, and Becky balanced on it, Gavin standing with his arm about her, and they talked for a long, long time.

The girl rested her soft temple against his, one arm was about his neck. The summer night was throbbing with small insect sounds; the white moon rode slowly over their heads. Now and then a great sigh went over the earth, and the high leaves rustled in the silver-spattered dark. Now and then a motorcar swept by, finding the fences with its burning bright eyes, flashing theatrically green on the grass, gone before it was fairly seen.

"Becky dearest, isn't this strange?"

"Oh, *strange!*"

"What's happened to us?"

"I don't know, Gavin."

They loved each other's names, said them again and again.

"And you're to marry Joe?"

She laughed ruefully in the dark.

"Oh, not now. It was to have been October—but not now!"

"You mean you won't?"

"I mean I can't. I *couldn't.* I've been thinking all day—trying to think all day . . ." She laughed wearily again; he felt her body move with a great sigh. "But I can't think!" she complained.

"I know. And I can't think. Or if I can," Gavin said, "it's that you ought to go ahead and marry him. After a while it'd come right. If you—if you tie up to me, Becky, it'll never come right."

"You tell me to marry Joe?" Becky asked in a laughing murmur, her lips against his temple.

"I say that that's the only happiness there is for you."

"The County Paris," Becky said dreamily. "Why, Gavin," she added with reproachful animation, "I could as soon marry Willy White! That's—*over.* It was my life; it was all arranged as short a time ago as Sunday morning. Now it's over. I've been trying to think of the easiest way to let Joe down. I think it might be best just to let things drift, and not name any wedding day, and eventually let it die."

"And meanwhile, darling, what will you be doing?"

"Waiting for you," she said.

"Becky, I swear to you it won't be long!"

"I know it won't," Becky said serenely.

"I'll get a job; I'll find a place and you'll come to me. But suppose it's months, sweetheart? Suppose it's September, October?"

"I'll live," Becky said simply; "they can't kill me."

"But they can make it so hard for you, darling. They're all set on your marrying Joe."

She was silent a moment.

"I won't marry Joe," she said then.

"And you'll wait?"

"Until I hear from you. I've six hundred dollars," Becky said suddenly. "I never thought of it. I'll bring it. We can buy tables and chairs."

"I'll send for you."

"We could," she said after thought when for a long dizzy moment they had clung to each other in silence, "we could get married right away and live on that until things were better."

Gavin turned suddenly and kissed her between the eyes.

"You are an adorable kid!" he said simply. "No, dear, we can't do that. It wouldn't last us very long. But when I get something to do . . . and I've never had any trouble getting a job . . ."

"You might be the kind," Rebecca said as he fell silent in a dream of the future, "who never comes back. We've only known each other since Sunday; you may not remember me by this time next week. In which case, the unluckier I!"

"No, I'm not like that," he said quietly.

"I'll tell Joe I've changed my mind about wanting to get

married. And he'll tell me," Rebecca mused, speaking as much to herself as to her companion, "that he's willing to wait until I feel sure. And by that time it'll be August or September, and you'll write for me to come."

"And suppose I don't, honey?" the man asked with a sudden honest doubt.

"Then I'll just live all my days in the memory of this week."

"Do you know, my darling," he said, "that you're the sort of woman who makes a man want to get on?"

"I hope I am, Gavin."

"Poor Joe!" the man said, rubbing his cheek gently against her chin.

"Poor Joe! He telephoned tonight to say that they were just in from Sacramento. They had a blowout, and he was tired and dirty and thought he wouldn't come down if I didn't mind. I told him by all means to get a good rest, and that I'd see him tomorrow."

"And then you came down to the gate? Not knowing I was there."

"Not knowing you were there. But just the same, it would have been desolation if you hadn't been."

"You'd have gone on to the Eldridges'."

"I wouldn't have dared for fear you might telephone!" They laughed, their faces together.

"I was going to walk about and watch the windows, and imagine which was yours."

A silence, from which she roused herself to sudden realization.

"Gavin, I have to go in. I never stay more than an hour at the Eldridges', and Mother might telephone over there to ask them what was keeping me."

"Then I'll walk with you back to the gate."

A sudden sorrowful mood possessed them both. Gavin's arm was about her shoulders. The moonshine was very bright now, but that only made the tree shadows more sheltering.

"It's too bad, isn't it!" she said.

"Yes, it's too bad that it had to come this way."

"You mean it, don't you?" the girl asked with sudden passion when they had stopped at the gate and could see the house lights a hundred yards away. "You *will* send for me? You will remember? I know that sometimes men—and especially if it's a country girl—a girl who believes everything that's said to her . . .

"Gavin, it's my life!" she whispered, clinging to him. And he saw tears wet on the face upon which the moon shone. "From now on it's my life! My fate to follow you and take care of you and have you take care of me. Don't fail me."

"I'll not fail you," he answered with an emotion almost matching her own. "We'll have a home, Becky, and a garden, and kids in it. We'll be happy!"

"For richer or poorer," she said unsteadily, tears running down her cheeks, "in sickness and in health, until death do us part!"

Gavin caught her to him savagely, and again she felt her very ribs crushed by his arms, and her lips stung with his kiss. Then they were parted, and she ran up the path and into the house. She did not turn to wave or to watch, for she was crying.

"That you, Becky?" her mother called from the kitchen.

"Yes ma'am." Her voice was thick; she made it steady.

"I phoned the Eldridges and she said you hadn't been over."

"No. I—I felt sort of tired. So I just walked around for a little—for fresh air."

"You feel all right?"

"Yes ma'am. But I'm going to bed."

"Well, I'll be up, and if you'd like a glass of hot milk . . . You didn't eat any dinner——"

"Oh no, thanks, Mother!"

"Girls in love never eat," her father's voice said good-naturedly. Then there was silence and she was free to escape upstairs and bury her wet eyes in her pillow and sob herself to sleep.

CHAPTER VII

IN THE DAYS that followed, unreal days filled with dreams and fears and wild unreasoning hopes, Rebecca tried to bring order out of the chaos of her spirit. But the tide was too strong. Memories of emotion, themselves arousing fresh emotion, swept over her in a brimming flood; languor possessed her, and she moved through the ordinary events and duties of the day abstractedly, hardly conscious of what she was saying or doing.

Joe, fortunately for her, was not an exacting lover. For one thing, he was absorbed and excited over participation in his first big case. For another, he had inherited something of his mother's Celtic reserve, her shy distaste and fear for any feeling that was merely of the body. He would be a possessive, a passionate husband. But his passion was held in check now, awaiting its legitimate hour, and Rebecca was the freer for it. Joe was not the sort of man who liked to park the car in a dark spot, expected cuddling and kissing in the shelter of the back seat. When he came to see Rebecca in the evenings he did not embarrass her before her own people. He kissed her when he went away as a brother might have kissed her—on her temple or holding her lightly by the shoulders, with a dozen light little kisses that fell on cheeks and nose and hair generally.

She had known kisses other than those now. The memory of them never died.

As the hot summer went its way she planned. She would tell her own family of her plan just before she went away, tell Joe at the very end. She would pack her trunk carefully on some Wednesday afternoon when Mother was away, and leave that very evening. There would be no long intervals for argument and reproach. She would see Joe for five hard minutes; her heart beat a little unsteadily, thinking of them.

"Joe, I'm so sorry, dear. It's been Gavin Flood ever since that day Ned McSwayne's car broke down. I promised then to marry him when he was ready, and he's ready now. Please forgive me."

Joe never said anything in this imaginary scene; Becky filled it with her own nervous volubility and turned away from him when she had said what she must say. Indeed, there was not very much that Joe could offer under the circumstances.

The trunk should be left, to be sent after her when she and Gavin had a permanent address. Her suitcase she would fill with necessities: her brown silk and her evening dress, all her stockings, her other purse, her fountain pen and silver powder box. She would go to the bank sometime between twelve and two that last day, an hour when Frank Pierce, who played poker with Dad and was insatiably curious, would be away, and she would take all but a little of her money and put it in an envelope, and later, in the teachers' rest room at school, pin that envelope firmly inside her girdle. She would wear her one good suit to school, and perhaps take her suitcase down to the station in the morning when she drove Dad to the store, and check it there with Perce Brannon. There must be no hitch in the final steps; her dinnertime talk to the family, her farewell to Joe— when would that be? Well, she could ask him to meet her at the station, and no matter how bewildered he was, he would do it. The trains, both the north- and the southbound, met in Salletts at eight. The station was about three miles from the Gibson farm, but there was a seven-thirty bus that would take her that distance if Dad refused to help her. A swift good-by kiss for Mother—her eyes tickled at the thought of it and she had to gulp—and promises to the boys, and the thing would be done.

And oh, the breathless relief of finding oneself in the train, alone at last, alone with dreams and prayers and hopes and joys, going to Gavin!

"What do you really know about him?" she would ask herself half amusedly in gayer moods. Nothing. The answer was nothing. Except that he looked and talked and dressed like a gentleman, and that she loved him. But it was through him that life out in the big world was waiting for her, and that at last she was going to find it!

Gavin wrote her immediately, a letter she kissed and wet with her happy tears and cried over. It was brief, but no longer letter could have said more to her hungry heart.

MY DARLING,

Here goes for the Big Adventure [Gavin wrote]. *The adventure that ends and begins with you. On the train from San José I met Lou Kreymeyer, as pleased to see yours truly as I was to see him. He's trying to put something over in San Francisco, and here we are! No more now, I'm late, but this is just to let you know that everything seems to be shaping well. "Yours truly!" Sweetheart, I'm a lot more than that I'm yours completely, eternally, adoringly,*

GAVIN

The address was of a San Francisco hotel. He was not so very far away after all! In three or four hours she might be with him. It comforted Rebecca to think of it. She slept with the note in her hand, pressed against her cheek.

For the rest she tried to act as if her life held no secret. She was more affectionate, more helpful than ever at home, moving through the days like an actress in a welcome part, her hidden plan running like a dangerous undercurrent to everything she did and said, her hidden love lighting her eyes with new fires and making everything she did thrilling and dramatic.

CHAPTER VIII

"BECKY," her mother said to her quietly on a hot Saturday morning, "sit down a minute, dear. I want to talk to you."

The tone was just Sarah's ordinary tone; perhaps even a little calmer than usual. But Becky, mashing hard-boiled egg yolks in a bowl, knew instantly that she was lost.

"Mother?" she said, turning a pale and stricken face toward the older woman, feeling her knees give under her as she sank into a chair.

It was almost noon; the day blazed above the little town in merciless white splendor. The boys had gone off with their lunches and fishing rods; Spencer had just telephoned from the Exchange that he would not be home for lunch. Becky and Sarah had put in a full morning peeling and cooking tomatoes; great pots of them, scented with sugar and vinegar and spices, bubbled slowly on the stove. Beside this and the usual household routine, Becky was stuffing eggs for a picnic at the Basin tonight, and had washed her hair, which was bound about her head under a tight strip of cheesecloth.

"Beck," Sarah said, "I want to know what's been going on between you and that Foote or Sloane or whatever his name is."

As she spoke she put upon the table with a damp hand a crumpled small sheet of hotel writing paper. Becky glanced at it; her color returned. After all, she said to her fast-beating heart, she was of age; they couldn't put her in jail for falling in love. She managed a rather scared laugh.

"I'm glad you know, Mother," she said with a deep sigh of relief.

"Know what?" her mother countered sharply.

"That Gavin and I like each other. That we're engaged," Becky said simply. She took the note, and after smiling at its few lines as if they had a personality of their own, put them in her apron pocket. "I was afraid I'd lost this in Joe's car!" she added.

"You haven't been writing to that fellow?" Sarah asked, unwilling to believe it, her eyes dark with pain and apprehension.

"Ever since he went away, when I've an address," Becky answered cheerfully. "I'm sorry, Mother," she went on with real feeling, "and I'm sorry to have kept it from you. I've hated it, really I have, on your account, and on Joe's, of course. Joe and I are engaged, in a way——"

"In a way!" her mother took her up instantly. "How do you mean, 'in a way'? You and Joe Feratta have been engaged for six weeks. You don't mean to tell me . . . You can't mean . . . What on earth does Joe think of this fine state of affairs?"

"Joe doesn't know; nobody knows. It's an absolute secret between Gavin and me. But we saw each other, just those few days, every day. He was up here and we talked in the barn, that day it rained so, when you were at the club, and he came up that night when I said I was at the Eldridges'. And the night Joe went to Judge Miller's to talk shop about the Chet Dark case, he and I had supper together at the Saddle Rock. And, Mother," Becky continued, gaining courage as she went along, "it just—happened. The big hawk lit, as Gavin said. He cared for me and I cared for him at first sight, that Sunday when I was up at Ferattas'. He's getting started now in San Francisco, and as soon as he's ready I'm to go down and marry him. We'll all go down, the boys and you and I——"

Sarah had remained immobile, looking steadily at Becky. Color had drained from the older woman's full, handsome face; she looked suddenly old and beaten. She spoke harshly with the air of seizing upon the uppermost of a hundred seething thoughts in her mind.

"He's getting started, is he? How old is he? Forty?"

"Thirty-one!" Becky answered, laughing over deep secret hurt.

"And he's just getting started?"

"He's done all kinds of things. He's lived everywhere. London, Mexico, New York. Now he's going to settle down."

"You believe that, do you?" asked Sarah.

"I believe him," the girl said simply.

"You don't know anything about him."

"I know enough." Becky spoke freely, conscious only of relief after strain. The answers were coming so easily, and such a weight was off her heart! Mother knew, and the skies had not fallen!

"Becky . . . my darling . . ." Sarah sat down with an air of despairing surrender. She had a skimmer in her hand, a skimmer that dripped a few red drops on her apron. "No, dear, you can't do this," she said gently, beginning all over again.

"Ah, Mother, but don't you see . . ." Rebecca left the sentence unfinished. She hung her head on one side, looking appealingly and yet without any real alarm at her mother. "After all, I'm nineteen," she offered mildly.

"That has nothing to do with it!" Sarah said in an absent undertone, her eyes far away. "It would be madness— there's Joe and all the Ferattas to think of . . . old friends of ours . . . and so kind to you! Your father . . . No, he'll never . . .

"And you wouldn't do it against us all, Beck!" she presently recommenced as Becky regarded her seriously, without speaking. "You couldn't throw away everything—home, and the boys, and your friends here. You wouldn't!"

"It wouldn't mean throwing away everything, Mother. Girls don't necessarily fall into pits just because they marry."

"Let him settle down here, make good here, and after a year or two everything might be different," Sarah said stubbornly, following her own train of thought.

"Mother, what would Salletts be able to give *him!*"

"When he works what does he get?" Sarah demanded irrelevantly.

"Well . . . I don't know," Becky answered, taken by surprise.

"You didn't ask him, of course?"

There was a hostility, a lack of sympathy in her mother's manner that was entirely new to Becky. She reared herself somewhat haughtily in return.

"No, I didn't ask him," she said coldly.

"I know I'm talking as if I didn't know how you felt, Beck," Sarah presently said in a softer tone, laying a hand on hers. "I'm sorry, dear. But if you do this you'll regret it as long as you live. It isn't the man, Becky. We don't know him of course. But it's not that. It's that—well, that things that don't count with you now will be so much more important in a little while. Home and your old friends and the feeling that you didn't run away from them. You can't look ahead now, you can't see what life really is. There might be a child; you've not thought of that——"

"Of course I've thought of that!" Becky said resentfully as her mother paused. "I want a child someday; I adore children. But a child can stand it if I can!"

Her mother hesitated for a long time, started to speak, thought better of it and sat staring at her again. Then she got up and without a word recommenced her preserving operations, skimming the seething dark orange mass in the kettles, setting clean empty jars to heat in the dishpan of shallow hot water that stood on the stove. Noon whistles sounded in the town. A yellow jacket buzzed angrily up and down the wire mesh panels of the door. It was hot in the kitchen.

"I'm sorry, Mother," Becky said sullenly, stubbornly, in the silence.

Sarah made no answer; once she sighed heavily. She was an unlovely figure, broad and dowdy in a limp kitchen percale and a big striped ticking apron, with her gray hair pulled severely off her face and twisted into a snug knot, but Becky saw only Mother, the dear and kind and beloved ruler and magician of her nineteen happy years, and her heart was torn within her.

"Becky," the older woman said suddenly, "when were you going to tell Dad and me?"

"Oh, I suppose when Gavin wrote that he had something definite," Becky said after a moment.

"And Joe then, too?"

"I suppose so."

Sarah sat down again, close to her daughter, and laid a persuasive hand on her arm.

"Beck," she said, "suppose you knew that this was going to mean unhappiness for you, poverty perhaps, loneliness, responsibility such as you've never known? Suppose it meant losing faith in your man, not knowing which way to turn——"

Again she interrupted herself and stopped, leaving her sentence in air. Rebecca, looking at her seriously, answered the question with another:

"Mother, why don't you like ·Gavin?"

"I—well, we saw him just that one time. I don't know him," Sarah parried.

"If it meant all that (but it won't)," Becky said, "still I'd go. I'd *have* to go. But to me it means something different," she went on with a dreamy half smile; "it means that my whole life won't be spent in Salletts. It means meeting people I don't know now, holding my own, finding my place! I could make a success of *any* marriage, Mother," Becky went on. "I could marry the white-headed Poteet boy and make a success of it! I could go down in Factory Town and take one of those awful cottages with the gate hanging on one hinge and the windows broken and the floors all splinters, and I could paint it and plant trees and have a supper table in the back yard and make it lovely! You know me. I *like* changing things, working them out! If I married Joe I never would have anything more serious than icebox cakes to think about, and whether my slip showed! Marrying Gavin, I'll have something to *do*—helping him and helping myself at the same time!"

"Icebox cakes aren't exciting maybe, to a girl your age," Sarah persisted, "but they're pleasanter than not having the rent, than having your husband drink and your little girl sick!"

"Gavin doesn't drink!"

"Not at all?" Sarah diverged to ask, surprised.

"Well, I wouldn't say that. I don't know. But I mean——"

"Exactly; you don't know," the older woman put in adroitly. She suddenly changed her manner and her tactics; her voice was loving, pleading.

"Beck dear, you'll not do anything suddenly? You'll not just run off?"

Becky was hard pressed. Her face grew red, and her mother divined instantly that she had planned something of the sort. There was a silence while the two looked at each other.

"Promise me, darling. You know we couldn't stop you. But after all these years—when you've been my only girl . . ."

"It'll just . . ." Becky altered the phrase: "To tell you would just make it harder to go," she offered.

"Truly it won't! Truly, dear. Promise me!"

So there was her deep-laid plan gone flat! With her unwilling nod Becky committed herself to an opener policy. She and her mother talked of other matters while they ate their luncheon, and at four o'clock, after a bath and a change, Becky went off under Joe's escort, looking her prettiest in picnic gear and laughing as she warned Joe to carry the cake and the eggs carefully.

"She's all right!" Sarah told herself over and over again. "But I'll have to tell her now, just the same!"

✿ CHAPTER IX ✿

Two DAYS later Sarah opened fire again. This time it was
night. The boys and their father had gone to bed. Becky
and her mother had lingered on, on the porch steps, under a
bright white moon, breathing in the cool air that relieved
the burning tension of the day, listening to the steady shrill
rasping of grasshoppers in the dry fields, marveling at the
miracle of moonlight that was tangled in the silver meshes
of a land fog and struggled in the oak branches with fila-
ments and streamers of mist.

Joe had come in earlier in the evening, half asleep from
a day spent in research for the Chet Dark case. Now he was
gone. Becky had made one or two halfhearted starts for
bed, had been dragged back by the coolness and sweetness
of the night. Now she was anchored suddenly to her seat
and turned an amazed face toward her mother as Sarah
said quietly:

"Would you be very much surprised to hear that Daddy
isn't your father, Beck?"

A silence of utter stupefaction on Becky's part held the
porch for a full minute. The girl, twisted about on the top
step, could dimly see her mother's face; her own face was
in shadow, silhouetted against the fog and the misty moonlight. The earth seemed to take a great jar under her.

"That surprises you, doesn't it?" Sarah faltered on.

"*Surprises* me!" Becky echoed in a sharp whisper.

"Yes. I—I had to tell you, my dear. We've talked over
your plans, Daddy and I, and we think it best that you
should—should know. Gavin Flood has brought a new
element into it. If you'd gone on and married Joe I think we

mightn't have told you. Dad might have told him only that you weren't our baby——"

"You were married twice, Mother?" Becky's voice was frightened.

"No, only once, Beck. I knew your mother, although I didn't know much about her, or even her name. That is," Sarah said with a peacefully reflective air carefully assumed to have a soothing effect on the girl's sensitive nerves, "I'm not *sure* I knew her name. She——"

"Mother," Becky interrupted almost angrily, "you're fooling!"

"I wish I was fooling," Sarah said.

"Go on," Becky said.

"I'll have to go back some way, then, Beck, to tell you how it was I met your mother. You mustn't look scared like that, dear. There's nothing to be scared about. I'll begin at the beginning, when I was working in one of Chicago's big department stores; I was about twenty-five. My parents were dead, but I'd met Dad, and we wanted to be married. But we had no money, and it seemed as if we must wait forever.

"One day in November—it was cold, I know, and looked as if it might snow—I noticed a lady standing quietly watching me for quite some time. When I was free she came up and bought some book, and we stood talking. She was handsomely dressed, but she looked sad and sick. She was going to have a baby very soon."

"Not married!" Becky said quickly.

"Oh yes, she was married. And somehow—I never knew exactly how—she drew me out to tell her about my being engaged and wanting to get married. Then she said she was in great trouble and asked me if I would help her. I was as puzzled as I could be, and I said that in any possible way—— I remember, Beck," Sarah diverged to say simply, "I remember wondering if she was a crook of some sort. We were always hearing about well-dressed women who were crooks.

But she didn't seem that sort. She looked like you, only smaller, and very frail. Her wrists weren't much thicker than one of my fingers are now!" Sarah added with a pitying little reminiscent laugh.

Becky, her face in shadow, her eyes two glints in the gloom, continued her intense stare at her mother's face and said nothing.

"She asked me what time I went to lunch," Sarah resumed, "and she waited for me. We had lunch together, and we talked. She was going to have a baby in a few weeks and she didn't want her husband to know; not that you were coming, nor that you lived, nor whether you were a boy or a girl. She'd left him, months earlier. I imagined that maybe he was a cruel, a dangerous man, and she wouldn't have any baby of hers left in his care. Of course I don't know whether he was like that or not. I never saw him. I never knew his name."

"You knew *her* name?"

"I knew the name she gave me. But I only saw her three times in this life, Beck. Lunch, that first day, and then a day we met at the bank, a week later. And then in the hospital."

"At the bank?"

"Yes. By that time I'd talked to your father—to Dad, I mean—and he'd agreed to change his name, and that we should be married right away and adopt her baby, whatever it was. It was like the skies opening, to us!"

"Change his name?" Becky, in her complete bewilderment, could only stupidly echo the amazing phrases one by one.

"That was the condition she made. We were to change our names, take you as soon as you were born, go to some completely strange city, live there for at least two years and then move to California. I'd told her our dream was to live out here on a little ranch. She said that was what she wanted for you. Only she always called you 'my little boy.' She said that under other circumstances she would have loved to have a son in her arms; that there had been times when she had longed and prayed for a child, to keep her from despair, but that now she was ill, she was afraid she would not live, and she could not leave her little boy to a father like that. She clung to my hand, Beck; she was like a crazy creature, and in the end I promised her everything, told her we'd take you and treat you as our own, showed her my new wedding ring. And that was the first happiness you brought Dad and me, Becky, that we could be married and plan for our California ranch!"

"And it was then that Dad had his streak of luck and you could afford to come out here?"

"*You* were our streak of luck, Beck," Sarah said, her concerned, loving eyes on Rebecca's downcast face and the young head aureoled by moonlight.

"Oh, I see! She gave you money?"

"That was it. That was how Spencer and I could marry and why we changed our names. We took a telephone book and took the top name on the left and the last name on the right of two pages. It came out Spencer Gibson. The money in the bank was deposited to the credit of Sarah Gibson. Twenty thousand dollars. All the time that you were coming —it was about a month—we were making our plans, and when you were five days old I went to the little private hospital and took you. I said I was your aunt."

"But she?"

"She died when you were seven days old. I saw her dead. They said she had known she would die. She had made arrangements to die."

"She killed herself?"

"No. She'd had transfusions—everything. But perhaps it didn't take very much to kill her. She had looked so ill!"

Becky looked up heavily.

"What was her name?"

"The name she gave me wasn't her own, Becky. At least

I don't think it was. She called herself Mrs William Davis. But of all the William Davises in the Chicago telephone book there wasn't one who took any notice of her death or came to the hospital. Dad and I arranged for the funeral—she had left plenty of money for that. We stayed only a few more weeks in town. Then we went to Brooklyn. We went there because it seemed a big place, a good place to get lost in. We were there two years—Dad had a job in a bank—and then we came here and bought the ranch."

"She hated my father?"

"Enough not to want him even to know you were coming."

"She'd left him?"

"She said so."

"And where was she living?"

"That I don't know."

"She just chose you at random? A person she didn't know at all?"

"Not quite like that. She said she'd watched me for three days, and heard one of the girls ask me when I was going to be married, and heard me say, 'Oh, not until we can afford a baby!' She said I looked 'wholesome,'" Sarah said. "I looked like someone she could trust. Someone who didn't have very much money and who couldn't easily be traced. She'd thought it all out. Anyway, she was desperate."

"My father was a criminal," Becky said slowly.

"I don't think so. I imagine they'd quarreled and she felt that if she died you'd be all his. Perhaps she hated his mother, wouldn't trust them with you."

There was a silence. Becky broke it in a somber voice.

"Then I really haven't—anyone."

"Dad adopted you legally," Sarah answered briefly. She was silent for a moment, her heart sick with pity.

"You've been—terribly kind to me," Becky said stiffly, her throat thick. "Money is money, of course. But money didn't buy what you've—what you've done for me."

She had to keep her voice low to hold it steady. Sarah spoke simply:

"No child was ever more loved than you've been by us. It wasn't only that you were such a wonderful baby, Becky. But it was everything else—our being able to get away from the city into this wonderful country—fruit trees and the creek, and then the boys. I think Dad loves his girl more than any of his boys, Beck. You know that."

Becky did not answer. After a moment she got to her feet and walked through the mottled shadow and moonlight to the side gate and stood there leaning on the bars, staring down the road. The misty meadows were wreathed in gauze; oaks stood out in mysterious flat surfaces, the village lights were merely a pink blur on the silver smoke. Sarah sat on on the porch in the deep shadow, trembling, afraid.

After perhaps ten minutes Rebecca came back. To Sarah's infinite relief she was not crying; she spoke almost in her normal voice as she resumed her seat on the upper step.

"Mother, what was your name originally?"

The older woman hesitated a second. Then she said:

"I see no reason why you shouldn't know that, Beck. I was Sarah White, my father was Robert White, a salesman in a hardware store in Chicago. I was the only child, and my father and mother both died in the year I was twenty-two. Father was killed, and Mother had been ailing for some time. Your father—Dad, I mean—was Frank Smith. I don't know much about his people except that they came from Buffalo. He came to Chicago and worked in a jewelry store; that was when I met him."

Becky's eyes were fixed on her for a long minute. Presently the girl said hesitatingly, finding words slowly:

"It's a strange story. It makes me feel—queer. It makes me feel—I really don't know how. I'm—horribly sorry, I think. And of course, of course," Becky stumbled on, laying a hand now on Sarah's knee, "I'm yours. You're the only mother I've ever had, and even if she'd lived she wouldn't mean anything to me. But she *is* dead?" the girl ended on a note of sharpness.

"I swear it, Becky. They'd told her she was dying. She made me swear, that last day in the hospital, when she was so weak, that I would treat her child as I would want my children treated when I had children. And I've not looked at one of them, Beck, when he was first born in the hospital without thinking of that."

"You didn't have to take any oath," Becky said thickly, awkwardly, her fingers linked in Sarah's fingers.

Sarah did not say: "Ah, my darling" or "Now you mustn't let this make the slightest difference, my dear." Becky, holding to her fingers, knew that she was too wise, too true for that. She felt the roughened hand tighten its hold a little, that was all.

"Mother, were you going to tell Joe this if I had married him?"

"Just that you were adopted before you were a week old and that all we knew of your mother was that she was a woman of—well, of fineness, Beck, much—very different from me!" Sarah said with a little apologetic laugh. "And that you were legitimate, of course."

"What made you sure of that?"

"What she was, Beck. How she seemed. Fine and very sad and not poor, you know. Her clothes were fine. And she gave me her wedding ring. This ring."

Becky turned the ring slowly in her fingers.

"I don't think it matters," she said musingly.

"I don't know that it does," Sarah agreed, a little puzzled but anxious to reassure her. "Keep it, Becky. It's yours."

"And my father, whoever he was, never knew I was born?"

"She said not."

Another silence.

"Why did you tell me this now, Mother?"

"Because—well, perhaps because I'm so much afraid of the world for you, Becky. It treated her so badly. We talked it over, Dad and I, and he thought I should tell you."

"Heavens, that's eleven striking!" Becky said with an effort to speak naturally, when they had sat on for a minute or two more, each woman wrapped in her own thoughts. "One more thing," she added, getting to her feet. "This has stunned me in a way. Would you mind—for a day or two—not talking any more about it? Then, if there's anything to say—and I don't see why there should be—we can talk about it again. I'll be more used to it."

"That's a good idea," Sarah said simply. She put out lights downstairs. She and Becky went upstairs together, kissed each other in the upper hall without further words, and parted for the night.

Becky went into her own room, went to the wide-open window that was flooded in white moonlight, knelt down and let the milky silver river flood over her. Thinned fog undulated gently in the garden; there was a sweet keen smell of dew on summer dust, and tarweed, and ripening apples in the air.

"Two months ago I didn't know Gavin," she presently said half aloud. "Now—this. Everything gone. All the past gone. And my whole life changed. My mother's wedding ring, eh? And another to go with it."

She had taken from its hiding place another ring. Gavin had given it to her. He had said: "Keep it until I put it on in church," and here it was, touching the gold ring that was all she knew of her mother.

Rebecca held the two warmly in her hand and looked out across the summer meadows toward San Francisco, and fell to dreaming.

"Well, Mother," she said, "you weren't afraid to trust me to a woman you hardly knew. It's not so strange that I'm willing to follow Gavin to the end of the world! I guess we're both runaways, you and I."

CHAPTER X

SHE, REBECCA GIBSON, was on the morning train going to San Francisco on a bitter cold day of keen winds and cold sunshine, white frosts and frozen wheel ruts. The fears that had been battering about her soul like beaked birds had drifted away, leaving behind them blessed peace. There was only the rumble of the train now, and the occasional jangle of a crossing bell to underscore her busy thoughts.

She was running away at last. It was half-past eleven. She had never planned to leave on a morning train; that would have seemed too hard to manage. But here she was, with Salletts behind her, her money snugly pinned to her inner clothing, her suitcase at her feet.

For the past two hours she had been frightened, and the relief from that fright was so great that she kept returning to the thought of it. Since exactly ten minutes after nine o'clock she had been escaping from everything, risking everything, fearing everything. Every familiar voice had held a menace in it; every familiar setting had seemed full of danger.

She had received Mrs Kinpaw's letter at nine. Becky had been, as usual, in the kindergarten, superintending the children's last quarter hour of play before marshaling them into the schoolroom, when the postman had arrived. A letter from San Francisco and not from Gavin, she had marveled, tearing it open.

It had been written in pencil on lined tablet paper, and signed "Mrs D. Kinpaw." The address was on Ellis Street in San Francisco. Mrs Kinpaw had written briefly.

Dear Miss Gibson,

Thought you might be the one to notify that Mr Flood is sick with flu and will not go to the hospital although advised. Has been laid up for a week now and no signs of improvement. Asked him last night if he would like to have anyone notified in case of fatal termination of his illness which frankly speaking is now pneumonia, and this morning he said you. Will keep you informed although hoping of course for the best.

Becky had read it, the solid earth wheeling upon its foundations about her as she read. She had put it into her sweater pocket and gone blindly toward the car, saying no farewells, leaving no explanations. She had gone straight home, finding her mother busy in the kitchen.

"What 'd you forget?" Sarah had called unsuspectingly. "My press key," Becky had called back. She had forgotten before this to take the press key to school.

She had gone upstairs, had commenced feverishly, swiftly to pack, fearing at any minute that her mother might come up. But Sarah had not come, and Becky had carried her suitcase downstairs unobserved. She had put it and her big coat into the back of the car, had gone to the kitchen.

"Mother," she had said with a quick kiss, "I'm parking the car outside of the Exchange. I'm going to San Francisco. Gavin's dying. I'll be back. I'll write if he lives. But he's got pneumonia, and the woman who runs the place where he's staying says he won't live. Good-by, darling. Don't be mad at me!"

"Becky——" Sarah had clutched at the girl's hand. "Listen! Promise me you'll write; you'll come back. My darling, I'll worry so about you! Let me know——"

"I will!" Another kiss, a message for the boys, and Becky had vanished. Sarah, after a moment's stricken immobility, had gone out to the dooryard, watched the car move away.

Becky had hastily planned as she went. First to the bank for the precious six hundred and twenty-one dollars, then to the station to check her bag, and then to the Exchange. Becky had smelled the good smell of the oiled floor and the bags of wheat; the peppermint candy and red-stamped rubber hoses, had wondered when she would come into the Exchange again.

"Your pa's out, Beck," old Cassell in the office had told her regretfully, pushing his eyeglasses up to his bald forehead, laying down his pen. "He and Lou Clark went over to Midden Ridge to see 'f they could get some beef. Seems the Masons want three hundred one-pound steaks for tomorrow night, and Spence and Lou are roundin' 'em up ev'vywheres they can git 'em! He won't be back for some time."

Well, that had been a relief. Becky had scribbled a message, had walked to the train. She had had twelve minutes to wait, an endless time in which imaginary obstructions had arisen on all sides, fears of her mother arriving reproachful and pleading; Mart Kane from the bank to say there was something wrong about the money; Joe Feratta, accidentally destined to go to San Francisco on the same train and amazed to see Becky there; the stationmaster to say that the eleven-thirty wasn't running today.

Nothing of the sort had happened. She had bought her ticket, found her seat, tipped old man Musto, who had placed her bag at her seat.

"We don't often have you with us, Miss Gibson!" David Fess had said, punching her ticket. "Return, hey? Comin' right back?"

"I think in a few days." He had brought her a detective magazine, had told her that Emily had written her mother to come down; not long to wait now.

"You want a girl, I suppose, Mr Fess?"

"Well, when you've got a boy . . . Two boys are nice, though."

Now she was safely on her way. She was going to Gavin. The train rushed on. The world outside the windows looked cold and bleak, with heavy clouds obscuring the sun, as they neared the city, and the little houses near the tracks withdrawn into themselves. Plumes of smoke rose from their chimneys and were snatched and torn to shreds by sudden winds. Shabby places, with garbage barrels and children's broken wheel toys in evidence, stripped trees, littered dooryards.

She must read her magazine. She must not think that Gavin could die. Oh, then what? Would she go back to Salletts and apologize for running away, and someday marry Joe . . . No, never Joe! What could she do that would not be desolation and emptiness? . . .

She opened her magazine. She would not think.

It was almost one o'clock when she crossed San Francisco Bay and found herself at the Ferry Building at the foot of Market Street. Becky was hungry, but she did not know it. The air struck her coldly as she left the warm train, and she felt shaken by chill, and nervous and anxious, but she did not think of hunger. She got into a taxi and gave the Ellis Street address. In five minutes she was descending before a dark-looking wooden building whose bay windows, draped in filthy soft lace curtains, were wedged tightly in between a languishing establishment which sold secondhand plumbing and a restaurant with a much gilded downstairs window full of steaks and green peppers. The side doorway was crowded with the cards of fortunetellers, dressmakers, foot specialists and passport photograph studios.

Becky rang, was admitted by a small pale Japanese woman in a dirty sacking apron who simply pointed upstairs. Lugging her bag and beginning to feel actually frightened now,

Becky obeyed the direction and reached a small upper hallway bounded by many varnished brown doors in the last
stages of peeling and chipping. One was open and in a room
beyond she saw a stout, dyed-haired woman working on her
nails.

The room was overfurnished in red plush, the woman's
house dress was red, her full wrinkled face was red. Red
crimps were pressed down damply upon her forehead with
a gauze rag; her nostrils were rouged. She looked sharply
at Becky as the girl came panting in, and said quickly, "Close
that door."

Becky shut it, smiled a faint, uncertain smile and asked,
"Does Mr Gavin Flood live here?"

"Oh?" the woman said in a rather flat voice. "You aren't
from Portland?"

"No. I'm from Salletts. Someone wrote me. A Mrs . . ."
Becky fumbled in her bag. "I've the letter here——" she
was going on, when the woman nodded and said briefly:

"Kinpaw. That's me. Yes," she went on after a moment
as Becky regarded her expectantly and did not speak. Indeed
Becky's mood at the moment was one of such utter panic
that she could not speak. "He's here," said Mrs Kinpaw.
"The Daniel House, next door, is full, and they sent him
over to me. I rent rooms downstairs."

She was leading the way downstairs as she spoke, and
Becky, picking up her bag, followed her. The girl felt almost
faint by this time, but she was too much frightened and
depressed to appreciate that it was long past her usual lunchtime. She was only conscious that the incense-scented, close
air of the horrible place was making her ill.

In what once had been the back parlor of a somewhat pretentious double house, a dark room lighted just now by a
narrow window jutting on a well and by the bulb of a red-
shaded dim lamp, she found Gavin. He was very ill, so ill
that Becky forgot everything else in instant desperate con-

cern for his life. Her brother Spin had almost died of pneumonia two winters before after a crazy fishing trip with the Butler boys; she had seen him look like this during the dreadful night when she and her mother and father had sat up in hourly expectation of the end. She knew there was not much to do, but, tearing off her hat and coat, she prepared to do that little.

"I want ice here, and a towel, and some milk. And have you a little stove? He ought to have hot milk every two hours. Where's the nearest drugstore? When was the doctor here?"

CHAPTER XI

GAVIN, almost unrecognizable, was lying on a couch whose dark day cover of mottled green and black chenille, heavily bordered with fringe, was part of his bedding. It was tangled in among limp spotted sheets and dirty blankets. His pillow protruded from a torn case; his rough, uncombed head rested on the stained ticking. He had not been shaved for days; a rough stubble, all but disguising him, covered his chin; his swollen lips were cracked and black and his eyes sunk into pits equally discolored. As Becky, with a little cry of love and pity, stooped just for a flying second to rest her cool cheek against his face, she felt the skin burn through the beard like the touch of a hot coal.

The room was hideous with cumbersome old furniture. "Bought when she bought the house, thirty years ago," Becky thought, even while she was thinking of a score of other things. The chairs were rockers fastened to heavy bases; there was a bureau with a marble top and a great mold-speckled mirror that doubled the gloom of the place. The lamp wore a red silk shade trimmed with bead fringe; there was a narrow bed of white iron, its posts trimmed with brass knobs. It had been slept in, was not made. Another assortment of dirty bedding was tumbled upon it, and a man's vest hung on one knob. Sunk into one of the walls, which were papered in chocolate with gold and red fleurs-de-lis spaced on the paneling, was a brown marble washstand scented suffocatingly from a piece of wet pink soap.

"There's another feller in here with him," the landlady volunteered. "I had to stick him in here just where I could."

Becky, in return for a bottle of milk and a grimy small

alcohol stove, returned to the lady several empty milk bottles, one empty whisky flask, three towels so dirty she touched them through a scrap of newspaper, and some sticky plates.

"Do you want to pay now, dear, or have me charge the milk?" Mrs Kinpaw, who seemed amiable and sympathetic enough as she saw Becky's concern, asked as she handed over the bottle. Becky felt a moment's check.

"I can pay now," she said, opening her purse.

"Thanks," the other woman said in a surprised, brighter voice. "He's run up a little bill at the drugstore, pore feller," she added thoughtfully, looking down at the unconscious and muttering Gavin.

"Well, I'll settle it later." Becky was not going to take out her money in this particular place. Intuitive caution warned her. She was absorbed in a score of duties as the landlady left the room.

No time to think or worry or reason or feel sorry for herself; it must be work now, straight-ahead work with no stop for anything whatsoever. She had straightened the bedclothes, shaken up the pillow; she had a sodden towel in her hand, was wiping chairs as she set them in order, was gathering scattered newspapers and cigarette butts from everywhere and anywhere, making them into packages with fluffs of dust and all the odds and ends of rubbish which accumulate in a neglected sickroom.

Ice arrived in a yellow bowl. Becky interrogated Mrs Kinpaw.

"The man who's rented this bed. Can you get rid of him, put him somewhere else? We can't have him in here. He'll get it. Get flu."

"He had it. I think he give it to him," the landlady answered, jerking her head in Gavin's direction. "Sure I can move him. It was just over the week end we was so crowded."

"Could Mr Flood be moved to a hospital, do you think?"

"Oh no. The doctor said yesterday it 'd be death to move

him or even open the window. As a matter of fact," Daisy Kinpaw went on, lowering her voice, "he didn't think he'd get through the night. Naturally I don't like this sort of thing— here. It gets my boarders nervous. I run a dramatic boardinghouse, you know," she added superfluously, for Rebecca had eyes and interest only for Gavin. "He's goin' on a long journey," she said with a shake of her head as her eyes followed Becky's to Gavin's dark face.

Becky seated herself on the edge of the bed, a glass half filled with warm milk in her hand.

"He hasn't taken any nourishment since Sunday," the other woman volunteered. "I don't know as the doctor wanted him to have none."

"They gave it to my brother right through everything," Becky said. She had a desperate need of help, deep in her soul. Dr Pringle from home; one of the nurses from the hospital; Mother, above all, Mother! Oh, if she could only come into the room, broad and comforting and sure of herself!

The warm milk went in through the cracked black lips; Gavin gulped, moaned and muttered for a second. He half opened his mouth for a fresh supply. Becky did not change her position until the glass was drained. She recommenced her labors with a lightened heart. Just that he had taken some food did not mean much, but it comforted her.

An investigatory tour to a dark kitchen downstairs and to a hall closet on the floor above resulted in a clean pitcher and glass and some fresh towels. Sheets there were none to spare in the house; Becky put on her hat and coat at three o'clock and went out to find some.

The unfamiliar street was dark and cold and grimy, but Market Street, filled with bright shops and markets and movie theaters, was only a few blocks distant, and when she reached it she saw the sign of the Emporium painted high on the massive sides of the big building, not far away. She could buy sheets there.

On her way she passed a restaurant and entered it in a sudden weakening realization of hunger. The good hot coffee, the sizzling ham and eggs she enjoyed there were a feast she never forgot. Not in all her nineteen years had Becky so relished food. It seemed to penetrate in warmth and strength to every fiber of her being, to the tips of her toes and fingers, to the tired head it cleared of a new vague pain.

Her last meal, an everyday breakfast of orange juice and brown toast and coffee in the home dining room, seemed ages in the past. The chain of events that began in the kindergarten with the letter's arrival, her rush home for clothes, her train trip, the taxi journey at the end of it, her arrival here seemed to have taken a long slice of life. Sitting back at the restaurant table with a great "Ah-h-h!" of relieved hunger, she meditated upon her present situation and wondered what she would do if Gavin died.

She could not go home. Not with her love destroyed and her life crippled forever. She'd have to stay here and find work, and perhaps after years, when Joe Feratta was safely married to someone else . . .

Meanwhile, the sheets. She went into the big warm department store with all a country girl's appreciation of its beauty and brightness, and bought eight cotton sheets and eight pillow slips, two warm blankets, a little stove with solid spirit to burn in it, a small cream-colored saucepan, a tall bottle of toilet water, drugs, malted milk, two all-enveloping hospital aprons and a pair of tennis shoes.

All this was exciting, despite the fear at her heart and the fatigue that she was now beginning to feel. She carried some of her purchases in a stout paper bag with a cord at the top—itself a ten-cent investment—and had the rest marked "Rush." And, walking home, she felt a sensation new to her nineteen years, a feeling of power, of self-reliance. Her old world was gone, swept away in a few short hours. But she could learn to live in this new world and master it!

The doctor came in at eight o'clock and was openly pleased to find the sickroom so changed and Becky in charge. She had managed with the help of a man who appeared to be a sort of porter in the house, a mysterious sickly-looking fellow everyone called "Heimie," to move Gavin into the bed, a bed freshly made and smooth. One of the new blankets and two of the new sheets were on the couch, neatly arranged for her own sleeping place. Clean and fresh herself, in a white apron and white shoes, she reported that her patient had had ice water and orange juice continually, and two half glasses of milk.

"Very good work, Miss Gibson. Get Heimie to shave him tomorrow," Dr Greer said. A fat, big, disorderly man whose face would also have been improved by a shave, he handled his patient briefly, expertly, holding the hot dry wrist, opening a drowsy eyelid with blunt fingers, listening with his stethoscope at Gavin's exposed chest.

"Tomorrow?" she repeated, sudden hope in the eyes she fixed on his face.

"Yip," the doctor said, closing his bag.

"You think he's better then, Doctor?"

"I think it may break, say around midnight. He'll be better then. You'll want to change his pajamas if it does. You his sister, what?"

"We're engaged to be married."

"I see. Well, I'll tell old Kinpaw to come in and help you if he begins to sweat. Got clean things for him?"

"Yes. He's got three pairs of pajamas here still in the package. She says he sent out for them when he was first ill."

"How about you? How about you getting it?"

"I'm not afraid."

"I'll tell you," said the doctor, departing. "I can send a nurse in here sometime tomorrow morning, and you two can give him a good bath. That'll make him more comfortable.

He's pretty sick, but I believe—well, can't tell. He might and he might not. But you call old Daisy if it breaks."

"I've been sponging him off a little with alcohol."

"Good idea. And any time you want to, you pile him way under blankets, just leave a hole over his face to breathe, and open that window. Have to have that radio going in the next room, I suppose?"

"It would seem so. It's been going since I got here this afternoon."

"Well," said Dr Allen Greer in a cautious undertone, "if he gets better you can get him out of here pretty soon."

Becky had borrowed two crime magazines from her landlady. When the doctor had gone she performed as much of an evening toilet as was wise for a nurse on night duty, putting on pajamas and wrapper, brushing her hair off her face, assuming comfortable slippers. Then she aired the room for three biting clean fresh minutes, and tried her patient with still another half glass of milk. Once again he took it obediently, murmuring a feverish whispered jargon in which she sometimes recognized her own name. But to the touch of her finger tips he seemed hotter than ever.

She moved the lamp, lay reading on the couch. The radio went on in the front parlor, separated from her own apartment only by a folding door. She could hear girls' voices in there, men's voices, the clinking of glasses.

Other unfamiliar night and city noises kept her long awake. Horns, the jangle and clang of streetcars, whistles on the bay. Men broke into loud arguments; women screamed with laughter. Somewhere near, she finally decided, there must be a dance hall; the stamp of feet to pulsing bass music began, stopped, began again, with an odd sound like the hammering of a mill.

But it only mattered to Becky that she was with Gavin again, that he needed her, that she could help him. After a while she fell into a light sleep.

She was awakened by his hoarse cawing call: "Becky!" He was awake and in temporary possession of his senses. Drugged with sleep, cold, bewildered, frightened, she staggered up, stumbled about the routine again. Ice, and a tablet in water, and the pillow shaken . . .

"Becky?" he asked in a puzzled whisper. For some reason she could not define, at this first sign of his recognizing her, she felt the tears press into her eyes. "What time is it?" the thick lips managed to say.

She looked at her wrist.

"Quarter to twelve." Her hand went down to his pajama collar; it was saturated, and she saw now that the thick hair on his forehead was matted with water. She ran from the room, found a light in the hall, met the landlady coming downstairs.

"I thought I heard you talkin'," Daisy Kinpaw said. "It's broken, has it? I'll see if Heimie's up."

CHAPTER XII

THAT WAS the beginning. A few days followed in which Becky lived in a nightmare of fatigue, anxiety, smells, strange duties, exhausting effort. Then the crisis came, after the fever was gone, and Gavin sank, sank with unutterable weakness into what looked like death.

That afternoon, a bleak November afternoon at about five o'clock, he and Rebecca were married at his bedside. He had whispered that he would be happier that way, and, like a woman of stone moving through a dream, she had made what sudden arrangements she could, had gotten a gentle old clergyman's co-operation, had secured a special license.

So now they were married, and during that evening she sat watching him, expecting that every weak breath would be the forerunner of last breathing. He would go easily, the doctor said, not the usual pneumonia death, and when he died she must telephone this number and the boys would come for him at once. "But looky," kind old Greer had added, "he isn't dead yet, and don't you forget it. He's got plenty of fight in him."

"Shall I go on with the milk?"

"Oh, sure, every hour, if he'll take it."

"Every hour."

And as the hours went by and the milk went down, and the thin, sunken, shaved face took on, she thought, a more peaceful look, the breathing grew just a shade stronger. Why, she could hear it everywhere in the room now, and at three she had had to stoop low to hear it. When Mrs Kinpaw came in they consulted in whispers.

"He don't look any weaker."

79

"I think he's stronger."

Suddenly there was a third voice in the room, a hoarse weak voice with a shred of broken laughter in it.

"Sure he's stronger! How about a beefsteak?"

She went, trying not to laugh, trying not to cry, to the bedside and knelt down, and laid her face against his. Gavin had shut his eyes, the sweat that even the little effort to speak had cost him glistening on his forehead. His hand groped weakly for hers.

"Who's this?" he breathed. "My wife?" And they cried together.

After that he had to be patient, to be quiet and obedient for many, many days. She could talk to him, but not of plans or worries, not of anything exciting. If he tried to question her or thank her the tears came too fast and, laughing at them angrily, he had to stop.

So they talked of indifferent matters, and Heimie came in and shaved him every other day, and Becky heated milk and malted milk and milk with coffee in it, and soup that was half milk. She went out to market, brought his clothes home from the laundry, read him newspapers, played games of dominoes with him, took her hour off for lunch and supper. There were scores of nice little places in the neighborhood where she could eat hamburgers or sausages, Italian cafés where there were minestrone and *gnocchi,* clean little dairies that served famous waffles and bowls of hot cereal.

On the eighth day after her arrival, which seemed the eightieth day at least, they quite suddenly left Mrs Kinpaw's. They went to a private hospital out on the Panhandle, facing the long strip of Golden Gate Park that led to Stanyan Street.

The hospital was managed by a warmhearted, noisy, flamboyant woman named Laura Tevers. Laura came flying into Gavin's dismal sickroom at Mrs Kinpaw's on the eighth day, and within an hour the feeble Gavin, Rebecca and their bags and boxes were on their way to Laura's house.

It was a large, handsome, wooden house, rather like Laura herself, with swelling bays and a white trim on clean gray paint. It was full, all but one room, but that one room happened to be the best of all, the first-story room with a bath behind it and a diet kitchen beyond the bath. All were nicely furnished, enormous in size and spotlessly clean. As for pay:

"Oh, for heaven's sake," Laura said, "let that wait!"

She had only chanced to hear that day of Gavin's wretched plight. For heaven's sake why hadn't he come straight to her? She wasn't supposed to take any contagious cases, but she would have taken him. And married, for heaven's sake! Well, his girl must have a sweet impression of married life!

If only physically, the escape from the squalor, the musty odors, the scent of incense, the filthy curtains, the incessant radio and the soiled blankets of Mrs Kinpaw's establishment was an unspeakable relief to Becky. It was wonderful to spread out in the old-fashioned spaciousness of Laura's house, and find clean towels in a clean big bathroom, and enter an atmosphere where invalidism was taken for granted, and where provision for it was the normal thing.

A nice stout nurse brought up a tray of "soft foods" for Gavin at half-past five; other trays were moving through the wide halls. Gavin went off to sleep, exhausted and clean and content, and Becky sat in a comfortable big chair at her bay window and looked out at the fresh green of the park and felt herself breathe freely for the first time since her arrival in the city.

But there were other than physical aspects in life, as she was painfully beginning to discover, and many of them presented themselves to her in this first hour of real rest and reflection, and filled her with misgivings.

In the first place, Gavin. She was puzzled and distressed about Gavin. He never should have been in a loathsome den like the Kinpaw place at all. Rooming with another man in a gloomy back parlor, unattended in what might so easily have been his last illness!

Then in his persistent weakness and exhaustion he was critical and irritable, not with her but with everyone else. Or if, as she had to admit honestly, sometimes with her, it was not often, and he would feebly apologize for it afterward. But what was he like, this husband of hers? He had said nothing about money. She had paid thirty-three dollars to Mrs Kinpaw; she had bought soups and drugs, paid for her own meals, for blankets and hot-water bottles and sheets. Her previous savings had gone down below four hundred dollars now. Dr Greer, dismissing Gavin today, had lingered in the hall to say suggestively: "Now the bill, Mrs Flood. Do you want to pay that now or later?" and she had unhesitatingly paid it. Forty dollars flat. That was perhaps to be expected, but Gavin's languid, "Dismissed, eh? Did you pay him?", his quiet acceptance of the fact that she had, these things disturbed her to an extent that she had never in her life before dreamed was possible.

Laura had disturbed her. Laura was forty-five, pretty in a dyed, flashy sort of way, her eyelashes dripping black oil and her breath, even at five o'clock in the afternoon, scented with liquor. And while Laura's house was imposing and clean and the nurse seemed nice and the colored cook seemed nice, Laura's talk was odd for the superintendent of a hospital. Laura talked races and roulette, and of a lawsuit between a man and his wife in which she was involved, and she urged a cocktail upon Rebecca before dinner, saying that she had been through a lot and it would buck her up.

Well, there was no crime in cocktails or lawsuits or roulette or races, and the great thing was that Gavin was safely housed and happy. Also at dinner Becky felt reassured somewhat by the presence of a few of such of the patients as could move about. A nice tearful old lady who was stiffening from hour to hour with arthritis; a nice gentle old man who

had once managed the Lockerwells' track, and whose talk
was wistfully of old track triumphs and old winners; a Swiss
gentleman, almost blind, waiting for an operation for
cataract; a nervous young woman who instantly told Rebecca
that it was a "joke," her being there, it was "rich." She was
going home as soon as she heard from her guardian. She had
been there, Rebecca learned later, four years, and there were
bars on her windows and a lock on her door.

"She'll yell tonight," said the nurse, Mrs Battock, as she
cold-creamed her face in Rebecca's bathroom and enjoyed a
confidential chat before going to bed. She had been most kind
in helping to sponge Gavin and change his pajamas and settle
him off for the night. He was now asleep, and she reported
that Mrs Tevers was also asleep. "If you want to call it
sleep," said Emma Battock significantly. "She wasn't so bad
tonight, because you were here. But she's lying right across
her bed with her clothes on. She'll get up, around eleven, and
go downtown and make a night of it."

Rebecca, cold-creaming her own face, turned horrified eyes
from the mirror.

"Does she . . . ?" She left the sentence unfinished.

"Sure she does," the nurse said. "Couldn't you smell it?
She's a smart woman, Mrs Tevers is. She could make an
awful lot of money out of this place, because she's got three
big doctors pulling for her—you know what I mean? They've
known her for years, and they like her. But she won't be up
until ten o'clock tomorrow. Then she'll do everything. I tell
you she's smart. She can cook invalid food so that they like
it better than regular food, and she babies them all—brings
them back puzzles and marshmallows and the favors she gets
at night clubs. But if that girl isn't in d.t.s before she's much
older I miss my guess. I'm fond of her," the nurse said, now
putting her short hair into crimpers. "But I tell you I'm
pretty sick of it," she went on, suddenly pathetic. "I'm a
widow with one of the loveliest girls you ever saw; she's

eleven. Jacky, we call her. Her father adored her. He never touched a drop in his life, except maybe if he was with his friends on a party or something, or he'd drink beer at home. He liked beer. I'm going to quit here and do something where I can have Jacky with me. I'm sick of never knowing how she's going to be, from one day to the other. I haven't had any money for two months. She hasn't paid the cook for seven. Rollie's husband was sick and Laura fixed him up in the basement and had the doctor see him, so I suppose she figures she doesn't owe Rollie anything. Well, Rollie sees it different. She told Laura right out she was going to sue her."

As she listened to all this Rebecca's heart sank—sank. It really did not affect her or Gavin, she tried to assure herself, but it was strangely depressing. It took her some days to ask the question she had wanted to ask immediately.

"Mrs Battock, do you know what Mrs Tevers charges for our room?"

The answer stunned her although she showed nothing; she knew she must not show anything.

"Forty," said Emma Battock readily. "But she may shave it a little for him. She thinks the world and all of him. But then there 'd be your meals extra; that's one-fifty a day. Call it forty a week."

"Forty a week." Rebecca gulped. Forty a week! With Gavin still sublimely indifferent to all practical details, never questioning anything! On the contrary he sent out for flowers, asked Becky to bring home a quart of champagne to celebrate his recovery.

"We'll ask Laura up to have some," he said.

"I wonder what we'll do when my money is spent, I wonder what we'll *do?*" Becky repeated in her soul, over and over again. She shrank nervously from the unpleasantness of explaining, of delaying her payment for anything. "You see Mr Flood's illness, coming so suddenly . . ." she could hear herself faltering. The words stuck in her throat.

CHAPTER XIII

DAYS WENT BY, and she came to know everyone in the sanatorium well. The sick ones who did not leave their rooms, the gentle old stableman, the handsome Ethel McCann. Ethel was physically well enough. She was by no possible standard insane, but she had to be in every night regularly. "The first night she skips she goes back to Stockton," said Emma Battock significantly to Rebecca, "and if you want to see that girl turn white you mention Stockton! That's where the asylum is, you know."

Ethel lived at the movies. She took a sudden fancy to Rebecca, abandoned it as suddenly and accused Rebecca of talking against her with Mrs Battock. She liked to slip into Gavin's room and talk to him, and confided to Mrs Buck, the little old lady, that he was a hard person to understand, and most people, including his wife, did not understand him.

Most of all Rebecca studied Laura Tevers, who knew everyone in the city's social set, called Burlingame's men and women Tom and Harriet and Linda familiarly, had apparently been present when crises in a thousand lives had taken place, when the Stokeses had discussed their divorce, when Belle Merriman's mother had forbidden her to marry Kane Callander, when Boyce Larue had killed himself. Laura Tevers, holding even in her drunkenest moment something of generosity and fineness, had evidently once been a loved and prominent member of the *jeunesse dorée*.

"Old lady Pierce used to send for me to sleep with her when the old man was on the rampage. Kate Kendrick? My dear, I was in the house the day that girl was born. D'you know, when they decided to contest Lloyd Rowley's will—

this was twenty-five years ago—that woman came to me . . ."

Every morning, if a little late in putting in an appearance, Laura descended to office and kitchen to prove herself a marvel of efficiency. Her income ran to a gross of some twenty-five hundred a month, and she earned it. She selected broilers and towels and glasses and flowers for the house herself; no one asked for oyster stew or iced bouillon without getting it in its perfection from Laura's own hands. All morning until her late lunch she went about in a white uniform, making arrangements and adjustments, answering the telephone, joking with some fashionable doctor, amusing her sickest and saddest guest with a fun that had tenderness behind it.

At half-past two she lay down for a rest and began on the gin. Often she was not able to appear at all at dinner; often when she did come she was tearful and self-pitying, telling the table group long tales of the injustices and handicaps under which she had struggled through life. Always she was interesting. Her own character, and the part she had played in all these lives she reported as forceful and influential. She had made Jerry Markham forgive his daughter; she had taken the Pitt child and defied the grandfather to kidnap her.

Many of her tales were of inebriates. She pitied and despised them in speech; Becky suspected she would be generous enough in act to them or to any other unfortunates.

" 'Jim Moore,' I said, 'you ought to be ashamed, getting yourself into this condition!' The old lady used to drink a lot in the afternoons. He was pickled to the eyes, of course," went the burden of her stories. Of the debutantes, those (to Rebecca) almost mythical figures being entertained at dances and teas and presentation parties innumerable, she was scornful. "One of her grandfathers was a minister who used to make us all kneel down with our faces on our chairs while he said grace for fifteen minutes," she would say, "and the other grandfather was shot by a Chinaman up in Oroville for cheating at cards. And now she has a coming-out party in a Vionnet model! Okeh. Okeh. Okeh."

Bewildered, eternally more bewildered, Rebecca moved through this group of strange persons, moved through the orderly uninviting halls of this big house, heard herself addressed as "Mrs Flood." Even to Gavin, lazy and languid in convalescence, the name sounded unfamiliar.

"So we were married, eh?"

"You remember it, Gavin?"

"Sure. I remember something. Old feller with a beard——"

"The minister, yes. They thought you were dying; in fact Doctor Greer said you were. And you thought so. You whispered to me that you'd die happier if we were married."

"Don't remember that. That was the day I was going down into a well, and coming up again, and resting awhile, and then going down, down, down into blackness again. Each time—I've told you this!—I'd feel that the next time I'd stop at the bottom. But each time I'd make that little jerk that started me up.

"But I remember you crying and saying, 'We're married now, Gavin. We're together now forever!'"

It hurt her to hear him piece together in his careless way the memories which were so sacred to her. It made her feel that she had been hysterical and hasty in deciding upon this dramatic marriage that was no marriage. He was looking on at the scene like an outsider; her money was slipping away during these days when he was so blandly unconscious of money's existence at all. She felt ashamed and awkward in this queer world, pretending to fuss over a tray that was complete with no help from her, offering to read to him who could now perfectly well read for himself, taking aimless walks through the park, lingering beside the swings and sandboxes where the children toddled and screamed and where the wooden horses plunged about in their endless circle.

At the end of the week she paid Laura forty-seven dollars, Laura writing a businesslike receipt. Despite her first careless: "Oh, for heaven's sakes, let the money question rest!" she had presented the bill with practical promptitude. Laura suggested that Rebecca make a little present to Rollie, the colored cook, and "get a little something" for Emma. Rebecca seized this opportunity to introduce the subject of money obliquely to Gavin.

"Give her two dollars," said Gavin, and apparently thought no more of it. Rebecca gave Rollie two dollars and bought an embroidered collar for Mrs Battock to give Jacky.

Laura saw to it that Gavin had a generous supply of eggnogs, rich chicken soup, milk, omelets, and such supplementary delicacies as creamed crab, artichokes, Roquefort cheese, persimmons. He grew stronger hourly. Rebecca heard him laugh again; heard Emma Battock go into something like hysterics of laughter as he teased her.

Suddenly there came one more change to add itself to the many that had stunned her ever since her arrival in the city. On the morning that found them beginning their third week at Laura's house Rebecca, who slept on a couch near the bay windows, awakened at eight o'clock to see Gavin smiling at her over his breakfast tray. He had been getting up and getting dressed for a day or two now, sitting for hours in the winter sunshine of the window, watching the life that streamed by in the street outside. But this morning, even though he was still established against heaped pillows in bed, there was a vitality, an energy, a naturalness about him that she had not seen since the long-ago days in Salletts.

"Hello, wife!" said Gavin. "What a sleep you've had! Nothing waked you up. I've had a bath and a shave, and the only reason I didn't dress was because you've hid my clothes! Come over here and see me."

She came over, tousled and red-cheeked as a child, in her woolly striped pajamas.

"Gosh, you're pretty, Beck!" he said. And something that had been lacking in these dreary weeks came suddenly back into her life, sang in her soul and ran warm in her veins. The touch of his hand as he laid it over hers was electrifying. They laughed into each other's eyes. "You've had a swell party, haven't you?" he asked. Rebecca, looking at him to laugh, found her eyes brimming instead and turned away her head.

"Oh well," she said thickly.

"Well, how about house-hunting today?" he asked briskly. "We've got to live somewhere. There's a new hotel on Geary Street where a friend of mine had a swell little place— kitchen and everything! You pay by the week; I think it's twenty-two fifty or something like that a week. You get dressed and go down and have your coffee, and I'll be ready by that time, and we'll get a taxi. And say, listen—say, listen," Gavin diverged, catching at her hand, drawing her back to a sitting position on the bed, "have you been paying for all this? What'd you want to do that for? How much is it? Where'd you get it?"

The blood came back into her heart. The winter day hummed and sang with the joy of reassurance and confidence restored. It wasn't the money; it wasn't just sordid financial anxiety. That had mattered as it must always matter when it was a question of everything going out and nothing coming in. But Becky's delight went deeper. It was because she had her man back again, vital and affectionate and willing to assume responsibility, because he was beginning to understand at last, at *last,* what she had done for him, because life was coming around into its right grooves. She was young and in love, and married in name to the man she loved, and to be his at last as he was hers!

"Look here," Gavin said, "I've been trying to say this for

days, but damn it, every time I started I got crying! It was enough for you to make beds and heat milk and sleep on that Iron Maiden that Daisy Kinpaw called a couch. You didn't have to dig down into your bank roll as well. I've got it. I thought, in a hazy kind of way, that Phipps had looked out for all that—that you were drawing on my money. Now Laura tells me you've paid up on the nail—why, my God, nobody ever pays up here, not for weeks and weeks! You crazy little nut, you!"

"Who's Phipps?" she asked on a shaken laugh.

"Phipps is the fellow I was having dinner with when all of a sudden the damn thing—the flu—hit me," Gavin said. "I'd been feeling cold and hot and achy all afternoon, but all of a sudden my head went *fizz!* and I flopped over on the table. Well, Phipps—mind you, I'd only met him that day to talk business!—took me to his place, the Kinpaw place. She runs a lot of chorus girls and near-actresses, that sort of thing, but she's his pal's aunt, and she took him in. That's why I had the couch; I thought I'd only be there overnight and go off all right in the morning, but I was in for it. I don't remember anything else much, except fighting them on the hospital thing."

"Gavin, I'm so glad to know all this—that explains it! I knew you wouldn't go to a place like that in your senses! But why not a hospital? It would have been infinitely better. You almost died," Rebecca said, childishly impressive, her eyes round.

"I'd have died if it hadn't been for you, my dear. Don't cry, Beck, you'll make me cry."

"I'm not crying," she said, gulping, trying to laugh, as she clung, half sitting, half kneeling beside him, his arm about her.

"Look here," he said, "do you realize that tonight we'll be in a place of our own? If I take you to lunch at the St Francis do you think you can cook me a steak for supper? Get pepper and bread and coffee and so on?"

"Gavin!" she said, her eyes stars.

His cheek was hard against hers.

"Realize that you're my wife?"

"Uh-huh," she said almost inaudibly.

"Realize what that means?"

"Uh-huh," Rebecca said again, on a little laugh.

"Scared?"

"Nope."

There was a silence, his lips against her temple, her head resting in infinite content and relaxation on his shoulder. After a while Gavin returned briskly to his abandoned tray.

"Well, you get started, and I'll finish this, and we'll go down to the bank, and find some place to live, and hunt up a market right near, and move in," he said.

Rebecca danced rather than walked downstairs half an hour later. Sunshine was streaming into the dining room; coffee scented the air; little old Mrs Buck was nibbling and sipping like a rabbit; Emma Battock was hidden behind a newspaper.

"Well, don't we look nice!" Emma said approvingly. Rebecca flashed her a radiant look. She knew she looked her best in her last winter's silk with its embroidered collar, and the brown velvet hat that brought out the gold lights in her eyes. "Where going?" Emma pursued, with her mouth full.

"House-hunting!"

"Well, I thought from the way he talked yesterday he's getting his feet under him," Emma said. "Mrs Tevers 'll be real sorry to have you go. So you're slated for a honeymoon, are you?"

Her glance—the significant glance of experience toward ignorance and innocence—brought the color to Rebecca's face. But it was happy color, part of a cloudlessly happy hour; there was no woman on earth with whom Mrs Gavin Flood would have changed places at that moment.

CHAPTER XIV

REBECCA HAD WANTED for herself a life better than any-thing that the girls had at home or were likely to have; she had despised Salletts, struggled to get away from it and from everything it could offer her.

Now she had to forget all that idiotic schoolgirl rivalry. She was handling realities now, and the peace and greenness of home, its luxury and fun, its simple problems and under-lying deep securities were gone forever. Rebecca was out in the world; she had chosen her path in it; she must abide by her choice. That only a few months ago her mother had been saying laughingly: "Don't you children ever get tired of fried chicken on picnics, Beck?", that she herself had been saying: "I'm going to wash my hair and read and loaf all day tomorrow," was like a dream.

A dream that made her heart ache, so she tried to put it aside.

She was desperately, amazingly lonely. Except for Gavin (and she was beginning to discover how very little she knew Gavin), she had no friend in all the city, no confidante, no one with whom to laugh and plan and go about marketing and shopping and wasting time in the way girls love. Gavin him-self had few friends in town, but there were clubs, places where men rolled dice and played cards and drank beer, and at these he was welcome. In the beginning he came home almost every night, but he often stopped at a club on his way, and Becky never put a steak on until he was actually in the house.

He liked steaks best of all—steaks and coffee and French bread—and would make a little disappointed face if dinner was not hearty.

"Brains? Spareribs? They look swell. But I hoped it was steak tonight."

"I believe I could give you a thick tenderloin every night of your life!"

"You know damn well you could!"

The tenderloin cost ninety or ninety-five cents, the cheaper cuts and meats half that. But Gavin would not eat stew or hash or sausages or minces or meat pies; he did not like fish. Lobster was as expensive as meat; and the amount of bacon he ate with eggs made them expensive too. Becky's little fussy dishes—fried tomatoes with cheese on them, asparagus baked in cream sauce, prune shortcake, stuffed peppers—he would merely taste. Meat, potatoes, coffee—that was his menu; he wanted nothing else.

If the dinner she had prepared did not happen to suit him he would say cheerfully enough: "Put on your hat and leave all this. We'll go down to the Lido."

Becky loved the Lido. But not after she had spent two hours in the kitchen making a veal loaf and a corn pudding. That was waste.

And even waste would not have been so bad if they had always had plenty of money. But she had not been married many weeks before she began to feel constant anxiety as to their finances, and it was at about this time that she realized that finances with Gavin never would be anything but uncertain. That particular worry never would be cured.

Disillusionment came so fast and so completely with her that she was never able in after times to analyze its processes, if indeed it did not fall like a blow, like something for which no possible preparation or expectation could have been made. Suddenly, hardly over her first bridal newness of wifehood, housekeeping, marketing, living the new life under a new name, she was hardened into a quiet, puzzled, patient yet unresigned creature who bore what she had to bear simply because she could think of no endurable alternative to it.

For she knew she could not go home, changed, saddened, silent about her experience since her runaway. She could not get a divorce and have Salletts presently saying: "Becky Gibson's left that man, you know. Looks as if he wasn't much good."

Indeed she did not want to leave Gavin. He protected her, and he was her husband; she was a married woman. That, balanced against all the advantages the other girls had in Salletts, was something anyway. And he was never consciously unkind to her.

That was just it. He was unkind and did not know it, and irresponsible and did not know it, and extravagant and did not know it. And he was selfish to a point that amazed her almost as much as it hurt her.

Rebecca had been praised in generous motherly fashion for unselfishness since she could remember anything at all. Sarah shrewdly developed in her children the qualities she desired in them by premature praise. Spin was "getting" so gentle; Bob had "almost stopped" teasing. And Becky, credited with kindness, thoughtfulness, generousness, had really grown to possess these qualities. It was natural for her to think first of others, to do what she could for their comfort and pleasure. That was a part of growing up in Sarah Gibson's household. One grew to enjoy service, to want to sacrifice self in small harmony-creating ways.

Gavin too evidently had never had that sort of training. He was as simply and completely self-absorbed as a cat. If he wanted a meal early he demanded it; if he wanted to be late or not come home at all he considered himself entitled to do so. That she had rights, feelings, sensitiveness, never occurred to him. Ruthlessly across the fiber of her being, mental, moral, physical, he drove his way, tolerant of her presence when he wanted her, forgetting her entirely when he did not.

Sometimes he was gone from home all night. Sometimes when she made shy appeals for money he went on reading the paper as if he had not heard her, folded it, jumped up and was gone for the day without a word. Sometimes he brought two or three men home unexpectedly for dinner, told her amiably enough to give them "any old thing," and let her slip out to the delicatessen store or the market without protest. He went on fishing trips, hunting trips, bachelor parties. They had not been married four months before he went on a party that was not a bachelor party. She heard some of the other men teasing him about it afterward, and knew there had been women on the party—women of whom she knew little and suspected much. It cut her to the soul that he would leave her for such a company, and made her angry. But under her anger and heaviness of heart was a more influential element. She knew that it would be of no slightest use to reproach him. He said repeatedly that he hated whining women and crying women and indignant women and curious women and argumentative women. They bored him supremely. No man in his senses would pay the slightest attention to them.

He took her to the races and she loved it when he won, as he usually did to a greater or lesser degree, and grew nervous when he lost. She knew they had no money to lose, and she was afraid of his dark moods, when he blamed everything and everyone for his bad luck. Coming home from the races after bad luck was a dismal business, and Becky usually spent those evenings alone. Gavin went off to find consolation in dice or cards.

She always lay awake until he came home, although when he got there it was usually wisest to pretend to be asleep. If he had lost again he would be irritable; if he had won he hummed while he was undressing and then she could open her eyes and smile sleepily upon him as if just awake, and he might kiss her and call her a sleepy little pussy.

Hunger for these moments of affection and lightness of heart was one of her troubles in these days. She was so much alone that his companionship was indispensable to her, and she got far too little of it. Silence, silence was everywhere.

She made an effort to talk to the German in the bakery and
the little French woman in the laundry. But bread lasted a
long time when Gavin was hardly ever at home to help eat it,
and in hard times Becky did most of her own washing.

The months went by, and she was still pondering, still
puzzled. She had been a giddy, carefree creature at this time
last year, surrounded by persons, little and big and old and
young, prosperous and less prosperous, but all loving Becky
Gibson, all helping to make her life full and happy. Now all
that was gone.

Gone. Becky was alone now with a handsome, careless,
selfish man who was neither kind nor unkind to her. She was
alone in a two-room apartment modern in equipment, an
apartment to be regarded by all the housewives of Salletts as
incredibly luxurious, with its lights and its refrigerator, its
elevator service and garbage service, its bells and signals and
conveniences generally. But there were hours when to Becky
it seemed a prison.

Why had she exchanged all that she had for this? And if
she could not answer, who could? Certainly not her mother
or father or the boys, certainly not anyone at the kindergarten
or at the Feratta dinner table! She herself was the only human
being in the world who might possibly remember or imagine
the answer. And to her it was now as complete a mystery as
to the rest.

Well, one must make the best of it! Cheerful, friendly
Mrs Flood went with her husband to races, cooked steaks for
"the boys," was seen at restaurant dinner tables sipping her
minestrone, breaking her chunk of toasted sour bread, lifting
her thick glass of red wine. She kept her own counsel. Nobody
knew much about her; she was just somebody's wife. The
grayness of it, the strange dullness of it enveloped her. She
felt that she had not only lost her old world, that sunshiny,
oak-shaded world that had held her mother and father and
the boys, and the Exchange with its good country smells of

sacked wheat and floor oil and new-ground coffee, but lost herself as well.

Sometimes she tried to break through the maddening meshes that seemed to hold her feet, her mind, her very spirit bound in a trap.

"Gavin, where are we getting to?" she might ask animatedly as she gave him his breakfast coffee.

"Gosh, I've got to remind Al that the fight's tonight," he might answer absently; "he said he could get tickets."

"I know. But listen, Gavin. We go on and on, and we don't get anywhere."

"What's the kick?"

"No kick. But we owe money—there's a regular sheaf of bills in there on the desk. I'll bet they total up to three hundred, maybe more. There's no sense to our going on this way. Your pay is—what?"

He might go on reading, murmur absently by way of answer. Or he might give her a slightly disturbed glance.

"Well, call it forty. But it 'll be more this week."

"Why should it be more this week?"

"Oh, extra work I've done for Greenway." Greenway was a commercial photographer whose cluttered study in City Hall Avenue was lined with brilliant studies of iceboxes and neckties, bouquets and weddings, and pictures of pretty girls in smart little tailored hats. Gavin had worked for Greenway before; they had quarreled, Becky gathered. But both seemed glad to be reconciled and associated in business again. Or it might be that he had won at dice or cards. "Don't you worry!" he would say, perhaps tearing a long strip out of the paper that would be left for her to read. "I may be home for dinner; I may not. Potts and Gibbs and some of the fellers were talking of going down to Halfmoon Bay after the fight. I won't know till late. Have something decent in the house; a couple of the boys might come out with me around six."

If she became imperative and followed him to the door, it was never to win a satisfactory answer.

"Gavin, I've *got* to know. I don't want to charge two dollars worth of steaks and have everything ready, and then wait and wait and wait indefinitely! Dinners take *cooking* and *planning;* there's no woman in the world who could be ready and not ready five nights a week!" Rebecca might say, hating herself for the irritated critical tone, and yet goaded beyond endurance at the prospect of another empty day, with the uncertain prospect of four for dinner or nobody for dinner at the end of it.

Gavin had a fashion at these moments of shrugging his shoulders and elevating his eyebrows as one perpetually puzzled by the vagaries of women. His amused smile never deserted him.

"Well, well, now isn't that interesting!" he would say pleasantly. "You tell me all about what women 'll put up with and what they won't put up with and then where are you?"

And he would saunter away, leaving her ruffled and upset, as angry at herself as at him for the remainder of the morning.

She wondered sometimes, in her desperate doubt and unhappiness, if he would be happier if she never had come into his life at all. The affirmative answer was inevitable. She was a parasite wife, clinging to him because he was strong and handsome and a man, enduring everything, slights and humiliations and injustices, rather than make a break. And what would a break mean for her? She couldn't go back to Salletts, not if the alternative were the poorhouse itself. And if she were to divorce him, get a job, support herself, she might just as well do it now when there was still the shell of her marriage remaining, when the fifty-five-dollar rent was being paid.

Becky began to look resolutely, steadily for a job. She had suddenly an interest in life. She read columns of newspaper advertisements; she received countless offers to sell filters, magazines, cleaning powders, brushes, sets of books. A bookshop took her on for Holy Week; she sold cards with lavender crosses and white and silver lilies on them at five and ten cents a card, worked for twelve days and was paid twenty-four dollars. The money vanished, her feet grew finally rested, and she began to look for work again.

She had written to her mother twice, loving letters, but letters that gave no address. Despite the heartsick longing she felt day and night to see her, she did not want Sarah, keen-eyed, sympathetic, to find her in the Eddy Street apartment. Sarah would see little to admire in a bed that swung into a dressing closet by day, an icebox that lighted brilliantly as one opened it, a garbage can about the size of one of Sarah's lard tins with a pedal to save one the trouble of stooping.

The neighborhood that surrounded the elegantly tiled street entrance also would find Sarah unenthusiastic. It was a grimy neighborhood of theatrical agencies and restaurants and cigar corners and liquor stores. All morning women in wrappers ran about these corners, with fur coats held together at the breast; there were fights here after dark, drunks in doorways. The lights of a burlesque show flamed up and down all night. It was an odd place in which to have put a building of seventy-two apartments, but here the Golcondita indisputably was, and from it Gavin resolutely refused to move.

It was in vain that Becky talked of a little place out toward St Francis Wood, beyond the tunnel, where there were beautiful big markets and little gardens set in the fresh foggy sweetness from the Pacific. Gavin liked to be within actual sound and scent of his associates and his interests; he had no feeling for a six-room bungalow with a patio and geraniums, and Becky, as the months steeped them deeper and deeper in debt, dared not take matters into her own hands.

CHAPTER XV

IN MARCH, a cold windy March that blew chaff and papers along the streets, she got a job as stock girl in a woman's dress shop on Market Street. It was a large place that sold hundreds of dresses every day, and put new dresses with new ridiculously low prices displayed upon them in six great angled street windows every night. The windows were slanted about to make a staggered arcade entrance; they drew shopping women like flies, women who lingered among the glass walls all day long, came hesitantly into the shop, looked, debated, consulted with the inevitable friend. For evening dresses they paid as high as eleven dollars and eighty-five cents plus tax; other dresses ran from one dollar eighty-five to seven dollars eighty-five, the latter often advertised with sketches in the papers as being "lavishly trimmed with stitching, fancy buttons, tucking, embroidery and fur." Sometimes one dress displayed all these features.

Rebecca was paid nine dollars a week liable to insurance, tardiness, emergency deductions. Emergency meant when one of the girls died and flowers had to be sent from the firm, or one of the girls was in the hospital and the firm was paying her half pay to hold her. For these expenses twenty cents per week was deducted from every pay check and held by the firm. It saved the trouble of collections, and nobody knew, as a girl named Willie explained bitterly to Rebecca, whether the beneficiaries ever received anything or not.

The girls here were of a very low grade—fierce, over-painted, overscented, overcurled girls who were also overworked and oversexed. They were without exception promiscuous in their relationships with men, savagely taking in money, dinners, dances, drink, everything they could, savagely discussing the disadvantages of carrying on their work by day and following an even older profession by night. Their talk had so far left behind in recklessness, vulgarity and stark frankness Becky's knowledge of terms that she could hardly follow it, could hardly believe that human creatures in a civilized city could live on such barbaric levels. Most of them had been married and divorced more than once; some were maintaining irregular establishments with the man of the moment; some boarded in places like the never-to-be-forgotten house of Daisy Kinpaw. The smell of their coarse cheap perfumes combined with that of their unwashed, perspiring bodies sickened Rebecca; the state of the dressing room with its wet floor, strong-scented soap, soaked, filthy towels, suffocating disinfectants and untouched disorder absolutely frightened her. To see them sitting there eating drugstore sandwiches and drinking beer from bottles was to wonder where they had been schooled, what sort of homes had given them their starts into life. Coarseness of speech and manner, coarseness in dress and in skin and hands, and over the coarseness perfume and powder and coarse dry crimps of hair. She felt sometimes that she could not breathe the air they breathed a moment longer. For twenty-six dollars a month—or a day—it would not have seemed worth while to her a very short time ago.

But Rebecca at twenty was a frightened pupil now in the great classroom called life. There was a lesson for her to learn, and if its beginning were here in this incredible and insufferable place, she knew she could not rise to the next class until she had mastered it. If she had been a fool, the only way to change herself was to work her own way out of this impasse.

So she reported daily at the Bon Marché, punched a basement time clock, put her hat and coat and bag into a locker, mounted filthy wide iron stairs littered with boxes and packing and paper cartons and strings, entered from the rear a second-story loft lined and crossed by frames from which dresses swayed in hundreds from cheap thin wooden hangers stenciled with advertisements of the shop.

Everything that was common and cheap and long ago eliminated from the code of respectable shops went on at full speed at the Bon Marché from nine o'clock until five. Rebecca and a few other housekeepers went home at five instead of seven, and were docked three dollars a week for the privilege. The others stayed for two more hours and were paid twelve dollars, less deductions, a week.

Snatching and crowding went on; those were unending. Women waged unceasing war around the racks. Dresses were torn, and disagreeable floorwalkers, hated by all the girls, tried to fix the blame on the customer and, failing that, fixed it irrevocably upon the saleswoman. More deductions.

Thievery went on, and hot-faced frightened women were eternally being herded up to the manager's office, their shrill protests coming back in the close, brightly lighted, suffocating air that was always thick with the smells of cloth and dye and dust and wet raincoats.

"My friend here and I were looking . . . I slipped the coat on; the girl was right there! Yes, I think I'd know her— no, I don't believe I'd know her. . . ."

Rebecca worked at the back of the loft behind a flimsy wall of beaverboard. She opened beaverboard boxes six feet square and three feet deep, lifted out dresses and coats, looked them over, piled them on the tag tables for the sore flying fingers of the markers to tag. The packages were from Eastern manufacturers; they had come crated, but the boys downstairs had knocked away the wood.

Two colored men carried away great canvas sheets loaded with gray coarse paper. It was their business to sift it all through their fingers to be sure that no belt or dress had escaped Becky's eyes. It was the business of Becky and several other perspiring, pale, breathless women to look for machine slips, buttons missing or broken, seams opened.

When these occurred, and they often occurred, the sales invoice had to be found on the file, identified with the garment, pinned to it, and the whole flung into a basket for Mr Costelli.

But the work at the Bon Marché went on at such breakneck speed, the pressure was so terrific, that many mistakes escaped, some stock was ruined in the handling and some was lost, and then there was trouble.

"The customer won't take it with the zipper broken, Flood. You girls should have caught that. She wants this dress, she wants to wear it tonight, the sale's made, and here it is with a spot on the hem. We can't have that kind of thing. Where's them four hundred flower patterns? We had 'em in the paper this morning. They're out there raving for them. Step on it, Flood; this ain't the day for you to have a headache."

They were all called by their last names: Flood, Neilan, Buckley, White, Payson. Another little coarseness that had troubled her at first, but to which she became rapidly accustomed.

For the girls on the floor life was even harder than in the stock rooms. They were on their feet all day, and they had to deal with the customers. Such cheap, unreasonable, exacting women Becky had not before known could exist at all. They were as fierce as the girls; they exacted fittings, disputed prices, they spoiled dresses with lipstick, perspiration, dirty hands; blamed the saleswomen mercilessly. They complained of the rudeness of the girls; they would never patronize the Bon Marché again until that girl was fired!

The red dress *must* be somewhere in blue. Here it was, but the wrong size. Well, see if they had it in green. "Excuse me, madam, I'm looking at this dress." "Excuse me, Harris, but the customer hasn't made up her mind." "Excuse me, Maxie, but you can't hold stock all morning that way! Mr Costelli won't stand for it. Excuse me, Mr Costelli, but my customer is waiting to see this dress——"

The "excuse me" was invariably as savage as the rest of the dialogue. Girls rushed into the stock room to cry and swear, blew their noses and rushed out again, a pale blue "formal" of shiny satin waving like a banner borne before them. For hours they nosed among the dangling hot cloth gowns.

"This is it, madam. Not exactly the same, no, but I think the collar is prettier, reely I do. Lemme get there, Morris, and see if a thirty-eight got on that hanger. You've seen that one, madam; it's just the same one."

High on columns ringed about with cheap balustrades watchers were perched. When they saw a theft they blew a shrill whistle and pointed, and the crowd drew away from some protesting angry woman who found a detective quiet and soothing and persuasive at her elbow. The whistle also blew when a large bill had to be changed, and the floorwalker who took it called its denomination loudly as he went with it toward the office. There was no credit at the Bon Marché, no deliveries. Customers showed at the street door a certificate of sale; checkers there made a cursory examination of purchases before plumping them on the wrapping desk behind the door. No customer was supposed to leave until a sale had been made, and the girl who could not wheedle, bully, persuade her into a sale very simply lost her job at the end of the day, was paid to the last closely calculated penny, watched the book-keeper's fountain pen make note of deductions, and disappeared forever.

But there were three or four girls better paid than the rest, who could be called in in any sales emergency and often dragged a hesitant customer over the line of sale.

"Miss Mildred," the girl would say. Nothing more. Miss

Mildred would come graciously up, would look at the coat or dress interestedly.

"Eva," she might say pleasantly, "I don't believe you've shown Madam that brown number—the one with the wooden buttons. We've just the one, madam—forty-two, that's the size? That's the right size. Get that, Miss Eva. It's a very beautiful little model, and not one of the expensive ones. Eleven eighty-five reduced to seven sixty-five; that's ridiculous, isn't it? But Mr Buck came in here yesterday and simply slashed through prices—— That's it. Isn't it dainty? It's an all-occasion dress, a Lina Krempff copy. I happened to be crossing the floor and it did seem to me to look like Madam."

To Becky, bringing out stock, making herself useful where she could, it was amazing to see with what docility, with what actual pride nine out of ten customers bought from Miss Mildred. Mr Maas was another emergency resource, and although different was just as good. His was the bullying method.

"Listen, am I crazy?" one could hear him shouting at all times and in all places along the great loft. "Tell me, some kind friend, if I'm crazy or is this lady with the new-model coat crazy? I tell her the dress makes the coat and the coat makes the dress, and from her gloves and hat and the way she talks I know she's got sense—she knows what's what, if you'll excuse me the liberty, madam, not knowing your name or nothing about you, except that this dress will make your husband sit up and take notice and give you the biggest kiss you ever got since the happy day! It flatters your face, it flatters your figure, it's the color or may God strike me blind . . ."

Mr Maas bored, angered, annoyed customers, even as he deafened, blinded and flattered them into a state of complete confusion. If a discouraged salesgirl was lucky enough to get him she was often reduced to laughter herself, and sent her customer off with not only the dress, but with two others and a midseason coat as well.

There was laughter behind the scenes at the Bon Marché; there was company, even if of a deplorable sort, and Becky had hungered for both. She tried to make herself the most valuable clerk among these poor, ignorant, dirty, defrauded girls; she had heard her father say years ago that in every group of employees there was always one who stood head and shoulders above the rest, who was selected for promotion by his superiors long before he dreamed himself anything but a cog in the machine.

But the only result of this was that the girls came to distrust her, and one of the bosses, a married man of middle age, made bold annoying overtures that even her ignorance and innocence could not misunderstand.

She was so tired these nights that she went home at five to lie flat on her bed for an hour or, if Gavin did not come in, for a second hour. When he was away she often lay broken until eight or nine o'clock, too completely exhausted even to begin to rest. Her feet and legs burned up to the bones of the knees; her back ached; the muscles of her neck ached. To soak in a hot deep bath, to drink a whole pint of canned tomato soup thinned with hot milk, to nibble a chocolate bar as she lay clean and fed, reading, in her bed afterward, these were her happiest hours.

When instead she had to stagger about getting a meal for Gavin, having bacon catch on the pan while she put cups on the table, or hearing coffee boil over in a froth of brown grounds when he was cutting the steak, her wearied nerves gave way, and she and he quarreled like all the other married couples in the apartment whose loud voices went up and down the air shaft.

These disputes frightened her. They seemed to affect her physically, upsetting her digestion, robbing her nights of sleep. If afterward he would be apologetic and forgiving she would always meet him halfway, thankful to feel peace and reassurance invading her spirit once more. Sometimes after a reconciliation they would sit without moving for half an hour in the apartment's one big chair, Gavin smoking his pipe and meditating with half-closed eyes, Rebecca almost asleep against his shoulder.

"You poor little pussy, you're having a rotten kind of time," he might say with unusual consideration, and when he did, and if while she washed the dishes he would stay and talk to her or even stay and simply read his paper, she was happy again, she loved him again.

It had its good moments, but it was not exactly a life; it wasn't building toward anything, getting anywhere. She hated her job, she hated being alone in the city, she hated Gavin to go away and was not much happier when he was about. It was unsatisfactory all around, and for the first time in her life Becky felt unequal to her problem.

Rather to her surprise (and, upon consideration, much to her secret hurt), Gavin made no protest against her holding a job. He didn't care, one way or the other. He was usually willing to take her out to dinner if he came home to find her flat with fatigue; or he would leave her, on her assurance that she wanted him to, and go off to find friends with whom to dine. She paid a woman now three dollars a week for two hours work on Mondays, Thursdays and Saturdays; on those days the house had a superficial cleaning and any accumulated dishes and pots were washed. It was not a satisfying way to live, but anything was better than sitting around at home idle from nine o'clock until five.

"I wonder what kind of a woman I am? I wonder if all my life is going to be like this? I wonder how people pull themselves out of it when they've made mistakes?"

She asked herself the questions tirelessly. There seemed to be no answer as the days went by and were weeks and months. Sometimes she and Gavin had pleasant lazy Sundays together and went to a movie, sometimes he was away and she spent the day alone, resting and reading. They had affectionate intervals, when he thrilled her with talk of going to Hollywood, of having a place of their own and a car, and they somehow got through long stretches when his complacent selfishness made her irritable and depressed, and when she hardly dared speak to him for fear of betraying it.

It seemed ages since the Kinpaw episode, the convalescence at Laura Tevers' sanatorium. Yet the time flew, too, and Rebecca counted the months on her fingers amazedly when in late July she knew that she was going to have a baby. This had not been a part of her plan; she had hoped to keep free of this complication of all complications for another year or two. But the fact was a fact now, and had to be dealt with like all facts. Her work at the Bon Marché was less tiring than it had been; the cool summer months were much more bearable than spring. But she could not continue there long with an early-February baby coming.

She waited a month, another month. Then she told Gavin. His honest consternation made her heart sink, and their first talk of the child left her in angry tears. One would think no one had ever had a baby before! They could fit him in somehow; certainly Gavin had made sufficient fuss about the Pringles' terrible muddy-faced little girl. It was Rebecca who was going to have the hard part of it after all.

"You'll see, you'll be sorry," he said. There was nothing that she dared answer. Pulses beat in her forehead and her back ached; she felt cold and tired all the time and could eat only late in the day. Wretchedly she gave up her job, crouched at home, stupid and dizzy, hardly caring that bills accumulated as fast as dust did, and that whatever charm she had ever had for Gavin was in eclipse.

One night when there chanced to be something of the old harmony between them Gavin suggested that she go home to have the baby. He had been all the evening before at the dog races and had won largely. He had given her a hundred dollars with which to handle some of the bills, and although she knew it would leave half of them unpaid, still the money looked comforting to her. A hundred dollars just out of the sky!

A few days before, as an alternative to actually moving out, he had paid up the rent. She could put this money on butcher and grocery bills and so feel free for a little while at least to charge afresh.

Gavin expected to go out tonight at nine o'clock for an evening of poker. Tony Reynolds was to call for him. Meanwhile he lay back in the big chair, smoking, listening to the radio, and Becky stretched herself crosswise on the bed, two pillows pulled under her head, and lay looking at him.

"Listen, Beck, what d'you suppose your mother 'd say if you went home in January?"

An odd hesitancy, a certain fear flickered across her face.

"I've treated them so badly."

"Oh, shucks, they'd forget all that. Hospital there?"

"A fine one. The Pennoyer Memorial." But still she was doubtful, a fine line drawn across her forehead.

"Your mother 'd be crazy with joy."

Rebecca felt tears sting at the back of her eyes. She herself, given rein to think what it might mean, would be the one to be crazy with joy! Home voices again, the bare side yard again, under the oaks, the coolness of her own room, up among the pear-tree leaves, the look of the hills toward the east, gauze blue against a paler blue sky! Even Main Street, with the women marketing and the little cars nosing in and out of the angled parking spaces, would be heaven after this!

But how take it? How reconcile her pride to going back, wearing the very suit in which she ran away; how put a bold face on disillusionment and fear and failure? In a moment of chill premonition she wondered if Gavin would come for her, would be there when the baby was born, would send the necessary money. The duty—but he knew no such word!—which lay close to Gavin he did not see; how much less would he see a duty that was out of sight, a responsibility that would be carried on by others if he neglected it.

To go to her mother would mean a constant apology for Gavin. Among friends she could perhaps put a bold face on the matter. But at home, at home where everyone knew what letters came, what money one had, what was worrying or pleasing every separate member of an intimate group, there would be no deception. Dad would pay the hospital bills, the doctor could wait, Rebecca would write and write to Gavin. And what if there was no answer?

"Gavin, when could you come to Salletts if I went home?"

"Oh, gosh, why should I go there? You'd be coming back."

"But you'd want to see . . . And I'd want you there . . ." Her voice was thickening into maddening tears. "I know you're—you're cross about it!" She stopped speaking, abruptly.

"You mean the kid?" he asked slowly. "Well, I've always thought I'd like a kid. The Johnsons had a little girl named Rose Marie; gosh, she was a cute little kid. Like a doll, with her hair all curled up. But I wish to hell this one hadn't decided to come along right now!"

"I wish so too!" Rebecca said, trying to make her tone philosophical, cheerful. But her eyes were wet.

"You and the kid could come back when you got ready. I wouldn't have any objection to having a cute little girl around here," Gavin said thoughtfully, over his pipe. "Keep you from places like that damn dress shop, anyway. But we may be moved to Los Angeles any time now. . . ."

She had to think the situation out, to answer the problem without help from him. Hour after hour Rebecca weighed one thing against the other. He *might* not fail her, of course. He was generous enough when he wanted to be. If she went home now in mid-November, he might come to Salletts for Christmas. They could give up this apartment, save a hundred a month that way. He could go south and see Lomita, the man all-important in the commercial photography business. No one in the world knew more about cameras than Gavin, and all Hollywood's business centered on cameras. Gavin had said a hundred times he wished that when he had been down south Lomita had been there. He knew Lomita personally, would have no trouble, he was sure, in getting a good job under him.

"But gosh, you can't drag a woman down there, pay hotel bills for three weeks while you're getting an appointment!" Gavin had good-naturedly grumbled. Alone, he could bunk with Wilson or Dave or any one of the boys. And after February she and the baby could go down.

She and the baby! Rebecca shrank from the care and responsibility that the baby represented. She had not adjusted herself to wifehood yet, had not solved half the problems that that state presented. Now this unwelcome baby! Sometimes in the nights she cried in pity at thinking how wholly unwelcome the poor little creature would be.

CHAPTER XVI

IN THE END she went home. Gavin gave her another hundred dollars one morning, the morning they would start a fresh week at the Golcondita. Quite suddenly Rebecca determined to pay off most of the remaining bills, even though it would leave her with less than twenty dollars in her purse, give up the apartment, send Gavin south with Wilson in Wilson's car to see the all-important Lomita. And she herself went down to the ferry and bought a ticket for Salletts.

She could not help thrilling with anticipation and hope as the cars slid along through the scattered villages and the railed open fields. The country looked just as it had when she had made her wild rush for the city and freedom a year ago. A year! It seemed ten years. Ten years of loneliness and anxious days and money worries. A year that had held the Kinpaw interval, the strange, whisky-scented days in the sanatorium, with Emma Battock solemnly cold-creaming a large plain face and telling her about Laura and about Jacky.

There had been happy days after that, when she and Gavin had lunched extravagantly at the St Francis, and looked at the debutantes parading in fashion shows for the Junior League or the Children's Hospital. When they had hunted houses in the very limited zone that Gavin liked, the theater and restaurant zone.

Then had come the bewildering beginnings of a constant evidence of his selfishness, that serene and sunny selfishness that never grew angry unless it was balked. His "Can't let you have any of this, lost most of it to Dan last night!"

when she had seen his pocketbook filled with bills and had asked for market money. His waking her in the middle of a cold night to make him some hot coffee. His lateness at meals, his unwillingness even to listen to her when she asked him please to let her know when he was going to bring men home to dinner. His quiet absorption of the paper or magazine; his quiet assumption that if he could only get one seat for a show that seat was his.

Rebecca remembered his going to market with her in the early days between his hospital convalescence and his resuming work.

"I'm leaving you here if you're going to pack that stuff home," he had said. He hated parcels; there was no use arguing about it. Recriminations bored him to the angry point, after which he became completely irresponsible, dragging up remembered omissions on her part, deafening her with furious words, finally slamming himself out of the house and neglecting her entirely for such hours or even days and nights as he needed to be brought to the point of a cheerfully forgetful reconciliation. "Look here, Becky, let's not be fools," was his usual approach. "If you're sorry, I'm sorry!"

And as he had all the money and was her only companion, she never had hesitated to accept the peace offering. After all, with a baby coming, a woman was heavily handicapped and had to take pretty much what life brought her.

Salletts looked oddly shrunken when she got out of the train in bleak midafternoon. There was a cloud over the sun, spread indeed in leaden solidity over the whole sky; all the little shops of Main Street looked countrified and small. At half-past four o'clock the electric sign in front of the movie theater, El Alcazar, was lighted and one or two of the smaller shops gushed light. A jay little town crawling up the first slopes of the Sierras, but the fresh air struck upon her flushed face deliciously cool and sweet, and when she half jumped and half tumbled out of the taxi at her mother's kitchen door Becky was laughing and crying together in excitement.

She heard her mother's unchanged voice: "Well, for the land sakes, Becky!" and the wild, excited cheering and shouting of the small brothers. She was somehow gotten into the warm kitchen among them all, and the happy, breathless questions and answers were flying about, the boys' entire unconsciousness of restraint covering what might have been awkward moments of embarrassment and explanation.

Becky thought at first that all that was over, that dreaded moment of adjusting present to past. But she found that as the hours went by it was not so. There was a gap, and all her mother's generosity and all her tacit apology could not quite bridge it. She was changed; they were all changed; life could not go back.

At six o'clock she was brushed and fresh and ready to hug her father and repeat her explanations.

"My rolling stone has rolled to Los Angeles for what really did sound like a good job, and I couldn't resist—I *had* to come home! I've thought of you all—I've *longed* for you all so. . . ."

But even as she spoke, with her hand holding little Gary's hand as he sat next her at table, her eyes shining at each member of the group in turn, she knew it was not quite enough. So many long months of absence with only a brief note now and then to say that she was well, that she would come, that she would write. It was not enough!

But the bliss that it was to be home again showed in every expression of her older face, sounded in every word she said, and they forgave her, without ever knowing or thinking that they must forgive her, because she was Becky and because she brought back to them something that was of priceless value in their lives. Becky, in her blue dress with the twisted white silk about the neck, with her soft bright hair ruffled and her gold-brown eyes filled with the old love and eagerness and happiness—well, they had missed her every moment, loved everything that was remembered or that reminded them of her; longed, as one longs after a loved child dies, for just this hour, this one hour of hearing her voice and being able to watch the emotions follow each other on her face again.

They had dinner in the kitchen; the dining room was being repapered. She must see a sample of the paper; she approved.

"And, Mother, you'll have to have new curtains!"

"Dad brought me home some samples last week."

The boys were eager to hear about the city. Gee, where had Becky lived? Gosh, movies all day long!

"We lived in a little apartment downtown—really nice rooms, and an electric refrigerator, Mother, and all that. But everything," Becky said with a rueful laugh, "everything that Gavin and I do is so sketchy, so temporary, that I kept thinking we'd change our address, and be in some little place with more sunshine to it, and a garden—like Lily Potter's place, remember, Mother? Out past the Twin Peaks Tunnel? Remember we went there about—oh, years ago, when they were first married? I kept thinking . . . And time went on . . ."

And her appealing look moved about the circle again, explaining and saying that she was sorry.

Her appearance immediately betrayed her condition. Becky sensed an odd reluctant satisfaction in her mother's lowered tones as Sarah asked her very first questions. A baby was welcome to Sarah under any conditions. Her father shook his head, lovingly, doubtfully.

"Little old Becky, eh? Well, well, well."

"Now tell me everything and anything," Sarah said seriously when Becky had had a night of delicious restful sleep, and when the two women were busy in the kitchen with breakfast dishes.

Becky felt a second's interior panic. But she had known this talk must come. And she had known from the first instant of thinking of this visit at home that it could not be quite a frank talk. Confidential, but with reservations her mother must not suspect.

Well, Gavin was a dear, of course, but he did jump from one thing to another, hated to settle down. He'd had a perfectly good job last year, but he was so lazy that he was always late, and in the radio business you simply couldn't be late. What exactly had he been doing? He'd been doing studio photography. He was really an expert on cameras, in his crazy way. Becky tried to make it all casual and laughing. It had a maddening way of sinking into what sounded like wifely whining, wifely complaint.

"Gavin's thirty-three, Mother, and he's simply not used to making allowances for a woman. Not in any way. Her comfort and her expenses and her feelings!"

"Selfish," Sarah observed thoughtfully, looking up over her grater. "How about money?"

"Well, Mother, if he had it! Or if he was lucky with cards or dice." It didn't sound very satisfactory. Becky had forgotten Salletts' simple countrified attitude toward gambling.

The talk rambled on and on in the heavenly quiet of home again, with chickens getting hungry and coming to eye the kitchen door expectantly, with noon whistles sounding far away and faint, the signal for all the kindergarten children to go rushing out like freed little wild birds, the signal for the Gibson boys to get out their lunch boxes and straggle into the cafeteria with their milk and ice cream nickels. Becky thought that she would sleep, sleep all afternoon. She could never get enough sleep!

"When do you go back to him, Beck?"

For some reason the quiet question struck her cold, and Becky looked startled as she said:

"Well, I thought after the baby comes . . ."

"But that's February, dear!"

"About eleven weeks."

Sarah shook a wise head, and Becky felt her happiness shrivel within her.

"That's too long to leave a man, dear, now in the beginning, when you're hardly settled even into being married yet. No; we'll keep you here a week or ten days, Beck, and then you join him again, and I'll come down to you in February."

Becky sat puzzled, hurt beyond words, her cheeks red.

"A man like that," Sarah was quietly, almost sorrowfully resuming, "has got to have marriage built about him, Beck. I don't know whether that's the way to say it exactly. But if he's anything of what you called him to Dad last night, he wants an anchor. A rolling stone needs a wife and child. You say he wasn't especially glad about this baby coming— poor little tyke! That's another reason why you ought to be with him all these weeks, let him see what it means to a woman. He'll not have any feeling for it or for you either if you stay here four months——"

"February isn't four months, Mother!" Becky said in a proud quick voice.

"No, but it 'll be another six weeks, it 'll be April before you and the baby are fit to move. It's a job, getting a small baby started—food and hours all have to be worked out. You'd want to stay right here near Doctor Pringle for that; they say he's the best in the state. No, Beck, you'll have to go down to Gavin next week, and get some sort of a home started . . ." Sarah left the sentence unfinished. She sighed heavily, and Becky sat silent, staring into space, a frown knitting her forehead.

"Dad and I'd rather have you here than anywhere else in the world," Sarah resumed in the silence, stooping to test the oven with a big capable hand, watching Becky over her shoulder, "but that isn't marriage, Beck. That isn't fair to you or Gavin or the baby either. You've got to start thinking of him. Ah, now *don't,* dear——"

The last was in a tone of infinite sympathy, infinite pity. For Becky had put her head down on the table and burst into tears. Sarah did not go near her, did not even lay her hand on the bright hair she had brushed and praised all through the happy little-girl days of school and plans and freedom. Becky cried violently for a few minutes, stopped between sulkiness and surprise at her mother's attitude, blew her nose and wiped her eyes, and looked measuredly into space again.

"It's just that I'm so *tired* all the time," Becky presently said, with her lips trembling and her eyes threatening to spill their tears. "And I'm so alone! And now—*this* coming, when we'll need money, and I'll be so clumsy . . . so good for nothing . . .

"Already," she went on with fresh tears, "already Gavin doesn't like to go out with me; I don't blame him! And it just seems as if I couldn't go down south, not this way—not to try to begin all over again this way!"

"Beck, that's marriage," Sarah said gravely. "When you married him what did you expect?"

Rebecca considered this for a long while, her brows still knitted, her eyes dark and brooding.

"I'll go down to him as soon as I know where he is," she finally said in a hard, resentful voice.

"And you'll see a doctor there?"

"Yep," the girl agreed lifelessly.

"Believe me," Sarah said, "it's the only thing to do."

It was a new tone from her. It was the tone of a woman speaking to another woman, not the motherly, protecting voice Becky had always known. It came to her suddenly for the first time, and with infinite bitterness of spirit, that this woman was not her mother.

"I'll go as soon as he writes me," Becky said. "And sends money," she thought.

But the days went by and were weeks, and Christmas came, and the new year, and he did not write.

CHAPTER XVII

BECKY WENT to the hospital on a bitter cold February day when the sun was brightly shining on frozen ruts in the road and on the nipped green of early grass. She went shakily, laughingly, apologizing to her mother for the bulky clumsiness with which she got into the car.

Sarah was quiet, efficient, nervous. She and Becky had been lingering over the breakfast table at nine o'clock when a startled cry had been wrenched from the younger woman, and Becky had said courageously: "Ouch, we're off!"

Her suitcase had been packed for days. They had only to pick up the coat which somewhat disguised Becky's figure, turn off a gas jet or two in the kitchen, and start.

"It's a relief to have it coming at last!" Becky said as they went toward the village and turned up toward the hospital street. But her teeth were chattering despite her tone.

"It's early, at that," Sarah said, not knowing what she said.

"Yes, he said fifteenth, and this is only . . ." Becky knew the date well; she had kept careful count of the days for weeks ahead. "This is only the thirteenth," she said. She was icy cold and shaking; she felt as if she were going to be nauseated and her head was spinning. "It's a lovely hospital," she said.

"It cost pretty near a hundred thousand," Sarah observed.

Not knowing what they were doing or what they saw or to whom they spoke, they went in and laughed and explained and were led about. Finally Becky was upstairs in a small plain room where a high, beautifully fresh bed slid about at the slightest touch on the polished floor. Minnie Cates came in and sat down with a fountain pen and a long blank, and filled in answers.

Mrs Flood was twenty-one. "My land, is that all you are, Becky?" Minnie said. Sarah said that she would go over to the Exchange and tell Dad that things had started. "Maybe I'll have something to show you when you come back!" Becky said gallantly. Sarah, her heart wrung with pity, stooped to kiss her forehead as Becky sat taking off her shoes and stockings. These hard months of hurt pride and uncertainty behind her, the rack just ahead, and she could smile, could think of her mother's fears.

"You'll have something pretty nice this time tomorrow," Minnie substituted. Sarah saw Becky's eyes blink with fright.

"It couldn't be that long," Becky said.

"Don't worry about time, just take things as they come along," Sarah suggested. "Get into bed and get reading and don't worry. You'll get through it, dear, like everyone else, and you'll have something lovely to show for it."

"I suppose the first's got to be a boy, Becky," said Minnie when, rather scared, Becky was left alone with her and various preliminary activities were under way. Her clothes were hung in the closet; oddly, she had on her nightgown and a loose cotton wrapper at ten o'clock in the morning. Dr Pringle looked in.

"Well, I shouldn't wonder if you're having a baby, Becky," he said. And then to Minnie: "Say, what's your brother on O'Neill's side of the fence for in this school business? You tell Dave to come round and see me."

"No, Gavin wants a girl," Becky presently answered Minnie. She brought in Gavin's name when she could, without seeming to force it. Minnie reflected, as she heard it, that her folks weren't the only ones in town who'd like to get a good look at Rebecca Gibson's marriage certificate.

"Well, whatever it is, you'll keep it," Minnie said.

Becky glanced at her wrist watch, her face twisting a little.

"Want me to time these pains, Minnie?"

"Lord, no," said Minnie, twisting something around her arm for a blood test. "You aren't having pains at all yet!"

Becky knew she was having pains, good hard pains. She thought it would be nice if they suddenly discovered that her baby was much nearer being born than they had thought. Becky Gibson, the town folk would say, got to the hospital at ten and fooled Minnie Cates good and plenty: the baby was born before lunch!

But time did slip by rapidly, that was one comfort. Even if the baby wasn't born until, say, five o'clock, that wouldn't be so bad. It was noon already, with Minnie bringing her chicken soup and a cracker. She was not hungry, and her hands and feet felt cold and her face burned, but when her mother came back at two she could say triumphantly: "I'm really having bad pains, Mother."

The main thing was to get it started and get it over with.

Sarah looked at the white face in which two spots of red burned. She sat down to talk and wait. She knew these were not pains, that Becky might not really begin the business of bringing a human to birth until this time tomorrow. Pitiful, courageous Becky, her ewe lamb, so changed, so lessoned and sobered, with her drawn thin face and eager eyes.

"We're really getting started, Mother."

"Min say so?"

"Min's gone off. It's just Lulu Cole, on the hall, now."

"How about some sleep, Beck?"

"Mother, you can't sleep when you're having *pains*."

"It's a nervous sort of time, waiting." Sarah sighed. The hours went by, and Becky's stream of chatter stopped. Her face went on burning; her hands were cold. She turned magazine pages, looked hopefully at the screen every time the door creaked. That might be the doctor. Or it might be Minnie to say, "Listen, this baby's practically here."

The clocks did not stop; that was one good thing. It was five; she had expected it all to be over by five! Her father came in to see her, and Loretta Cross, who was in training.

It was eight o'clock when the old doctor really did come in and say cheerfully that he thought she ought to get some sleep; he did not expect that baby until sometime tomorrow. Becky was agitated and wakeful now; she was sick of her magazine and hungry and wearied unto death of the impersonal little room and the eternal waiting.

But she had learned something in the past three months. She had learned a sort of protective gentleness; she had given everyone who loved her a good deal of trouble and anxiety and disappointment; she was now adding to it all the supreme strain and expense of a baby's arrival; it behooved her to save them what she could. She said very meekly that she would try to sleep.

At three she was awake again, and the hot bright little room took shape, and the dark starry night looked in at her high window. The night nurse came in yawning and smelling of coffee; Miss Cates had told her not to call her unless it was important, she said.

To Becky it was important. She was seized, flung about, hammered. She did not look at her wrist watch now, nor at the clock whose hands stood still on the wall. Her voice was gone, and she was soaked and panting. Minnie Cates was looking at her thoughtfully through a red mist.

"My God, I just had the most awful dream," Minnie said in an undertone to the night nurse. "Don't throw yourself around that way, Becky. Take hold here. Yep, we're started all right."

Becky said something in a hoarse whisper.

"Doc? He'll be in," Minnie said soothingly; "he always comes round early."

It went on and on. A nurse looked in and said, "Miss Cates, my patient is being terribly bothered by the noise in here."

"You tell her to tend to her knitting," said Minnie Cates.

There was a lull. Rebecca panted; Minnie sponged off her forehead and told her to take it easy.

Suddenly, as it all recommenced, Rebecca felt herself settling down to it. It was not a question of avoiding pain now; it was a matter of something to be done. Her wet hair was swept back from her forehead. The merciless light burning on, the merciless rack seizing her, she looked expectantly at Minnie. What was she supposed to do? She would do it.

Sarah came in at six, in the straggling dull dawn. Rebecca heard her mother's little gasp of pity, heard Minnie say, "She's working hard now. She started in an hour ago. We're coming on fine now."

Oh, that the love of a man could put a woman's supersensitive body through this! Devils, not men. Devils, all of them—oh, God, she could not stand it. . . .

"Oh, I'm sorry, Mother, I can't help it!"

"Don't mind anything, darling, except that it's coming to an end."

"Well, well, well," said Minnie. Rebecca felt Minnie's hand on her forehead; she could not open her eyes. "The doctor's here," Minnie said, "and here we go. This 'll prick, but in about five minutes . . ."

Rebecca felt a needle in her arm, she felt the blessed silence closing in over her own voice. She was only crying now, audibly, sobbingly, moaning through her nose, but not with pain.

"Oh, that's better. Oh, Mother, make them keep that up."

The wheeled stretcher at last. The God-given bewildering halls at last; a student nurse smiling at her. The elevator, strongly scented. And the pain held under, smothered under —there, but under . . .

"Well, now, what would you like? A baby?" It was old Dr Pringle. Rebecca, crying already, began to cry afresh. Tears streamed down.

"I guess I'm broken!" she faltered with a smile.

"Let me fasten your arms down, Becky. You aren't going to have any more pain, dear." This was homely old-maid Dr Mary Saville, but what an angel she looked, bending down! Becky could summon up enough manners to whisper, "Thanks," and that was all she remembered.

CHAPTER XVIII

SHE CAME BACK from far places and by degrees. First it was someone being soothed, someone with a cold wet rag on her forehead. Then it was hands lifting her, changing hot blankets. "Thanks, Miss Pierce, I've got her." And there was the miracle of no pain, blessedly no pain.

She was going to sleep. But afterward her head hurt and she opened her eyes and saw the top of the window curtain and a rainy sky. Long, long ago she had been Becky Gibson come to the Pennoyer Memorial Hospital to have a baby. I seemed very sad; so long ago. Everyone must be dead.

The time clock, and the girls crowding about her. "Maxie, I'm late. Cars blocked." Raining in the city streets.

"That hurt. You're fine, Becky. Proud of you," Minnie Cates said suddenly in a warm bright hospital room.

"Oh?" Becky said with a sore dry throat. "Oh, thanks, Minnie." For that was a sliver of ice, deliciously cold and wet.

"Becky, you've got a beautiful boy." That was her mother, close beside her, crying and smiling.

"Oh no," said Becky as the full miracle broke upon her. It was over; she was flat and weak and out of pain and back in bed. Ether hung about her, slightly nauseating; breakfast trays clattered in the hall. It was over. "Oh, Mother, is he nice?"

"He is simply a darling. They're all laughing at him, he's so saucy," Sarah said.

"Stay," Becky whispered.

"I'm so proud of you, darling. They said you made it all so easy for them."

"I was a flop and a quitter and I lay down on my job," Becky breathed with something of her old smile. Her mother had missed it all these months. "But now I'll come to and be a model mother," she whispered after a pause.

"It's all over," Sarah said. "You've got to sleep now, and then you're to have some breakfast."

"And not see him?"

"Oh, Lord," said Minnie. She went away and brought the baby in, tunneled in blanket, wrinkled, deep orange red, with black mop on the top of his scowling face.

"Is he really handsome?"

"Oh yes, he's a fine baby."

"Oh, Mother, I'm so happy!" Becky said. Her head aching faintly from anesthetics, her throat rasped, her eyes drenched, her body sore and wearied, her stomach caved with hunger, every bone of her slowly receding to normal position after hours of wrenching and straining, she went peacefully into the deepest sleep that even her twenty-one healthy years ever had known.

And for a few lazy comfortable days she was content.

"Mother, we'll have to find Gavin, Gibbs and I, and go to him," she said one day seriously, and with a little effort.

Sarah looked at her gravely, made no denial.

They were at home again. They had moved the baby, dainty and sweet and fed, pink-blanketed in the bottom of a wash basket, out into warm spring sunshine. Now the two women were sitting near him for a moment, in the old side-porch chairs, glad of an interval of breathing and resting.

It was almost eleven o'clock. Since Gibbs's first little awakening whimper at five minutes of six Becky, who had slept even before that but lightly, had been flying from one thing to another without an instant's respite.

The day had followed its usual pattern. She had stumbled

up in the early cold to patter downstairs for his bottle; she had set it in a saucepan of hot water to heat, the complaining baby meanwhile balanced firmly on one hip, and had waited the endless moments until a squirt of milk, on her wrist, had matched in temperature her own bodily warmth.

Then upstairs again to a room warming to the first heartening crackle of a fire in the airtight stove, to tear every soaked stitch from the crib and from the baby's small person, pull a fresh dry microscopic shirt over his head, pin things, fold things, wrap him in a new warm blanket and settle down to getting his morning meal into him, a serious business and one that usually took almost half an hour. Afterward Spencer Gibson Flood was turned on his face, warmly covered and left to go off to sleep again, but Becky, at twenty minutes before seven, had other things to do. She must straighten the room, make her bed, take her bath and get thoroughly dressed for the day. Any neglect of hair or girdle or shoe-laces was bound to react later in the morning, when some caller would find her disheveled and sloppy.

After that masses of baby linen must be gathered into a great bundle, and if Becky was already perspiring and a few minutes late for the eight o'clock breakfast it was because she had seized a minute in which to soak all these in the tub and soap some of them thoroughly. Then breakfast, with her old sunshiny greetings for her father and the boys, her old eager help for her mother at the stove. Only somehow this eagerness, this cheerfulness seemed infinitely more valuable, seemed to her parents, at least, to be more touching now, now that Becky was a woman and had put a woman's experiences, passions, tears behind it.

She and her mother dared not loiter after breakfast now. Becky's share of clearing was confined to carrying dishes into the kitchen, wiping the table top and putting back the strip of colored embroidery and the flowers, running a carpet sweeper over the floor. Window shades were evenly drawn, chairs aligned against the wall, and she was upstairs like a flying swallow to see if Gibbsy had stirred.

Downstairs again with all the bottles, which were sterilized while she mixed his formula.

"Is this the new milk, Mother?"

"That bottle there, Beck." Sarah had an assistant now, a morose big peasant girl from some Balkan country, who worked with something like three horsepower. Sophy had a child, too, a pale shy little creature called Anya; her one interest in a life that had treated her hardly. She was hence expert in handling Gibbs and often helped Becky with the last of the ironing or with folding the clothes.

When the bottles were all filled with the smooth pure creamy mixture and set away in the icebox, Becky rinsed out the forty or fifty pieces of laundry work that Gibbs demanded daily. Shirts, diapers, bibs, sheets, everything that came into the remotest contact with Gibbs had to be washed every day, wrung out, shaken out, hung flat, sunned, unless there was a cold wind that shortened matters, for at least three hours.

Becky put on a sweater to hang them out; the yard was cold these March mornings. She snapped the springs of small wooden clothespins, snapped the diapers by their corners, and felt the fine fog from them strike her warm face. There would be a tremendous satisfaction in working so hard if only one's back wouldn't so maddeningly get tired in mid-morning!

At ten Gibbsy had another bottle and another complete change. Again the crib was torn apart, another bunch of discarded clothes began to gather like a snowball on the bathroom floor. This time he might be wakeful for half an hour, and Becky would carry him down to the kitchen.

Sarah always stopped her stringing of beans or cutting of cookies to stretch eager arms for him; while she crooned and cuddled him Becky dragged out the basket, put it either where an angle of sunshine came into the kitchen or carried it out into the yard, ran up- and downstairs to get blankets and pins.

Eleven o'clock now, and two of the boys, who had been moved to the Union High School since Becky left home, would be back in an hour on their flying bicycles for lunch. Sarah had to get baking potatoes started. If it was a Tuesday or a Friday she had been to market and would only be getting back now with her loaded car. Becky would go indoors, half blinded by bright sunshine, and set the kitchen table. The boys' meal was an altogether hurried affair, no use in formality. They seized their sandwiches, took great bites between gulps of chocolate or milk, stuffed cookies or gingerbread into their pockets and were away again, flinging apple cores behind them as they went.

Becky and her mother, as the racket and whirlwind died away, settled down more comfortably to their own meal. Sophy ate never and always. A saucerless cup on the very edge of the kitchen table at some odd hour, a scraped saucer that had once held the remainder of spiced herrings or wilted salad in the sink, a few doughnut crumbs on Sophy's dark face were the only evidences that the family had of Sophy's eating at all, except for the fact that Sophy always gulped something down before she morosely answered a question. Little Anya had careful meals given her by her mother, but she was always asleep at noon.

After lunch Becky gathered in her wash, stiff, dry and sweet, and much of it was folded at once and carried upstairs to go into Gibbs's bureau. What had to be ironed was dampened and rolled and put back in the basket, and when Becky was not so tired and sleepy that she could not keep on her feet, she started ironing immediately. It was pleasant work, especially when every slip and sheet and tiny shirt made her think of the brown sturdy baby with his mop of black silk hair. But her back would be tiresome again; no help for it!

She had made a solemn compact with Sarah that the older woman should not touch the ironing, although Sarah protested, and Becky knew it was true that she loved to iron. But Gibbs and his mother had quite sufficiently disorganized the household without that, Becky said, and she meant it so earnestly that Sarah dared only sneak in a little surreptitious service here and there. Becky insisted that her mother go to her clubs, keep up with her village interests, but with all her efforts she knew that Sarah had too much to do at home and that the augmented housework was a burden to her, whether she admitted it or not.

At two and at six there must be a full hour out again for Gibbs's bottles, for more complete changing of raiment and bed linen. Sometimes at the later bottle he roared inexplicably. Becky was sorry that that was his troublesome time, for her father was rather awkwardly and shyly fond of the baby and was quickly regaining his old adept touch with a tiny infant. The boys also liked to gather about their nephew and comment with laughter upon his inadequate equipment of intelligence. Gosh, he din' look at 'em, and gosh, what a hand, and gosh, didn't he hear anything, Beck?

Sometimes after dinner she brought down whatever rumpled and wet baby linen had accumulated and set it to soak overnight. She was usually so tired at eight o'clock that she went blindly upstairs to bed, setting her alarm for Gibbs's ten o'clock meal, and hardly awake while she gave it to him.

For with all his demands the household demands went on steadily too: bedmaking and dishwashing for a family that now numbered ten, cutting of bread and setting of tables, picking up gum wrappers and detective magazines in the boys' rooms, keeping them at their homework, clearing up after them when they polished their shoes or took their baths.

And all the time Becky must endure the nagging humiliations of Gavin's treatment. No letter, no money, not even a dollar to tip Sophy, who so obviously expected it, or to indulge Gibbs in the little white coat at McGee's Linen Shoppe. Nothing for her but heartsick wondering and lame explanations to her own people, and what face of courage and confidence she could present to the world.

CHAPTER XIX

So on this particular sweet warm morning, when she said seriously that she and Gibbs must go to join Gavin, Sarah, who understood all these things, made no protest. She only gave one quick glance at the baby, or rather at the lock of silky black hair that was all that was visible of him, and faintly nodded, her face very grave.

"I'll miss him so, Beck!"

"Ah-h-h!" The long-drawn syllable was like a sob. Becky had been longing, only a short two years ago, to get away from home. Now it seemed to her a very haven from the cold winds of the world, a place filled with peace and love, roofed with blue skies and apple blossoms, where Gibbsy could grow safe and strong. . . .

"If I don't go now, I never will," she said. "And then what?"

"But you don't know where he is, Beck?"

"I've thought of a way to find out. I almost hoped it *wouldn't* work," Becky confessed, ashamed, "but it's going to. Ned McSwayne, the San José man Gavin was with when he first came up here, was up here to see Mollie White on Friday. I met him when I took Spin to the dentist. Apparently he thinks everything's——" Her throat closed on a dry bitterness. "Everything's fine between Gavin and me," she began again. "He asked about Gavin, said that he was baching it with a man named Cotton, down there in Hollywood, a movie photographer, I think he said. He said he'd send me the address; it probably wasn't in the telephone book. So I wrote Gavin."

Her voice stopped on a level note. She looked away into space.

"I wonder we didn't think of him before," Sarah commented, trying to make her voice sound simply concerned and natural.

"We might have thought that, if I didn't know, Ned McSwayne wouldn't know." Becky spoke dryly.

Sarah was silent for a while, troubled.

"Beck, I hate to talk about this. Don't think I'm curious," she presently said. "But you—you don't hate Gavin?"

"No, I don't hate Gavin," Becky answered, not moving, speaking in a lifeless voice.

"It's just . . . ?" Sarah left the question in air.

"It's just that I can't depend on him, Mother. I never know what his mood will be, what his job will be, how much money I'll need and how much I'll get. No," Becky said, still looking away, and now with a sudden flush on her face, "I—he could so easily make me love him again. He can be fascinating. I know he's smart; if he'd only just—just apply it to something. Everyone likes him. That is," she amended it with a reluctant little laugh, "everyone he wants to make like him does like him. But I'm never—comfortable with Gavin! I think perhaps—I think perhaps I love him," Becky went on uncertainly, speaking as if she were in pain and with a frowning brow, "I love him without liking him. When he loves me, when he needs me, everything goes right somehow. I despise myself for it," she finished, "but he can—can tease me into loving him, can win me back to him by just putting his arms around me. I go—all soft and—and kind. I want him to love me. That's what makes me feel I'm such a *fool!*"

"But that's the way it ought to be, when you're married, Beck."

"Yes, I know. But not with all the other things wrong. Not when you're resenting unfairness, resenting being left alone, resenting extravagance and bills and ill temper and criticism!"

Sarah sat pondering this, her own forehead lined, her lips pursed.

"Yet I'd hate you to talk divorce, Beck," she said finally. "A girl your age, with this beautiful child."

"I'm not thinking about divorce," Becky answered grimly. "I'm thinking of failure. I've made a failure. I suppose it always takes two to make a failure in marriage, and I'm one. But how—*how?* What did I do or what didn't I do that made him want to marry me and be so wonderful during that week here, and then let me down this way? It isn't Gavin or even Gibbsy I'm thinking about. It's me. What have I done?"

"Well, you just married a man who—who hasn't acted up to his promises, Beck."

Becky's thoughts were adrift. She spoke somberly.

"I saw Joe Feratta yesterday."

"Back in town, is he? He's been in Sacramento since Christmas."

"Yes, I know. He asked so pleasantly for Gibbs, and was so nice."

"Not any feeling—I mean love for Joe left?" Sarah asked in a new anxiety.

"I never did love Joe, Mother. It just isn't there. I see Joe just as he is, a big, fine, clean, nice man with all the good points of the Irish and the Italians combined, clever and successful and rising in his profession, and I wish—I wish to God," Becky said with sudden warmth, "that everything Joe has could stir in me just one tenth of the feeling that Gavin used to manage with one look or the lazy way he used to say one word!"

"D'you think Joe's still in love with you?"

Becky answered hesitatingly, reluctantly.

"Yesterday I would have said no, Mother, because when I met him at Christmastime, that week that he was home, he seemed just like—just like anyone else. Of course I was enormous, not exactly the laughing girlish beauty that men follow. And I was glad. Lucy said something about a girl he liked in Sacramento, and I was really glad. But yesterday there wasn't any question about it. He—of course one knows. His voice was shaky and he—well, I knew. He asked me to go and have a soda at Luchein's, and I said no, I had to be back for Gibbs' bath at half-past five, and he asked to bring me home. But I said I had the car and was picking Dad up, and he walked with me to the car and asked me if some night, 'before Gavin came for us,' I'd go to the movie with him."

"Joe Feratta asked you that!" Sarah said, shocked.

"Yes. He was—was all shaken up. It made me ashamed." Becky dismissed it with an impatient jerk of her head.

"His folks would die if he went out with a divorced woman," Sarah said ruminatingly.

"There's that to think of too. I don't fit here any more; it's just eternal food for gossips, and God knows this town has its share!"

"But, Beck, you haven't the faintest idea what you're going to!"

"I know. But just the same, if Gavin's working——"

Both women turned. A man, well dressed and groomed, with a light overcoat folded and belted about a slender figure, had come in from the front garden, past the bare whips of the berry bushes.

"Hello, Becky!" he said cheerfully, advancing toward them.

"Gavin!" Becky said faintly. She got up, and he put his arm about her and kissed her.

After a confused moment of forced laughter and surprise and greeting, they all sat down again, and Gavin smiled keenly at his wife. Becky's hair was in disorder; she wore a cotton morning dress belted with Gibbs's big bath apron.

"You're thin. Think she's thin, Mrs Gibson?" Gavin asked.

"Look here, Gavin. Don't make too much noise; he's beginning to hear things." Becky raised the baby's blanket.

"He looks all right!" Gavin said, laughing. "Well, tell me everything, and how's everything?" he added, resuming his seat, taking out his cigarette case and looking from one woman to the other. "Smoke, Mrs Gibson? I know Beck doesn't. What's all the news? Ned McSwayne wrote me he'd seen Beck, and I thought the best thing I could do was to come up. I'm not much of a letter writer."

"I'll say you aren't!" Becky felt an odd prick of self-contempt beneath her rueful little laugh. This forgiving, casual manner wasn't the way to treat him after all these months. But what else could a neglected wife do? Make a scene in these first minutes of reunion, embarrass Mother with recriminations? Instinct told her that at the first break, the first loosening of her tongue, she would lose all restraint and begin to cry. She must hold tight to her self-control.

"But, Gavin," she said, trying to speak lightly yet with a touch of bitterness already in her voice, "where've you been? Why no letters? I didn't know where to write, or what was happening to you——"

"Beck was worried," Sarah put in gravely.

"I didn't know where I was myself!" Gavin assured them cheerfully. "They sent me to Yuma; hell of a place. I was in Calexico for three weeks, being fried by inches. I kept thinking I'd sit down and write the whole thing out for you, Beck, and then, by George, it'd all bust up and I'd be off somewhere else. Well, but here I am now, with a few days to consider about sixty-seven different propositions," Gavin concluded with an air of humor, "and meanwhile the kid's arrived, eh?"

To Becky, even in this first moment, it was not humorous. Nothing was right from then on; not his suggestion that he take a bath and a shave while they were getting lunch ready, his characteristic procrastination until too late, nor her father's kindly, quiet greeting of him, nor the boys' surprise, nor the meal to which they all presently sat down. Gavin did most of the talking, telling them amusing little episodes of the helter-skelter days of a movie cameraman, acknowledging their goodness to Becky and the baby somewhat indirectly with a good-humored: "Say, I've loaned you my wife long enough! I knew her mother 'd want her to be here, but there were lots of times I could use a good cook down there!"

He had some money; was quick, almost ostentatiously quick, to pay the small bill that was presented when the drugstore boy brought the boric acid and the Castile soap which had been ordered for Gibbs. Becky felt mixed emotions when she saw his hands on the green five-dollar notes.

CHAPTER XX

BUT SHE COULD SAY nothing then. Indeed, she was presently to discover the extreme difficulty of criticizing Gavin at all, anywhere, under any circumstances, for anything.

He came into the kitchen when the boys arrived for lunch, enjoyed his own lunch, gossiped entertainingly as she and her mother and Sophy cleared the kitchen afterward. When Becky carried the baby upstairs he followed her and sat in her room—that old room of her girlhood with the Louisa Alcott and Little Colonel books in the bookcase and her carnival hat of fringed tissue paper still perched on the bureau pole.

Gavin sat there, seeming embarrassingly out of place in the immediate hurry of her care for Gibbs. Smoking a tenth cigarette, he watched her as she changed and fed the baby.

"I thought it was much better for them when their mothers nursed them?"

"I couldn't."

"And what's the big idea of naming him Gibbs? Who's Gibbs?"

"For Dad. He's Spencer Gibson." She was afraid again. She was afraid of him again.

"Ha!" he said. "He's not been christened?"

"Oh no."

"Well, why not think it over and name him after me?" Gavin murmured. "However . . ."

A silence. Becky pulled the rubber nipple from Gibbs's mouth; it was flattened. It expanded with a little hissing sound and the baby began to drink again. Fresh cold air had made him hungry; Becky tipped the bottle; the last film of white drained away.

"Now what does he do?"

"Well, he's beginning to stay awake a little now. He'll drop off about half-past three and sleep until five maybe." She was getting nervous. She wanted to ask Gavin his plans, to review with him these months during which they had been separated, but he seemed interested only in matters of the moment, seemed content to watch and smoke. Once he said he hoped her mother would have that pot roast for dinner.

"Yes, that's for dinner. And applesauce cake. She and Sophy made it after breakfast."

Separated for months, and they talked of applesauce cake!

"Who's Sophy?" he asked, and they talked of Sophy. And later: "Weather been like this? It's been hot, down south. Spring, down there."

Becky carried Gibbs back to his basket in the yard. She and Gavin sat on the porch steps in afternoon sunshine and talked. But even now she could not bring herself to an open, honest forcing of his confidence.

"How long will you be here, Gavin?"

"Tired of me already, huh?" It was his old teasing way.

"No. But I didn't know whether you were working now, whether you had a job."

"Sure I'm working. That is, I could be the minute I wanted to go back. But I think I've seen enough of Yuma, and of Frenchy Cotton too. Did me out of about six grand, Frenchy did."

"Six *grand!* You mean six *thousand?*"

"Yip."

The weak spring sunshine came down through the oak branches; chickens pecked nearer and nearer, cocking their sleek little heads, watching with beady eyes. Becky felt a sickness of spirit, not at the loss, but at what she suspected was the lie.

"How'd he do that?" she asked against her will.

"Oh, we had it in common, and what does he do but sink it all in a well! Dust well."

"What's a dust well?"

"It's a well that puffs up a lot of dust instead of oil."

"Can you sue him?"

"He'll be damn lucky if I don't," Gavin growled. She knew that the whole thing was a fabrication, reflected that it would be senseless to criticize any one part of it.

"So now what do you plan?" She tried to ask it brightly, naturally, as if she were just another of the town's secure, everyday young matrons who wheeled babies to market, discussed bridge games, picnicked and camped up at the lake in hot weather.

"Well, I don't know," he said. "Rest for a while, I guess."

No answer could have filled her soul and heart and mind, her very being, with a more complete dismay. Becky was unable to make any response. A dismal prevision of what would follow silenced her.

"Well," he said after a while, with a jerk of his head toward the shabby little car he had parked around the corner of the house, near the front door, "I'm going to take my bag upstairs and unpack. What's the chances on a bath? Where's your mother?"

"Mother had to go to the Baker funeral—old lady Baker. She'll be back."

"Will I wake the kid unpacking?"

Of course! He was going up to her room. Where else? There was no other available space now, for Sophy and Anya had the big room at the top of the kitchen stairway; Robert, sixteen, had the attic room to himself; her mother and father occupied, as always, the big front room; the younger boys more than filled the two small chambers that finished the hall at the back of the house. Becky's room, abandoned by her, had been turned into a rarely used spare room; now she and Gibbs used it. A comfortable old double bed had been substituted for the couch she had used in winter. In summer she had always moved out to the awn-inged porch. But no one could use the porch hammock as a bed these cold spring nights.

"Gavin," she began, seizing her courage with an almost physical effort, "let me explain something. I've—you've made it very hard for me. I've had——" She swallowed angrily, lowered her voice to keep it from breaking. "I've had a hard time these last months. Christmas and all."

"For criminy's sake! Didn't they want you?"

It was like him, her lightning thought flashed, to put it on her people.

"Of *course* they wanted me. Of course they've been won-derful to me. Of course I had my own room and my own nurse in the hospital!" Becky said, warming. "But do you think it was *easy* to take it all from them, to have no money, not a dollar, to call my own? Week after week with no word from you, no letter, nothing to tell these village gossips who were wondering and watching and saying what they liked——"

"Lissen, lissen!" Gavin interrupted as she paused for breath. He put a drawling accent upon the first syllable of the word. "What d'you think *I've* been doing? Going round the world in my private yacht? If I had money I'd have sent it. I've been having a rotten time, borrowing every-where . . ."

It was a long story. At the end he flung away the stub of his cigarette and hunched himself across to sit close beside her on the step and put his arm about her.

"Don't be mean to me, Becky," he pleaded.

She felt her mood yielding to his and hated herself. She made herself say sulkily and stubbornly: "You might have written," but even as she said it she felt her own weakness.

At dinnertime she watched him nervously, watched the other faces to see what impression he made, laughed wretchedly at his jokes and hastily and eagerly explained whatever seemed confused or doubtful in his easy talk.

Her father and mother and the boys responded readily enough, were interested, listened, replied. Apparently they felt no strain. She wondered when they would begin to feel it, how soon he would wear out his welcome, destroy the last shred of her peace of mind, almost regained in these quiet weeks at home.

Gavin was restless. He had always been restless. After dinner he asked the boys what movie was playing in town. Bob and Spin looked up eagerly, but Sarah said pleasantly enough that there must be no movie for them on a school night.

"I have to be here for Gibbs' ten o'clock," Becky, a hot glass and a dishtowel in her hands, reminded him. Spencer Gibson, in his kitchen rocker, looked up across his eyeglasses from his evening paper but did not speak.

"We'll have a fire in the parlor in a few minutes and sit in there," Sarah said, mixing oatmeal for breakfast. Sophy ran the carpet sweeper in and about the boys' heavy muddy shoes as they studied at the dining-room table. Gavin sat smoking in the kitchen, evidently bored.

In the city, she knew, he would presently have gone forth when he felt like this to find a game of something somewhere: dice, poker, roulette. Salletts offered him no such amusement. Or if it did he had not found them yet; in another day or two he might. She felt that she could not endure this situation for many days.

Andrew, eleven years old, and struggling with long division, called on her for help. Her mother brightly suggested a game of dominoes; did Gavin play dominoes? Becky, dropping with weariness and need for sleep, protested that she was "terrible," but somehow the dominoes appeared, and they played a languishing game. Gavin apparently was not interested. Why should he be? His domino stake was usually "twenty and two"—twenty cents a point and two dollars for the game points. Her parents never played any game for money. They liked "five hundred," had played it with neighbors for many years on occasional winter evenings with great enjoyment, their only reward the hospitable one of offering their opponents coffee and doughnuts afterward.

Nine o'clock came; the boys stumbled up to bed, clumped noisily about the upper floor. The black night outside the farmhouse was bitterly cold. Sophy stamped up the kitchen stairway and was heard singing heavily and talking to Anya. Becky did not want to go upstairs. She did not want to be Gavin's wife, shut into his room with him, conscious that the airily indifferent mood he had shown to her anxiousness all day long was changing to a mood of affection, of willingness to please her, sympathize with her. She did not want his arm about her, his kiss against her bare neck as she undressed.

Sarah was miserably aware of the situation, too, and Becky knew it. Her father and the boys had been receptive to Gavin's talk at dinner, had accepted unchallenged his indirect apologies and explanations of his long silence and absence, but Sarah had been watchful and wary. However strong the case he had made for himself with them, he had convinced her of nothing but his selfishness and neglect.

Now Sarah was suffering with Becky afresh. The older wife sensed perfectly the difficult position of the younger one. To rebuff Gavin, to send him off to the hotel to sleep, would be to precipitate an unpleasantness that might, by some miracle, not be in prospect at all. He might really intend honestly by his wife and child now. He might really have had a difficult and uncertain time during these long five months, struggling to find work, losing jobs, ill. Perhaps his breezy manner was the covering for a conviction of defect, a consciousness of having failed her.

If that were the case, and if Becky angered and estranged him, it must be Becky who would pay, stranded with her child in her old home before the watching eyes of gossiping townsfolk.

Sarah could not interfere here; no one could interfere. Twenty-two-year-old Becky must solve this problem herself; go to his room with him tonight and shut the world out. That was marriage.

"Everything all right now, Sally?" Becky's father asked, vaguely uneasy, half an hour later, when he was snug in bed. Sarah's whole body had been strained into an interrogation mark since they had all come upstairs. She had heard Becky's murmur over the sleepy, whimpering baby, heard Gavin's laugh and her reluctant half laugh in reply. They had been settling Gibbs for the night, as proud young parents everywhere were settling off small children at ten o'clock.

"Seems so," she had answered Spencer briefly. All her thoughts had been with Becky, never lovelier than she had been tonight. The hard business of bearing her child had thinned the girl's body to a new fineness; joy and pain and trembling responsibility had put dark amber lights into her eyes; Becky's old gaiety and generosity where her parents and the boys were concerned had gained an infinitely touching grace and gentleness now.

All through the evening Sarah had been conscious of her beauty; the beauty of the smooth neck and the low forehead against which little feathers of dark gold curled carelessly; the beauty of the smooth skin, the deep-set eyes, the wide, eager, expressive mouth. All the warm golds and browns had mingled together, brown in the gold hair, gold in the brown eyes, brown thin hand, brown, curved young breast where the striped cotton gown fell open at the throat. Her girl, her lost little girl, whose husband was seeing all this sweetness and beauty, too, watching it, glorying in it, growing kinder to her, more affectionate and responsive and appreciative every moment.

"Poor little Beck!" Sarah said half aloud.

"What say?" Spencer roused himself from a first doze.

"Nothing," she answered. But she lay long awake that night, worrying.

Gavin could be kind, and his kindness was the weapon against which Becky had no defense. In the first days of their marriage his mood had made the difference between joy and pain to her: his happier tempers had found her eagerly receptive; when he had been silent and cold Becky had drooped like a flower in a frost.

Tonight the old power reasserted itself. Gavin was amiable tonight, good-naturedly interested in Gibbs, amusing in his help with and comments upon the baby. Lord, he was a queer little fish! Was he honestly a pretty fair little specimen? An unusually fine baby, and already above the average in length and weight? Aw hell, didn't they tell every mother that?

"But you can compare him to the chart, Gavin!" Becky was so eager in her earnestness that Gavin felt an impulse to put his arms about her. But he did not show it; he was apparently completely absorbed in watching the child.

"What d'you do? Just slam him on his poor little mug and slap him down?"

Becky laughed. She had not laughed too often in the past months.

"He goes right off."

"Well, what do you know?" Gavin was innocently surprised as Becky fastened great safety pins adeptly on either side of the baby's small dark head, tucked in pink blankets, hung a piece of dark cloth on the outer side of the crib to shut off the light. "Y'know," Gavin continued, beginning on his shoelaces, "I've been seeing—I swear it struck me for the first time tonight—what a rotter you must have thought me for not writing. I feel terribly about that. Time went awfully fast, and I kept thinking I'd have a steady job and could take a place for you and the kid. I knew most girls wanted to be with their mothers when a baby was coming, so that was all right, but it never struck me you could be worried about me; I'll swear it never did. Now tonight," he went on, walking about the room, busy with the folding and hanging of clothes, "tonight, when your folks were so kind, and your mother cooked such a swell dinner, I began to see what a family can be like—I never had one, you know. I never had anyone to help me with homework and wipe dishes, that sort of thing. I'd have been a very different sort of person if I had. By George, I envied your brothers tonight. I thought: 'You don't know anything about loneliness and having to fight your own battles, the way I did!' I wish we were going to stay here longer. But three or four days are about all I ought to spare if I'm going to start in with Cooper."

"Three or four days!" Inextinguishable hope sprang in her heart. If they could really get away in three or four days! "But I thought you hadn't a job, Gavin," she said.

"Well, I haven't the job I want. But we can get along on thirty-five a week, to start with, can't we? This loafer Yelland, who's doing exactly the same work, gets a hundred. Yep, that's what that bum signs up for every week. But I wouldn't get that. I'd start off for thirty-five or forty, and work up. Because we want a little home, Beck," Gavin went on, sitting on the edge of the bed now, scowling into space as he spoke. "We've got to get going, with this feller to look out for. I'd rather have less, and have it sure . . ."

She came, fresh and soap-scented with her damp curls brushed loosely from her face, to sit beside him. Her eyes shone.

⁷Oh, Gavin, that's what I want so much! I want so terribly some little place with a garden and maybe a patio, where we can have his sun baths and someday a sandbox. I'd not mind being poor. We could live wonderfully on thirty-five a week—that's a hundred and forty a month, even in the four-week months!" He put his arm about her.

"I've treated you like a dog, Beck," he said in a lowered tone. "But I never saw it! I thought of us as—well, kinder having a fight to fight out, you carrying your end here, and I mine there. I ought to have written, and I ought to have sent you money. But I didn't have it, and I hated to write and say so. It's one thing to write and send a hundred, and another to tell a hard-luck tale."

His story was strengthening as he elaborated it. Some cold little corner of her mind told her so. Plausible as it was, it was not quite plausible enough. But smothering, engulfing that tiny area of reason, was the stronger argument of the senses, those betraying senses that were so conscious of the dimly lighted room, the scents of young grass and turned earth that stole in on moonbeams through the pear-tree blossoms, the warm, heartening hold of a man's arm about her, his hard young cheek against her temple.

"Don't ever again be mean to me, Gavin," she whispered. "We've got to stay together. Whatever happens, we've got to face it together!"

"I love you!" he whispered, deeply stirred. Becky saw the glint of tears in his eyes.

CHAPTER XXI

HALF-PAST FIVE o'clock on a June morning. The valley was already simmering in burning heat. Becky, coming downstairs with Gibbs, looked out into the dry yard, looked toward the barns and the woodpile and the straggling line of paddock fence, and saw no drop of dew, even in the shadows, no shadow itself that was not reflecting back the merciless light of the day's heat.

The flanges of the windmill were motionless; cattle grouped on the north side of the sheds were motionless. Yesterday's washing hung dry and stiff and motionless on the line. Chickens, pecking their talkative way from the chicken house, gathered under the porch; a calf bleated, was still, bleated again somewhere out of sight.

The kitchen reflected the day's dry warmth even now. In through its two southwestern windows poured the glory of the risen sun. Becky, drawing shades, wondering who had let them up after she had drawn them last night, took one blinking look at a mountain range that had already vanished into trembling lines of dazzling opal haze. The sink was hot and dry. There were smells about; a smell of yellow soap curled and cracked beside the laundry tubs; a smell of peaches rotting on the porch; a smell of food drying and souring in the cooler.

All the milk had soured, and the cream was just on the turn. Becky left Gibbs in his pen and stepped over to the dairy. No sourness here; the earthy coolness of it met her like a breath of the sea; the delicious smells of wet wood and new milk were mingled in that dairy sweetness that is like no other in the world.

She went back, stepping carefully, the big shallow pan in her hands. Gibbs was watching for her anxiously; he smiled a broad toothless smile at her. She had to catch him up, when she had set down the milk, and kiss him once, twice, three times before she could go on with her work.

There was plenty of it. The steadily mounting heat of the day brought perspiration to her forehead and set a faint pain between her eyes as she moved about.

With a small wooden paddle she loosened the leathery sheet of the good Jersey cream and poured the thick clots of it into a blue pitcher. The pitcher went on the ice; the milk was set on the stove. Gibbs had cereal now after his orange juice; the cereal had been simmering in the double boiler all night. Becky caught the child up, nude except for his pinned undergarment, and felt his lively little perspiring body wet against her own as she dribbled the food into him. Then he had his bottle and went back into his pen, and Becky pulled on an old straw hat and went into the yard to gather in the wash. She had been too tired after yesterday's blazing hours to bother with it last night, but everything that concerned Gibbs must move on schedule, and to break that schedule meant extra work the next day.

Coming back, she took a long drink of well water, chilled in the red earthen *ojah* that hung on the side porch, and, going to the sink, let the cold water run on her wrists.

"Whew!" she gasped, pushing back the hair on her forehead with a wet hand.

She folded most of the hot dry linen, dampened some of it and set it aside, set the breakfast table, cut bread, put on the coffeepot. The remains of a joint were in the icebox. Becky cut the meat into cubes, found onions and turnips and potatoes to put with it, covered the whole with water, scraped cold gravy in for a finish and lighted a bead of gas

on the stove. Lamb stew; Gavin hated stews. Only two
nights ago, finding that the main dish of the evening meal
was corned-beef hash, he had excused himself and gone
downtown for dinner. Rudeness to Mother . . .

Inexcusable. But she would not think. One could train
oneself not to think. Becky put a heap of folded baby linen
on the lower step of the front hall stairway, settled down in
Dad's rocker to drink a cup of coffee just as the clock struck
seven.

There was ironing left from yesterday. When Sophy
came down with little blonde delicate Anya, Rebecca went
vigorously at the ironing. Gibbs's nightgowns got two swift
smacks apiece; Gavin's socks and handkerchiefs and underwear demanded a little more. Becky had learned to be
much more economical with her own clothes. A few thin old
shirts, a cotton gown or two, the minimum of shorts and
brassières and nightgowns were all she allowed herself. Old
shirts and slacks of the boys were comfortable summer
wear; she never wore stockings now. But Gavin was as extravagant as ever; he went into town every day; he must
look presentable.

Some of her brothers' stockings were in this wash. Sophy
had been scrubbing and wringing all day yesterday and had
gotten heavy work, like Gibbs's blankets and the boys' jeans,
out on the line. There was always a tremendous lot of it to
do, and Becky wanted to save her father not only the expense of her own and Gavin's washing, but was always
eagerly trying to do a little more.

But with the unconscious Gibbs and the hardly less irresponsible Gavin both contributing a constant stream of discarded garments to the wash basket, it was hard work.

She was finishing her ironing when her mother, corseted,
shod, stockinged, severely combed as always, came down,
and they had a second breakfast together, from which
Becky leaped up to serve her father and the boys. The air

in the kitchen was suffocating now, and scented with fried eggs and bacon, toast, burned cereal. For a while Gibbs sat in his pen, looking interestedly on. Then he wept, and Sarah took him up and mothered him.

Dishes accumulated in the sink. Sophy fed Anya weak coffee and rye bread. Anya would not eat cereal or vegetables; she liked an orange sucker before every meal. The kitchen was in an uproar for a while; then Becky's father and the boys disappeared, peace came back, and the women could set about the morning's work.

Sophy washed clothes; Sarah washed dishes; Becky cleared the table, set the dining-room table for lunch, answered the telephone, dusted the parlor. At half-past nine she carried Gibbs upstairs for his bath; he could have it in the regular tub now. When she went into the bedroom to put on his fresh clothes and amuse him until it was time for his ten o'clock bottle, Gavin was waking and usually ready to take Gibbs in hand while Becky straightened the room.

If she could at this time, she slipped into the other rooms, whipping beds together, hanging up her brothers' clothes. But if Gibbs was fretful she generally had to feed him a little early, and subsided gratefully into a chair, breathing deep, glad of the fifteen minutes rest.

When he was off for his nap she went downstairs, set Gavin's place at the end of the kitchen table, found the newspaper and folded it with its sheets in order, set the coffeepot back on the stove and made toast. He liked orange juice very cold and fresh, poached eggs on toast, two cups of coffee. Almost every morning he told one or other of the women that he never ate cereal or hot cakes or waffles, nothing like that. Not this weather!

This breakfast time of his was a hard time for Becky for many reasons. One of them was that at this time more than any other she felt keenly her mother's total disapproval of Gavin. Sarah tried—Becky knew how generously!—to disguise it and hide it. But it could not be done. To have Becky, already tired after four hours steady work, wait on him in this fashion made Sarah's blood boil. It was only for Becky's sake that she held her tongue, that she forced herself to endure his serene acceptance of these attentions day after day, forced herself to listen to his interested comments upon the news of the world.

Now that the summer heat was upon Salletts, Becky's labors and Gavin's impositions seemed redoubled. But Sarah knew that Becky was as helpless as herself, and she never broke.

When the dishes and pans from Gavin's breakfast had been piled in the sink, and Sarah and Sophy were peeling peaches in the darkened kitchen, Rebecca took the car and went to market. It was a bad time to go to town on a broiling summer morning, but it was the time Gavin wanted to get to town, and one that gave her a little interval between Gibbs's imperious needs.

The butcher shop at the Exchange was deserted and odorous at this hour. Rice and noodles and beans looked and smelled dryer than ever. The very thought of food was disagreeable. One only wanted iced tomatoes and crisp lettuce and iced tea. . . .

Becky consulted her list, went to another counter for spools and tape and dish toweling and writing paper, went to talk to Joe Werry about the bulbs that continually burned out in the hallway socket. Oh, and Mother wanted a trowel. . . .

Very few customers were in the Exchange at this time. The two showcases of the bakery department would be almost empty, the last loaf, the last cooky sold until the fresh lot came in at four. Millie Delaney at the stocking counter would be fanning herself with a yellow palm-leaf fan with "Rajax for Torpid Livers" printed in purple upon it.

" 'Lo, Beck. Some weather!"

"Awful. Makes me feel so limp all the time!"

"Yep. And Pa was sayin' it don't even cool off at night."

"No. I know. The baby was terribly restless last night. I hardly got any sleep at all."

"Well, you'll get worse if you and Mr Flood go down south. Chess was sayin' he was talkin' of goin' down."

"I suppose so. But I'd like to stay here until it gets a little cooler."

With casual friends, met here and there, it was always the same. Becky got tired of answering, never could show how deep the neighborly questions cut her.

"I hope your mother realizes how lucky she is to have you and the baby here for this nice long visit, Rebecca," Mrs Carmichael, the minister's wife, said kindly. "I do wish Anna could come home to me for six months!"

"Say, when you folks goin' back to San Francisco?" demanded Alma Pettit, at the post office. "How long 've you and Gavin been home? Six months, ain't it?"

"Becky, the girls want to give you a good-by shower, so be sure you let us know two weeks before you go," Helen Bradley, who had been Becky's chum in high-school days, said affectionately.

Some of her mother's club friends asked even more searching questions.

"Rebecca, what does Gavin do? A photographer? Is he really? And do you mean that there isn't a demand for that sort of thing down in Hollywood?"

Or it might be:

"Becky, will you forgive old Auntie Belle Mason for saying that Mamma is getting a little tired? I noticed it, and Vi noticed it too. It's a big household, dear, with you and the baby and the boys and Mr Flood, and your father home sick for a week; it's too much, dear. If you and Mr Flood could take her up to the lake for a month, it'd do her a world of good. . . ."

And then finally her father mildly joining the chorus:
"I'd encourage Gavin to take anything he can get, Becky,
since he isn't particularly interested in getting into business
here in Salletts. It is—it isn't particularly healthy for a man
his age to be idle. No harm in a billiard game or a poker
game now and then. My uncle Ray, my mother's brother,
used to be what they called lucky at cards. He got over it;
he settled down. But at Gavin's age——"

"I know, Dad," Becky would say in nervous agony of
spirit, "I know you're right. And I *do* talk to Gavin about
getting a job."

She talked to him continually whenever they were alone.
She had long abandoned any consideration for his feelings;
he had no feelings. Quietly, incessantly, Becky kept at him.
But the impression she made was small.

"Gavin, don't you see we can't go on this way? It isn't fair
to Mother and Dad to land on them like this, to go on costing
them money. And as long as you're out with that Perry gang
down in Chinatown half the night, you'll never get a good
job. Mother's been wonderfully patient, you know that, but
it does make her mad to have you always late for dinner, and
always coming downstairs in the middle of the morning."

"What's it to her? You give me my breakfast."

"It's her *house*, Gavin. Naturally she likes things to go
her way."

"What's she afraid of?"

"Just that—that things aren't *right* this way." And sometimes she would add: "You ought to have more pride, Gavin.
Everyone knows you're being supported by my people. Everyone knows I haven't any money except what my father gives
me."

"Because these hicks won't get into a real game," Gavin
might explain simply.

"But you oughtn't to be gambling with a lot of day labor-
ers, Mexicans and Portuguese and Chinese and everything

else! Lin Perry—why, he was tried for murder once! And that loathsome Snyder!"

"I'm going to get a job. I've got something swell lined up," Gavin would say if he were in a good mood. If he were dissatisfied and impatient in the dry wearying heat of the relentless summer days, he would fling away impatiently, to go upstairs and sprawl on their bed for a sleep, or catch the bus and go into town.

Becky grew thin and anxious, worrying about him. Sarah saw her draw more and more into her shell. The younger woman wanted to see none of her old friends now; she was rarely persuaded to leave the house except for the three-times-a-week shopping round. She was ashamed.

CHAPTER XXII

ONE DAY when Sarah was away on an all-day business trip with her husband Becky seized an afternoon moment when Gavin was away and Gibbs asleep to take from her purse several strips that had been cut from a San Francisco newspaper. Her father got this paper regularly and in bygone years sometimes she had glanced at it idly, amused by a columnist, interested in a puzzle or diverted by the pictures of the members of the social set.

But the strips that she had torn out today were want advertisements. Stenographers, cooks, chauffeurs, housekeepers, housemaids, saleswomen, agents. Becky settled herself in the desk chair and went over them carefully. Three she tore out roughly, taking the remaining papers to the kitchen woodbox afterward, where their mutilated condition would arouse no interest. The three clipped notices she studied thoughtfully, her brows knitted.

"Wanted. At once. Young woman, good cook, no objection to small children, mountains, general housework. Salary $60."

"Wanted. Strong, good-natured girl. Piece work at home. Good pay."

"Houseworker wanted in small San José hotel. Cook and waitress kept. Must be clean, capable, willing. Permanent place for right party. $45."

"That first one," Becky mused, half aloud. "Somehow I like it the best. I can't see myself doing very well with 'piece work.' Gibbs and I in a hot room somewhere, sewing on overalls. No, that won't do. And a small country hotel? It mightn't be so small. It would be frightfully hot, whereas the mountains are cool all summer long. 'Good cook.' I'm a good cook. 'Small children.' Well, God knows I've got reason to like small children! It might be bedlam. But it might be that if I offered to work for, say, thirty dollars a month, she'd let me have Gibbs."

Her face grew serious; her thoughts wandered.

"It 'd break Mother's heart. I wish I knew what to do. Maybe I'd not get away with it. I haven't gotten away with much. And his naps and his bottles and his clean clothes! It might kill me, and then he'd belong entirely to Gavin of course. . . ."

She had been groping in the old desk for a pair of shears that would trim her newspaper clippings cleanly. Suddenly under her eyes were several scattered small papers; they had been clipped together; her rummaging hand had broken them apart.

They were acknowledgments of small loans—loans of fifty, of ten, of forty dollars. There were five—six—seven of them. One for only two dollars. They were I.O.U.s from Gavin to her father!

Becky sat perfectly still, feeling the blood churn up into her face and throat. Her eyes, fixed on the papers, glazed slowly. Her heart pumped—pumped.

She would not believe it; she could not believe it. She put her hand slowly over them, shutting them from sight. Oh no, Gavin could not have added that to all the other obligations he had incurred here in her own home! He would not do that!

Spreading them on the desk, she stared at them for a long time. The largest one had the earliest date: fifty dollars. Then came the forty, and after it, in May, two for twenty-five dollars. Then a ten, another ten, and the two!

It was all very clear. He had told Dad some cock-and-bull story in April, and Dad had advanced him fifty, and afterward forty, probably for one purpose—for the job which Gavin was eternally sure that he could take if he had a little "spot cash." The rest had been mere concessions to Dad's love for Becky, his anxiety lest she learn too much about this husband of hers. Petty loans, whining and borrowing . . . She put sudden hands to her eyes, sat bowed and broken under the utter hopeless ignominy of it.

The latest date was more than a week old. That accounted for Gavin's bad temper these last days. Dad had stopped short. Two dollars, and then no more. If Gavin wanted money after that he could earn it.

But what made her face burn with a fresh shame—she who had thought she had reached the very depths of shame! —was that three or four times in these weeks since his return Gavin had given her a little money; once five dollars, then later two, and two again. And she had been grateful and had hastened to pay her mother some infinitesimal bills. Ten cents for safety pins; fifteen for vaseline; six for stamps.

That had been Dad's money! And Mother and Dad had been too generous to let her know that he had taken it from them to hand to her.

Fifty and forty were ninety, fifty more, twenty-two more. Gavin owed them one hundred and sixty-two dollars.

Becky sat quite still, thinking about it. She felt as if she had a clean wound straight through her heart. If she moved she would feel more pain.

She was still tranced when her mother came unexpectedly in. Becky started, and turned to face Sarah with the promissory notes still in her hands. Sarah was frightened at the expression on her face.

"Mother . . . look here . . ." Becky said indistinctly. "I was looking for the old desk scissors and I happened to see them."

Sarah, still wearing her hat and black silk coat, took the notes into her hand.

"Yes, I knew about these," she said slowly.

"Oh, Mother!" Becky's tone was despairing.

"I know," Sarah said simply, sitting down. There was a silence. Becky, stricken, looked at her mother. Sarah looked away.

"Mother," Becky presently said, "this can't go on. It—simply, it can't go *on!*"

"H'm!" Sarah muttered, shaking her head, still not meeting the younger woman's eyes.

"What do *you* think, Mother?" Becky demanded despairingly.

"Well, I think there will have to be a change; I agree with you about *that*," Sarah began guardedly. "Gavin—it's only reasonable to suppose that Gavin will get something to do sooner or later. . . ."

Her voice wavered away doubtfully.

"Meanwhile," Becky said in the silence, "meanwhile I have to bear every possible humiliation with all of my old friends —that's nothing! I can bear that. It would have killed me a few years ago, but it's nothing now. I have to worry, worry, worry about myself and Gibbs! I can't have the joy of him, the pride of him, because I'm always afraid—afraid of what Gavin may do or not do. I'm sponging on you and Dad for every mouthful I eat and every one the baby eats, and now Gavin's added to that—now he's settled down here comfortably too, eating and drinking as if it were a hotel and borrowing money from Dad to gamble with! Mother, I can't stand it! I don't want to stand it! Can't you and Dad get him to go away? I've tried. I've kept at him for days; I've said everything, insulting things, maddening things . . ."

"You may as well know, Beck," her mother said in a troubled, reluctant voice as Becky paused, "that Dad *has* tried to—to spur Gavin into something like ambition. He doesn't seem to have it. At first Dad looked for photography work

for him here, but there wasn't much chance of that. Gavin
. . ." Mrs Gibson hesitated delicately. "Gavin wasn't interested," she finally said. "And now lately," she went on,
"Dad's been very firm with him about going away and getting work somewhere, so that he can send for you and the
baby one of these days. But Gavin—he was quite rude to
Dad," Sarah finished, and was suddenly silent.

"Rude to Dad!" Becky echoed, aghast.

"Yes, he—he said that if he went he'd take you and the
baby and that we'd never hear of you again," Sarah answered. Sudden tears ran down her full, plain, middle-aged
face and blotted out her courageous smile.

"But that's nonsense!" Becky said stoutly. "I could always
come back and bring Gibbs with me. He's simply—bullying.
He gets that way. And if he's being rude to Dad . . ."

Both women sat silent, thinking, for a few long minutes.
Then Becky said abruptly:

"I've threatened divorce. You know how I feel, Mother. I
hate it. But if I've been a fool there's no reason why I should
go *on* being a fool!"

"Claiming nonsupport?" Sarah asked, eyes narrowed in
thought.

"I suppose so. But Gavin says that he'll fight that. He'll
fight for his half year of Gibbs. He'll claim that I left him
and came home with the baby to my parents. He says he'll
never consent."

"What could he do with the baby?" Sarah asked, paling at
the mere thought.

"He has a married sister at Whitney. She has two daughters, about seven and ten, I think. He says she'd take Gibbs."
Becky's tone was unconcerned; this was not even a possi-
bility.

"Oh well, that's out of the question. If he talks like that
. . . No, we can't permit anything like that," Sarah said.
"We'll have to think it out some other way. If you went with

him, Beck, just till he gets settled?" she suggested doubtfully.

"He doesn't want to work, Mother. He's perfectly comfortable here. He'll merely put up objection after objection until we stop arguing," Becky answered hopelessly, "and then he'll settle down here. Like Jud Mason after he broke his leg," she added. "The girls and Ray have been supporting him ever since. And like that big handsome loafer of a Buckley boy. Mrs Buckley and Alma are always saying that Johnny isn't so well this spring, and Johnny is going to see a man about a position, and Johnny's older than I am and has never earned a cent!"

"Well, it's too bad," Sarah said after long thought on a deep sigh.

"What does Dad think?"

"He's—he's troubled."

Becky displayed the newspaper clippings.

"I was seriously thinking of taking a job somewhere," she said.

"What sort of a job, Beck?"

"Housework, I suppose. Cooking, maybe. Like Sophy. She has Anya with her and manages it all right."

"No," said Sarah, shaking her head, "you can't do that."

"Anything's better than a shop, Mother. They almost killed us at the Bon Marché."

"Dad only pays Sophy twenty-five."

"I know, but she and Anya get their meals and rent. That's more—more than Gavin's earned since he came here."

Bitter tears stood in Becky's eyes; her lips trembled. For a while Sarah could not seem to find anything to say.

"If you're going to do that, Beck, how much better to stay here!" she offered at last.

"But as long as I stay here, Mother, Gavin will stay here! And as long as I stay the whole town will know and watch and criticize. It 'd be so much easier with complete strangers.

I'll come back," Becky said, speaking cheerfully, but with tears running fast, "I'll come back someday. But I seem to have made such a—such a horrible mess of things! I suppose life can be pulled up, and some of it saved, somehow, at twenty-two——"

"Becky!" Sarah protested between a laugh and a sob.

"Yes, I know it sounds young to you, Mother. But with Gavin forever in the background like a—like a terrible shadow, and now my baby to care for, it seems as if it never could come straight again! Only—only I feel as if, when I'm gone, Dad can send Gavin away without being afraid of hurting me. And if other women have taken care of themselves and their babies, I can do it!"

"Beck," said her mother, "don't give up yet, dear. You've had a terribly hard year since first you knew the baby was coming. But what's a year out of a lifetime, Beck? Thousands of women have to endure conditions just as hard, year out and year in——"

"Not with their husbands doing nothing!" Becky interrupted hotly. "Not when they are ashamed before everyone they know, everyone they love! Not when they haven't a penny to spend—even for safety pins and bus fare!"

"Thousands of 'em, Beck. And worse."

"Well, I'm not like them!" Becky said, her breast heaving. "I'm not going to let one mistake—one man—spoil my life for me! I—I'll do something—*something*. . . ."

There was a silence. It was Becky who broke it, impulsively.

"Mother, *you* don't think we'll get anywhere, going on like this?"

"No, Beck," Sarah answered slowly. "I see how hard it is for you, dear. I see what you mean. It's hard for all of us. If things go smoothly, then Gavin is so pleasant—amusing the boys and playing dominoes with Dad. And if there's the slightest criticism . . ."

"When was he rude to Dad?" Becky asked from a moment of brooding thought.

"Well, he said something like—— Dad doesn't talk much, you know, and he only gave me the impression that Gavin said something like what was his daughter and her child worth to him. 'If I go, they go,' I think he said, something like that. It made Dad feel very badly. He said to me that he didn't see how we could—could get Gavin to take his responsibilities seriously. The minute we criticize him he gets so mad."

"The minute I talked nonsupport he'd get a job, some sort of a job," Becky said. "I'd be advised kindly by some domestic relations judge to give him another trial. Don't expect me to say what I think of myself for letting us all in for this," she added with sudden passion. "I think it all day long, you know that! I suppose it was love. It was what fool girls of twenty think is love! And the worst of it is," she added, her cheeks suddenly reddening, "the worst of it is that when he puts his arm around me and says, 'Ah, Beck, we love each other, give me another chance!'—the horrible part of it is that I—I——"

"I know," her mother said hastily, as one avoiding pitfalls. "That's only natural, Beck. You're his wife, and whatever your reason says, it's natural for you to forgive him. . . . Beck," Sarah asked, suddenly off on another topic, "did you ever tell Gavin what I told you about yourself? About your mother, and your being adopted?"

"No," Becky said, her quick look riveted on her mother's face.

"You're sure of it?"

"Positive, Mother, why?"

"Because there was money given us, Beck, spent long ago, of course, but it meant this home. It meant California, for us. I wondered if he knew."

"No." Becky's thoughts went back across the months.

"No. You see he was dying, or almost dying, when I got there," she said. "We had no chance for any privacy or confidences. Then we went to the horrible Tevers place—that's the woman who drank or doped or both—out near the park. And I was homesick there, and I remember crying myself to sleep thinking that I didn't really belong to you and Dad. I didn't want to think about it myself, much less have him ever remind me of it! And then," Becky went on somewhat hesitatingly, "from the beginning I knew that if he heard of any money—money that was spent long ago in giving me the happiest childhood any girl ever knew . . ." She faltered and was still, tears thickening her voice.

"You were afraid he might ask for it?" Sarah finished the sentence for her.

"I don't know. He'd have no claim."

"Becky," her mother said suddenly, as one coming to a resolution, "you know my white gloves that Daddy brought me home for Ida's wedding? You know, I wore them about four years ago and I haven't worn them since?"

"I remember!" Becky laughed shakily.

"Well, there they are. Some of the women wear gloves to the club," Sarah said leniently, "but all I do is to take 'em off and work 'em into a ball. They're in my lower drawer at the back, beneath my mother's Spanish shawl. And in them, Beck, are five twenty-dollar bills. I won them in a newspaper contest years and years ago—you remember?—and I've never found anything good enough to spend 'em on. If you ever really need them, I mean if Gavin should get a promise of a job and you should want to go—— Now don't cry, Beck. Why, what else would a mother want to do with her money except spend it on her children?"

Becky's head was down on the desk; her face was buried in her hands. Sarah stroked the bowed bright hair for a moment. Then she went upstairs to change her clothes and peep in on Gibbs, who was stirring.

"Beck!" she called down. "Baby awake!"

"I'm coming!" Becky gulped, put the clippings into her purse, went upstairs. She looked in at the bedroom door; saw sitting up in his crib in the dim light the red-cheeked baby with his cockatoo crest of silky black hair. "Ah, Mother, come see how adorable he looks!" she said. A few minutes later Sarah heard her laughing as she busied herself with Gibbs's bath preparations, and breathed easier.

And again the days took up for Rebecca their unending, throbbing undertone. What can I *do?* What can *I* do? What *can* I do?

And again Gavin slept late, shaved, bathed, dressed himself carefully, drifted downstairs to an eleven o'clock breakfast, sat reading the paper and amiably discussing the news for half an hour, got a lift uptown from Becky on her way to market or sauntered forth to catch the noon bus.

He would come back in the late afternoon perhaps to play ball with the boys in the yard for an hour, wander about picking up a pear or a few prunes, make to Spencer Gibson some helpful suggestion about the car or go up to the orchard to chat with the fruit pickers as he smoked a cigarette.

But sometimes he did not come back for dinner or went away immediately after it. Then he might not be home until three or four o'clock in the morning if he came home at all. If he went with some of the men to San Andreas or Stockton he might not put in an appearance until breakfast time on the following day, when he would be heavy with sleep and stumble upstairs after his second cup of coffee to fall heavily into bed. At such times Becky's wisest course was to make sure that Gibbs did not disturb him, not because she was not fully conscious of the utter injustice of his demand for silence, but because Gavin's shouted angry protests over the baby's "infernal damn racket" upset the whole household while they lasted, and upset her mother and herself for the entire morning.

It was extremely inconvenient to move Gibbs's morning routine into the boys' rooms at the back of the house; towels, bottle, clothes, pins, blankets. But more than once, in the hot dry summer mornings, she did it rather than cause added distress in a situation that at its best was distressing. And all the while furious arguments went on in her soul; all the while she was mentally battling with Gavin, flinging at him the long-repressed bitterness, the scalding reproaches, the raging condemnation that seethed eternally in her heart.

❧ CHAPTER XXIII ❧

ONE VERY HOT AFTERNOON Becky and her mother went into town to see Judge Miller. Judge Miller was fat, good-natured, fond of fishing, of a mild poker game, of sitting back in a broad tipped revolving chair in his office swapping stories with his contemporaries.

His father, old Nat Miller, had owned the mines to which Salletts owed its existence; he had left his son a modest fortune, the charge of a maiden sister and a large wooden house set prominently at the mountain end of Main Street, bulging with bay windows, cupolas, columns and turrets.

Joe Feratta worked in Judge Miller's office, the judge's own son having failed repeatedly to pass his bar examinations, but Joe was in Sacramento now, watching the famous Chet Dark case. Becky knew there was no danger of an encounter with him on this particular afternoon.

She had dressed herself as coolly as she could. Sarah wore her aged black grenadine made over into simpler lines and deprived of its once impressive sateen lining, but both women looked hot and pale with the heat when they went into the cool big office and faced the lolling, fat old man. He seemed pleased to see them.

They talked weather and lake fishing and the sudden widowhood of the judge's daughter Jean, who was coming home with the two little girls, and then Sarah, who was very nervous, said abruptly:

"Judge, this girl wants to talk to you. She's in real trouble."

Becky's eyes, fixed on the old man, filled with tears, and her lip trembled as she said:

168

"It's Gavin, Judge."

Judge Miller swung about in his chair, leaned so far back that the spring creaked, fitted fat finger tips together and shot a glance over his big rimmed spectacles at Becky. And suddenly, and with an unpleasant little chill, she knew that he was going to lecture her, that he was, as she disrespectfully phrased it deep in her soul, "going Doctor Lavender on her."

"Wha's trouble, Becky?" he said with his favorite fatherly air. Venetian blinds had been dropped at the windows, but dazzling lines of blazing heat split them here and there and showed motes moving in the shafts of light against the background of old leather books. Far below the lessened noises of afternoon Main Street sounded faintly.

"Everything!" Becky answered with a forlorn laugh. "He's just—not anything," she went on, weakening with every word. "He's not working, he goes away and I don't know where he is, he's—well, not satisfactory!"

"Ain't satisfactory, eh?" the judge said, narrowing his eyes, twisting the big heavy lower part of his face about slowly to dislodge corn silk from a tooth. "Not satisfactory. Well, I don't know how many of us are, Becky. We're a pretty poor lot, we men, ain't we, Sarah? I s'pose that's why they put it into the contract, 'better or worse,' eh?"

She hated him. With all her heart Becky hated him, the big fat, comfortable, smiling old man who could loaf about this office having the stenographers flatter him, having other lazy, comfortable old men come in and talk to him, having Jean come back with two babies and make much of darling Daddy, having that cabin and that launch up on the lake for fishing whenever he felt like it. What did he know of the burning needs of a woman of twenty-two, longing to be protected, to be sheltered, to have a home for her child, to have some support for her pride and dignity? All it meant to him was a chance to be paternal and wise!

"Got t' the point where you want to talk divorce, eh, have

ye?" Perry Miller asked. Sarah looked stricken, shutting her lips tightly together. Becky's color rose under her transparent brown skin.

"I *have* to, Judge," she said feebly.

Sarah had tried to brace her for this meeting, had told her that she must speak up, make her case strong. But it was very hard, especially as Becky was inclined to cry, here and now, in the very preliminaries.

"Oh, toe-toe-toe, now! Maybe 'tain't so bad," the old man said, good-humoredly soothing, as if speaking to a small child. "Le's look into this. Sometimes we get all riled up . . . hot weather . . . nerves, eh?"

"He's trying to talk like Will Rogers," Becky decided bitterly.

"Gavin hasn't treated Becky right from the very beginning," Sarah put in firmly. The judge moved a fountain pen with a fat hand on the desk blotter, puffed his lips out into another unconvinced "Oh, toe-toe-toe-toe, now!"

"Wha's trouble?" he said again. Becky began to speak, more bravely and composedly this time. She had been married for almost two years. In that time Gavin had gambled, had borrowed money, had left her for five months without any knowledge of his whereabouts, had come to her mother's home to idle, to borrow more money . . .

"You ain't been married two years?" Judge Miller asked, looking up from apparent deep study.

"Well, in November it 'll be two years."

"But 'tain't but August now, Becky. Now looky here," said the old man with an air of reason, "I don't know's you want to get any divorce from Gavin. He ain't been any too successful, but most of us kinder racketed around when we were kids, and it didn't keep us from settlin' down. What *d'you* think of this, Sarah? It ain't goin' to help Becky with her old friends here if she kicks this feller out."

"Things can't go on as they are, Judge," Sarah persisted.

"It's just getting so we can't any of us stand it. It's money, money, money, and it's gambling——"

"Don't drink, does he?" The judge looked up shrewdly under bushy great white eyebrows.

"No. He isn't a teetotaler," Sarah admitted grimly, "but you couldn't say he drank."

"*I* could say he drank," Becky thought, remembering dark early morning hours at the Golcondita, remembering his heavy snoring while she lay awake in the room, his breath scented with sour fumes. But she said nothing aloud.

"Drink's bad," the old man said, shaking his head. "Yes sir, that's bad. If a feller gets drinking hard . . . I have the women in here all the time . . ."

He rambled into reminiscences of divorce cases, repeated at length his advice to the injured parties. The heat of sunset attacked the blind at the western windows like an army with banners.

"Now Gavin come in here yesterday—or maybe 'twas the day before," Perry Miller presently said, returning to the case in point. "He kinder suspected that you's thinking of something like this, and he dropped in and we had quite a talk about it."

"Gavin came to see you?" Becky asked, incredulous.

"Yes sir. Sat right in that chair where you're sittin'."

Light seemed to break upon her. Oh, if he would—if he only *would* . . .

"But—but he didn't want a divorce?" she stammered.

"Nope. But he suspicioned you's thinkin' of one," the old man answered. Becky's heart quickened to anger. He had forestalled her!

"He doesn't want it," she said dully.

"No sirree, bob!" Judge Miller answered with an air of triumph, an air of having trapped her. "That's just what he *don't* want, Beck. He wants his wife and his child and his home, same's any other man. Why, you'd feel ashamed," the old man went on, dropping his voice to an affectionate and re-proachful note, "knowin' you as I do, and knowin' your folks, I just know you'd be ashamed, Beck, if you could have heard him talk and seen the tears in his eyes. 'I've not been much credit to her,' he says. 'She married me when I was just about dyin' of pneumonia. She stood by me, and I haven't had much luck since. I was to Arizony, and workin' down there in the movies when my little boy was born, and I just couldn't wait to get up here and see him, and see my wife,' he says. 'She ain't got no right to divorce me for non-support,' he says. 'I'm lookin' high and low for work—at Jackson and Placerville and Sonora and everywheres.' You'd-a felt sorry for him, Beck. Ain't it Scripture teachin' to give him another chance? I'll tell you what you do, Becky. You and your mother go home and think this over. Gavin's a nice feller. He's out fishin' with me coupla times last month, and I's sayin' afterward to Mrs Miller that I don't never want no nicer company. If you left him, and got custody of the child, he'd want his son a coupla months every year, and who's benefited by that?"

"Why waste words on this old chucklehead?" Becky thought, icy scorn at her heart. "He just adores to hear him-self talk. He doesn't handle divorces anyway; Ike Lansing does."

"You see, Becky, you divorce this feller, who's a perfectly harmless feller, and liked by everyone," the old man said as the two women presently rose to go, "and the whole town talks. I'll grant ye Gavin's a little gay—a sport, as they say these days. But if you wanted a husband that 'd come home every night and read the paper, how is it you give Joe the boot?"

White-faced, silent, Becky descended with her mother to the street and the car with smoldering rage in her heart.

"The old fathead!" she stormed, jerking the gears.

"Well, he didn't help us much!" Sarah agreed disconsolately. "There was a time when May Miller was just about ready to divorce *him,* to hear her talk," she added darkly.

"What he feels for himself is the *grande passion,*" Becky said viciously. "We could see Ike Lansing?"

"I don't know," Sarah said dubiously. "Ike takes such terrible cases."

"But a divorce case is just a divorce case, Mother."

"Oh no, it isn't, Beck. Not when one of the parties is a man like Gavin. He might get ugly, and then you wouldn't know where you were. With that awful—what was his name, the man who brought a countersuit——"

"Oh, Bundy, yes. Bundy."

"Yes. Lansing took that, and brought charges of goodness knows what against her, and they say she really died of a broken heart. She'd gotten religion, and she'd written him a note saying she was terribly sorry for it all and wouldn't he forgive her and Ike twisted it all round and made it seem as if she was confessing to something. She was one of the finest girls I ever knew, Vera Bundy was. But Bundy got the baby, and she never got over it. Ike did that."

"Well, we won't go today," Becky conceded, turning the car toward the home road. The unending question began in her heart again: What shall I do? "There can't be any fix so bad that you can't get yourself out, Mother," she presently said. "What would *you* do?"

"I suppose just—let it go on," Sarah began hesitatingly. Becky made a sharp sound of dissent and shook her head, without moving her eyes from the road ahead of her engine.

"It might go on forever," she said.

"Oh, I don't think so." But Sarah's tone was one of doubt.

Nothing more was said. They reached home, and Becky rushed upstairs to see that Gibbs, left in Sophy's charge, was safe. The evening went on its way like all their evenings.

But a night or two later the crisis came.

They were talking in their room before dinner, Becky and

Gavin, when something that he said made her face him suspiciously with the sudden almost frightened question: "Gavin,
you've not borrowed money from Joe Feratta?"

Gavin was lying across the bed with the pillows piled under
his head. He had been idly watching Becky as she settled the
baby off for the night with a sponge bath, a bottle, cereal, the
inevitable change of raiment. Gibbs looked his sweetest in his
crisp little cotton nightgown, with his sun-tanned face fresh
and clean and his damp dark hair combed smooth.

"What makes you think I did?" Gavin asked, unalarmed.

"What you said," Becky said in a voice of steel.

"What 'd I say?"

"Then—just then. You said that you wished you had Joe's
money, that his pocketbook was filled with twenties. You said,
'I'd like to get hold of a few, and my note with them.' "

"Did I?" Gavin asked, seemingly amused. But she knew
from his tone that he was chagrined at having betrayed himself. "Well, I've been kinder rambling on here about Joe because I think he's a mutt," he added, "and I think he gets all
the breaks."

Becky, the child in her arms, came to sit on the side of the
bed. Her eyes were tragic.

"Gavin, you didn't borrow money from him!"

"Hell, why the heck not?" Gavin demanded, hunching
himself up on the pillows to face her better. "He's got it."

"You didn't!" Becky said.

"Oh, I happened to run into him. He was down here for
his mother's birthday or something, and I saw him downtown. I was coming out of Miller's office. The old man is *for*
me, see? He says that as long as you came home of your own
free will to have your baby, and your folks won't put me out
—I'd like to see them try it!—you haven't got any kick
coming. I ran into Joe in the hall and told him we'd been
having a hard time—— Why not? It's true, isn't it? He had
a crush on you and he'd do anything for you. Shucks, I'll

pay him back. Men do these things all the time, don't think anything of them. He'll get his money. . . ."

Becky was not listening. She was breathing hard, her face red. She had carried the child to his crib, kissed the back of his little neck, put him face down on the smooth sheet and pinned his light blanket snugly.

"Sh-sh-sh!" she said sharply to Gavin. "Keep quiet now, until he's off."

In the dimly lighted room she moved about softly, brushing her hair, changing her dress. Gibbs hummed like a bee, bumping his head up and down. Gavin lay silent, scowling.

"I'm sorry I told you," he presently said sulkily. Becky spoke in a sharp whisper.

"If you get the baby roused you'll have to stay up here with him!"

Gavin got to his feet, put his arm about her as she opened the hall door to go down to dinner.

"Don't be mad at me, Becky," he said.

"I'm not mad," Becky assured him wearily, indifferently.

Three nights later, fifteen minutes before the late bus went through to Jackson, Becky sat at the kitchen table, writing a brief letter. A packed suitcase stood beside her; she had brought the small car to the end of the barn lane before dinner, parked it there, where no one in the house could hear the engine. Gibbs, shawled and blinking and pleased with the novel procedure, was on her arm.

"My own dearest Mother, I am running away again. . . ."

CHAPTER XXIV

BECKY RAN UP two flights of narrow stairs scented with boiling onions, dirty clothing, unwashed bodies, filthy kitchens and garbage barrels. She opened a certain narrow doorway on the third floor and was at once in a cold kitchen in which with other kitchen furnishings there was a couch bed. The room was dark in the late December afternoon. A thin woman in a wrapper, who had been bending over the couch, turned to look at her as she came in.

"How is he?" Becky flung off her coat and hat, sank to her knees beside the couch and laid her cold hand over the hot little hand of the baby whose dark head was moving restlessly on a pillow.

"He's awful sick," the woman said in a whisper.

"I don't know . . ." She wouldn't believe it. Gibbs, quite himself only a few days ago, just a "little upset" yesterday, couldn't really be ill today. The leaden weight that had tugged at her heart all through the long day in the shop sank deeper, heavier. Gibbs was sick.

"He'd ought to be in a hospital," said Mrs Devvins of the floor below.

"My darling," Becky said in a low hoarse tone to the baby.

"You've got a cold yourself," said the other woman.

"Yes, I know. I gave it to him, I think. Thank you for watching him," Becky said. She had ice and orange juice in a cup now; she put the drink to the child's lips, her arm supporting him, her voice tender in his ears. "Drink a little, my darling. It will make you feel better," she murmured.

The other woman stood watching. The room, which was

one of two composing the apartment, had two narrow windows on a crowded street in a Bronx cross street, near Bergen Avenue. It faced southeast and had full benefit of the sun, when the sun shone. But there had been no sun today, nor for many days. The street was grimy and dark, and the house darker and grimier. There seemed to Becky no light in the world.

"Mis' Gibson," said Mae Devvins, "how'd you happen to come to New York?"

Becky was changing her clothing now; she was buttoning on a sleazy but comfortable bungalow apron, of the sort that Rheingolder's sold for forty-three cents to the public, twenty-one cents to the trade, and ten cents to the employees when, as in this case, there was an obvious flaw in the application of the rickrack braid which trimmed it.

"Oh, New York sounds so good, to girls anywhere else!" she said in an abstracted undertone. She sat down beside the couch as she spoke, and laid a cloth wrung out of ice water on the baby's forehead, brushing back his rich black hair as she did so. "I had a chance to come," she added. "A woman wanted to send her little girls to their father, who lived here. She didn't mind my bringing Gibbs, and it seemed a great chance for me. That was more than two years ago. I got my fare and two hundred dollars; I was sure I could get along. And I did get a job right away; I'd had some experience. I can always get along. Last winter wasn't so bad. But then I began to get so tired—summer tired me horribly, and the woman I was boarding with didn't want the responsibility for Gibbs; he got too active. So I came here and things"— her voice thickened—"things haven't gone so well," she added in a low tone. "Or at least," Becky went on with a desperate flicker of her old gallantry, "things were all right until I got this last cold, and then he got it. I think if the weather 'd get warmer," she said, her voice trembling impatiently, her fingers continually touching the child's forehead and his wrist as if she were unwilling to believe their testimony, "I think if once we could get *warm* . . ."

"Oh, it's awful," the other woman agreed in the pause. There was a moment of forlorn silence in the forlorn room.

"Do you think we ought to have a doctor, Mrs Devvins?"

"Well, it's two dollars. And all he could say is to keep him quiet. That's all he said about our Johnny. I had him once on the Monday and then the day before he died."

Becky felt a chill run down her backbone like the tip of an icy finger.

"Where's your folks, Mis' Gibson?"

"California."

"Hard up?"

"No. We lived on a ranch." Oh, spreading oaks and warm home comfort and blue winter skies! "But I cost them enough," Becky said on a bitter note. "I ran away, first, and worried them sick. And when I went home there was the baby and myself . . . and after that another person—my husband—and *he* worried them sick! I've failed them, I've hurt them where they couldn't strike back, because they loved me. And that's why, last summer and this winter, when things have been so bad for Gibbs and me, I couldn't wire them, I couldn't ask help! I was afraid that if I went back he'd show up again. There 'd be no peace for any of us. I couldn't do it! But now," she finished almost inaudibly, laying her cheek for an instant against the child's burning cheek, "I'd do anything. I'd not have any pride now. My sweetheart —my little brave boy who's stood by me through it all . . ."

"Ain't the store open tonight?" the other woman asked after a silence.

"They want me back tonight," Becky said. "But I can't leave him! My God, I don't know what to do!"

"He'd be well took care of in the hospital," said the visitor.

"I haven't the money!" Becky whispered, no eyes except for Gibbs.

"They'd take him free at the Lincoln."

"In a ward," Becky said, and shuddered. "No, I couldn't do that. His mother couldn't do that to him!"

Mae Devvins stood silent for a minute, watching. She had three children of her own belowstairs: Pete, Loretta, a baby Gibbs's age called Buddy. Gibbs and Buddy had played for many hours together in her odorous kitchen. Becky paid her three dollars a week for the six-day accommodation, and knew that Gibbs would have the same affectionate if insanitary and slipshod care that the small Devvinses had. But now for three nightmare days Gibbs had been alone upstairs, tended only when Mae could steal a few minutes to run up to him, give him a drink, straighten his bedcovers.

"They wouldn't let me see him in the hospital!" Becky said.

"Haven't you any religion at all, don't you ever pray?" the other woman presently asked unexpectedly.

"No, never. Prayer," Becky said, not looking over her shoulder as she opened a can of soup at the sink, "didn't save your oldest little boy."

"No." Mae was perhaps nonplused for a moment. But presently she said bravely: "But I've sometimes thought God's hand was in that, too, that Johnny should go before he ever knew what sin or sorrow was. My brother Johnny lived to be a terrible heartscald to my mother and all of us. If he hadn't died of the pneumonia Johnny might have gone to Sing Sing. Well, they won't ever get my little Johnny there!"

"I wouldn't pray now if I'd been praying all my life," Becky said. "I wouldn't want Them—Whoever's up there—to notice me. To decide that my innocent beautiful baby would be better off—safer—somewhere else! What *cruelty!*" She interrupted herself, fell silent, and once more went to lay her hand on Gibbs's forehead. "He's not sleeping, really," she whispered, speaking half to herself; "he's just heavy with the fever."

"Just the same, if you went down on your knees and said

the 'Our Father,' " Mae Devvins persisted mildly, "you'd get up from your knees feeling better, whatever happened. And if you said it every hour, or every ten minutes from now until ten o'clock, you'd sleep and maybe he would too. And maybe he'd be better in the morning. It isn't the things that happen to us, it's the things we think are going to happen to us that drive us almost crazy," she finished simply.

Becky, pouring milk from a bottle into a small saucepan, looked at her sharply, struck by the simple philosophy.

"Anything that could keep me from—from tearing my heart out about him tonight," she said, "anything that could keep him with me would seem to me a miracle tonight! I know he's going to get well—it's only a baby cold, and he's strong—he's always been strong! But I don't know the Lord's Prayer, not all the way through—I don't think I do—and I don't believe in miracles."

"There's miracles just the same," Mae Devvins persisted without heat. "Frank's a miracle. He made the Nine Fridays with his mother and I, and he hasn't touched a drop since. He says he hates the smell of the stuff. If you was to say maybe only one prayer you'd change your ideas, and you'd let me run over to the drugstore and telephone Lincoln Hospital. It's pneumonia, that's what he's got. I know, because 'Retta had it. 'Retta and Frank had it over one Christmas. They won't move him if it's pneumonia, but they'll take good care of him here."

"Charity," Becky whispered. "I don't mind for me. I don't mind anything for me. But it doesn't seem fair to him. What's he ever done that he should be a charity patient?"

"Well . . ." Mrs Devvins said, departing. Becky made a quick step to arrest her with an outstretched hand.

"I do thank you!" she said. "No money would ever pay you for what you're doing. If I go back to the store in a few minutes will you run up and see him now and then?"

"Oh, sure. I'll lay down on your bed in there, when I've cleaned up after supper," Mae said.

"And will you—seriously, I mean this—will you pray for him?" Becky asked, a shamed little flush rising to her tired, colorless face. "I don't know how."

"You don't have to know how; it's just ask and receive," Mae told her, going on her way.

Becky drank her bowl of hot creamy soup, ate two slices of buttered toast, found a chocolate bar. Then she tried to tempt Gibbs with the iced orange juice again, sponged the hot little face.

After that she washed her own hands and face and ran a comb through the brush of her gold-brown hair. And then quite suddenly on her knees beside the couch, her hands gathering together the child's burning hands, she groped tearfully for the first real prayer of her life.

"Our Father who art in heaven . . . forgive us our trespasses . . . If You really are anywhere, help me to find You—oh, God, help me to find You! Forever and ever amen. Our Father who art in heaven . . ."

She knelt for a long time, incoherently repeating the jumbled words and phrases, shutting her eyes and turning her face up to the ceiling, opening them to bend her anxious adoring look upon the child who was all her world.

On her feet again, she reached for her coat, ran downstairs and into the ice-cluttered, feebly lighted street where poverty brooded all day and all night, pushing sickness and crime and fear and suffering into their predestined places.

The drugstore was warm and pleasantly scented with peppermint and cigars and rubber. Becky turned the pages of a telephone book worn into a woolly ball tied on a chain. Instantly she was being answered by a pleasant female voice.

"We'll send right away. We'll send the ambulance, but if the doctor thinks it is a home case they'll leave him there.

In about twenty minutes I should think. There'll be no charge."

Running back to Gibbs's bedside, Becky felt a strange lightening at her heart. Much bigger persons were going to share her responsibility. The office nurse had sounded kind, concerned. Someone else was going to care that the precious spark of life that meant Becky's life as well as Gibbs's was held in the small fever-thinned body.

While she waited she knelt down again by the bed, prayed again.

"Oh, God, please make what I am doing now the right thing. Oh, God, help me to find You and give me back my little boy. Oh, Gibbsy—Gibbsy—do you know me, my darling? This is Mummy. Mummy's taking care of you. Oh, God, make him well and get us out of here . . . get us home to Mother. . . ."

The thrilling clang of the ambulance and the intrusion of a white-clad intern and two stretcher-bearers so enthralled the entire tenement that Becky and Gibbs found themselves with an escort when they went down to the street. Gibbs, rolled in a blanket, was muttering and feverish; he made no objection to the strange arms, the strange voices. Becky's one feeble protest against the hospital was met by the intern's so definite "No, we've got to get him over there right away," that she offered no further objection. It was only hopelessly that she asked if she might ride with the child. The life-saving, pain-saving, colossal machinery of the Biggest City had little Gibbs Gibson in its grip now, and no one was particularly concerned for the quite usual and expected fears of his mother.

"Jump in," the intern said after a glance at the tawny-headed woman with the gold eyes burned deep into a white face. Becky went along, saw Gibbs carried away from her in a group of strangely interested white-clad folk of both sexes, sat in a brightly lighted, drug-scented receiving room talking to a handsome woman on whose desk a metal triangle announced, "Margaret Cole, R.N., On Duty."

Margaret Cole took data: Father Gavin Flood 36, Mother Rebecca Gibson 24, separated, using her maiden name. Spencer Gibson Flood, born in Salletts, Calif., in February almost three years ago. Dates. Weights. Ages.

"Can I see him?"

"I think you'd better not wait tonight."

"Would you find out if he's—pretty sick? If they think . . ."

"I'll have Doctor Dinsmore come down." Miss Cole telephoned, murmured unconcernedly yet conscientiously. "She's worried," Becky heard her say.

Dr Dinsmore did not come down. But a pleasant young nurse did, told Becky to telephone in about an hour and she would have a full report, assured Becky that children's temperatures didn't mean much, "although he's a pretty sick little boy."

Could Becky pay a little something? Indeed she could. That would mean better care? No, just the same care. She opened her purse, found she need only sign a card instead. She went out into the night.

It was quarter to eight. She should have been at Rheingolder's at seven. But there was a shift that went off for dinner at seven and came back at eight; by walking fast she could get there and slip in with that group. If she were found out she would be found out, that was all, and probably discharged. Or, since Christmas was close, she might be only fined; girls at Rheingolder's were fined for absence without leave, seventy-five cents an hour or for any fraction of an hour, although they were paid only three times that for the nine-hour day. Some of the smartest girls, however, Becky among them, almost doubled their salaries by selling "plugs" and handling difficult customers by breaking in at the hopeless moment on the sales of other girls with suggestions, flattery, good salesmanship. When she did this the second girl got two per cent of the sale and the original saleswoman nothing. But no supersaleswoman could break in on a sale unless sent to do so by the floorwalker, so the girls felt no personal resentment of the system, against the "takers," as they were called, and saved their biting criticism for the system.

Tonight Becky reached the bedlam that was the immense department store a few minutes before eight, entering by the great damp cement-smelling basement and, because Miss Tinney's eyes were upon her, boldly advancing to the time clock and punching against number 544 the eight o'clock slip that should have fallen at seven o'clock. They might discover it and they might not.

"Oh, God," she said, hanging up her coat, rubbing rough, cold-bitten hands together, "don't let them find it."

She slipped into her own department: little girls' dresses. It was buzzing with women pulling the cheap little frocks in every direction, considering the blue with the collar, the red with the belt, the green with the glass buttons. Which would a very happy sweet little girl of ten like? She was the most popular girl in the school, and her composition . . .

Becky went to and fro under the blinding lights, her arms piled high. She lost her sales book, discovered it, lost it again. Her pencil broke; she borrowed Miss Blum's knife. Miss Blum was in a frightful state of worry because she feared she was going to have a baby. Becky's heart was lead, thinking of her own baby in the strange big smelly ward, perhaps shouting, "Mom!" this minute in a hoarse little feverish voice.

No one came up to ask her why she had checked in at eight instead of seven. Becky prayed for Gibbs, prayed that she would not lose her job, found herself absorbed in this new secret business of prayer. Her thoughts came back with a jerk to Gibbs again, but she had had the moment's lightening of spirit.

"Pray without ceasing." Where had she heard that? You could hardly pray without ceasing. Or could you? "Oh, God, help me to find You."

At half-past ten, aching in every limb, her head stupid and heavy from air thick with the smells of woolen and cheap dyes, Becky went downstairs again and asked Miss Tinney if she could charge a telephone call.

"They took my little boy to the Lincoln tonight. I came out without my purse. Pneumonia. I just wanted to ask. I'm to ask for branch—I've got it written down—and ask for Doctor Lichtenstein."

"For the Lord's sake, I'll lend you a nickel. And I'll ask Ma to pray," Josephine Tinney said. "You poor thing."

Becky waited, waited. The report came. The little Gibson boy was asleep; he seemed more comfortable. He hadn't cried at all; he'd been just a little angel.

"Oh, God bless them, he's warm and safe and at least they're watching him!" Becky said, tears running down her face as she walked bareheaded under the cold stars on her way home. It was a long way, through dirty streets with snow piled high against the curbs. The city cleaned the big avenues fast enough but sometimes on these shabby back streets the snow mountains stayed for weeks, with garbage and the dirt the dogs left there spoiling the children's only playgrounds.

"God bless them!" That was a prayer too. Her heart was strangely light and comforted. The fresh sweet air was doing her good; the bitter despair and anxiety of only a few hours earlier had disappeared.

She was poor, obscurely employed in a shop which gave small hope of real promotion to any of its thousands of employees, her son was desperately ill, her husband a ne'er-do-well of whose very whereabouts she was in complete ignorance. And yet somehow, for the first time in weary months and months, she was walking on air. When she got to the tenement she went into Mae Devvins' rooms and reported.

Mae lived in exactly the space Becky and Gibbs occupied upstairs: an entrance kitchen measuring perhaps fourteen feet by sixteen, a bedroom not so large. Almost the entire bedroom space was occupied by two beds. Mae and Frank put the bedroom chairs on the beds in the morning so that they and the children could move about, dressing. An enormous chest and a couch were in the kitchen. There was no bathroom, but there was a small ice-cold lavatory with a sink washtub on the stark iron stairway that connected the rear entrances of the flats with the street.

Buddy, three years old, was awake in his high chair when Becky entered the kitchen; Mae was ironing a boy's shirt; little Pete was sound asleep on the kitchen couch. The women talked in low tones not to disturb him. Mae was touchingly, generously pleased that Gibbs had been taken to the hospital. She asked Becky what had decided her so suddenly to change her mind.

"I don't know," Becky answered, ashamed to make the flat statement. "I guess I found God."

Had she found God? She did not know. She only knew that when despair and doubt and fear touched her she could banish them by plunging blindly into prayer—any sort of prayer. A dozen times a day, twenty times, she tore her thoughts from some avenue of discouragement or doubt to repeat her formula: "God, help me. Help me to find You. Don't let Gibbs die."

And strangely, strangely, the eternal magic worked, and she was comforted, comforted even when he was still very ill, when she went home to the empty rooms and opened for herself a can of soup and pressed her aching bare feet hard, hard against the cold iron of the sink props to cool them, and read her book. When her mind wandered, when fear crept into it to shake her to the soul, it was always there, the prayer that she thought meant nothing to her and that meant so much.

"Oh, God, help me."

CHAPTER XXV

THE EIGHTH DAY after Gibbs had been taken away was a Sunday, and she could go to see him in the hospital. She had crept in every night for a report; she had telephoned every day; but he was better now. There was a joy in this meeting that Becky had never known in her life before. There was joy in the very air of the still winter-locked city, joy in the dark streets where men and women and children were loitering in Sunday leisure, joy even in those hospital corridors that had once so horrified her, the waiting room so sickeningly scented with poverty and illness, the bare clean halls that smelled of iodine and ammonia.

Gibbs was lying languid on a pillow; he was pitifully thin, and his big eyes seemed to take up all his face. But his small hand was cool, and the forehead that Becky's lips touched was cool. She sat beside him talking quietly, telling him his favorite story of the white rat that was good and the black rat that was bad, and he listened with all his old absorption, sometimes supplying details with vigor. "So his mommy din' give him any ice cream?" or "And hurted his leg so it bleeded?"

"Mrs Gibson," a nurse said. Becky turned to smile. "Doctor Dinsmore, the head, is here," the girl went on. "He would like to see you for a moment. He took charge of your small boy when he was brought in. He'd like to see you in his office. Fourth floor. I'll show you the way, if you like."

Becky followed, praying as she went. It couldn't be that anything was wrong with Gibbs. Not tuberculosis or anemia . . . She was so white when at last she faced the famous physician in his lair that he made her sit down, and himself brought her a paper cup of water.

"You're all right?" he asked anxiously. Becky sat facing him, trying to smile. But she had been under a heavy strain since the first of the month; the daily hospital visits, the constant concern for Gibbs, the hasty little insufficient meals at home, the long day and evening hours in the thick air of the shop had worn her down. She felt the room spinning slowly about her and gripped the chair arms for support.

"I'm all right," she said shakily, "but Gibbs, my little boy . . . ? She said he was really out of the woods. She said that perhaps he could come home next Sunday."

"He is. He's made an astonishing comeback. Well, not for a baby, come to think of it. No, he's all right. But now, Mrs Gibson, where do you live?"

Dr Stephen Dinsmore, nearing fifty, was dark, tall, lean, spectacled. Becky liked his voice. It was unalarming, cultured.

"Where do I live? I have a little apartment in 149th."

"Go to work in the subway every day?"

"No. I work at Rheingolder's. It's not so very far from here. I've been able to come to the hospital every night at dinnertime. Before that a neighbor took care of Gibbs while I was away."

"I don't think," the doctor said thoughtfully in his consulting-room voice, "that little Gibbs ought to go back to that neighborhood. Not now. He ought to have a month or six weeks in an even warm temperature and very careful building up. Any epidemic now, measles or whooping cough . . ."

"Oh, God help me!" Becky said in her soul. Aloud she added:

"Could I take him to California?"

"Could you get to California?"

"My people are there. But there are circumstances . . ." Becky began, and hesitated. "They haven't a great deal of money," she explained. "I've four younger brothers, all in school. I thought . . . I knew so many people had made good here . . . I ran away from home——"

"What I'm suggesting," said the doctor in a businesslike voice, "is that you bring the child down to my house on Long Island and keep him there until after Christmas. My sister is there, widowed, with two girls—grown girls; she's visiting me. I think she'd be very glad to have you. After Christmas we are going to Florida for several weeks. That would build him up perfectly, and I don't imagine you'd have any further trouble."

Becky looked at him in stupefaction.

"I'm not believing my ears," she thought. "You hear of that all your life, but you don't think it ever happens. But I'm really not believing my ears."

Aloud she said dazedly:

"But, Doctor Dinsmore, why—why should you do this for me?"

"Because I want to," the doctor said composedly, looking at some scribbled message on his desk pad.

"But—but my job?"

"You would have to give that up."

"But what—what would I do in return? I couldn't just—just *take* it."

A glance was flashed at her through the strong glasses.

"Why not? I would of course guarantee you your fare to California in March, in writing if you like. You could safely move him in March, I believe."

It was as if the dark December skies above the grim old city had broken into the blue of June. Flags were waving and birds singing, and the air was sweet with flowers. Rest now, and the divine right to care for her child! Florida's palms and sunshine for him! And afterward home again and her mother's voice, boys racketing in for lunch, and Dad coming forward in the oil-scented coolness of the Exchange to say, "Better take your mother some asparagus, Becky. Just in."

"What do you say?" Stephen Dinsmore asked.

"Why, but, Doctor Dinsmore, what can I say? Except that I didn't know that people could be so wonderful—so marvelous. I was—I was—sort of at the end of my rope," Becky faltered, "and it doesn't seem true!"

And suddenly abandoning an attempt to hold back her tears, an attempt to turn them into a laugh, she put her head down on the desk and burst into wild sobbing, sobbing so uncontrolled, so exhausted and abandoned that the man presently rang for a nurse, and Becky had to be quieted with something powdery and white dissolved in water, and made to lie down in one of the waiting rooms on a wide leather couch.

She saw Dr Dinsmore again before she went home; he was quiet and businesslike and unemotional. Gibbs could be moved on Friday; that was the eighteenth. If Becky would be at the hospital with his clothes and hers on Friday afternoon, they could be driven straight to the Locust Valley place.

"My sister will take charge of you; she's done this sort of thing for me before. You're to do nothing but rest and eat for a while. I'll be down Saturday and see how you've settled in."

Her face colorless, her lashes soaked, her voice shaking, Becky caught at his hand.

"Doctor, you don't know . . . you don't know . . ."

He blinked at her, stirred himself.

"I do know," he said.

CHAPTER XXVI

ON FRIDAY GIBBS, well rolled in a big soft tan blanket with S.D. lettered upon it in brown silk, rode in his mother's arms away from the city into the clean sweet winter country. Becky, herself luxuriously wrapped in rugs, looked out of the limousine window and watched the congested streets sink away under the bridge, and saw the cold walls of the island prison ruffled by gray water, and great cakes of ice drifting in the East River.

They went under mighty girders and through a shabby, snow-spattered town or two, and then they were out on the open roads, and the beautiful homes of Long Island began to slip by one by one, mansions standing proudly on the rolling hills with great stripped trees and clean white barns and fences, with empty tennis courts and stable yards where famous racers lived their protected lives.

After a while they came to the water again—cold gray water strewn with blocks of gray ice. Becky drank in the beauty of the road thirstily; the prosperous breadth and spaciousness of it enchanted her. It was good to see children riding on ponies, to see smoke rising from comfortable brick chimneys, to realize that all life was not the crowded griminess, the biting, incessant, burdening poverty that she had seen in every day and hour and minute for all these two long years.

The big car turned in at an iron gate; it was not a pretentious house at which they stopped, but Becky thought she had never seen a more inviting one. A square plain brick building, painted a cream white, on which bare vines etched delicate patterns; french windows with curved tops; a door-way severely Colonial with fine-fluted columns and a fan-light. There were window balconies of green ironwork; there was a fire in one of the downstairs rooms: she could see the pink hospitable light of it flickering on primly drawn net curtains.

Another fire, in a fireplace of white tiles, was burning briskly in the great upstairs bedroom to which she and Gibbs were immediately taken. Mrs Lafayette Lee, Stephen Dinsmore's sister Harriet, a faded, sweet woman of some fifty-five years, escorted Becky there, as did Carrie-Sis, an enormous gentle young Negress, who performed all the offices of nurse for Gibbs so kindly that even the shy three-year-old did not feel strange with her.

A pretty girl of twenty, Harriet junior, did what she could to make Becky feel welcome. There was a butler, who went off for milk and toast for Gibbs, a big motherly gray-headed cook and a thin little eager maid. All these, as Becky was to learn later, composed the house staff, but so comfortable and friendly and understanding was the relationship between them that the domestic machinery at Hillover ran as if by magic, and she was never conscious of their presence again unless she needed them.

She was presently left alone, to sink panting into a great ruffled chair by the fire and wonder—and wonder—and wonder what had happened to her. Her big room was still with that complete stillness that only a country winter knows. Outside her windows great stripped trees stood motionless; beyond them the bare garden stretched down to the water. Shrubs had been muffled in burlap and were powdered with snow; the iron gates, that might have come from some old French château, were touched with lines of virgin white.

But in the room all was warmth and comfort. The air was as soft and fresh as on a spring day; the dull blue and dull ivory notes of chintzes and carpets and walls made for infi-

nite coziness as well as harmony. Gibbs, refreshed with bread
and milk, warmly blanketed, slept deeply. The fire crackled
and was still; Carrie-Sis came in noiselessly to lay another
log or two upon it, to murmur sympathetically: "I raik'n
you's jus' played out, havin' yo' baby so sick!"

"It's good to sit still," Becky admitted shyly, on a long con-
tented sigh. "I don't know what sort of angels live here," she
added, "to let me bring a sick child in on them!"

"Dey angels all right," Carrie-Sis agreed. "En Doc," she
added, "is a son of God. Yas'm, he sho' a son of God."

God again! Becky leaned back in her chair, when the
Negress was gone, and smiled deep within herself. "God, I
thank Thee. Whether it lasts two days or two weeks, I do
thank Thee."

After a while she got up and explored her domain, reveling
in the spacious country generosity of its proportions, in the
bathroom as big as her Bronx bedroom, that bedroom she had
left only this afternoon, forever; in bureau space, closet
space, big towels, fragrant soap. Becky had known comfort
all her life, but she had never known anything like this.

Her clothes were shabby, deplorable. No matter. She could
only make herself look as neat and fresh as possible. A dancing joy stirred in her whole being as she went about, reveling
in the first deep hot tub bath she had known for more than a
year, reveling in the softness of the bed and the brocade-lined
fur rug she pulled over her feet when she lay down to watch
Gibbs as he slept.

There were children's books on the lower shelf of the bookcase; surely, surely not even Dr Stephen Dinsmore's inspired
kindness could have thought of that! But there they were:
Sambo and Jemima Puddleduck and the intrepid Nils, and
Osma. Some were worn, some new. Becky and Gibbs had a
wonderful hour with them before dinner.

Then Gibbs's supper of chicken soup and custard appeared
on a tray, and afterward Becky went shyly down a curved,

gracious white stairway to dinner and sat with the two Harriets over a meal so simple, so perfect, so delicious that she felt that the daughter of a California farmstead was taking a lesson in table service.

Afterward they had a library fire and talked, while the elder Harriet played solitaire with tiny cards that matched her small ivory hands, and the younger Harriet debated tirelessly the arrangements for a Princeton week-end party.

"But, Mother, if I go by train it means three suitcases—that is, counting my hatbox! And if Rhoda takes my bags, then I can't change until late. And I *can't* wait for Rhoda, because she isn't going to the rehearsal."

Gordy's car and Davy's car and staying overnight with Yvonne. But then she'd have to telephone Isabel—well, she could do that! Becky, listening, smiling, looking dreamily into the fire, thought of Mae Devvins' problems tonight, and wondered in her soul.

The older Harriet Lee advised, planned, indulgently attentive. She must have been very pretty once, Becky thought, with her blue eyes and sensitive mouth. Now her curled hair was gray and her thin face wrinkled, but still it was a pleasant face. Her dress of white and gray checked silk, trimmed with real lace and touches of blue velvet, suggested an earlier day. Perhaps, Becky thought, she had once had a dress like that for some especially gala occasion—a White House dance, a wedding—and she liked the fashion still.

Hatsy, as the daughter was called, was of larger build than her mother. She had ostentatiously avoided fats and sweets at dinner. She told Becky that when she even sampled them she became "gross." She had fair lusterless hair, cut, rolled and curled in the latest mode, wide-open brown eyes, not a pretty face exactly, but smart and aristocratic, her expression, her manner, the tones of her voice assured and confident.

Some friends of hers came for her; they were dancing at Sally's.

"Now you take good care of her, Donald," Mrs Lee said to one of the boys. "Hatsy hasn't got any brother, and I've got to trust you."

"Mother, why not make him an offer of me in writing?" suggested Hatsy. Her mother was unabashed.

"Well, I may get that far yet!" she answered cheerfully.

Then she and Becky were left alone.

"Steve has a heart of gold," was Harriet Lee's only acknowledgment of what Becky tried to say. "It gives him the greatest pleasure in his life to do what he calls 'playing God.' "

Again, Becky thought. God again.

She told her hostess her own story of the past few years. The girlhood on a California ranch whose prune and oak and eucalyptus trees ran up toward the high blue mountains. Her mother and brothers, and the father who kept the store. Of the man who had casually drifted into her life, whose enchantment had been so strong upon her that no other consideration, no other tie mattered at all.

"I felt that way about Colonel Lee. Never looked at another man for one second!" Harriet Lee, understanding nothing, put in sympathetically at this point.

"We were engaged, but I'm not sure Gavin would have come back for me if things hadn't happened as they did," Becky resumed. "He got frightfully ill—dangerously ill— and I went to him. We were married in his sickroom; he was hardly conscious of what went on, I think. Then we were very poor, it was always a struggle. Gavin—my husband— used to play cards a good deal. I never knew where I stood. So before the baby came I went back to my mother, and he followed me there, and it was worse than ever. He's not an easy person to influence—not vicious, but lazy, easygoing. It embarrassed me, for after all, those were the people I'd known all my life, and I came away to make a living, somehow, somewhere, for the baby and myself. It seemed so easy. Just one woman and one child. But from the very beginning it was running downhill—everything was slipping, faster and faster. Almost immediately I had this chance to bring two little girls to New York to spend their half year with their father. The mother had remarried and was expecting another baby, and she couldn't go.

"But that was a terrible trip. I had no rest at all for four days and nights, and even when I got here, and had my two hundred dollars, I was terribly frightened. And since then it's been a nightmare. . . ."

"Well, you'll get a real rest now," Harriet Lee said comfortably. Becky had already discovered that the one real treat life could bring her little hostess was a good listener. Mrs Lee loved to talk, to ramble on endlessly of the glories of the old South, of her family's possessions and privileges all through America's history up to the present moment. She had always been rich, gentle, generous, good, proud of her place in the world. She wished she had had a son, she told Becky, because with Barbara and Hatsy one branch of the fine old family died out.

Barbara was the older daughter, now on her way home from a two months stay in Hawaii. Hatsy and her mother had gone over with her in September, but they had come back to arrange for Hatsy's formal bow to society, a great ball on the day after Thanksgiving. Four hundred had come to the ball, some from Richmond and Asheville and Washington, some from Boston. Lights and music and champagne and terrapin for four hundred. Becky thought of the woman in the drugstore the night she had been telephoning the Lincoln Hospital about Gibbs. A woman trying to prove to the clerk that he had given her a bad dime.

"Stephen, of course, wouldn't come," said his sister. "He

had some poor old thing dying over on Blackwells Island, and he had to be there all night. My brother is—well, we call him a social outlaw, Mrs Gibson. But the longer you know him the more you'll admire him."

"I haven't any doubt of it," said Becky.

Portraits in colored chalks of Barbara and Hatsy flanked a large handsome oil portrait of their mother and father over the mantel. The late Colonel Lafayette Lee had been painted in uniform with decorations. He sat at a library table, looking at papers; his wife, a slender young creature in plain black velvet, stood at a window in the background, half turned toward him, as if she had looked back from the lovely view beyond.

"I wasn't supposed to be in that picture at all," the widow confessed, seeing that Becky was studying it. "But I just couldn't bear to see Lafe being made immortal without me. And afterward I was glad I insisted!"

Barbara was evidently beautiful in very much her mother's type. Hers was a small sensitive face framed in loose gold-red curls. When at half-past nine Becky said that she thought she would go up to Gibbs, Mrs Lee took her about the room and showed her other portraits: elderly Dinsmores handsome in buttoned alpacas, lace collars, stiff-skirted black cloth; a great friend of President Cleveland, that one; married to Senator Buckholt, that other. Hatsy and Barbara when they were babies, sweet in bare arms and white ruffles and blue ribbons with a white kitten and a brown setter.

Gibbs was his lively, interested self when she went in; in that fact alone there was heart solace for Becky. After she had settled him off and gotten herself ready for bed she suddenly, unexpectedly, sank on her knees again. And this prayer was one of pure gratitude.

It was all wonderful. It was a miracle of peace and security to awaken in the warm stillness of a winter morning and see snowflakes coming steadily, gently down outside, and to think of Rheingolder's "big, bright, busy basement" as a thing of the past. All gone, the stifling heat of the shop, the damp cold of the basement, the smells of cloth and wet raincoats and bad dyes. All gone, the aching of leg muscles and chill of roughened hands, the smell of unaired apartments and the taste of rancid butter preserved too long on a chipped pink saucer.

A miracle to go downstairs quietly, exploringly at eight o'clock, and find a fire crackling in the little white and blue breakfast room, with the snowy garden making a Christmas picture of itself outside of the deep-silled windows, and the coffeepot smoking invitingly. A miracle to rest and rest and rest through all the hours of the dreamy day and the next day, reading to Gibbs, telling him stories, lying cozily tucked under the fur rug, dozing when he dozed.

For a wonderful week Becky steeped herself deep in the wonder of it, the thankful, all-absorbing novelty of ease after strain, peace after strife. The snow fell steadily; Harriet Lee puttered with potted plants in her green-glassed conservatory off the side porch; Hatsy departed for her house party; Barbara sent a radiogram to say that she would be home on the twenty-third. And it was all peace.

On Saturday the whole house stirred with an expectant ripple to meet the master's arrival. Carter, his driver, brought him through the flattened snowy roads, and he came in, breathless and rosy, while Becky and his sister were at luncheon. Hungrily falling upon his own chop, his own plate of salad, he had little to say, but he smiled at them through his strong glasses and somehow his merely being there seemed to Becky to add comfort and safety to the world. The boy was going on well? Good. Barbara getting home for Christmas? Good. And how was Mrs Gibson? Too good? Well, that was a nice thing for a doctor to hear.

After luncheon he had to go to a consultation in Oyster

Bay. His snowy topcoat and wet cap had disappeared, another thick fur-collared coat was ready for him; he pulled on a dry new pair of thick gloves.

"Is it Senator Lawrence who's sick, Steve?" his sister asked. "She telephoned this morning."

"Yep. I brought you home some boxes," Stephen Dinsmore said to Becky almost absent-mindedly, pulling on his gloves. "I asked Carrie-Sis to put them in a spare room somewhere for fear your boy was asleep. You might look 'em over; Miss Sachs, in the office, picked 'em out. She dresses well, they tell me——"

Becky, her fork arrested, was facing him with widened eyes and suddenly reddened cheeks.

"Me?" she said a little thickly, breathing almost as if she were frightened.

"Frocks," the doctor answered briefly. "Girls have to have 'em! You and Harriet go up and look at 'em, and if you don't like any one, put it back in the box and Carrie-Sis will wrap it up to go back."

"Ah, Doctor . . ." Becky's voice, the note of reproach that deepened it making it richer than ever, said protestingly.

"Well," said the doctor, "go look at 'em. You may not like any of 'em! I'm on my way."

Dessert lost its taste for Becky. Her heart beat high. He had sent her a dress—he had known that she would not have the right wardrobe. . . .

But how ever to thank him! How ever to pay him back! The burden of gratitude was heavy upon her as she and Mrs Lee went upstairs.

"I don't know what makes him—what makes you all—so kind!"

"Stephen's always been like that," the sister said.

Carrie-Sis had opened the boxes and laid out the clothes; the room looked like a smart frock shop. Becky caught one audible deep breath and stood stricken, staring.

There was, to begin with, a dark brown coat of some silky warm cloth that felt like a kitten's ear, a coat big enough to banish all the chill one could possibly feel on a winter's day, and possessing a great soft beaver ruff of a collar that would come up about one's ears. With it was a brown hat trimmed with two balls of beaver, and lying on the table two pairs of soft white gloves, two pairs of soft brown, one pair deliciously fur-lined.

Spread on the bed were a plain homespun suit with a sweater blouse, an evening gown of maize-gold taffeta exquisitely corded and severely plain, a house gown of delicate brown velvet and two all-service dresses of black crepe, one patterned here and there with small scarlet cherries, the other smartly tailored and trimmed only with a fall of rose point. Carrie-Sis, very much enjoying the job, was opening boxes filled with filmy peach and cream underthings when the other two women came in.

Becky stood speechless. Tears smarted in her eyes.

"Not for me? Oh, he shouldn't! Oh, why did he?" she whispered. And because it was habit with her now, something within her added, "Oh, God, how good You are to me! I do thank You!"

And the next hour was one of rare delight, the rarer because her life, the long years that had gone before, had known nothing to equal it.

That night at seven, when Stephen Dinsmore came into the library before dinner, Becky got up from her chair and went to meet him. No one else was in the room. She was wearing the brown velvet gown; its rich darkness set off her own golden-brown beauty, the warm smoothness of her smooth cream-brown skin, the amber lights in her eyes. There was embroidery at the throat of the dress, and against it her breast showed soft and brown; firelight behind her aureoled her head with gold.

"Doctor," she said, "you are very good to me. I never

knew anyone so kind. They've been telling—Hatsy and Carrie-Sis and all of them, all this week—that I'm not the only one. But that doesn't make it any easier for me to thank you! I think it's—it's like God, to do things like this, with money. It makes—everything *right*."

She knew she was saying it awkwardly, clumsily. But it was all the more eloquent for that. Her hand in the doctor's chilled hand was warm, was trembling as every fiber of the whole vital, beautiful woman was trembling with feeling. Dr Dinsmore smiled behind his glasses, took them off to wipe them.

"You look lovely," he said, clearing his throat.

It was several hours later that Stephen Dinsmore went into his sister's bedroom. Harriet had not started to undress; she was standing staring down into the fire. Both faces wore a strange look as their eyes met.

"Well?" questioned the doctor.

"Oh yes, yes, yes!" the woman said quickly, speaking in a hushed, cautious undertone. "In spite of your telephoning to warn me, the instant my eyes fell on her I thought I would faint. Her voice, her coloring—nobody else in the world ever had Madeleine's coloring!"

"Does anyone else know, Harriet?"

"No one. Not Hatsy nor Carrie-Sis nor anyone. Better so, Steve. It would only stir up all that old agony again."

"Oh, far better not! She'll not think it strange?"

"Even if she does, you've done so many things like it nobody else will. She'll very quickly accept it. Look, Steve!"

She had a handful of old photographs. They looked at them together.

"That one," he presently said thickly.

"That one. And look at this one! How did it happen, Steve? Not the detective agency?"

"Not the agency. I suppose I never told them to look for that gold color. It didn't follow that the child would have it. No, it was in the children's ward at the hospital, one night last week. I suddenly heard her voice—Madeleine's voice. She was just going away; I followed her, but I didn't talk to her until Sunday. They sent her in to the office. She looked at me with Madeleine's eyes. I suppose we talked of the child, I don't know; I told them—it seems to me that almost immediately I told them that the little Gibson child was not to be discharged until I had seen the mother again. Or perhaps I telephoned that later from the office; I have no idea. I know I asked her to come down here, that first day."

He sat down, suddenly unable to go on, and his sister, equally silent, watched him for a few minutes.

"She was working in Rheingolder's," the doctor presently recommenced, "that big department house up in the Bronx. You don't know it? Well, I went up there twice during the week and watched her; she didn't know it, of course. This was after the Sunday I talked to her. I didn't need proof, but she gave me proof. Quite innocently she said to me, 'Doctor, it might make a difference in Gibbs' constitution—inherited tendencies, you know, that sort of thing—but I don't really know anything about my own people. No one knows this, but I was adopted.' And, as if it concerned the child, I asked for dates." He put his two hands over his face, bowed his head. "My God, my God, my God, they matched!" he whispered.

The woman was in tears. She smiled shakily.

"Congratulations, Steve!" she said.

CHAPTER XXVII

BECKY CAME DOWNSTAIRS to the library early. The doctor had said he might rush in for an early dinner; he could not stay for Barbara's formal eight o'clock affair.

He liked to play dominoes with Becky. She rarely beat him, but she played well enough to avoid too overwhelming defeat and to concede him only a narrow margin of gain. Sometimes Harriet Lee would be reading near the fire, and now and then Gibbs could come down for a few joyous minutes; Hatsy, if she were dining at home, always was early, being ravenous by dinnertime. Becky, to whom all hours were wonderful now, thought this special hour one of the happiest of them all.

On this wintry night of winds and crackling branches and wild snow, a week before Christmas, she came downstairs with Gibbs to find Barbara alone in the library. Barbara, taller than her mother, spirited, even a little rowdy, was even lovelier than her portrait. It was practically a flawless head that was crowned by the red-gold curls; the eyes were wide, thick-fringed and very blue; the mouth's only fault that it was a little too perfect, a little too completely the Cupid's bow.

Spoiled, selfish, a good deal of a snob, followed and admired wherever she went, rich and of America's finest lineage, Barbara had not shown Becky a very attractive side at first. She had arrived unexpectedly, having left the yacht on which she had been traveling at San Pedro and flown home. She had shown no special enthusiasm at finding a small boy and his mother, a woman of just her own age, snugly installed at Hillover. At the first dinner table Becky had heard a good deal of Barbara's marvelous friends on the Islands, her marvelous good times, the perfectly marvelous men she had met there, the simply marvelous invitations that she was now considering: to go to Europe, to London, to Palm Beach, to Nassau.

But quite suddenly, a few hours later, Barbara's attitude had changed. In their few brief encounters when she rushed home to sleep, dress, telephone, make fresh engagements, she had been pointedly friendly with Becky, and tonight, as Becky came into the library, and Gibbs made a straight frontal attack on the doctor's setter and her litter, lying on the rug, Barbara rose with a welcoming little cry and burst at once into feverish speech.

"Becky, thank heavens we have a minute alone! Listen, I'm in trouble and I've got to talk to you! Mother 'll be along any minute and then it 'll be too late."

Becky laughed a little at the other girl's intensity, but it was an understanding laugh, and as they sat down together on the great leather davenport that faced the fire their hands were locked.

"You see," Barbara Lee said, "thousands of people are coming to dinner tonight."

"Twenty-four," Becky, who had helped with the planning of menus and arranged the seating at dinner, altered it quietly.

"Well, twenty-four. And Pedar Granger with them. And you know I am supposed to be engaged to Pedar Granger."

"But nothing definite." Becky nodded at the information, for little gentle babbling Mrs Lee had mentioned this man's name in connection with Barbara from the very first. Pedar van der Venter Granger was an important figure in the older woman's scheme; Becky knew that he was rich, and prominent in Long Island's socially influential group.

"Mother told you so?" Barbara asked in quick suspicion.

"She said something about it."

"Well! It's been more or less understood. You've seen him?"

"I don't think so."

"Thin and small and yellow-haired, but nice, and always talking," Barbara supplied, always in the same urgent, hurried manner she had used in first speaking. "He was here on Sunday."

Becky laughed again.

"I think I know which one it is."

"Well, this morning, shopping in town, I met Larry Moulton," Barbara said, and stopped with an air of having launched a bombshell.

"I don't think your mother had him on tonight's list," Becky said, instantly concerned.

"No, I should think not! But he's—he's *the* person. I mean I'm madly, desperately in love with him and there's no use lying about it," Barbara said in a luxurious rush of frankness. "He's—I knew him in Paris a year ago, and Mother met him and disliked him. Then he was in Honolulu; he left two weeks before I did. But it's—at least with me it is—I mean, everything's over, the ship's sunk, the marines have positively *landed!* He's thirty and he's absolutely marvelous-looking in a completely and definitely marvelous way—— I haven't time to tell you about him, but anyway, here's the thing—he's coming to dinner."

"Tonight?" Becky asked, aghast.

"Of course. I met him, d'you see," Barbara continued, glancing occasionally toward the hall door to be sure of not being overheard, "when I was lunching at the Park Lane today. He came over, and of course I was lost. I babbled and mewed and everything—I mean, things just go round when he's anywhere in the picture! And being perfectly terrified that he'd vanish into space, I asked him to dine with us some night and he said, 'Tonight?' That's the way he is;

that gives you some idea of him. He's going to Boston to-morrow for days, so it was now or never. And of course I had my lamé in mind; I know I'm going to look for all I'm worth tonight. And everyone will be here, and Rudy's silly color movies or whatever it is afterward, and Sandy to keep the games going—you know what I mean."

"He's never been here before?"

"Oh no. I told you we only met him in Europe last year, and Mother only saw him once and didn't like him so much. Perhaps she was afraid he might make me feel differently about Pedar. Differently!" Barbara interrupted herself to add on a scornful laugh, "He makes me feel differently about everyone, including myself! And here's the extraordinary thing. See if you don't think this is strange," she went on. "He lives right down here at Glen Cove, so all he has to do is run himself over in twenty minutes."

"You told him not to dress?"

"Oh yes. Of course"—just a touch of her characteristic snobbishness colored the girl's voice—"he probably hasn't any idea of the sort of place it is," she said.

"You're engaged to him too?"

"I'm not engaged to anyone. The Pedar affair is just family stuff, and no such luck as Larry's asking me! It's a perfect *mess,*" Barbara said with relish. "Did you ever know anyone to be such a stormy petrel as I am?"

Becky reserved any expression of opinion on this, spoke simply.

"Isn't it just a question of asking Bonfacio to put another place at the table?"

"No, because nobody 'll know him, and Mother 'll make him feel like the Ness monster! She has no idea how far things have gone! You're going to be way up at the other end of the table. Won't you take him next to you, and make much of him, and tell him what a wonder I am, and then after dinner I'll manage to get next to him, at the pictures, and snuggle a confiding little hand in his and all that," Barbara said eagerly. Becky began to shake her head.

"You'll have to tell your mother," she began doubtfully.

"No, *you'll* do that! You'll just say casually: 'I'm going to ask you to let me rearrange the table, Mrs Lee. It seems that Barbara met a man you used to know in Paris'—be sure you don't mention that he was in Hawaii!—'and I'm putting him up near me.' You'll do that, won't you? I mean sort of encourage him along, and tell him how domestic I am, and how different from modern girls!"

"Doesn't he like modern girls?"

"My dear, I'm so desperate to find out what he does like and what he doesn't that I'm dizzy day and night! To see him walking across the room at the Park Lane—it was enough to drive the breath right out of your body! He's an artist, you know," said Barbara.

"Artistic, do you mean? Or really an artist?"

"Really and truly an artist, studying at the Beaux Arts. His uncle's an artist—Fox. Duane Fox. Larry's an orphan, the darling, and lives with his uncle in a place called Foxaway. Isn't that adorable? It's a barn, the most adorable old place—rocks and long roofs; he had a picture of it. They work there together. Here's Mother; I've got to go dress."

Barbara vanished as the older woman, formally gowned in brocade and lace, came in.

"You look lovely, Becky. I dressed; I can't get used to these sweater dinners."

"Not exactly sweaters! And so much more comfortable," Becky pleaded.

"I don't know. P'pa had us dress every night, when Lou and I were girls. . . ." Mrs Lee was well away on a rambling dissertation upon the vanished glories of her father's home; Becky presently made a little ejaculatory sound.

"I forgot! Barbara met a man she used to know in Paris,

today, and asked him to dinner. I must send word to Bonfacio to put on an extra place."

"Oh, I hope it wasn't that Moulton man!" Harriet Lee said.

"I'm afraid it was. You don't like him?"

"I don't like him to like her," the other woman said, accenting the pronouns. "Otherwise he's a charming man. Handsome."

"Is he handsome?"

"Stunning. But he hasn't a penny, and Barbara's twenty-four, and it's high time she made up her mind, especially as Pedar——" Harriet's voice dropped to a cautious note. "Pedar is *wild* about her," she said.

"Perhaps he's in a profession that makes money?" Becky suggested.

"Painter!" Barbara's mother answered scornfully. "Wants to do portrait work. I wish to goodness she wouldn't pick up such *freaks,*" she said fretfully; "she got hold of a Roumanian prince or something, and then it was a young Scotch officer—adorable boy, but not serious! And Babs ought to settle down; she's not the kind that can go on like this forever!"

Becky sat half listening, her eyes on the fire, as the stream of plaintive phrases poured on and on. Gibbs had tired now, and when Stephen Dinsmore came in, chilled and weary, the small boy went to him and climbed onto his knee.

"You're too tired to hold that baby," Becky protested. But the doctor, without a word, sent her the glance that told her he was utterly content to feel the small head resting against his shoulder, the small fingers in his, and they all sat so for a while without moving, while Harriet's babble died away into silence, and logs crackled and dropped in the heart of the fire.

Then Carrie-Sis came for Gibbs, and Harriet went away, and Becky and the doctor sat on in dreamy peace with only the firelight and the glow of one dim lamp somewhere back in the shadows of the room to break the comfortable darkness. Winds continued to blow fiercely out in the wintry night, and branches to crackle about the house, but here in the narrow, charming, book-lined old room there were warmth and shelter and peace.

"No Decembers like this in California, Becky."

"No. But up toward the Sierras we have snow. Only we're apt to have a hot sunshiny day right in the middle of January or November, a day like real spring. I've seen alfalfa that high——" She stretched a smooth hand in illustration; her topaz eyes met his. "What is it?" she asked, surprised at his look.

"I was thinking of something—miles, ages away," he confessed. "You were happy when you were a little girl, weren't you?" he asked.

"Too happy! I didn't know unhappiness could exist," she answered soberly. "I didn't know agony could exist."

"Like losing faith in someone you love?"

"Ah, not that. A good many married women experience *that*," Becky said whimsically, "without despair. They can go on eating their meals and going to the movies and having their hair done without wanting to commit suicide. But it's when a small feverish baby is sick in bed, and you are in a great crowded shop trying to sell bargain dresses at one forty-nine," she said. "It's the dark cold streets and the stairs and having to wait in the grocery, when every second counts, when you know he's crying for you . . ."

She was silent. After a while the doctor said slowly, as if thinking aloud:

"That sort of thing never should be."

"No. But ignorance and stupidity create it, as well as poverty," she reminded him eagerly, hating to see the face she loved so grave.

"Then we have to fight ignorance and stupidity as well as poverty, don't we?"

"Well, they do," Becky said vaguely, remembering the social workers, the school inspectors, the great army of workers who had climbed up to the Bronx apartment, eternally vigilant on the subject of youthful tonsils and adenoids, angering and arousing laughing scorn in tenement mothers, but pursuing their work steadfastly nevertheless.

"Oh yes, they do. Schools, clinics, government bulletins. Something gets done." But the man sighed and was silent again, and Becky, looking at him solicitously, asked with sympathy:

"Hard day?"

"Interesting, interesting," he said. And then, in a different tone, fitting his finger tips together in consulting-room fashion:

"You're happy here, my dear?"

"Happy! I'm in heaven." The sensitive, earnest face she turned to him was very lovely; her whole slender, well-built body, outlined in the soft thin folds of the silky velvet, was the incarnation of youthful beauty. "To be with people who are good and loving *is* heaven," Becky persisted. "That's all heaven can be. And when there's warmth and books and wonderful food and deep soft beds . . ."

She left it unfinished, shrugging.

"So that it's a divine prerogative to supply them to those who haven't them?" the doctor finished it, amused. "By the way," he said, "I think I've got something better for your little friend Mrs Devvins—or for the husband, rather. He came to see me. He's driving a taxi now—bad hours and poor pay. I think they'll give him an ambulance. I'm not sure."

Tears came into Becky's eyes.

"You!" she said in a whisper.

"Well—but he said it was answer to prayer—that his wife had been praying," Stephen said dryly.

"Prayer brought me here," Becky said on a sudden impulse of shamed loyalty, her cheeks very red.

"You believe that?"

"I have to."

"I didn't know you were a churchwoman. Harriet is."

"I'm not. I've never had any teaching. It's just—just that this same Mae Devvins that you're helping told me to pray one day. And I did pray. At least I didn't know how to pray, but I prayed to be able to pray!" Becky laughed. "It was a dark bitter night," she said. "We were in a two-room apartment in a Bronx tenement, Gibbs and I. His fever was up to a hundred and three. I was working from eight until ten-thirty at Rheingolder's, and I had to leave him all day. My clothes were soaked to the knees and my feet ached and my back ached. That was the night I prayed."

"That was when they brought Gibbs to the Lincoln?"

"The same night. That was the beginning. Not three weeks ago. Good heavens! It can't be only that!" Becky added under her breath.

"And you say God did that?"

"I have to. It wouldn't be decent," Becky said vigorously, "to think anything else. I was quieted even before I knew Gibbs wasn't going to die."

Stephen Dinsmore ruminated upon this for a moment. When he spoke it was of another matter.

"What's the plan now?"

"I don't know, exactly. If I went home it would be to just the old situation," Becky said, frowning a little in concentration. "I'm praying about *that*. I pray all day long," she added with a little laugh, "which is ever so much more convenient than having to wait for Sunday or having to go into a church to pray! It's for my mother that I'd go back. She knows I love her, she knows nothing will change me. But she probably wants to see Gibbs."

"You've written her?"

"Only twice. Once from Chicago, not telling her what I was doing, or that I was on my way to New York. Just to reassure her. And then the day after we came here I wrote and had Hatsy mail it from Boston. She was going up for the Swann wedding and I knew it would be safer with that postmark."

"You're so much afraid of your husband's following you?"

Becky was silent a moment, staring into the fire. Presently she turned to him a troubled face; there was no other reply.

"I wish you would stay here," the doctor said. "We go down to Florida next week. I'll only be there a week, but Harriet and the girls will stay on for a while. It's a quiet place where we go, with fine swimming, not much style, but there are a good many of their friends in the neighborhood. Gibbs will fatten up in no time, and you'll like it. And when you come back I wish you'd stay on here. They're going back to Baltimore, Harriet and the girls; but there's no reason you shouldn't stay.

"In that case you might have your mother come on here," he presently resumed, as Becky, being entirely unable to speak, merely stared at him with eyes that glowed and deepened and welled with amber lights. "She and your father might come on and see you, and go back without arousing any suspicion, I suppose. You don't know whether that man, your husband, is still hanging about?"

"I don't know anything. I've never dared send an address, get in touch with them at all."

"There were a hundred ways you might have done so, Becky."

"Not without risking his seeing the letter. I thought of writing Dad at the Exchange. That's our big general store at Salletts. But then I thought Dad might be employing Gavin there."

"You might have wired your father to ask for mail at some post office."

"And had Sylvia Cutter, at the telegraph station, hand the wire to Gavin!"

"Why don't you," the doctor began, after giving this a moment's consideration, "telephone your mother some night?"

His answer came in the sudden glow in her face, the eager lights in her eyes, even before she stammered:

"Telephone! From *here?*"

"Why not?"

"I never——" Becky gulped with a dry throat. "I never thought of it!" she gasped. "I suppose," she added, reflecting, "that I never would have considered it on account of the expense, anyway. But to telephone! To hear . . . to hear . . ."

Her voice thickened and stopped, and she turned to the fire suddenly brimming eyes that made rockets and flashes of the lazy flames.

"Barbara's having a dinner tonight, isn't she? I know Bonfacio's to give me something in my study in a few minutes," the man said.

"Not a party; they're not dressing. But twenty-four or -five, and movies afterward, movies somebody took of a house party last summer, and then games, I believe. Anyway, I know that I sharpened a thousand pencils on the little grinder today!" Becky said, laughing.

"And are you involved in this event?"

"Well, yes. Mrs Lee and I are at the table, and Barbara has commissioned me to amuse a certain man that she likes, until she is free to take him on."

"Pedar, eh?"

"No, some man she met in Paris."

"Harriet won't like that," the doctor said dryly. "Well, come up to my study about ten. It 'll be only seven o'clock out in California then; it won't frighten your people."

"Mother 'll be doing the dishes with Sophy, and the boys doing homework!" Becky exclaimed, her heart warmed with

the mere mention of the names. "Oh, Doctor—to hear them
. . . But I can't believe it! Tonight—just whatever they're
doing . . ." Becky's tears started afresh.

"Well, here's where I make good my escape!" The man
was on his feet as a jumble of loud and cheerful voices surged
in from the hall. The company was arriving. He stopped to
pat her shoulder reassuringly and disappeared through the
narrow fireside door which was one of the old house's charming features; the "bride's door" that had given many a shy
young wife the same means of flight that he was taking tonight.

CHAPTER XXVIII

WITH CONFUSION, noise, laughter, with cocktails and sherries and tomato juices and cigarettes, the dinner party got under way. Becky said little now, but she could not help laughing a great deal, for it was a gay crowd and many of the witticisms that were wearisome and stale to the group were fresh and funny to her.

She did not really notice Laurence Moulton until just before supper, when everyone was churning madly about the long table finding place cards, and she saw a tall, lean, nice-looking fellow moving away in the wrong direction.

"Mr Moulton? Are you Mr Moulton? If you are, you're right here." Becky laughed at his frankly disappointed face. "Yes, Barbara's way down at the other end," she conceded. "But there's a reason. Her mother," Becky added in a confidential murmur as the man settled himself beside her, "had arranged all the seating with great care. For no matter how informal or impromptu these parties are, certain persons *must not* be together!" she added seriously. "And as you are the last comer, you are put down here below the salt."

He was looking at her intently.

"And who are you?" he asked flatly.

He was the sort of man who could speak thus flatly, the sort of man all women trusted instantly, liked instantly. He was a gentleman; his hands, his voice, his manner, the way his clothes rode his lanky tall figure all said that, and yet there was somehow a suggestion of hoosier strength and bigness and leanness about him, infinitely likable. His hair was the tawny color of Becky's own, but without the gold lights that danced in her loose waves and scrolls, his voice delight-

215

ful, his eyes a clear gray; altogether his face had something lumpy, homely, angular, fascinating in its contours that added up almost into fine looks.

"Rebecca Gibson, visiting here," she said.

"Miss Gibson, as one old married woman to another——"

"You're guessing better than you think: married woman is right," she interrupted, laughing. "It's Mrs Gibson."

"Married?" he asked, surprised.

"Married, and with a boy racing around to three."

"How definitely disgusting," observed Laurence Moulton.

"Try to bear it," said Becky, busy with turtle soup.

"Old friend of the family?"

"I feel as if I were. As a matter of fact my small boy was one of Doctor Dinsmore's patients, and Mrs Lee invited us to stay here while he was getting well."

"Isn't that rather unusual?" Laurence asked.

"More unusual than it ought to be," she agreed, and turned to the man on her other side.

"And what do you think of this rat race?" Laurence presently asked her, recapturing her attention.

"These people?"

"Yes."

"That—well, that they're terribly nice and that they have a—a marvelously good time."

"I wonder if I'm beginning to talk like Barbara," Becky thought. And then in satisfaction to herself as she glanced about the table: "This is a nice party, everything going beautifully. Fish perfect. Thank God. Thank You, God."

"Here's a funny thing," Laurence said. "I never saw you until tonight, did I?"

"I don't suppose so."

"But I've seen you somewhere. What do you know about that?"

"Very little."

"Been in France? Honolulu?"

"Never. California, and then New York City, and then here. I was a saleswoman in the little girls' dresses in Rheingolder's. Have you any little girls?"

"Not that small. I begin on the seventeen sizes. But I've seen you somewhere with a bang."

"Why with a crash?"

"No, no, I mean the other kind of bang, hair down in a fringe into your eyes. You'd look cute that way, by the way."

"Cute!" said Becky, squaring her fine slender shoulders, arching her brown rounded throat. "The cute female giant."

"Where do you get this pongee color of yours, Mrs Gibson?"

"Born with it, I think. I was browner a year ago, living in the country. But I'm always mulatto."

"Octoroon, the loveliest color in the world," he changed it courteously. "And as for being a giant, you're the perfect height. You're just about up to my heart."

"Hold everything!" Becky said, laughing. She turned away again, devoting herself to the rich, rather uninteresting husband of one of the brilliant women present. Courtney Forster, as all the world knew, was interested only in polo and tarpon fishing, but Becky did what she could with him before Laurence pulled at her sleeve peremptorily.

"Listen, do you like that lad?" he demanded plaintively. "Have you ever seen him before tonight?"

"I've never seen you before tonight," Becky reminded him.

"That's a very different thing. Tell me, are these Lees rich?"

"Very rich. They have trustees and guardians and all that," Becky answered, thinking less of him for the question.

"I didn't know that," he said with an honest, baffled note in his voice that did something to restore him to her favor.

"Well, when people travel in Europe and go to Honolulu for months at a time . . ." she offered significantly.

"I suppose so. She acts like a person who's always had too

much, too," Laurence mused. "Ha! But then who's Dinsmore?" he diverged to ask abruptly. "She said 'my uncle's place.' I didn't know but what he was taking care of them."

"No, they have two or three places of their own. A camp somewhere, in the Adirondacks, I think they said, and an apartment in Baltimore that is rented now, but Mrs Lee always talks as if she meant to reopen it, and a farm somewhere. It sends us up apples and pumpkins and cream and things. And the hunters, whatever they are, are there," Rebecca finished on a laugh, "but I haven't any ideas about hunters!"

"They're horses."

"I guessed that much."

"And Doctor Dinsmore's the uncle?"

"Yes, and he's quite different from them, from all of these!" Becky said innocently, and colored, hearing her own words. "I mean, they are lovely, all of them," she amended it hastily. "But—but he's just—a saint. He's a very great doctor, and he spends his time taking care of people, being wonderful to them! He saved my small boy's life—at least if he hadn't taken care of Gibbs he might have died—and now he's—but I can't talk about him!"

She stopped, unable to go on. Laurence Moulton looked at her speculatively before he said:

"Is your husband here?"

"No, he's in California."

"Divorced?" Laurence asked with so simple a note of hope in his tone that Becky laughed in spite of a little sense of vexation and confusion.

"Oh no. Things—things got a little difficult," Becky confessed, "and I ran away. I'd run away to get married, and this time I ran away from marriage. I'm a terrible coward, I suppose," she added lightly, "but there seem to come moments when anything is better than facing the music. Edifying, isn't it?"

"I dare say it seemed sound at the time," the man observed pleasantly. "You'd lived in California?"

"All my life until two years ago."

"San Francisco?"

"Not very far from it. Off toward the northeast, toward the mountains."

"God, I love those mountains!" he said.

"I love them too. Hillmen desire their hills," Becky said.

"Kipling."

"Do you like Kipling?"

"No, I couldn't say that. Not like. Adore," Laurence answered soberly. Becky's eyes brightened.

"Oh, I'm so glad you do! I've battened on him all my life. Mother bought Daddy a set at some sale years ago, when someone died and left a lot of books, and I've worn them thin. Do you know . . ."

They could not match quotations fast enough; the minutes flew. Becky was only aroused to a sense of time when the whole group suddenly rose and began to stream toward the game room, where backgammon and domino tables had been set out, the billiard table uncovered, the slot machines supplied with slugs, the fire piled high.

She lost Laurence deliberately in the confusion, and ran upstairs to look at Gibbs, and to cross the upper hall to the study. Stephen Dinsmore was alone under a cone of green light, working at some papers against which little tufts of green and red silk and tiny curves of wire were visible.

"Nothing important!" he said as she hesitated in the doorway.

"Flies," she exclaimed, surprised. "Fishing flies! Dad has them at the Exchange."

"Ever do any fishing?"

"Lots. In the river and up at the lake. The river is only a stream. You keep crossing and recrossing it," Becky said, "but it's great fun."

"Trout?"

"And salmon trout. And bass, if you go down as far as the bay. But I've never done any bass fishing. My father does."

"Hunting too?"

"Duck hunting and deer hunting. Just a few days every year. But Dad makes them last by planning and packing and fussing with guns for months beforehand."

They laughed together.

"What's your home telephone number, Becky?"

"Salletts 83. It seems so funny to be saying it again!"

He had the telephone in his hand.

"Salletts 83; it's California," he said. "One special person, I suppose? Your mother?"

"Mr or Mrs Spencer Gibson." She was trembling, lights flickering through eager tears in her gold-brown eyes.

CHAPTER XXIX

THERE WERE TRACES of them left, despite her efforts to efface them, when she went downstairs more than an hour later, to be sure everything was all right before going to bed. Hatsy and a beau had disappeared from the party rather early and Barbara, for all her animated sophistication, was a rather awkward hostess. Becky feared she might possibly have also disappeared with Laurence Moulton.

Mrs Lee, ascending, met her as she went down.

"Becky, will you find Hatsy and tell her I want to see her? She's not been in sight for—well, since right after dinner, and now it's almost midnight."

"I thought she was all for ping-pong."

"No, she wasn't in the game room at all. I *wish* she wouldn't be so rude!" Harriet went on up, and Becky descended to meet Laurence in the dim square lower hall.

"What you been crying about?" he asked her abruptly.

"Oh—you?" Becky stammered. "I didn't see you!"

"I've been waiting for you. What you been crying about?"

"Talking to my people."

"Your people? What made you cry about that?"

"I've not heard their voices for more than two years."

"Oh?" He dragged out the monosyllable, comprehending. "I see. They're in California, are they? You telephoned?"

They had reached the deserted drawing room where chairs were in disorder, lights glaring, fire sunk to red ash. Becky snapped off a switch, pulled furniture about, clicked ash trays on the hearth as she emptied rubbish on the fire.

"Could you put that big log on? Thanks," she said. She

seated herself on a great cream-colored davenport, and Laurence sat down beside her. The room was soothingly dim now; the noise of the game players came in intermittent hysterical bursts from the distant billiard room.

"So you heard their voices?" he asked.

He could see her eyes flash in the firelight.

"Mother, yes! Oh, and Dad first," she told him eagerly. "And all the boys, all four of them, even Gary. First Dad asking, 'Is everything all right? Who is it? Is everything all right?' And then *'Becky!'* and I heard Mother say, 'Spencer Gibson! It isn't!' and I couldn't talk fast enough, and we were all crying!"

"And they're all well?"

She liked his sympathy. It was nice of him to see how much she cared.

"All well. Spin and Robert both in junior college, now, and Sophy still with them, and bitter cold weather; they've never had it so cold. And Mother said, 'Ah, Missy, do this soon again!' "

"They call you Missy?"

"She used to, when I was little." Becky's eyes were still wet. "Oh, they sounded so delicious!" she said. "I told them that I was well, and that Gibbs had been terribly sick but was all right again——"

"Who's Gibbs?"

"My little boy."

"Oh. And where's he?"

"Upstairs asleep. I just went up to tuck him in."

"Somehow I don't see you with a baby."

"You would, if we ever met in the daylight."

"And your husband—was he there?"

A shadow fell on her bright face, and she looked thoughtfully into the fire.

"No. But they expected him back any day," she said in a

subdued tone. "He went into the mountains this year, my mother said, helping a guide. Harry Grace. He's a professional guide; he takes tourists and strings of mules and packs into the Sierras every year—back and forth. And this year Gavin went with him. Now he's gone up to stay with Harry and make plans for next year, my mother says. Harry's tall and he has a black handlebar mustache and he swaggers around and tells Indian stories, and I suppose it fascinated Gavin. Gavin was working in Hollywood when I met him, and Harry Grace is a perfect movie cowboy."

They were silent, looking into the flames.

"And you ran away twice?" Laurence presently said musingly.

"Yes. Cowardly, but I'm made that way."

"There doesn't seem to be anything especially cowardly in taking a job in Rheingolder's and supporting your little boy," the man said in his understanding, pleasant voice.

"He remembers everything!" Becky thought, liking him better every minute. "Ah, but you see," she said aloud, "I didn't know what I was running into! I ran into marriage, ran away from home to do that, and then ran away from my husband, and then ran away from the awful mess I'd brought down on my people."

"He was an awful mess, was he?" the man asked speculatively.

Becky laughed, shocked.

"I didn't mean Gavin! It was just that he didn't fit. And it was hot weather and I had a small baby and it just—didn't fit. My people are very simple country people, and he was from the city, where men gamble for high stakes and go to races and drink a good deal. Oh, a hundred times since," Becky went on as the man listened without interruption, not even turning his head toward her, "a hundred times since I've wished I could run back! If I'd had the fare—any time this last year—when it was so hideously hot, and I had a head-ache for days at a time. And lately, when it's been so cruelly cold . . .

"But I didn't have the fare," she finished, "so I had to go on. It broke my heart—it sickened me to think that but for my pride Gibbs would have been out there in the California sunshine with Mother keeping an eye on him! But then I never could have dreamed things would go so wrong."

"Doctor's bills, hospital bills, eh?"

"He was in a ward," Becky said. "Oh, it was all as bad as it could be! And that only makes what Doctor Dinsmore did for us the more wonderful," she added under her breath; "that only makes the miracle more wonderful. And now, what do you think of my going upstairs to bed, and you going in there and playing games with the others?"

"Can't you think of some program for yourself that includes me?"

"You've been included in my program for the last twenty minutes, and now I really have to go upstairs. And Barbara will be expecting you."

"Why do you say that?"

"Why do I say that? Because you're Barbara's guest, aren't you?"

"Well, I'm the guest of the house, I should think."

"And I should think you were very specially Barbara's friend. She's been telling me about you, and moonlight in Hawaii, and a picnic out on an island," Becky said.

"You can imagine that after tonight I am not apt to bother Barbara very much," Laurence said. "This—this isn't my kind of thing. And isn't she engaged—aren't they pretty well taking it for granted that she's engaged to this—what's his name? Peter Something?"

"It's a family understanding. I don't think her heart's in it at all. You know very well that her heart isn't in it," Becky said.

"I know very well that there isn't the shred of an understanding between Barbara and me," the man said definitely. "I sell two pictures a year for a few hundreds. I live with my uncle, who is the bachelor of the world. There never was anyone so against the idea of a woman in the house as Duane. It isn't a house; it's a high-hipped grand old barn with a little furniture in it. The idea that I'd look at a girl who has—what all was it? Trustees and hunters and places at Bass Rock! The idea, I say, is fantastic."

"You didn't know she had those until I told you."

"I'll say I didn't!" said Mr Moulton fervently.

"You mean," Becky asked curiously, "that you didn't realize that she was rich?"

"I don't think I thought it out at all."

"Yet you liked her well enough to—to fall in love with her?"

His look was surprised in its turn.

"I didn't fall in love with her. We liked each other; we like each other still, very much. But there was nothing more to it than that. As a matter of fact there's another woman."

Becky was affronted; she straightened up on the wide leather seat, looked at him sharply in the gloom.

"Another woman!"

"Yes. Since five minutes past eight tonight there's been another woman."

Staring at him suspiciously, Becky said uneasily:

"I don't think I understand you."

"I don't understand myself," he answered promptly.

"You mean you . . . since tonight—since just before dinner . . . ?" She was fumbling when he helped her.

"Yes, just tonight. And that's where you come in. And the thing is to make you believe it."

"That's where I come in," Becky stated rather than said, in a cool tone faintly ironical. "Are you trying to say that I'm the other woman?"

"That's the exact fact. Take it or leave it, and of course I think you'll leave it."

A silence. After half a minute Becky broke it with a definite, impatient "Nonsense!"

He was sitting looking into the fire, his long lean body somewhat slumped toward it, his linked fingers dangling between his knees. In his charming careless voice he answered seriously:

"Isn't all love nonsense? Is there any reason to it?"

"Do you always start an acquaintance this way?" Becky asked after another pause.

"No, and I'm sorry to prejudice you against me by saying this," Laurence answered simply. "But it's taken possession of me like a—like a dust storm, and I can't see anything else."

"You know I'm married, of course?"

"But as good as divorced. You've left your husband. That could be arranged."

"Oh, that could be arranged?" she echoed, scandalized and amused.

"You think I'm fresh," the man said. "I want to tell you something. I've been waiting all my life to meet you. I've seen a picture like you somewhere, I don't remember where; in some gallery maybe. Lots of Renoir's models wore their hair that way. But wherever it was, it stuck in my mind, stuck in my heart. When I saw you tonight, the first minute, I knew that you were the sort of woman I wanted to have smiling at me the rest of my life, you were what I wanted to have my arms around, your hair was the hair I wanted to kiss.

"Now this may take time," the pleasant cultured voice went on as Becky, staring at him transfixed, made no remark. "You've no money and I've no money, and I can't ask my uncle for any—not that he has much himself. He gave me my education, art schools here, Paris for two years, and since then I've been on my own. As I say, I make a few hundreds now and then, and take a trip, and come back to the barn and work like blazes and make a few more. That's what I've been doing for six or seven years. But now that's over. Now I'm going to work for you. It's all come to me in a rush; I've been in a dizzy dream since dinner. You're for me and I'm for you, forever and ever. Amen."

"I wish you wouldn't talk in quite this way," Becky said uncomfortably when he stopped.

"I know. I've no business to. I didn't mean to."

"It isn't fair to Barbara, for one thing; she likes you very much," Becky pursued. "And of course as far as I'm concerned or could possibly be concerned . . ."

"Well?" he asked in the pause, turning his head to look at her with an encouraging smile.

"Well, it's out of the question—— But here I am answering you seriously," Becky broke off impatiently, "when it's all such utter nonsense!" Her cheeks were red with distress as she faced him. "I wish you hadn't said all that!" she said.

"I wish I hadn't. I didn't mean to."

"For if I were divorced—if Gavin were dead," Becky went on with spirit, "it wouldn't make any difference! I think," she added in a lower tone, her eyes returned to the fire now, "that I'm done with men forever."

"*That's* nonsense if you're going to talk about nonsense!" Laurence protested.

"No, it's not nonsense. I don't think I like men—as husbands. Men like Doctor Dinsmore or my father, that's different. You can love them; you can adore them. But when it's married love, it's too hard on the woman, it's too unfair to her. She gets all the bad part," Becky reasoned, not looking at him, frowning a little as she reached for words. "She does the waiting at home and crying and wondering, she has to ask for the money that he eats up in rent and food as fast as she does, she has to keep still when it's drink or gambling or being away nights, or even other women; she mustn't ask questions, she mustn't start rows. And if it's children, she bears them; she's twisted out of shape, sick all the time, tired and heavy, and wanting to cry, wanting tenderness as she never does at other times . . ."

She was talking to herself, half aloud, her somber eyes narrowed, not seeing the sleepy fire on which they seemed to be fixed, seeing instead a dreary little dark flat in a winter city, a homesick girl cooking steaks for men who waited for dinner with dice in their hands and cigarettes between their lips.

Laurence spoke soberly.

"It isn't always like that."

"No, of course not," Becky agreed, returning to the present with a little apologetic laugh; "but we were talking of impossibilities anyway, so we needn't go any further."

Laurence sent her an oblique glance over his shoulder.

"You don't believe me, do you?"

"I believe that you like me, and I'm very glad," Becky said composedly. "And now how about joining the others?"

"How old are you?"

"Twenty-four."

"I'm thirty. And I'm in earnest, Becky. I'll get you if it takes ten years."

Something in his voice, something in his eyes shook her defenses suddenly, and she could only look at him, fascinated, and make no reply.

"You know that, don't you?" he asked in a low voice.

Becky sat helpless under a rush of emotion as unexpected as it was unwelcome. Every fiber of her being responded to him; as surely, as inevitably as the falling of a tree whose base has been severed, she knew herself completely under the spell of this new voice, this new touch, the look in these keen, friendly gray eyes.

She was conscious of backing away a little, of the soft movement of the brown velvet gown, of withdrawing her hand from the smooth leather of the davenport, where his hand touched it, raising a shoulder almost as if in self-defense.

And at that moment, welcome as even he had never been to her before, Stephen Dinsmore walked into the library and came up to them, smiling and blinking, polishing his glasses.

"Is it you, Becky? Where are the others?"

"Struggling with papers and broken pencils in the game room," Becky said, on her feet, eager and radiant. "We were going back this minute." She presented her companion; Stephen gave him a keen look.

"I came down for a book. Did you see it?"

"*The Murder in a Walnut Shell?*" Becky laughed.

"Not quite so bad. But it was a crime book."

"Here it is. Ah, but don't go!" she pleaded, a folding card table already in her hands. "Two games—one game? Two games. Thank you!"

The last words were to Laurence, who had taken the table from her and was opening it. Becky moved a tall lamp, pushed a chair. Dr Dinsmore, well pleased, had the dominoes and the pegging board in his hands. When Laurence left the room the other two were already deep in their game. He heard Becky say triumphantly, "Now listen, *listen!* Who skunked who Sunday night? *I* skunked *you.* I took one hundred and four points from you. At a dollar a point, if we played for money, that would be . . ."

She did not glance at Laurence again as he walked quietly away. He turned into the hall and found his coat, and went out unnoticed into the black snowy night.

❧ CHAPTER XXX ❧

IN THE SHADOWY blue light of the cold afternoon of the eve of Christmas Eve the studio was mysteriously lovely; its old rafters and high windows took on a strange beauty as the last chill light of the day moved and lingered on the dim beauty of tapestries and brasses, on pottery gay with Spanish color, on the tooled leather of antique books, the age-softened wood in Colonial chairs and chests.

Outside, snow mantled the world in true Yuletide fashion, and trees and shrubs were bowed under it. But in the barn the great airtight stove had been burning all day and for many days, and now there was a tempered flatness almost like warmth in the air.

For all that, the woman who stood against the great many-paned north window was bundled in furs; the man who was her companion wore a long leather coat belted about his tall lean figure, and held a fur cap in his gloved hands.

Behind them in the studio a lingering luncheon for three had just been ended. Crackers and cheese and fruit still littered the round table; two cigarette stubs sent lazy spirals and lines of gray-blue into the twilight softness of the waning day.

"Well, did you like Duane?" the man asked.

The girl turned to glance toward the stove and the great chair that stood empty beside it.

"Oh, he's gone?" she asked. Then quickly: "Of course I like him. But the question is why he tolerates me. I thought you said he couldn't stand women?"

"He can't. But you're not 'women,' Becky. You're you. And he's mad about you."

"I can imagine. I've been here twice."

"Well, that was enough. I can assure you he is completely yours, my dear."

To this Becky made no direct answer. She stood for a moment looking out at the blue wintry afternoon. Then she said simply:

"You say such nice things, Larry."

"Nothing to what I *can* say!"

"I suppose not. I've been thinking," Rebecca said, suddenly more serious in tone, "that I'll not come here again, Larry. I felt badly coming today. I knew I shouldn't. But nobody was at home. Mrs Lee is at a tea for the Daughters of Old Virginia or something; Hatsy's in town staying with the Baggs girl (they're going to a dance); Barbara's still in Washington. And Doctor Steve isn't coming home. I'm meeting him in town."

"For the opera?"

"For my first opera. *Lohengrin.*"

"Going up after dinner?"

"If I want any dinner after this enormous lunch, with sandwiches and biscuits and everything. Do you do this every day?"

"I tell you this was a great occasion for Duane, Becky. Ever since you were here on Monday he's been talking about you. You were a real girl. No nonsense about you. If I liked women like you he'd never object to having 'em around."

"He's nice," Becky said, touched. "Tell me again. He's your uncle?"

"He's my mother's stepbrother. She was two and he was four when his mother married her father. So he stands in the position of an uncle. I never knew he was alive—at least I'd met him, been to his studio as a kid and all that. But I mean I didn't know him at all well when he showed up after my father's death and offered me a chance to work with him for a while and see if I had anything. I had a job on a printing press at eighteen a week. You can imagine what it meant to me. That was eight years ago. I stayed here and tried to paint, and he helped me and finally sent me to Paris, where I got on to—well, got onto whatever I have. It isn't much, but it tickles him to death to think that I've got it at all. He and I are alone in the world and we like each other; he's a grand old guy."

"He's a dear." Becky fastened her coat collar. "I have to go," she said in an odd strained tone.

"Don't go." His own voice was strange. There was a silence. One of their moments of quivering emotion was upon them, when any jarring word or note might shatter the exquisite communion that existed without visible sign.

Becky wrenched herself free of it, turned toward the door, made her way down the old wooden stairs to the lower barn, big and shadowy and unfurnished in the twilight. Outside the garden door a lamp of old Italian design shed a half-light; by this she could see the path to the gate, lumped and molded in snow in the early dusk.

Laurence was walking beside her; he did not speak.

"Don't be cross," she said.

"You don't love me!" he countered fiercely.

"Ah, please, now . . . !"

He gripped her arm under the elbow, held it tightly and firmly, guiding her along the road. They came to the parked car, and he opened the door for her, but before she could step up his arms were about her and his half-savage kiss hard on her mouth. Becky struggled with fur-clad arms, gasped for breath, was free.

"Well!" she said when she was seated beside him and they were driving. "That was—unexpected."

"It wasn't unexpected at all. Why the hell do girls say things like that!" Laurence growled. "You know I'm mad about you. You don't care. You're going away in a few days to Florida; sure, why not? Have a good time. The old man's in love with you, I know that. I hate him. God, I loathe him! With all his money and his fur coats and his opera box!"

"You couldn't help loving him if you knew him," Becky said as the angry voice paused. "He's old enough to be my father, and you know it. But twenty fathers couldn't be kinder to me."

"Has he introduced you to Hilda Heinrichsen yet?"

He could hear the astonishment in her voice.

"Hilda Heinrichsen?"

"Yep. She's singing in the opera tonight, with Flammavilla. The other part, whatever it is."

"And he knows her?"

"Yes, darling, he knows her. She's one of the old warhorses of the outfit. Doctor Stephen Dinsmore has known her for many a long sweet year. Barbara told me all about it. Her husband got consumption and he sent them to Arizona, and after he died she came back and was down and out, and he got her into the Met; she'd only done church singing. She's sixty if she's a minute. You can imagine she thinks he's a god."

"You sound very bitter," Becky observed composedly, over some inward twinge of hurt.

"Well, it gets me the way you adore that man."

"You'd adore him if he'd done for you what he's done for me. Why, Larry, look at your loyalty toward Duane Fox! You're like a son to him. Why shouldn't I give the doctor whatever pleasure I can? He likes me, he likes to—to simply bury me in kindness. Why not? It doesn't hurt anyone."

"And what does he expect to get out of it?"

"Now you're being unpleasant," Becky said firmly, coldly. "I've told you that immediately after we come back from Florida I'm going home to my mother, for a while anyway. And when I come back you and I are not to see each other any more."

They had reached the Dinsmore gate; Becky could see the

ιpleasant home lights shining out in pink streamers across the pale blue snow. Laurence stopped the car and turned to face her. His bared hand found hers and stripped the thick glove from it, and again she felt herself trembling, felt herself overwhelmed with some emotion as frightening as it was delicious.

"Don't be cross at me. I love you so much!" he said.

"Larry, I'm not cross at you. I like you a lot more," Becky said, laughing a little excitedly as he jumbled her in his arms, her lips close to his face, "I like you more than I'm willing to admit! It isn't that. But I have a husband in California, and I have a child who belongs, partly, to that husband. I'm going home in about a month to see my mother, to talk to Gavin, to see what I can do to free myself from the feeling that—in a way—I still belong to him."

"You mean you're going to get a divorce and marry me?"

"Don't squeeze the breath out of me, dear."

"I can't help it! I'm insane about you. My darling, you must like me a little if you call me 'dear.' "

"Don't be so *wild*. Please, *please*——"

"Will you marry me, Becky? Duane admires you too; he said only yesterday that it was grand to have you around. We could manage on what I have; we could skip over to Paris and I could work there, if Duane would go. And when he dies I'll have something——"

"It isn't that, you idiot! It's that, in the first place, I'm married."

"You can drive to Reno in about five hours. You said so!"

"I know. But there's Gibbs to consider. Gavin will never give him up. Not that he wants him, or could take him for three months a year. He'd have to leave him with his sister, and Gibbs' heart would break. But Gavin knows that he can hold that over me."

"But Lord, if he's that kind of dog in the manger he ought to be shot!"

"A great many people who ought to be shot aren't shot."

Laurence laughed delightedly, and again she was caught in his smothering arms.

"So my affairs are all in a mess," she said. "I seem to have been saying that all my life, but it's true. I hate divorce and my mother does too. I would hate the idea that Gavin was alive in the world, and I living with another man."

"But sometimes, Becky, it's the only way. Promise me that you'll kick him out and come back here and marry me?"

"Ah, I can't promise you anything."

"But you will?"

"Doctor Dinsmore is going to Europe this year to study the sanitation situation or something. He's to take Hatsy and her mother and he wants me to go."

"For the Lord's sake! When?"

"In March. Ah, and I'd love that!" Becky said provokingly.

"What pipe dream is this?"

"It's all like a dream to me. But that's what he told me last night. In that case I wouldn't go home at all."

"I thought he only came down here week ends?"

"No, oftener. Three or four times a week."

"Well," Laurence said after a moment's thought, sulkily, "I can't offer you anything like that, of course. You'll naturally not want to turn Europe down. Ever been?"

"Ever been! Of course not."

"Becky," the man said in a different, a pleading tone, "don't be mean to me. I love you so! And you could love me, if Barbara and the doctor and your damn husband were out of the way, couldn't you?"

Her voice was very low; her amber eyes glinted very close to his own in the dusk.

"I'm afraid so."

Again he had her jumbled up close against him on the leather seat, tumbling hair and hat, pressing his mouth against hers. When she could break free Becky slipped from the car and ran up the path and steps to the door, being joined there by him, breathless and laughing, and once again imprisoned by his long arm.

"Becky, may I come in? Nobody's here."

"No, no. I have to give Gibbs his bath and supper and dress for the opera."

"I could watch Gibbs have his supper at least."

"No. You'd confuse me so that I wouldn't know what I was doing."

"Please let me, Becky!"

Bonfacio had opened the door.

"Doctor telephone, Missy Gibson," said Bonfacio, "and say he come home now, and Carter drive you in to opera tonight. He say have litty supper happass six. He on way now. I say you take walk."

"Oh, goody, he's going to have Carter drive us in!" Becky exulted. "I've got to fly if we're to have early supper Good night!"

One laughing nod at Laurence and she was shut into warmth and light and flower-scented airs. Laurence stood on the step irresolute for a moment, then turned and went down to the car. But within half an hour he telephoned her.

CHAPTER XXXI

BECKY LAUGHED joyously at hearing his voice.

"Larry, I haven't an instant! I've got the baby in the tub, and I'm pinning up my hair so it'll be gorgeous tonight! Doctor Steve is here, and I'm so excited I'm afraid I'll break right out and sing a solo myself from the box!"

"I just wanted to remind you that I love you," he said.

"Thank you!" She replaced the receiver and turned to see Barbara coming into the room. Becky gathered her wits together with all speed.

"Hello!" said Barbara. "I knocked and Gibbs said, 'Come in.'"

"I didn't know you were home."

"Just got here. Where's Mother?"

"At the Daughters of the South thing. And Hatsy's in town with the Baggs girl for the Christmas Junior League dance."

"And Uncle Steve's home? What's he doing home on a Wednesday night?"

"We're going to *Lohengrin!*"

"Oh, of course. Mother going?"

"He asked her. But she's having dinner with Mrs Cromartie, who's coming back with her, and they said they'd be too tired. Barbara, he'd probably simply love to have you go."

"I couldn't. I'm dead. I thought—I was just thinking that I might telephone Larry Moulton and see if he's free for dinner. I suppose not. But if everyone else is away it might be fun. Have you seen him since I went away?"

"Met him today," Becky said, toweling Gibbs vigorously.

"You got your hair all wet, darling. I met him and went over to the studio with him, and met his uncle," Becky further volunteered, her back to Barbara as she nightgowned Gibbs on the bed. "Don't keep turning over and crawling away, baby. You didn't meet anyone you liked better, Barbara?"

"I met scuts, pikers, twirps, lice and underdogs. In all my life I've never been on such a lousy house party!" Barbara said frankly, lighting a cigarette as she lolled in a chair. "Is this his supper? Why is it that babies get better food than we do? Look at that rice! I could eat every bit of it. I had an honorable offer. I could be Mrs Colonel Fisher."

"Colonel! Isn't that rather high up?"

"Well, he's rather low down. Five feet flat, I should say. But nice. He's smearing string beans on his face."

"Gibbs, eat nicely."

"No," Barbara said, returning to her favorite topic. "I'll never like anyone as much as Larry. If he'd just go *definite*, I'd drop Pedar like a hot brick. But Larry's afraid he hasn't anything to offer me. What rot! Half the girls support their husbands nowadays and nobody thinks anything of it! Let's be Victorian, yes. But let's not bound back to the Middle Ages!"

Becky returned from the closet with a brown lace garment dangling from a hanger.

"Recognize it?" she said.

"For heaven's sake!" Barbara said simply.

"You gave it to your mother for the rummage sale; I saw it, and Carrie-Sis altered it a little—made it longer and lengthened the shoulder straps. Wait until you see it on!"

"It ought to be lovely on you. It was a gorgeous dress, a Paris model—isn't it a Leneau? But the color always made me look like something sitting up on a slab in the morgue," Barbara said.

"I love it!" Gibbs was in his bed now, studying the two women with thoughtful sleepy eyes through the bars. Becky proceeded with her dressing and Barbara tried various telephone numbers, finally finding Larry at the club.

"Damn it!" she said after an unsatisfactory conversation. "He's got a date. He's going to the opera too. Did he tell you so today?"

"No. He didn't happen to. Then why don't you come with us, Barbara?" Becky said, trembling inside. "There's sure to be another seat in the box."

"No, it isn't that. But Pedar 'll be there with his mamma and his uncle Thomas, and I refused to go with them. He'd be sure to see me and it 'd only make trouble. No, I'll stay home and do something. I think I'll take up ceramics. I wish I'd married at eighteen. A boy was mad about me when I was eighteen. I'd have a kid of six now and be divorced. So much simpler than this dangling around on the family tree."

"That isn't the pleasantest program," Becky said thoughtfully. "Divorce sounds simple. But it's horribly complicated and you never quite get done with it."

"You do if the man dies," Barbara observed.

"Well, then you might just as well wait for that to happen first."

"Damn it, what does he want to go to the opera for!" Barbara muttered under her breath.

Becky turned from her mirror and stood smiling at the other girl. The café-au-lait lace was trimmed with an intricate embroidery of coral and pearl; it was severely plain down to the knees, where it broke into a very foam of delicate ruffles and scallops that trailed out beyond Becky's trim brown satin slippers on the floor. She had coaxed her soft gold-brown hair into a bang on her forehead; the quaint unfamiliar style, combined with the gown that somehow suggested a day of hour-glass figures and ruffled bustles, quite transfigured her, and Barbara burst into genuine enthusiasm.

"My dear, there's no one in this world like that filthy robber Gaby Leneau! That's the way that dress ought to look, and that way of doing your hair is simply inspired. I hope nobody recognizes it as mine, Becky, for it's simply a knock-out! Make Uncle Stephen wander around with you between the acts. Honestly, you're stunning in that getup!"

"I never have looked like this before!" Becky murmured, eyes on the mirror.

"If anyone looks snooty, as much as to say 'Where have I seen that dress before?' you yawn and say that Leneau's models are getting so common that you're going to get your things over here after this."

Becky laughed joyously.

"Imagine my trying to get away with anything like that!"

She kissed Gibbs, with that floating dramatic feeling that only the consciousness of looking her best before an important party gives to a woman, and went downstairs. Stephen Dinsmore was waiting for her in the library. He explained that a second earlier he had felt a sharp pain in his eyes, and when she came in was pressing one of his fine clever surgeon's hands against them. Becky was aghast.

"You've a headache?"

"No, no, no! I'm all right." He had risen to meet her; now he sank back in his chair, and she saw beads of water glistening on his forehead.

"You mustn't go! I don't care about the opera! If you've a headache——"

"It won't last a moment," he said, taking his fingers from his eyes and smiling. "It's nothing. I've to speak to Harriet, and then I'll be back. Bonfacio just said that our supper was ready."

"Mrs Lee's in town, you know. She's having supper with that old lady who lives at the Waldorf, and they're coming out together."

"I'd forgotten. Well, then let's go right out and eat. *Lohengrin* begins on the stroke of eight."

And suddenly he was quite himself, if a little pale after

what had apparently been a sharp onset of pain, and they could enjoy their meal in great felicity.

Barbara loitered in to join them; she was going over to Kate St Michael's to play bridge.

"Give my love to that crook Laurence if you see him!" she grumbled.

"And what does that mean?" the doctor asked when he and Becky, warm in fur rugs and big coats, were being smoothly rushed toward the city.

"Barbara likes this artist, Laurence Moulton. You met him."

"Did I? One way and another Barbara makes herself rather miserable about young men. We're stopping here for the Holidays, Becky. Judge Holiday is a real musician, and she used to sing. You'll like them."

The elderly couple were ready; came down immediately from a great stone house upon which the winter moon was coldly shining. Becky moved to the middle of the seat; felt Stephen Dinsmore's arm go part way about her as they adjusted themselves to make the most possible room. She fell silent as they went on their way; glad to be free for her own thoughts of her first opera.

Well before the rise of the curtain she was seated in the front of the box, watching with fascinated eyes the gathering of the brilliant audience, the slow filtering into the boxes of other fortunate girls in beautiful frocks. The violins began to whine, and as the lights fanned lower and were gone, and the first hush of silence fell on the house, her heart began to beat with a heady rapture. With a great shattering sigh she settled down to an evening of ecstasy.

Afterward she could not join in the pleasant confusion and laughter in the box. She was dazed, stunned, her eyelashes wet. All the others went away, and Laurence Moulton came up to talk to her. The lights were bright now, the orchestra pit and half the seats and boxes empty.

"Gorgeous, isn't it?"

"Oh!" Becky breathed feebly.

"Listen, did you enjoy that lunch today? I was in heaven."

"Oh, Larry, what music!"

"Yep, it's gorgeous. She's in great shape tonight, everyone says. I've never heard her before."

"I never . . . dreamed . . ." She was still bewildered, speechless. After a while she asked him the position of his seat.

"I have no seat, darling. I'm standing, and I may go home after I come up and see you again. I mustn't miss the eleven-fifteen."

"You didn't tell me that you were coming tonight."

"I wasn't, when I talked to you. I came because I had to see you, had to hear your voice again. I've got you under my skin, Becky. There's just you and nobody else in the whole round world. D'you know what that means?"

"It can't mean anything," she said. And then in an under-tone: "I was there when Barbara telephoned you tonight at the club. I felt so horrible. It all makes me feel horrible. I—don't like it. And if Doctor Dinsmore comes back, don't say that I had lunch with you and your uncle today. I didn't tell him."

"Why shouldn't you tell him? Doesn't he expect you to make any friends of your own?"

"It's not that. It's Barbara."

"Oh, Barbara!" he said moodily. "That's all imagination. She's not in love with me."

"She'll probably get over it in Florida, or if she goes to Nassau," Becky said, reflecting. "But just now she wants to see more of you, and it makes it uncomfortable—impossible for me to go on seeing you. So please—please help me!"

Groups were sauntering back into the boxes; the aisles below were streams of slow-moving figures. Laurence departed, stooping to kiss her hand before he went, leaving her fluttered and uneasy, glad of the returning dark.

But the witchery of the music captured her again, and she forgot him and forgot everything under its spell. After the second act the doctor took her to stroll along the balconies and the wide passages, where hundreds of other folk were wandering and chatting, and introduced her to old friends here and there. She was nervously on the lookout for Laurence, but he did not come upstairs.

"I went down to see Madame Heinrichsen a few minutes ago," Stephen said. "Would you like to meet her after the last act?"

"You mean go behind the scenes?" Becky gasped.

"No, at her own apartment. It's right in this building." He saw the disappointment in Becky's face and laughed. "Would you like to go behind?" he asked. "Of course we will. I'll send her a line."

Taking out his fountain pen and a doctor's prescription pad, he wrote a few lines and handed them to an usher, and Becky watched him and thought what a strange thing is power.

Mme Heinrichsen was not alone in her dressing room when they went to it; Mme Flammavilla was there. Both women greeted Stephen affectionately and smiled at Becky for his sake. Mme Heinrichsen, wig and costume gone, and figure wrapped tightly in an old discolored cotton kimono, sitting at her dressing table, was smearing her pleasant, full, middle-aged face with cold cream, while a maid handled her heavy gray-streaked gold hair. The other woman was still in full costume, with beads of perspiration squeezing through the heavy oily make-up on her face, her long blonde wig and veil still in place, her voluminous white-and-silver gown looking a little rubbed and tarnished at close view.

They turned at once to Stephen and the conversation was

evidently taken up at some point the three had discussed before. Becky, dazzled, sat in a corner, looking at the costumes that were hanging on the wall, at the big German maid, at the mirror that flung back a very blaze of lights, at the smeared and sticky litter of pots and jars on the dressing table.

"Well, aye sing and sing and sing even ven dey don't pay me vun zent!" Mme Heinrichsen presently said, laughing. "Steef knows it, don't you, Steef?"

"Oh, they couldn't shut you up!" Stephen conceded good-naturedly. "You are always retiring to that delightful farm at Helsingfors, only you never retire."

"Yes, this year aye go!" Madame had somewhat surprisingly put a magnificent chinchilla wrap over the kimono, and now she caught youthfully at Becky's hand. "Come on, ve go upstairs and eat; aye don't eat since yesterday!" she said gaily. "Elena, come and have something goot to eat."

But Mme Flammavilla had an engagement. "I will get cold chicken when I want good hot *gnocchi*," she complained, "and I will have to sign my name for sixty or seventy keets, but I say I will do it and I do it!"

The other three with the maid followed somewhat tortuous but spacious passages, entered a large gloomy elevator, were carried up to an apartment filled with souvenirs of the singer's triumphs, and otherwise furnished with old-fashioned stuffy elegance. Fringes, antimacassars, tassels, draperies impinged upon each other; there were a great many signed photographs, and the proportions of the room were so generous that space was allowed for two grand pianos, fitted into each other and cluttered with vases and scarfs. There were a great many flowers; there was a supper table by a coal fire, and much good hearty food, and plenty of beer.

"Steef, you were early tonight. You were in box before overture," Madame said, with her mouth full. She was enjoying her supper with all the gusto of a child. Becky had declined everything; Stephen was at the table, but only making the gesture of eating.

"You saw us?"

"Aye always look for you. If he not there when I sing Ortrud," the older woman said, turning toward Becky, "then aye can't sing. Von't sing."

She was sixty, but magnificently handsome still, with a clean sweet peasant face that was younger than that of many a woman half her age. The heavy hair must have been glorious once; it was thick, straight, twisted into gold-gray ropes about her head. She had discarded the priceless coat and the kimono in some inner apartment and wore a flowing house dress of white velvet roped at the belt with a gold cord.

Tired, hungry, traces of grease paint still lurking here and there on face and throat, she was evidently happy, and sat enjoying her meal and smiling at her guests luxuriously.

"In this opera aye sing my first time," she told Becky. "And Steef sents me flowers—white violets. Aye am so frightened, so big, aye am like big horse galloping out to footlights. But aye know Steef dare, croying for fear I big flop——"

She looked at him, and the doctor said to Becky:

"She was so much of a flop that one of the finest managers in the country tied her up the next day for concert work for the rest of her singing career."

Becky laughed, and the singer looked at her approvingly.

"Aye sing now twenty-six times, Steef."

"Yes, I noticed that they had you pretty well dated."

"Den, in April, six farewell concerts."

"Farewell, ha-ha!" said Stephen.

"In my home," Madame said pathetically to Becky, "aye have bought a farm. My brother—he is lame since the war —he run it for me. Aye have ten white cow, chicken, two horse."

A large blond young man in white took away the supper table; Madame gave Becky an immense leather portfolio filled with loose photographs, settled back in a deep cushioned chair, lighted a cigar and began to talk fluently to Stephen in German. Some hand unseen extinguished most of the lights; the stuffy Victorian drawing room took on more gracious lines in a soft red glow.

Becky looked at pictures, stopped and looked about her instead. The other two murmured vigorously for perhaps fifteen minutes, Madame gesturing with her smoking cigar. Then Stephen laughed, got to his feet, kissed his hostess on the forehead and brought Becky her coat. In five minutes Carter was taking them rapidly through the dark winter streets toward the bridge into the fresh cold quiet country again.

"Well, did you like your first opera, Becky?"

"I have never," Becky said solemnly from the rugs and the warm darkness, "I have never had such an evening in my life! I can't believe it's me. It 'll be days—*days* before I get over it!"

"She's interesting, isn't she?"

"Madame Heinrichsen? She's fascinating. And is she really going to retire?"

"I don't know. She gets here and begins to rage at the expense of living and the noise and the waste, and she gets terribly tired before the end of the season, and she goes back to Helsingfors and drinks pure milk and breathes pure air and is the celebrity of the neighborhood. And then after a few months of that she begins to wonder if she really has a foothold in New York, if she really has a car and a chauffeur and her pictures in the Sunday pictorials, and back she comes to see if it's all true. It's my belief that she'll keep on doing that until she cracks on a high note and hasn't any choice!"

"I'll do that when I go back to Salletts," Becky said musingly. "I'll wonder if I ever wore a Leneau dress and sat in an opera box and saw Flammavilla come out in her long white dress!"

"You think you must go?" the doctor said, clearing his throat.

"Oh yes, I must go back. For so many reasons! I only had to have a full meal and a hot bath to know that I must go back," Becky said on a rueful laugh. "To gather up the dropped threads, to clear up the situation with Gavin, once and for all. To manage, somehow, that he won't keep turning up in my life, humiliating me by borrowing money from the people I love."

"I see," the doctor said on a reluctant note. And for a moment or two neither spoke.

"You'll go with us to Florida?"

"Oh yes! If you want me. I'm going to write Mother that, for that's an address Gavin couldn't trace. Then after that we'll go home again. And you'll always know," Becky said steadily, "that somewhere out there in the West are a woman and a child whose lives you saved. I don't know how many lives could be saved, Doctor, by just a few weeks of spoiling. But I know that just rest and good hot meals and warm blankets pulled me out of a hole that might have gone deeper and deeper until neither Gibbs nor I *could* get out!"

"It doesn't take much sometimes," the doctor said cheerfully. "Then there's no Europe this year, Becky?"

"Not this year. It's enough this year that you want me."

"Ah—that," the doctor said with a quick look. Becky's eyes met his for a second but she did not speak. There was a moment of silence.

He thought perhaps that she was crying. After a moment he groped with his hand to find her hand, and she pulled the glove from it and slipped the warm smooth fingers into his, and they rode so the rest of the way, without speaking.

CHAPTER XXXII

WHEN HE WAS at Hillover Becky always came down at
eight to breakfast with the doctor, bringing Gibbs, who con-
sumed orange juice and played with toast while his elders ate.
Afterward she went to the doorway to watch her host drive
away. Sometimes clear bright sunshine laid blue clean shadows on the snow, and the trees sparkled in crystal casings;
sometimes there was a leaden sky and a furtive wind that
rattled branches and snatched the smoke from distant chimneys; sometimes the snow was softly falling, twisting down
silently in pale blue and cream and pink and lavender flakes
that blended themselves into a veil of living white.

After that the day in the solid, secure old brick house went
pleasantly, serenely, with women going up and down the
delicate spiral of the stairway; flowers appearing here and
there in clear glass vases; Hatsy's telephone trilling; Barbara's late breakfast scenting the bedroom floor with coffee
and toast.

Gibbs had his blocks and trucks and heavy little iron
motors on the rug by the fire; Harriet Lee's big white cat
and old gray cat came lazily in to lie down on Becky's bed;
the doctor's hunting dog lay in the study, waiting, or went
out to follow leaping squirrels across the snow.

If Becky went into town she was apt to report at the office
at about four, sitting among the waiting patients until Miss
Mills saw her and sent her in without formality. She never
kept the doctor more than a minute, despite his obvious pleasure in seeing her, his obvious willingness to waste a little

time. She put but her one question—was he coming home tonight?

"Well, let's see what I have to do here, Becky. Yes, I can be done here in half an hour. Where's Harriet?"

Mrs Lee, or Barbara or Hatsy as the case might be, had gone home earlier. Becky and the doctor would presently drive out into the country, the man sunk back wearily, smiling and listening, Becky on the edge of the seat, turned sidewise to face him, her eager story of all the day's adventures, and of the adventures and experiences of many other days, making the trip short.

From Florida she wrote him that she missed him. He had gone down there with the family but had stayed only for a few days; Becky and Gibbs, who was once again his strong little Indian-brown self, finished the five weeks stay.

While Barbara moved about to neighboring estates, dancing, flirting, involving herself in a hundred different engagements, Becky and Gibbs lived quietly in a roomy shore cottage with Mrs Lee and Carrie-Sis, the older woman spending long hours on the sand gossiping and murmuring over her petit point with old friends who were established in the same colony, Becky and Gibbs rioting in glorious warm sea bathing that made every other consideration secondary to Becky. She cared not what she ate or wore or did between the hours that were spent in the sparkling champagne that was the Atlantic.

"Barbara's friend Laurence Moulton has come down," she wrote to the doctor. "We all swim together in the morning, and even Gibbs does pretty well. I am very brown; my nose, which was peeling when you left, is now completely peeled and browning again, so I will be Cherokee three layers in. My mother sent me a letter that made me cry; she is happier than she ought to be to have her bad penny turning up again. Gavin has been in town, is away now with Harry Grace in the mountains, but returns every now and then. My old beau

Joe Feratta has married a darling girl and they are going to have a baby, and she is a Catholic—the wife, I mean, not the baby—which must be a great satisfaction to Joe's family. . . .

"I have had almost enough sunshine," she wrote later, "and am thinking too much of a certain old white brick house near the frozen Sound, and the way the red-berry bushes at the gate look when ice forms like lace over the berries. Laurence has gone; he stayed only four days. We leave in three more, and it will be good to see you again! But there's a cloud. Gibbs and I ought to be starting West almost immediately."

"What do you think will happen when you get there, Becky?" he asked her on the night of their return from the South.

"To Salletts? Oh, crying and kissing," she said, laughing, "and gossip. Mother telling me everything, and the boys and Dad and Sophy chipping in. And then everything going a little quieter . . ."

She fell silent.

"You're a wise child to expect a reaction," the doctor observed, watching her.

"Oh yes, then there'll be all the bad news," Becky said with a resigned sigh, "that a chain store has come into town and is cutting into Dad's business; that Bob wants to go to Stanford. He had a straight A rating at the junior high, but that Dad feels he can't send him; that somebody's died and somebody else was in an accident. . . ."

"You don't want to go back?" he asked with a keen look.

"I want to see my mother, but I hate the thought of the news of Gavin, whatever it is. It won't be good. I'll have to see him, to hear it all again, the reasons why he didn't keep this job or that, and that he's always loved me, and won't I—won't I give him another chance, be kind to him." Becky's face burned. "After all, I'm his wife," she said, looking away.

They were in the library alone after dinner. They had been

playing dominoes while Hatsy and her mother hovered about. Now Hatsy's crowd had carried her off and Harriet had gone to bed. The Florida party had arrived in midafternoon, but unpacking and caring for Gibbs and all the varied activities attendant upon a return had occupied Becky fully until now. This was her first moment alone with the doctor.

"That too?" he said now, knitting his forehead, looking into the fire.

"His attitude is always one of 'forget and forgive,'" Becky went on with a desperate little laugh. "He'll say that he knows he's treated us badly, but that a lot of it he couldn't help, and won't I be generous, because he's never looked at another woman since he met me."

"And is that true?"

"I don't know. I've no way of knowing. I don't know any of his friends down south. I was with my mother for five months without hearing from him, and then he sauntered in, pleased to see the baby, informing Sophy that he liked his coffee poured up to the top of the cup, as much at home as if he were the son of the family and I the irresponsible daughter-in-law!"

"Hard!" the doctor muttered.

"Oh, hard to deal with! When he's playing with Gibbs, when he's coming down from the woods with wild strawberries, and saying to Mother, 'I know you like these, Mrs Gibson,' it's impossible not to feel friendly. But it's no *use*," Becky broke off to say, growing more nervous every minute, "it's no use listening to him, believing in him! He doesn't mean any of it. And now, now that I've been here, that I love this life so, that you've all given me a new—a new viewpoint, and new feeling about life——"

She stopped, her throat closing with tears, and came across the rug and took a low fat square cushion of red leather, close to his knee.

"I *cannot* go back!" she whispered. "There must be some

way in which I can get free. I don't mean instantly; I'll be patient. But it sickens me to think of his kissing me again—now—now when I know——"

Again she broke off short, turning away from him, looking into the fire.

"What do you know?" the doctor asked her in a low tone.

"Know—but we didn't mean to tell anyone for months," Becky said, "that Laurence Moulton and I like each other."

It was very simply said, and the face she turned toward him was not a happy face. Immediately she began to explain.

"From the beginning he knew—he says he knew, that he —he cared for me. But Barbara had talked to me so much about him (she knew him in Paris and in Hawaii) that I never thought . . . I never dreamed . . ."

She left the sentence unfinished and started again.

"That very first night he was here, before Christmas, just after Barbara got home, he told me. They were all playing games, you remember? And he and I were in here alone. He told me then. But I didn't believe it," Becky said, her troubled eyes never leaving the doctor's serious face, her hands knotted on her knees. "I didn't want to believe it. I thought I was finished forever with men. And there was Gavin, you know. For even if we'd been separated for months, as we had been, we were still man and wife. So I tried . . .

"I did try terribly to fight it. But it couldn't be fought. Two or three times, when Barbara was away, I went to his uncle's studio, and we talked. Once we took a long walk; it was snowing. And then he came down to Florida and we had a few days together. The others were around us all the time, of course, but we managed a few hours together, and I said —I said that when—that if I could honorably free myself from Gavin, and if my mother was happy about it, and if I had the custody of Gibbs, except perhaps if Gavin wanted to visit him, take him to movies or the circus or anything, later on—I said that if all that happened," Becky finished on a long breath, "I'd come back and we could be married."

The doctor sat quite still, looking at her.

"I'm sorry," he said after a silence. "He seems—and if you and Barbara like him so much, he probably is—a nice fellow. But I'm sorry! I lose you and I lose my little boy. I'm to be in Europe most of the summer, so that I'll be busy. But this has been a happy little interval for me, my dear. What does Barbara think of this plan?"

"Barbara knows nothing about it," Becky said in alarm. "Nobody will know anything about it. Not even Mother, until I have settled everything with Gavin. It's not an engagement—it's not a promise; it's only 'if' and 'if' and 'if.' It's only that we discovered that we were thinking of nothing but each other, and that Laurence, who is about the most jealous man I ever knew, wanted something—something to go on. But if things go wrong at home . . . And anyway, it's only probable . . ."

"Jealous, is he, eh?"

"Oh, jealous!" Becky laughed indulgently. "He's always saying I don't love him, I never really loved him," she said. "I look at other men, I like good times when he's not around."

"He says all that?"

"To the exclusion of almost everything else."

"Then what about Gibbs?"

"Oh, he—he concedes me Gibbs. He likes him. He's only seen him for a few minutes, twice, but he thinks Gibbs is grand."

"Jealousy can be a pretty serious thing in marriage, Becky."

"I know it can!" Her clasped hands were on his knee now, her beautiful gold-brown eyes suddenly serious. "But when a woman loves a man very much," she said, "she keeps him too happy for jealousy. Once we are married he'll be quieter, he'll understand that there are other things in life than just love-making. Meanwhile," Becky went on, "I'm hoping, I'm *praying* that Barbara will come to like Pedar or someone else. Every hour of my life I'm saying, 'Please make it come right, please guide us to do the right thing!' "

"To God? I remember your telling me that in your very darkest hours you did that. But I didn't think these days exactly—er—called for it."

"I think one should do it all the time, to be ready," Becky pronounced. Stephen Dinsmore was not listening; his eyes were far away.

"I think I'm a little sorry," he presently said in a musing tone. Becky, hypersensitive to his moods, fixed her eyes upon him anxiously. "Sorry to lose you, Becky."

"It can't be for more than a year!" she told him eagerly. "Even if Gavin is manageable, even if it goes through quickly, it can't be for more than a year."

"No, and we can plan for that year. Yes," the man conceded, "I suppose you must go home. But you'll be back."

In her turn Becky was inattentive, her thoughts far away.

"Will you tell me something?" she said suddenly. Her face, which had flushed hotly, turned pale. She fixed her eyes on his face. "Are you my father?" she asked.

The doctor looked at her steadily, his own color changing. "Why—why do you ask me that?" he stammered.

"I know something about my own history," she said. "Do you?"

"Something," he answered slowly. "I didn't know that you knew anything. You told me in the hospital that you had been an adopted child. You know more than that?"

"What my mother told me before I was married. When she thought I might do something rash—something foolish. We've never talked of it since. And she didn't know much, not what my real mother's name was, nor anything about her."

"They were friends?"

"They saw each other only a few times. The last time was the day my mother died in a hospital. She gave me to—to my own mother, to the woman I've always called 'Mother.' "

"How old were you then, Becky?"

"Only a tiny baby. A few days old."

"And she died? I hoped she might have lived, after all."

"My mother saw her dead. I know, I know how kind you are to everyone," Becky said, "but it isn't you. Not you alone. It's everyone in this house, your sister and the servants and the girls. They know there's some other reason for having me here, for making me a daughter of the family!"

"The girls and the servants know nothing," Stephen Dinsmore said quickly. "Harriet knows, and the girls know you are the child of someone I once knew. I told Harriet that first day in the hospital when I heard your voice, when I saw you walking away, that you were found. I told her not to be shocked when she saw you."

"You were shocked, when I came downstairs dressed for the opera, at Christmas time," Becky said. "The night you said your eyes hurt. Remember?"

"Yes. I was looking through the doorway toward the stairway. And in that dress, with the ruffles around the knees, and the way you had your hair—well, you weren't merely like your mother, Becky. You *were* Madeleine."

"Madeleine!" Becky's eyes filled, yet she was smiling. "Was that her name? You loved her? You *are* my father! From the beginning I think I loved you that way. Was that it?"

"No," he said. "I'm not your father. I wish—God knows how I wish I were! I loved her, Becky, from the time I wasn't much more than a little boy. I idolized her. She was like you, but slighter, a slender little woman. Her color was exactly yours. And everyone who saw her loved her, I think. But she didn't love me. I was a little younger—two years, three years, something like that. And so many older men wanted her!

"And then I had a chance to do her a service, Becky, and I failed her. Her asking me came absolutely without warning, and she'd hurt me, she'd hurt my pride! I said no, and she went away, and I never saw her again.

"But it was about you, her unborn baby, that she'd spoken to me, so I knew you were somewhere in the world, if you hadn't died. And I knew she was gone, for she sent me a little note to say good-by. I tried to trace it; there was no tracing it. It had been sent by some hand she could trust. It had been mailed in St Louis, but it hadn't been written in St Louis. I went there, I searched. It was no use. Babies and mothers and babies and mothers, and clue after clue failing. She had covered her tracks too well.

"So you slipped through my hands. But I took a vow that if ever I could help Madeleine's child every penny that I had should be hers. And time brought you straight to me."

Becky sat perfectly still, her tearful eyes fixed on his.

"Now I'll tell you my side," she said. "What Mother told me."

His hands were tight over hers on his knee. Ashes fell in the fireplace and the room grew chill. But still the two voices murmured on and on in the silences of the old house in the depth of a winter night.

It was after midnight when he sent her, tired and white, upstairs to bed. At the foot of the stairs he said:

"If I were your father, Becky, I think I should tell you to wait—wait a long time before trusting yourself to any man again!"

She did not answer. But he saw the stricken look in her tear-wet eyes; saw the slow weary drag of her feet as she turned and went upstairs.

CHAPTER XXXIII

"AND WHEN do you go, Becky?" Duane Fox asked in the voice of one who knows the answer.

"Tomorrow night. We drive into town at about nine, wake Gibbs up to take him in—he'll have supper as usual and go to bed—and are on the train at midnight. Then I'll put him right to bed. We're in Chicago at ten tomorrow night and make close connections with the Overland. And home on Friday!"

"That's San Francisco?"

"Sacramento. We get off at Sacramento. Mother and Dad ought to be there."

"You like the prospect," Laurence said gloomily. "My God, if I were leaving you for six or seven weeks I couldn't sing about it!"

"I wasn't singing," Becky said, laughing. "Larry, if you could see your face! But I've not seen my mother for two and a half years. When she last saw Gibbs he was a little baby; he couldn't even sit up in a high chair. And of course I want to show him off to everyone I know!"

"Including Gavin Flood," Laurence said briefly. Becky, seated on the arm of his chair, leaned over to touch her cheek to his thick fair hair.

"I believe this poor little nitwit is jealous," she said dreamily.

"You know it!" Laurence said, twisting about to kiss her cheek.

"Yes; I'm glad to go home and say that I'm sorry I've given them so much trouble," Becky presently said in a more

serious mood. "And I'm glad to get the other thing started.
I don't feel that I belong there any more. When I come away
again I want it to be all cleared up and closed behind me. And
the sooner the better!"

"God, I wish you didn't have to do it. They may pull that
interlocutory year on you!" Laurence muttered.

"Oh, they will!" said Becky. "That's California law. I
know, because I——"

"It isn't Nevada law," Laurence interrupted in a low voice.

"No; but why should I go to Nevada? It's expensive, and
it would be lonely, and it would distress Mother terribly. If
I have to do that," Becky said, "I'll come back here and make
this spring trip with Doctor Dinsmore and Mrs Lee, and
then go back to California in the fall."

"And what would that accomplish?" asked the older man.

They were having tea in the studio on a wild February
afternoon of wind and sleet. The afternoon was spent; the
high windows were almost dark; Laurence had finished the
sketch in pastel he had been doing of Becky's head, and they
had gathered around the stove whose iron sides glowed red
against the encroaching cold of the dusk and the bitter
weather.

Duane Fox was a stout man with a rosy face and silvered
hair. His gray eyes were covered with strong-lensed glasses;
when he smiled he showed handsome white teeth. He wore
loose wide slacks of well-worn corduroy streaked and spotted
with odds and ends of paint, and a ticking smock faded and
equally paint-spattered but stiffly ironed and recently washed.
Under the open collar of the smock a heavy brown sweater
showed itself; his ankles were bare, his feet thrust into heavy
fur slippers. Laurence as always was picturesque. His fair
loose hair was tumbled, a smooch of vermilion chalk lay
across one cheek, his old white silk shirt and sleeveless
sweater, his disreputable blue cloth slacks were all informal,

and yet he looked his best somehow, comfortable and right in his own setting.

"Well, it would accomplish this," Becky said in answer to Duane's question; "it would mean that for once in my life I did something deliberately, didn't run away from one thing to plunge blindly into another. Doctor Dinsmore has been an angel of goodness to me. He loves Gibbs, he's taken a tremendous fancy to him, and I think he loves me. He wants— he really wants the fun of showing me London and Paris. He said so in so many words the only time we talked about it. He's taking Carrie-Sis—she'll run Gibbs—and we'd be gone until September. That doesn't seem too much to give him! Then I want to be with Mother for a while. She loves Gibbs too."

"What is this, a marriage or a farewell tour for Gibbs?" Larry demanded. Becky laughed again, unalarmed.

"Why not do this," said Duane, thinking it out. "Becky goes West and gets a Reno divorce. I know you don't like the idea, my dear, but it only takes six weeks, and in the kind of life you and Larry here are going to live nobody's going to raise eyebrows at you. Then you come back, join the Dinsmore family here, make your plans to go abroad and get quietly married to Larry right away. You go to Europe, have your trip, and when you come back announce your marriage. Then a certain fat old fool gives you a check for, say, three thousand, and you and Larry are off by way of Panama to California for a honeymoon! Your being married will keep Iago here quiet; you can have a few weeks in California, leave the small boy there with your mother since she loves him so, and come back here to paint great masterpieces in this very room."

"Ah, you're awfully kind!" Becky said, more touched by his thoughtfulness than convinced of the wisdom of the course he outlined. "That—that would . . ." she began, feeling her way. "Wouldn't that make you worse than ever?" she asked Laurence with a little helpless laugh.

"I'm much more civilized than you think I am," Laurence told her, rubbing his cheek against hers. "I want my wife. I grudge every moment that we'll be separated. But when the old boy here makes a plan as reasonable as that, and goes to the trouble of having the Lodge all done over for you and me——"

"You're not doing that?" Becky interrupted, turning toward Duane. She was familiar with the snowy exterior appearance of the Lodge, a small tenant house that had been spared when a great fire had swept away the old Colonial house to which the studio-barn had belonged.

"It's not very interesting," Duane said. "Four rooms downstairs, two rooms upstairs. But since we're only renting, it doesn't seem worth while to knock down walls and build porches. Someday we'll go further down the Island and find a place big enough for us all."

"I don't think I'd want to leave Gibbs very long with Mother," Becky said, anxious to make that clear in the very beginning of planning. "There's his father, you see, who might make things unpleasant."

"It would only be if you two decided to run over to Paris for a few months. Paris is no place for children," Duane said.

"Oh, this is such fun, planning!" Becky laughed. "A year ago I was working in Rheingolder's, and now—opera, and Florida, and a drawing room to California! Doctor Dinsmore brought the tickets home last night——"

"And what does he think of this idea?" said Duane.

"My going West?"

"Well, and marrying Larry?"

"Oh, I only hinted that. I said 'if' and 'if' and 'if.' I said I wanted to be free, and I do. But I didn't say anything definite about Larry simply because I'm not free. Not yet.

You see, Doctor Dinsmore doesn't know Larry. He's met him—you remember, Larry? That night when you and I were talking by the fire and the others were all playing games. But then he only thought of him as a man Barbara liked."

Duane Fox chuckled.

"He'll have to come to know you better, Larry," he said.

"You said it," Larry agreed on a quiet little laugh of his own.

Becky felt her skin prick for a second on an inexplicable feeling of discomfort. She could not see Larry's face, for she was seated on the arm of his wide chair, but she could look at the other man. Something about him frightened her for just a fraction of time; it vanished almost before she was conscious of it, but she remembered it afterward and wondered about it.

Duane Fox was about Dr Stephen's age, but he seemed older, she thought, because of a certain careless disorder in dress, a certain effect of not having been quite completely groomed. Where Stephen was erect, businesslike, frowning in concentration upon some problem, Duane was lax and indifferent or contemptuous, talking a great deal, habitually eating and drinking too much according to his own confession, interested supremely and primarily in himself, and secondarily in art as he saw it.

As a portrait painter he had had a certain vogue many years earlier, had made large sums of money rapidly and easily. He had studied in Paris, learned to jabber certain French phrases readily. For years he had collected bronze and copper trifles, filled his walls with not quite good pictures bought for almost nothing at sales in Brittany and Flanders. In conversation he was racy, amusing, often vulgar and sometimes shocking, but his was a personality that carried off with good grace what might have been offensive in another type of man.

Of women he had nothing good to say, although his frank

and rambling recollections testified to the fact that there had been many in his life and that they had been more than kind to him. A beautiful English model, an Austrian woman doctor, a Russian dancer, countless affectionate little Parisiennes —he spoke of his careless possession of them all; and Becky never doubted that a certain fascinatingly ugly trained nurse of some forty years, who once came to the studio and showed under her gallant rattle of unrelated matters a pitiful desire to win him back to some previous status of friendship and feeling, was one of them.

But she couldn't help liking even if she didn't admire him. From the moment of Larry's introduction, when Duane, who was suffering from a serious eye trouble, had peered at her with his heavily glassed eyes, she knew he had put her in a class quite apart from the rest of her sex. He had drawn her to talk of herself, and in return had made himself so convulsively funny with his own memoirs that both she and Larry had had to put their heads down on the luncheon table and cry with helpless laughter.

Like all good storytellers he was inspired by the right audience, and went from yarn to yarn with an air of naturalness and simplicity, with much ingenuous revelation of his own stupidities and amusement at his own expense. Larry told Becky later that he had never seen his uncle in better form, and Becky could truly answer that she had somehow known that the older man was in high and unusual spirits, even before Larry told her.

Apart from this flattering beginning of their friendship, he showed her and Larry in a hundred practical and generous ways that he was delighted with the prospect of the introduction of a new niece, and even of a small noisy boy, into the family. With the rehabilitation of the Lodge in mind he had seen painters and plasterers immediately after Larry's confidences regarding Becky had been given him, and on the evening before this very day, when the three of them sat about the hot stove and drank the tea with which the painters always finished their working day, he had had a long talk with Larry as to the actual details of the affair.

From their seven o'clock dinner, served by a neighboring farmer's daughter who often cooked them a meal or spent odd hours cleaning the studio-barn, until the small hours of the morning the two men had discussed the situation, and at the end Larry's one word for his uncle had been that he was a prince.

"We'll go way down past Good Ground and the Moriches," Duane had said; "we'll find some old place that 'll seem more like a home to her. I can turn in a few bonds and launch you, and if I were you I'd persuade her to make it Paris for six months or a year, and leave the child in the West. Better for him, and better for her than trying to make a go of it with a kid and an old codger like me in the picture. Then, say in the fall, or maybe next spring, come back and we'll house-hunt. Meanwhile I'll hibernate here, listening to the radio and getting too fat, and having my little chuckle to myself in the dark!"

Larry had listened, impressed for the first time, as a man must be at some time or other in the course of an engagement, with the fact that he and Becky really were to be married. With Stephen Dinsmore informed, with Becky seriously talking divorce, with his uncle in this astonishingly co-operative mood, matters were moving fast. He had thought of himself and Becky in some picturesque studio on the Left Bank; had thought of winter dinners with her in the warmth and excitement of the Dome; of summer afternoons at the awning-shaded tables of the boulevards, and his heart had warmed in eager anticipation.

Becky, coming in with him after a cold bracing walk for tea the next day, had not been quite so sure. The California tangle that he could dismiss so easily, as concerning only a few names with which he had no associations, was a very real and vital thing to her. The break with Dr Stephen hurt her, even in her thoughts. He had been a father to her in the hour of her bitterest need, and he had of course hoped that the association so welcome in his lonely life would go on, that Becky and Gibbs would always be in a sense his find, his special possessions.

To have her so immediately deserting him, off to California, off to France with a husband, off to some other town to live, seemed hardly fair. He had loved her mother; he had been loyal to her mother's memory, and she was like that mother, and so dear to him for reasons that went far back beyond her own beginnings.

She thought of him now when some faint intonation in Duane Fox's laugh made her wince deep within her soul. Stephen, the finest product that American soil after three hundred years could boast, cultured, traveled, brilliant, loving everything that was good in letters, music, life; Stephen, whose line had given eminent men to statesmanship, to science, to social service of every description, would never like Duane. She knew that. Duane was the cynical, lazy, clever, irresponsible type; he became blasphemous when anyone like Stephen was under discussion.

Duane was lawless. What decencies and conventions he observed were included in his scheme of life merely because they were convenient, personally desirable, or, in earlier days when he had had a fashionable patron to please, expected of him. He loved to use words and do things not usually permitted in refined society, and could tear to pieces with a few brilliant phrases the code which years of stumbling human effort had painfully composed.

Stephen lived by law. It had been ingrained into him generations before his own birth; he followed it without ever knowing how or why he came to do so. The law of careful speech and act, the law that gives each man the responsibility to make of just one man a loyal citizen, an honest and self-controlled contributor to the good of the commonwealth, the law that leaves untouched another man's goods and his good name, that shelters the homeless and counsels the doubtful, this had been a commonplace with him through all his days. He was a Christian of the type that finds endless and inexplicable joy in every day's labor, and that cannot see suffering or need without swift willingness to help. Becky sometimes went to church with him and Harriet on Sunday, and sat with them in the pew that had been marked with the family name of their great-grandmother when that church had first been opened, a hundred years earlier. She knew that hypocrisy and indifference and affectation were all about her; she knew that Stephen's own motive in churchgoing was a strangely mixed one, that it was' partly because it seemed to him vaguely a good thing to do, and partly family custom, and partly the need to set an example; she suspected that he had not ever really analyzed any of these feelings and would find little enough beneath them if he did.

But it was part of the whole plan and procedure that had made him what he was—the finest man she ever had known, the kindest, the most simply winning and lovable. Becky resolved in her heart that even though her marriage temporarily separated them she would never lose him. She would telephone just so often from that studio-farmhouse of which Duane had spoken today, to ask if she and Gibbs might come up for a visit. And every year she'd remind him to ask "Madeleine's daughter" to join him for the *Lohengrin* night.

"He's as dear as a father," she said to herself. "Dearer. I'll never fail him."

"*Now* what are you thinking about?" Larry demanded. Becky came out of a dream with a start. Of course! She was in the studio of Foxaway. They had been having tea; the delicate sweetness of Oolong was in the air; twilight was blue against the high windows; the gale had dropped; there was a complete hush out of doors.

"Thinking that I must go!" Becky said. She went to lay her hand on the older man's full big hand as it rested on the arm of his winged chair. "Don't get up," she said. "And good-by. You've been awfully good, for a woman hater, to Larry and me! I'll not see you again until I've gotten things straightened out at home, so it may be weeks. But I'll come back!"

"And we'll put a secret marriage over on them, Becky," Laurence said as he and she went down the narrow wooden stairs and emerged into the last cool light of the February afternoon. "What d'you think of the old boy's idea?"

She laughed at him, glancing up obliquely over a furred collar.

"Are we walking?"

"Will you? It's all cleared, and it's only three miles."

"But how 'll you get home?"

"I'll walk back, thinking of my girl. I'm so damn restless," Laurence said pitifully. "I don't know how I'm going to get through it. You off tomorrow night—I suppose I won't see you tomorrow at all?"

"Doctor Dinsmore wants me to go into town with him in the morning. I'm to fill in time with last shopping, and lunch with him at half-past twelve. He'll have to keep his two o'clock office appointments but Carter's bringing me back immediately. I'll have packing to do, all Gibbs' packing."

"You couldn't call him off and lunch with me, darling? Ah, do! Think what a long pull it's going to be!"

"Oh, I couldn't!"

"Tell him it's our last chance to be together. He'll have you tomorrow night."

"But the others will be there too."

"Ah, I see!"

Laurence's face was grim, his jaw set. They walked rapidly along the cold darkening road without speaking again for some time.

"Larry, you're not going to be silly enough to be jealous of Doctor Dinsmore?"

"I'm going to be silly enough to be jealous of anyone! Who does he think he is, monopolizing you this way?"

"But you'll be continually miserable, and make me miserable too, if you're going out of your way to imagine things like this! Why can't you just be happy because we have found each other in such an extraordinary way, and because I am coming back, and then nothing will separate us!"

"Nothing? Ha! You're going off to Europe!"

"But, Larry, you wouldn't want me to get a divorce one minute and be married the next?"

"Why not?"

"Well, it's just too—too sudden. Too rash, too unadvised, too sudden. I've been too precipitate all my life. Give me time to—to get my breath, to try to realize all that's happened!"

"You certainly don't think you're going to get much time to breathe, running round Europe with the Lees?"

"Europe!" she said in a dream.

"Becky, play fair with me," he pleaded. "I'm in love with you. I'm counting the days until we can be married. Don't let this old boy throw a monkey wrench into the works."

"I think it's perhaps a fortunate thing that *someone* slows us up a little, Larry!" They had reached the Dinsmore doorway now. Becky, breathless and rosy and exhilarated by the rapid walking, stood on the step above Larry and framed his handsome dissatisfied face in her two gloved hands. "Barbara doesn't know anything about this," she said. "Doctor Dinsmore agreed with me that it would be much simpler to let any explanation, at least as far as I'm concerned, wait until I come back. You'll be seeing less and less of her, and she'll be seeing more and more of other men——"

"You mean you haven't told her!" He was outraged.

"I mean I haven't had a chance. She's hardly ever home, you know. You see her almost as much as I do."

"I don't see her at all," he said darkly. "She telephoned me a night or two ago, wanted me to take her to some damn treasure hunt or something! Said that everybody had to take an animal and that Sonny McGee had gotten an elephant somewhere! They never grow up, that lot. I said I'd just had a tooth out. I think you might have told her, out of justice to me. It leaves me in a deuce of a situation to have you go away and leave me here holding the bag!"

"Larry," Becky laughed, speaking in a mother's low monitory tone, her fresh cold cheek against his, "whenever I see Barbara she wants to talk of you, tell me all the things you said in Honolulu, ask me if I've seen you. It'd be utterly impossible suddenly to burst out with 'Oh, I like him too. As a matter of fact, when I get my divorce, of which there isn't any prospect at all at the moment, he and I are going to be married!'"

Larry was not proof against the fresh cold kiss with which she finished speaking. He caught her to him, in the shadows of the doorway, and for a moment they clung together, breathless and laughing.

"God, don't I see you again?"

"I've been thinking how we might manage it. If you could be at home in the studio tomorrow at about four I'd stop in on my way home. For just about two minutes though!"

"I'd be anywhere!" She loved him in this fiercely devoted mood. Her power over the tall lean casual man she had met so short a time before was a continual marvel to her.

"Be at the studio then, and I'll come in. Carter 'll wait."

"I'm damned if Carter 'll wait! I'll take you home."

"No, now, honestly, Larry! If we begin *that*—where the car is and what time it is and whether the clock is right or not,—I'll die of nerves! After all, Gibbs and I are leaving for California tomorrow night. But just let me come in for five minutes. And now, darling, I've got to go in. Gibbs' bath, you know, and I've got to change."

"Do you realize"—he was holding her so tightly that she could not draw a full breath—"do you realize that in a few weeks not Gibbs' bath nor anything else will keep me from coming up to your room and watching you change and watching Gibbs' bath, and putting anyone else out who wants to come in, and telling old Steve Dinsmore when he wants to take you to lunch that he can go roll his hoop?"

"I've thought of it," Becky said demurely.

"Why can't I come in?"

"You can!" Her laughing face was laid against his again. "Barbara's having some people in for cocktails and she'll be perfectly delighted."

"Oh hell!" he said. "Well, go on in and be daughterly with the old man. Does he kiss you?"

"Really, Larry, you are too horrible!" But Becky was still laughing as she went upstairs.

CHAPTER XXXIV

THE NEXT DAY, driving into town with the doctor over fresh fleecy snow, she asked him if he specifically disliked Laurence Moulton.

"No," Stephen said hesitatingly. "I think I only feel that it would be very soon, another marriage. You're young, you've your fine boy, and you've hardly had time to accustom yourself to all the changes and moves. Sometimes in love we do things—as we do, for instance, in fresh grief—that are inexplicable to us later on. I'd be glad—I'd have been glad if this hadn't come up quite so soon. I hope you'll wait—wait until winter, perhaps. . . ."

"Larry is perfectly frenzied with impatience," Becky said in explanation as he paused. "He wants—but it doesn't really matter what he wants! All the California business has to come first."

"You're pretty sure you love him, Becky?"

She laughed, with the little sound in the laugh that only women who love and know themselves loved ever reach. The face she turned to him was bright with color and radiance.

"Pretty sure!"

"He makes a fair income?"

"His uncle is going to help us at first. We'll all be together in a perfect bohemian mix-up!" Becky explained, shyly eager. "The idea is that Larry and I spend a little time in Paris, just as a sort of honeymoon, and then come back and find some place further down the Island where we can settle. Mr Fox—Duane Fox isn't painting now, because—— *What is it?*"

The last words were interjected on a note of fright. Becky

put out her hand quickly as if to protect herself from what she saw in his eyes.

"What—what did you say?" Stephen asked quickly. "What name did you say?"

"His uncle, Duane Fox," she repeated, bewildered and frightened. "Why? Do you know him?"

He had recovered himself, but he was staring at her with a strange expression.

"Yes, I knew someone of that name once," he said somewhat breathlessly. "It was many years ago, but it must be the same. There could hardly be two of that name, unless it was—was a cousin perhaps. I'm sorry to have frightened you, my dear. He—this man, Duane Fox, is your Laurence's uncle?"

"The uncle who's done everything for him. He adores him. Larry didn't have much of a chance, you see; his people were dead, and he'd hardly known this stepbrother of his mother when Duane sent for him and—well, his whole life changed."

She talked on and Stephen listened, or seemed to listen. But Becky fancied that he was hardly hearing her, and it was with an abstracted manner that he left her when they reached the hospital, merely reminding her that she was to call for him there at half-past twelve.

Becky went off on her shopping round alone; her list included little gifts for her father and mother, for the four brothers, for Sophy and Anya. It was fun, this winter exploring of the big shops, stopping to glance at leather displays, at rows of thick plaid socks, at neckties and belts. Bob and Spin and Andrew and Gary—she would see them long before this time next week, and smell the delicious fragrance of winter-soaked eucalyptus and pepper trees again, and feel the crisp dry leaves of the oaks crackling beneath her feet in the big bare yard. Fogs again, drifting in from the west and wreathing Main Street in creamy veils every morning; tarweed again, ragged and pungent between the bare orchard trees; great pools along the dirt road into town reflecting the wild blue and ballooning white of March skies.

At quarter past twelve she and Carter were back at the hospital again to find only a message. Dr Dinsmore had been called to Spuyten Duyvil for a consultation. Would Mrs Gibson please pick him up after office hours at half-past three?

"Oh, dem! I could have lunched with Larry!" Becky thought. Aloud she said: "Well, Carter, I'm going to have a sandwich in a drugstore and see a movie. Suppose you come to the office about three?

"I'm becoming a cosmopolitan," she thought, going on her way. "I call my chauffeur by his last name and lunch in a drugstore! I love it. Stephen," Becky reflected over a swiss on rye and a cup of scalding tea, her elbows on a sticky counter, the world whirling around her at its maddest hour and pace, "Stephen knows Duane Fox. Queer! Are we in such a tiny little globe of space, really, that we keep meeting each other and mixing into each other's lives? Perhaps Duane Fox admired my mother. Perhaps she liked him better than she did Stephen? She *couldn't*. But perhaps he wasn't always fat with his eyes like that. We think we live among millions of people, but we really only live among a few! Anyway, I don't believe Stephen wants me to talk about it. I'll tell him what I got for the boys' presents. . . ."

When he came down from the hospital to the car she looked at him sharply. He looked very tired, but he smiled at her affectionately and answered her first concerned question with the assurance that he had had some coffee and a sandwich. He was not keeping his late office hours today; he was to have four operations tomorrow morning and wanted to go home for a rest.

"And you're *not* coming into town with Gibbs and me tonight," Becky stated firmly.

"Oh yes; I must. They're bringing this Spuyten Duyvil

case into town, and I've got to see her again. I operate at seven tomorrow."

"Did you tell them how to save her life, Doctor?"

"I hope so. It was something a little out of the ordinary. Healthy, sweet type of girl, with two babies. Strange."

"Then you'll stay in town tonight?"

"Oh yes. And you, unfortunately, won't!" Stephen said with a whimsical half smile. "You'll be rushing past Albany and Buffalo . . . Becky?"

The last word was said with a change of tone. Becky looked at him with instant prescience. He was going to say something . . . something . . . Her heart closed on a little spasm of fear.

"Becky," he repeated, "are you to see Laurence Moulton again?"

"Oh——" Her expression turned to one of consternation. "Oh, I was to have seen him!" she exclaimed. "I forgot. I thought I would be going out alone earlier, and I said I'd stop at the studio for a minute, just to say good-by! He'll have been waiting—it's almost four now!"

"How hard would it be for you to——" Stephen interrupted himself and fell silent. After a while he began again.

"Becky, if I asked you, could you do something for me?"

Color rushed to her face. Wrapped in her big soft coat, with gold-brown fur touching the gold-brown waves of her hair, and her eyes shining, she faced him squarely.

"Do you think there's anything I couldn't do?" she asked.

Stephen laughed, flushing a little in his turn with touched pleasure.

"I believe you would. It isn't that that stops me," he said hesitatingly. "It's whether I have a right to ask it."

"You!" The simple monosyllable, half whispered, was sufficient answer. But still he was doubtful.

"It would be for you as well as for me," he presently began again, finding words with difficulty. "It would be this:

would you—would you break with Laurence Moulton?"

Her eyes did not waver. But he saw the color drain slowly from her face. Becky swallowed with a dry throat.

"Break with Larry?" she whispered.

"Not forever. Just now. Just for these months when you'll be with your mother in California, and with Harriet and me in Europe. Would that be frightfully hard for you?"

"No!" Becky said courageously. She seemed unable to say more.

He went on speaking seriously, as if unaware of the betrayal in her eyes.

"I mean for you only to tell him that you won't—you won't consider yourself bound, you'll make no promises until, say, next autumn."

"But I have done that! He knows that! He knows that I'm not in any way free now." Her eyes narrowed. "Doctor, do you know anything about Larry?" she asked.

"About Larry, no. But his uncle—I knew something of him many years ago. It's not an association that has—that has any pleasant memories for me, and the thought of you belonging to it is hard. I wish, in all this time, that Duane Fox's name had come up before," the doctor said. "I wish I had known who he was. It seems extraordinary—not that I ever talked to Barbara about it, or that you and I discussed it except that once—but it seems strange that I never knew until now! And I can only ask you," he went on after a pause, "because you've come to be so very dear to me, because you've come to be—so very dear to me—to consider this—this marriage. To wait. To tell him that nothing can be considered settled until you come back from Europe."

"Of course I will do that," Becky said simply. "If you will have Carter drive around that way (it's not much of a detour), I'll—I'll see Laurence today. Now. I'll not have another chance. It's all been said, you know," she went on. "It's nothing new. But I'll make it clearer, since his uncle is planning on it and having the little cottage fixed for us. He even suggested that I marry Laurence as soon as I get back, before we go to Europe. And that—that 'll have to stop, of course."

"Duane Fox suggested that?"

"Yes. At least we were all speaking of it at tea yesterday. And afterward, walking home, Larry wanted me to promise it. But I didn't. I couldn't."

"Becky, if you love him, it isn't fair to ask it. And it isn't possible to explain——"

"No, no!" she interrupted him eagerly. "It's such a *joy* to have you want me to do anything! I'll feel happier this way, truly I will. I'll feel better about the divorce and everything! It *should* be this way. If you'll have Carter drop me at the end of the lane here——" She stopped, frowning a little. "But Larry 'll have to take me home then," she offered dubiously.

"I'll send Carter back immediately."

"It's only to go in there," Becky said, "and say good-by, and tell him it's over. They'll be at tea, he and his uncle, and I'll say I don't want tea, that I've packing to do and that I'm late. And then I'll simply say, 'Larry, you understand that nothing is definite between us. You mustn't make plans or count on my coming back in six or seven weeks or going to Reno or anything. That's got to be clear before I go away, and I know you'll understand that perhaps we'll have to wait a long time!'

"And then," said Becky, who had turned a little pale while outlining this course, "I'll just—go. So be sure that Carter isn't late, for after that there won't be anything to say."

"Could I wait for you?" Stephen asked.

"Would you?" Becky ejaculated incredulously. "Oh, if you *would!* I'll be so scared—so cold—when I come out. And if I know you're here it 'll all be so much easier!"

"You really think that you will have the courage to say that to him, Becky?"

"Oh yes. For it won't be disagreeable or angry. I'll just say it as simply as I can."

Stephen Dinsmore was watching her closely.

"It's all tiring you; it's exciting you terribly," he said as if half to himself. "I'm so sorry to put this to you!"

"No, no; truly it isn't that way. Your feeling as you do has made it easier for me," Becky said. "It's made it—clearer. I don't want to go away leaving him to think that it's all settled. It's *not* settled, and it may not be for months. It's always been—my trouble," Becky added youthfully, with an appealing look at the man, "to jump into things without looking."

They had stopped at the studio-barn now. She got out of the car.

"Will you really wait for me? I'll tell them you're waiting; that 'll make it shorter. I'll only be a few minutes."

"I'll wait."

Becky went in through the always open downstairs door, mounted the inner stairway, stepped into the big studio. Afternoon light was gray at the high windows; the stove glowed red; Duane was in his usual place beside it. Opposite him a handsome woman dressed all in dark red was leaning back in a big armchair, Laurence on a hassock at her knee. A cocktail shaker and a tray of glasses were on a near-by table.

Laurence jumped up as Becky came smiling in, and there were introductions. Mrs Huntress; Mrs Gibson. Wasn't Mrs Gibson going West? Yes; she was leaving at midnight tonight.

"You utterly adorable darling, I thought you'd forgotten!" Larry said in an undertone, pushing a chair forward for Becky. Becky seated herself on the edge of it, loosening her furs, her swift glance moving from one face to another. The presence of the stranger upset all her plans, but she must do what she could.

"I've only five minutes. I've been in town all day, and I've packing to do. But of course I had to come in to say good-by!"

"Not for long," Duane Fox said.

"We'll hope not for long," Becky agreed. Laurence had transferred himself and his hassock to her knee now; one of her hands was clasped in both his big ones. His adoring eyes never left her face.

"Isn't she marvelous?" he asked the visitor.

"She's grand," Mrs Huntress said in a man's hearty voice, made moist and rich by the drink she was enjoying. "And I understand you're going to take this boy in tow?" she added, eying Becky and Laurence with an understanding smile.

That the matter was being generally discussed gave Becky a moment's alarm. She seized the opening.

"Ah, nothing's definite about that!" she said with a little flush. "You see, the difficulty is—the difficulty is that I have a small boy——"

"A superfluous small boy and a superfluous husband, of course," Mrs Huntress agreed easily. "We all have 'em! Can't you tuck the child into school? My small boys adore their school." She turned to Duane. "Ridin' horses and scout camp and all that," she said.

"I couldn't call Gibbs superfluous," Becky protested, a faint emphasis on the last word. She said it not for her listeners but to satisfy some demand for loyalty deep in her soul.

"Tuck Gibbs into school? She'll put me there first," Larry said. "Everybody else is out of step but Gibbs."

"Well, he *is* adorable!" said Becky, laughing.

"And what'll he say in April when Mamma gives him a new daddy?" Mrs Huntress asked amusedly.

"Oh, not April!" Becky felt as if a net were closing around her. Duane Fox spoke from the shadows over his big chair.

"I thought we were going to manage a surprise wedding party as soon as you got back from the West?"

"Before you go to Europe. You said so, Becky," Laurence added, half turning at her knee to smile at her.

"Ah, Larry, how could I, dear? When nothing is settled?" she protested, trying to keep the conversation light and amused.

"Everything's settled unless Reno closes shop," Larry argued, himself good-natured and unalarmed.

"Nothing to it," Mrs Huntress said, stretching an over-ringed hand to the cocktail shaker, filling Duane's glass as well as her own.

"What difference does it make? We get married in April and tell people when we get ready," Laurence argued. Becky, her face reddening uncomfortably, forced herself to protest.

"But we weren't going to tell anyone that we were even engaged, Larry! It might make the greatest difference to Gavin—to my husband—if he heard any such talk! And that might affect what happened to Gibbs."

"Gibbs again!" Larry said, laughing. "Never mind, don't be frightened. Nobody knows but Sissy here, and she won't tell!"

"Me talk? You needn't worry about me!" Mrs Huntress said. "I'm the original sphinx."

Becky turned toward her her anxious, apologetic smile.

"There are other reasons why I don't want to hurry it. They've told you that Doctor Dinsmore has been a perfect angel to me, has done more for me than anyone else in my life?" she explained. "I was in real trouble—my little boy was dying—when he came along and befriended us. He's been like a father, only a father with infinite—infinite wisdom and power." Becky stumbled along, smiling with suddenly wet eyes.

"It sounds like God!" the other woman said, exaggeratedly impressed.

"Well, that's God's way, I suppose," Becky countered simply.

"And Dinsmore doesn't want you to marry?" Duane Fox asked. His finger tips were touching; his face turned toward the stove.

Becky started to frame some conciliatory phrase, save the situation with tact and pleasantness. But quite suddenly she seemed bereft of any power to do so. She began inwardly to pray as she answered in a flat low monosyllable:

"No."

"Says so?" Duane asked.

"We talked it over. He asked me—or at least he said it seemed to him wiser not to do anything too fast, not to decide at all now . . ."

She faltered to silence. Duane asked dryly:

"Oh, it seemed to him wiser?"

Laurence gripped her hand, spoke in a hurt tone.

"What's he got against me, darling?"

"This is a nightmare," Becky thought. "We're all trapped in here in this stale warm place, everyone so careless and amiable—and all steel and poison underneath! I wish I were out. I wish I were out!"

Aloud she said eagerly:

"Nothing against you, Larry! Of course not! But you see, he—he knew my mother. That's one reason he's been so marvelously kind to me. He was fond—was fond of her years ago, and so when he had a chance to help me he did everything! *Everything!* For her sake."

"Ah? But I thought your people were Californians?" Duane asked smoothly.

"They are. At least everyone thinks they are. At least," said Becky, looking about the circle with the strained smile that asked for sympathy and understanding, "I thought so myself until a few years ago. And then my mother—that is, I always thought she was my mother—told me that I had been adopted. That my people were from this part of the world somewhere, but that she never knew them. Only my real mother, who had left home and had gone to a little private hospital, in Chicago it was, I think, and died when I was born."

"Why is my voice sounding on and on in this place?" an undercurrent of her thought ran nervously. "What are we all doing here? What is it that I don't understand? They're all thinking things and I don't know what they're thinking."

"Doctor Dinsmore," she went on aloud, "happened to come through the hospital ward where Gibbs was, and he saw me and knew me right away because I look like my mother and my voice is the same, and he asked us to come down here until Gibbs was well. And then we went to Florida and—— But of course you know all the rest, Larry," Becky interrupted herself, her appealing smile turned to him now. "And so you know why I have to—and want to!—do everything he thinks right."

"And he thinks it right to keep us waiting? But surely, surely, we're the ones to decide that," Larry said. "I mean, darling, I'm not trying to rush you or anything like that, but what's so dangerous in a man and woman settling that for themselves? Duane here has kind of gotten his heart set on it; we're making plans to move out of here in June; everything's in line. What the hell?"

Unexpected firmness came to her, and although she laughed it sounded in her voice when she spoke.

"Larry, I'd give him five years instead of five months if he asked for it! It's only because he wants me to be happy, he wants me to be sure. I told him, only today, that I'd let it all wait until after summer. You and I can trust each other. We can afford to wait. Think what he's done for me and for Gibbs!"

"But he hasn't any right to ask that, Becky," Laurence persisted. "And as for Gibbs—darling, you take Gibbs too seriously!"

"I don't think I belong in this talk," said Mrs Huntress. "I'm going to beat it."

"No, no; it's not a talk!" Becky said hastily, rising. "I only stopped in for a moment to say good-by. We're leaving to-night, and I've a lot to do. Good-by, Mr Fox, and thank you a thousand times for being so good to me and Larry," she added, going to the older man and extending her hand. "I'll see you in April, if I'm back, and if not Larry 'll have letters."

"Oh, he's going to let you write to me, is he?" Larry asked. Becky flushed suddenly, although his tone had been merely amused and ironic.

"He hasn't said anything about that," she answered.

"And Gibbs doesn't object?" the man pursued in the same tone.

"Ah, Larry!" she said in reproach.

"Good-by, all!" Mrs Huntress said, rising.

"Well, we want to be sure that neither Gibbs nor Stephen Dinsmore is going to horn in on our honeymoon!" Laurence said. And quite suddenly, standing helpless in the middle of the floor, fumbling in her pocket for her handkerchief, Becky was crying.

The other woman slipped away, and Laurence put his big assured arms about Becky and shook her gently to and fro.

"Here, stop it, stop it!" he said. And as she had been unable to find a handkerchief he substituted his own, drying her eyes for her.

"I left my bag in the car!" she said with a childish gulp.

"Evidently what Stephen Dinsmore exacted from you in the way of a promise to throw Larry down hasn't made you entirely happy," Duane Fox observed with an air of speaking amusedly.

"Evidently n-n-not!" Becky laughed, Laurence's big arms still about her. "I don't know why I'm so silly," she said, "but I've had a long day and I'm tired, I suppose, and I hate

—I hate to go away to everything that I have to face in California!"

"He didn't want you actually to break the engagement?" Laurence asked. Becky, her coat and herself jumbled in his embrace, leaned backward to look into his eyes.

"It isn't an engagement, Larry! It can't be!"

"Come, we were talking housekeeping," Duane reminded her reproachfully. "But he knows, Larry knows, why Steve Dinsmore would go out of his way to cut my throat," he went on.

Suddenly there was an interruption.

"Good evening, Mr Moulton. Good evening, Mr Fox," Stephen's voice said from the darkness by the door. "Sissy Huntress just came over to my car to speak to me," he added, advancing into the circle of the lamplight, "and I was afraid Becky was getting too—tired. How about coming home, my dear?"

Becky had left Laurence's side; she joined him now, put a hand into his.

"Oh yes, Doctor!" she said quickly, relief rising over her soul like the rising of healing waters. "I was just saying good-by."

"Well, I scored last time, Dinsmore!" Duane Fox said lazily from his chair, "and perhaps I'll score again. These two are in love with each other, you know. You can reason, you can delay things maybe. But in the end this girl and boy will be in each other's arms as Madeleine was in mine, eh? As night after night she and I watched the moon rise, and wakened to see the dawn creeping in. She's promised to him; she won't break her promise."

"She's another man's wife. She's not likely to have promised him anything," Stephen's voice said incisively, "until she is free."

"That's all!" Becky said eagerly. "Only that—if I were free, perhaps——"

"Oh, come, there was no perhaps about it!" Duane said sharply. "We were talking of a studio down the Island only a few days ago!"

"If I were free," Becky said. "I said 'if' and 'if' and 'if'! Didn't I, Larry?"

"But you were positively going to be divorced, Becky. There wasn't going to be much 'if' about it," Larry said, gentle and hurt.

"I'm sorry!" she said simply. "But—it can't be definite. I came in to say that today. Didn't I, Doctor?"

"And Steve Dinsmore told you why it bites him to have you marry my boy, didn't he?" Duane asked. In the soft light of the room he turned a strange look toward Becky and the doctor, who stood facing him. "I'm almost blind, you know, Steve," he said. "Didn't Becky ever tell you that? I'm losing the last of my sight. That's a point for you, isn't it? A painter, and going blind! But I'll have my laugh. I'll have my laugh when my girl here comes back to this boy. He's like a son to me, but he isn't a son. No. He's no blood kin of mine, my stepsister's son!"

"There's no blood tie at all, Becky," Laurence said quickly. "I'd have told you if there had been. If I'd been Duane's son I'd have told you."

He had taken an eager step toward her, just as Becky, her face ghastly with unnamed terror, had stepped backward toward Stephen. She felt Stephen's arm firm and strong about her.

"What are you talking about, Larry?" she whispered.

"I supposed that Stephen there had given you a hint," Duane Fox's voice said smoothly. "I knew you the moment you stepped into the studio, just as he did, by your voice. It was only Madeleine who had that voice! Then Larry described you, the gold-brown hair and skin and eyes, and I knew. I've pictures of her; Larry saw the likeness when he met you, but he couldn't place it. You see, I loved Madeleine too, my dear. We both loved her, and she loved me! Too bad, wasn't it, with so much wealth and position and respectability on his side? She wouldn't give herself to Stephen; she gave herself to me. And she was as beautiful as you are, wasn't she, Steve? And she gave me what all his wealth hasn't given him: a child."

Becky's whisper came as sharp as a flash of steel.

"Larry?" she breathed confusedly, the world going around her dizzily. "Larry's the child?"

"No. You," Duane Fox said.

Again, without moving her eyes from the man by the fire, she stumbled a step backward, reaching unseeing for Stephen's hand. It was ready for her; she clung to it without looking at him as she said in a quick frightened whisper:

"Don't let him say that! Don't let him *dare* say that! He's nothing to me or mine; he never will be! I'll never come to this place again, or speak to him again. It's not true!"

"Tell her it's true, Steve," Duane Fox said amusedly.

"It is true, Becky," Stephen said. "He's your father."

For a long minute there was complete silence in the shadows of the studio. To Becky the whole world seemed to have died into dimness and stillness and coldness. She turned; Stephen put out an arm to brace her.

"Take me away from here!" she said in a hoarse low voice. They went out of the door and down the stairs together.

CHAPTER XXXV

"How do you feel?" Stephen Dinsmore asked, coming into her room.

"Fine," Becky from her pillows said with a languid smile. She stretched out a hand. "You missed Gibbs. Carrie-Sis has just taken him off to bed," she added. "I thought he might as well get some sleep before we go."

"Still think you'll go?" the doctor asked, sitting down.

"Oh, I think so." Her eyes were widened with alarm. "Don't you think so? I only fainted, didn't I?"

"That was all. Just as we reached the car. And I got you away immediately."

Becky shut her eyes, shuddered.

"I remember being in the car."

"Oh yes, you were all right. It's too bad, Becky," the doctor went on slowly, "that you had to hear it this way. I'm sorry. I'm terribly sorry. I hoped you never would know."

Becky, lying flat in her bed, gripped his fingers. She did not open her eyes.

"Did you have some supper?"

"Oh yes, delicious. I'm all right. Only," Becky said in a whisper, "only I don't want ever to see him again!"

"I don't think you ever need."

"Laurence knew. Laurence knew and he didn't tell me. He would have let me marry him, and not have told me!"

"I would have told you."

"And after I had married him, then he would have told me that—that Duane Fox was my father. *Is* my father," she amended it under her breath.

"Becky, I would have told you."

"Yes, but they wanted me to marry Larry before I said anything to you."

"You wouldn't have done that, my dear!"

"Ah, I've been such a fool! You don't know what I would have done." She opened her eyes, drenched with sudden tears.

"You're pretty sure you want to start West tonight?"

"Oh, sure! I don't want ever to see them again!"

"Poor Larry! He really loves you, Becky."

"Perhaps he does. Perhaps he does. But I've been feeling strange—uncomfortable about it all—about him, for days! And I don't think I want to marry—not anyone—ever again. It makes me feel like such a *fool* to say this so soon after telling you I loved him. But it's true, and I'm horribly sorry. But oh, I so want to get away! I want to see my mother. I want to put time—time—time between me and that—that voice of his, saying that he is my father! Doctor," Becky ended, staring into his eyes, "could there be any mistake? Was that true?"

"I'm afraid there isn't any mistake. I'm afraid it's true, Becky. We've all been so stupid, so blind," Stephen Dinsmore said, "and you're paying for it!"

She looked at him for a long moment in silence, amber eyes flaming darkly in a white tired face.

"Tell me about it," she said. "Funny!" she added in a musing voice. "I always used to think the only troubles in the world were money troubles. But this—this is *trouble*."

"Not necessarily. Take it just as one of those things that —that happens in this life. In a few days, in a few hours, your mind will get used to it; you'll accept it as we all have to accept changes and shocks. You'll be safe on the train tonight, my dear, rushing away from it all; you'll be with your mother and father in a few days, and it will all seem a dream."

"My mother was married to him?"

"I'll tell you the whole thing. But first I want to say that I had no idea that Duane Fox was in this neighborhood, that Laurence Moulton was anything to him. If I had, I'd have gotten you out of it; I'd never have risked your meeting. I haven't heard of him for years and years; now and then I'd see his work in a magazine. I put him out of my mind as much as possible."

They were alone in Becky's bedroom. Only one lamp was lighted, her bedside lamp that threw a soft apricot radiance in the little circle that held her face and their interlocked hands.

"I came home from medical school one Christmas," the man presently began, after a pause when he had sat silent with a knitted brow as if trying to find the right thread with which to begin to unravel the story, "and my mother was giving a house party and a dance for Harriet. I was working hard, had spent my last vacations in Europe, taking special courses, and I didn't know many of Harriet's crowd well. But at dinner I sat next to a girl from Boston—Madeleine Satterlee. She seemed to me quite a sophisticated woman of the world then; twenty-six years old—I was only twenty-three. A good many men were mad about her, for she was very lovely. Smaller than you and lighter, with the softest little satin hand I ever touched. And eyes—they were like gold light.

"I was instantly, completely in love. I was a driveling fool. She took possession of me; there was nothing else in the world. For days I made myself ridiculous, trying to think up presents, meetings, notes that would win me one hour with her. An hour!" The doctor laughed ruefully. "A moment!" he said.

"She laughed at me, of course. We were skating and sleigh riding and dancing all the time, and she was the queen of all the girls. Everyone wanted to be with her, to be doing what she did, to look like and act like Madeleine.

"On the last night, incoherent and crazy and with no hope at all, I asked her to marry me.

"She took it very seriously and nicely and told me it wasn't possible. I stammered out something about her liking another man and she said very gravely yes, that she did like another man, but that there was no chance there either. I said I would give her everything—travel, clothes, everything women like. And very gently she said no, that she couldn't marry a poor man, because she was too spoiled and too extravagant, but that all the same she wouldn't marry a man she didn't love for his money. I pleaded, I said that after we were married I'd be so good to her she'd have to love me! An old argument. She wouldn't listen to it, but she kissed me before she went away, and I went back to college almost out of my senses. Just the look of a girl's coat or some voice, or the sight of some little thing that brought her to me, made me tremble for hours.

"This was at New Year's. Six weeks later I had a letter from her. It was a courageous letter, written in a sudden impulsive mood. She wanted me to know that something had happened that destroyed her chance to marry the man she loved, or had fancied she loved, and she asked me whether I had meant what I said. Her father was dead; for years she had been living with her mother in the house of an aunt who was a business woman, buyer for one of the big department stores. It wasn't Madeleine's kind of life; she was sick of it.

"She was quite honest with me, Becky. She quoted me back to myself. I had said that love would come to her after she was my wife; she was willing to take the risk. My mother and father were dead, I was rich. We were married in just another month, in the afternoon, here in this house.

"After the ceremony I was to go back, and she with me, to Philadelphia, for my medical work. I had another year before graduation, and of course intern work after that. But I had found one of the loveliest old houses in Philadelphia, small but beautifully complete, and I planned that we should have a maid, have a home, even though I was so busy at the hospital.

"There were only a few at our wedding, forty perhaps, but there was a shoal of telegrams, and as we had a train to catch —that was before I had a car—I put them into my overcoat pocket and we said we would read them on the train. But we didn't; we dined on the train and got to our little house at about eight at night. The maid had another supper for us, but we weren't hungry, and during the meal we went at the telegrams, Madeleine reading some, I reading others, passing them back and forth and comparing notes.

"Presently I came to one simply signed 'D.' I couldn't understand it, but I'd been reading so many, and I was in such a confusion of joy and love that I thought it was just some joke. I read it to her, asking her if she identified 'D.'

" 'It can't be done,' it read. 'Freda has gone back to Vienna and freedom. What do we care for the world's opinion? I am coming to you at once. I know you'll wait for me.'

"That was all. Madeleine laughed as she took it from me, glanced at it and stuck it into the pocket of the brown suit in which she had been married. But when we went upstairs she told me that it had come from the man she loved, that he had determined to end his marriage with a beautiful German singer who had been in this country that winter. There was something irregular about their marriage—she had been married before, or something. Anyway, now she had gone away. And he was coming after Madeleine.

"She laughed about it. She said, 'Of all strange things to happen on my very wedding night! I've not seen him for weeks!' But in a few minutes her face grew troubled. She came over to me and put her hand on my shoulder. She said —and she seemed so frightened, so small and troubled and young when she said it!—that she was not ready to be my wife, that it was too soon to be off with the old love and on with the new. 'Give me time!' she said. 'I'll come to you some night; I'll love you—I love you now. But Duane and I had parted forever from each other. I thought that was over. And it's not over.'

"It had upset her horribly—terribly. I could see that. He had sent it to her old home, her old name, and they had forwarded it, thinking, I suppose, that it was just another joking telegram of congratulation. She said it could change nothing. It was too late. But days and nights went by, and instead of growing nearer, she slipped further and further away from me. She was shy, affectionate, but aloof and afraid, and I was only twenty-three. We would talk together, breakfast together, have our dinners by the fire and perhaps go to a movie or to call on someone, but she never let me come any nearer than that. I was working hard; we were living very quietly; we had planned to go to Bermuda for my Easter holiday. I hoped I might win my wife then. But at Easter she went away; she didn't say good-by. It was just that she was gone.

"I went to Germany that summer, worked like a madman. It was after I came home in October that Madeleine walked into this house one night and asked to see me. I came downstairs and we went into the library. She looked badly, and within a few months, I could see, she was going to have a baby.

"She did not tell me that she was unhappy; she did not need to tell me. Quite simply she said that she must have a divorce from me now; she must go to Reno; she had no time to spare. 'He will get a divorce too,' she said. 'He has never felt that we need marry, but it is different now. We must get married for the child's sake.'

" 'He will go to Reno too?' I asked. 'He won't have to,' she said. 'He says he can get it here.' 'How on earth can he get it here before this baby is born?' I asked. 'I don't know, I don't know,' she said feverishly, 'but he *must*. And you must help me, Steve! Help me—against him!' 'Against him?' I said. It was all terribly distressing to me; I can't tell you how distressing! Her manner, and the change in her, and the knowledge—what I'd always suspected—that he was not kind to her.

" 'You see,' she said, crouching up close against me on the davenport, her hands holding tight to mine, 'he doesn't want this baby, Steve. You can't blame him! It's stupid, it's so terribly stupid of me to have let him in for this! I love it. I'd love to have my own dear little son in my arms,' she said, 'but his work is all-important, and he's nervous, and if he fails he'll have to go back to bookkeeping, or selling life insurance. He can't do that, Steve! And I can't be a drag on him! And unless I force him he'll not push his divorce—it isn't really a divorce, it's only an investigation into some sort of ceremony he went through with Freda in Vienna. It may be legal, it may not be, but it will cost money to find out. We haven't money; that's why he's hesitating. We're living in one big room with no bathroom; the bathroom is on the floor below! It's not a good place for a baby, and he doesn't want to move.

" 'Oh, he sounds selfish,' she said as I looked at her, 'but he's not! Not always. But this thing has taken us both unawares. Steve, can you help me? Must I have this baby?'

"I told her yes, there was no way out now, and she put her face into her two hands and cried. I told her that she should have more than enough money to go to Reno, but that I couldn't see that her divorce would be much good unless he was free. I suspect now and suspected then that the marriage with this German girl never took place, but as it turned out that didn't matter.

" 'Steve, there's more,' she said to me when I'd made her drink some hot chocolate—she'd always loved chocolate— and take off her hat and coat, and make herself more comfortable by the fire. We were talking then like old friends, except that she cried now and then, and once she caught up my hand and kissed it. 'The terrible thing is,' she said, 'that as things are now, this is your baby.'

" 'Not my baby, my dear,' I said. 'I wish to God it were!' And I thought of this old house, Becky, in which there have always been Dinsmore babies, little kids running up- and downstairs. . . .

"But it came as a shock, you may well believe! She said it again and I asked her what she meant.

" 'Legally this child will be born in wedlock. You and I are still man and wife under the law.'

" 'I never thought of that,' I said. 'How did you happen to think of it? I never thought—of that.'

" 'Duane told me,' she said, the look of fear and horror coming into her eyes again. Becky, not until you came to this house was I able to forget it. But your eyes are your mother's eyes, and I've seen them laughing, I've seen them happy, happy at the opera, proud of Gibbs, and it seems to have washed all that memory away.

"What she told me then I don't think I can tell you, for she didn't use many words. She stammered and stopped, and I helped her, and the thing was somehow said between us. He had told her that if her child was born while she was still legally my wife, that child someday—his child—could claim something of my property after my death. She said he had laughed about it; her eyes were sick with pleading with me to understand. 'He's an artist, Steve. They're different. He takes everything so lightly—his attitude toward his mother, and the dreadful things he says of his father, who's dead, and of life and—and sacred things, and everything! He's not like us. He never had a real home or love or tenderness or training. He thinks it would be just as well for us to marry a year from now or never marry. And he said something about our being foolish to let go our claim on the Dinsmore money.' "

Becky made a sudden involuntary ejaculation.

"Yes, I know," Stephen said. "I was sick for a minute, too, just hearing it. But I suppose we have to make allowances for the artistic temperament."

"He'd give up his child!" Becky breathed in the pause.

"He was—he is—a strange man. But she saw it as it was. She was beside herself to clear the whole thing up, to get her divorce and be married to him, to give her child his name. Poor little Madeleine! She was so helpless. She couldn't hurry matters, couldn't save herself.

"I said, 'He told you that? That this child would have a claim on me?' Oh no, she said quickly, it wasn't exactly that. He wasn't mercenary. It was just—it was just that he had been so poor all his life, and that he had said—oh, idly, carelessly—that a Dinsmore child would inherit a fortune, that if she had never gone to him it would all have been so different. It stung her to the very soul, and yet, knowing that his child must be born within a few months, she could see nothing clearly except that she must be married first. 'I never could look my son in the face otherwise!' she said more than once.

" 'He doesn't want the child?' I said. 'Well, he's always talked of a boy, someday,' she answered as if it hurt her. 'But he's working so hard, and we have so little money, and it wasn't in the bargain that there should be children—not for years anyway.'

" 'Well then,' I said, 'suppose I take the baby? If he can take my wife from me, why shouldn't I have his baby?'

"She looked at me as if she were going out of her senses. 'You couldn't do that?' she said, her voice almost gone. 'You wouldn't do that!' 'Why not?' I said. 'The child would be better with me than with him. He'd bear my name.' Her voice went up into a sort of cry. 'Ah no, Steve, you'd not do that! A child you hated! A child who reminded you of everything you want to forget!' 'But legally my son,' I said. I wasn't thinking of her, Becky, of what she must be feeling. I was thinking of him, of the fury he'd be in when he realized that I could claim his flesh and blood as mine. I was young, you know, and she was very beautiful, and I'd loved her so long, agonized for just one of the kisses he threw away.

"And now she was to bear him a child! I knew, even while I talked, that I would never take it from her. But there was a rage within me, a need to frighten her, so that she could frighten and anger him. I'd dreamed of a child. My life was bitterly lonely. And to see her, thin and shabby and despairing, and all for nothing—all for him, who wasn't worthy to tie her slippers—well, I suppose I went a little mad for a while! 'You tell him that he need give the child no further concern,' I said. 'It is my child, born of you, whom I've loved since I knew you at all. It will be mine!'

"She looked at me as if she would go mad. 'Oh, what have I done, what have I done to all of us, Steve, you, and Duane, and my baby too!' she wailed.

"I went on talking insanely, thinking only of him. 'You shall have money in the bank as my wife,' I said. 'You must take care of yourself and of the baby. But he, Fox, is never to see the boy. I'll have nurses waiting for him——'

"'Ah, stop!' she said. Suddenly she was very calm; it was as if she were trying to quiet me. 'No more of this tonight. I'm tired, Steve,' she said, 'and you don't know how delicious it is to lie here in this comfort, and drink my chocolate and not think at all! We'll talk of it again. I've been cruel to you, but you'll not be cruel to me. Let me rest here a little while, and then take me home, and someday help me to go West and get my divorce, and tell me what to do to clear up Duane's marriage, if it was a marriage!'

"'I've got to go to the hospital; I'm on call,' I said. 'Will you just lie here and rest until I come back?' 'I'll go to sleep,' she said, laughing: She drew my face down to hers, and I had one kiss—the only real kiss she ever gave me! I never saw her again."

There was a long silence. Becky came back to the room with a start, and heard the fire crackling in the grate, and the tickling noise of rain on the windows. She was Becky Gibson Flood, in the old Dinsmore home at Cove Bay listening to this, watching the grave fine face of the man who told the story. Her boy was asleep in the next room, her bags packed; she was going on her way to California tonight.

"When I came back," Stephen presently resumed, "she was gone. I thought she had gone to him, but she never saw him again either. A day or two later she drew money from the bank—twenty thousand dollars. And after that I had no news for weeks—weeks. I telephoned him; I couldn't help it! I wanted to hear her voice, to know that she hadn't succumbed to fear and weakness. But he suspected me of hiding her. It was genuine; he knew no more than I.

"Then came a letter, mailed in New York City. Her baby was born and had been adopted. He would be safe, she said. And she was dying and wanted to say good-by. 'If you love me, don't try to find him,' she said. And there was a penciled note, unsigned, at the bottom. 'The writer of this letter died one hour ago. She asked me to mail it.'

"I went away. I lived in Europe. But I know he tried to find her and failed. He didn't believe she had died. But I knew. Madeleine was gone. And it was only last year, Becky, when you spoke suddenly in the ward, that I knew that she had fought to protect you from our blundering stupidities to the very end. You were 'the boy.' She wouldn't risk saying 'my daughter, my little girl,' for fear it would be a clue. She had probably given the letter to some head nurse, asked her to keep the secret. Or perhaps to a priest. From what you tell me now it was a month old before it was mailed; perhaps that was part of her plan.

"And now I think," ended Stephen with a great breath of relief, "you know all that I know. A strange, strange story, but it brought you to me in the end, and I thank God for it.

Whatever you do, Becky, wherever you go now, I can make things easier for you. And one more thing," he said. "Don't be in too much of a hurry to judge Laurence. After all, Fox has been very kind to him. It was natural for him to see things in Fox's way."

"They were trying to play a practical joke on you, Doctor. They were counting on my marrying Laurence without your knowing it, and on taking Gibbs and me away from you, just as he took my mother! He's—he's sinister," Becky said, shuddering. "He's dangerous! And yet," she added in a whisper, with a sudden pitiable air of collapse and tightly shut eyes, "he's my father! Isn't it strange? Isn't it *strange!*"

"You'll have quiet weeks at home, time to think it all out," Stephen said, his fingers firm and warm on her languid hand. "They can't touch you, you know. You're of age, married and with a child, and your destiny is in your own hands. It isn't as if you'd been discovered when you were a little thing, taken away from your father and mother then."

"No, no, no, and I'm grateful for that!" she said fervently. "But—but suppose I had secretly married him this spring, and we'd gone down the Island to live, and then I'd found out! They wouldn't have wanted me ever to see you; that would have been part of the plan."

"But if you loved him, loved Laurence, Becky, you'd not have minded that."

It was suggested mildly, almost timidly. Becky answered with sudden force.

"But I don't! Or at least, if I do, it's all mixed up with not loving him but loving"—she floundered, looked at him for help—"with loving this house, and being here, and not worrying about money . . ." She began again. "These last few days—oh, for a week, maybe—I've been feeling that I didn't want to go too fast; I didn't want to promise! You see," Becky went on, "Laurence was the first man I met after the—the nightmare of Rheingolder's and the hospital, and immediately—immediately he took possession of me; he was definite and I was flattered and excited. It was all like a happy dream!

"And now I'm sorry to hurt him. It's just another of the stupid things I do! But I'm going to write him as soon as I get home and tell him it was only part of the wonderful—the wonderfulness of coming here, belonging here! And then," Becky finished, looking straight into her benefactor's eyes with her own shadowed amber ones, "I'm going to be at home for a long, long time! Years, perhaps. It isn't going to be Europe, it isn't going to be Hillover. I've not earned that.

"I've a husband," she presently added, as he did not speak but sat holding her hand in his, his steady look upon her. "And being here with you and Mrs Lee has changed what I feel—about him. I don't mean that I ever could love him again; I don't mean that I think he treated me fairly. It's not that. It's that I've come to see that we can't run away from things; there's no satisfaction, there's no dignity in that. It might be that I'd have to go away with Gavin, wherever he had a job, make a home for him, be a wife to him. That's what I bargained to do.

"And it might be ten years, it might be twenty, before I could come back to Hillover," she went on in a lower tone, her fingers gripping his tightly now. "If he wanted to leave me, if there was another woman, I'd come straight as a bird. But if he wanted me, if he needed me, then it might be for most of my life!"

"It won't be that," Stephen said, clearing his throat.

"I know it won't be! I feel that it won't. This is home to me, as no other place I've ever been in has been home. The fires, and the wide window sills, and the snow coming down over bare trees, and the—the feel of it is all in my blood. You met my mother here, you were married here. I don't know how long it will take me to get back, but sooner or later I'll get out of the car at the door and hear Carrie-Sis say, 'Yo' ole room is waitin' for yo'!' And then I'll never go away again. So you see—you see, you win out in the end, Doctor," Becky faltered, her eyes brimming. "Duane Fox doesn't have the last laugh after all!"

The man spoke slowly, quietly, his thumb moving on her hand.

"I'll be waiting, Becky."

"And you think I'm right to give Gavin his chance?"

"I don't know, dear. I suppose so."

Silence. Presently she said:

"What time should we start for town?"

"At nine, we said. It's after eight now. Do you want to dress? I think Carrie-Sis has done most of your packing."

Becky sat up in bed and put her hands to her disordered hair. The short sleeves of her nightgown fell away from her young smooth arms. Her eyes were still ringed with the shadows of fatigue and tears, but her face was flushed with apricot color.

"You know that I love you as no woman ever loved a man before, don't you?" she said.

Stephen Dinsmore said nothing. He stood looking down at her for a moment with a strange expression on his face. Then he turned and left the room.

CHAPTER XXXVI

SHE HAD NOT BEEN at home ten minutes before she felt that she had had the cream of the news and that all the strain of meeting and of explanation and apology was over and forgotten. Her father met her at the train, her mother in the side yard where the car stopped; there were tears in Spencer Gibson's eyes as he kissed her at the train and picked the small boy up in his arms, and when Sarah knelt to envelop little bewildered polite Gibbs in a great embrace, she was crying.

But the first emotion of meeting passed quickly, and as the familiar kitchen odors came to Becky once again and she tied a great blue apron about her waist and proceeded to lift steaming asparagus from the pot to the toast-lined platter, she felt as if she had never been away.

The boys came clattering in to lunch; Gibbs, potato and spinach and mashed prune sauce wiped from his serious, rosy little face, was taken upstairs for a nap; Spencer went back to the store when the school bells rang again, and Becky and her mother settled down to the business of dishwashing and gossip.

The day as she had seen it from the car windows on a heart-shaking morning had been flooded with bright sunshine on new green fields and mustard tops and the snow of prune orchards. But in the afternoon clouds gathered, and the two women, when the last spoon was dried and the last crumb swept away, sat on in the warmth and coziness of the kitchen, talking, talking, talking.

Sarah was knitting busily. To Becky her mother seemed older, grayer, changed somehow, completely the farm wife. Had she always talked in quite this way, with the careless "ain'ts" and "don'ts" and "my lands"? Well, perhaps she had. In any case, Becky rapidly lost all sense of strangeness in it and was listening, talking, interrupting, smiling sometimes in the old way.

"Well, Beck, I don't see's you could believe that if you read it in a book!" was Sarah's comment when the story had been sketched. "So it wasn't her husband your mother was afraid of, but the man she'd run to!"

"I come rightly by my runaway blood," Becky said rather sadly.

"And this Doctor Dinsmore—he sounds so nice—what on earth could she have had against him?"

"Just that she didn't love him. And she did love—she'd loved for years—this other man."

"Your father."

Becky winced.

"I hate to think he's my father. I hate to have anything to do with him!"

"But you do like Doctor Dinsmore?"

Becky narrowed her eyes, looked into space.

"I wish you could know him, Mother. He's so simple and quiet, and he works so hard that all the rest of his life has to be really resting, operas and symphonies and Shakspere," she said, talking to herself rather than to the other woman. "Everyone adores him; he's got that—that authority about him that makes you know when he comes into a room. Men ask him his advice, and hundreds—thousands of his patients feel that he has saved their happiness as well as their lives. They're wonderful people—the Hydes and the Dinsmores and the Frelinghuysens; they've been statesmen and ambassadors and judges ever since there was an America. And you feel it in—in Doctor Dinsmore."

"If he wasn't old enough to be your father, looks like you'd be in love with him, Becky," her mother said with a shrewd look.

"I hope that 'll save me!" Becky said dryly.

"You *hope* it 'll save you?"

"Yes. I'm not good enough for him. Nobody's good enough for him," Becky explained.

"And you're married."

"And I'm married, of course." It had to come. They must cut to the cankerous heart of it sooner or later. "Tell me about Gavin," Becky said bravely, locking her hands before her on the table, facing her mother.

"Well, Gavin's doing real well!" Sarah said with obviously forced enthusiasm. Gavin's name had not been mentioned previously; Spencer had made no allusion to him. Becky's long recital of her adventures, of Rheingolder's and Lincoln Hospital, Hillover and Florida, had not included any references to him.

At her mother's first phrase her heart sank. He was doing well; he was still in the picture. Becky had not realized until this moment that she had been secretly hoping that Gavin had disappeared, had been disgraced in some way, had definitely widened the breach between them. Evidently it was not to be that way.

"He's here in Salletts?"

"Off and on. I believe he's off with Harry Grace now. They've got a cabin in back of Huntington Lake somewhere, and he didn't say when they'd be back. Gavin worked real hard on the school census," Sarah went on, "and he was out at Lenharts' helping with the books most of December. Lenharts' went through liquidation or something, and they've sold the factory. Then Gavin went down to the city for a spell, but now he's off with Harry. He made good money last summer, taking parties through the Sierras, over Muir Pass and up to Granite Basin, and you'd laugh to see him put it in the bank and tell Dad he was saving up so's he could go get Becky and the baby. But I don't know but what he

spent most of it playing cards and trying to make more!"
Sarah finished with a philosophic shadow of a laugh.

"It's a terrible problem," Becky said somberly.

"Well, folks round here really like Gavin," Sarah said
encouragingly. "Seems like he's pulled himself together and
determined to settle down at last. Of course he didn't know
you were coming back, Beck, or I believe he'd have been here.
But all his talk lately has been about when Becky comes
back."

Becky was staring into space with darkened eyes.

"What 'd you tell people, Mother, when I went away?"

"Why, Gavin came right here, Beck, and he and I and Dad
had a regular council of war about it. We thought we'd hear
from you, and that you'd come back. Gavin suggested that he
go away for a while, too, and we could tell folks that you
were trying your luck in the city. So I'd tell anyone who asked
me that you were all trying to work the thing out, and I never
let on how worried Dad and I were.

"Well, in a few months Gavin showed up again; he'd been
sick and had some bad luck and I put him right to bed. After
that I didn't make any explanations at all; I let 'em think
what they wanted to think. Now and then one of the women
at a cake sale or apron sale or something would ask me what
I heard from Becky, and I'd say I thought you were working
a little too hard and that I wasn't a bit pleased with you being
away so long, and they knew I was as much in the dark as
they were. But nobody said much."

"I'd nothing but bad news to write you," Becky said
slowly, still looking away. "Life is terribly hard for a woman
with a baby and no training! I always thought I was equal to
it, that I was beating it until quite suddenly when Gibbs got
ill, when I saw him playing in a dark winter kitchen with his
poor little hands chapped and his little nose wet. Then I got
suddenly, frightfully scared that it was beating me! And it
came pretty close to beating me."

"Well, it's over, and you're home again, and I believe you've got a much better husband than you had when you went away. And if Doctor Dinsmore does as he says, and you have a regular income of your own, Becky, there's no reason in the world why you shouldn't take one of those little places in the Bruce Salletts Memorial Park," Sarah said cheerfully. "Dad says it sounds like a cemetery, and I b'lieve they're going to change the name to Bruce Salletts Hampton Court, but you wait until you see those houses! Electric refrigerators and indirect lighting and hardwood floors and two baths and patios. Kate Seagreen and I walked over there after club on Tuesday, and I declare—— That's Gibbs crying, isn't it? You'd better go up!"

The old gray hopeless feeling was creeping in with the afternoon fog. There was no world outside of Salletts, the little mining town wedged up against the high blue eastern mountains that had been forgotten for so many years, and that trickled a feeble tributary of pears and apples today into the world's great fruit supply.

Becky picked up the red-faced, perspiring, tearful little boy and put on his small buckskin shoes and brushed his thick mop of dark hair. They descended to Grandma's kitchen, and Gibbs drank sweet rich Jersey milk and stared over Gary's old mug at the stove and the sink and the windows and the fascinating mysteries of the closed pantry door. Everything smelled and looked and sounded just as it used to smell and look and sound. Foggy spring stillness over fruit blossoms and lilac out of doors, the occasional forlorn caw of a chicken or honk of a motor horn the only sounds from outside. Everything purring within, cats and stove and the chicken stew that was bubbling slowly on the stove.

She might have been a little girl of ten again, home from school jaded and hungry after the long walk and the long hours, drinking milk and talking to Mother in the kitchen.

Gibbs approved of the ranch. He went with his mother

through quiet afternoon stillness to the barn and hunted for eggs. He saw the cows milked by young Knut Pedersen. He was held firmly on the top rail of the corral fence to watch the great horned creatures file out again toward the new sweet grass. His four young uncles made much of him.

"Grandpa, I yike dis place!" Gibbs said, friendly and entertained by the kitchen confusion, on Spencer's knee.

"We like you too, sonny," Spencer said. "I guess you've come back where you belong!"

"What shall I do?" Becky thought as she laughed and chattered and explained, as she fitted herself once more into the home pattern that seemed to have grown so tight, so narrow, so dull. "God, help me. I can't do this alone. Help me!"

And every hour was like a fine impalpable net, tightening, tightening about her, binding her closer and closer to this world that had once been hers, and to which her soul could never belong again.

CHAPTER XXXVII

THREE DAYS LATER Gavin came home, pathetically pleased and surprised to find his wife and child there and in such good health and spirits.

He arrived just before supper, looking browned and well, and seeming in manner and aspect somehow more definite than Becky remembered him. He sat on the old kitchen settle, talking of his stay in the mountains and making overtures toward Gibbs.

"If I don't pay any attention to him he'll come round," Gavin said, and he was right. Gibbs was presently on his knee, playing with the big elk tooth on the gold chain and entirely reconciled to "Daddy."

Dinner went off pleasantly enough; afterward Gavin and Spencer played dominoes. The older boys were away; the younger ones did their homework in the old fashion while Becky and her mother cleared and washed dishes. Sophy had long been gone. Sarah was doing all the housework herself. There was nothing to it, she said. The boys were trained to hang up their pajamas and leave the tub clean, and on ordinary days nobody came home to lunch.

When they all broke up, before ten o'clock, Gavin came upstairs to Becky's room.

"I believe you're sleeping upstairs with the boys, Gavin. Mother moved the other bed out to put the cot in here."

"Gosh, I know that!" Gavin laughed and lighted a cigarette. "You're terribly afraid I'll stick around too long!" he said in amused scorn. "But the truth is, I don't think you've given me a square deal, and I don't care who knows it!

Running off with the kid, leaving me holding the bag; it was a hell of a note!"

The old blustering, whining tone. The old skill in laying all the blame on her. The old necessity on her part, if she spoke at all, of rushing the war into his camp, pouring out the stored anger and resentment of the years, bringing up his defects and injustices, one by one, talking him down.

"You didn't support me; you gambled and drank; you borrowed money from my father and from my friends . . ." It could go on forever. A long story.

But she wouldn't begin it. Instead she said patiently:

"I was ashamed to go on here as we were, Gavin."

"How d'you mean, *we?* I was trying hard enough for a job!"

"Gibbs and I."

"Oh? Oh! Well, then why the hell didn't you tell me you were worried?"

No use following this line. Rebecca was silent. In one minute the interval of more than two years was bridged. Gavin was just what he had always been, the situation unchanged.

But Becky was changed, and she felt the change within her. This was exactly what she had come home to face. She had a despairing feeling that she couldn't carry the thing through, but she could try.

"You've been making trips through the Sierras, Gavin? Was it fun?"

"It wasn't fun at all. It was damned hard work. But I had you and the kid to think of, and I took what I could get! I understood from your mother," Gavin went on with a slight change of tone, "that this man in the East, this doctor, has fixed you up with some money. How come?"

"Yes. He was very generous. When did Mother have time to tell you that?"

"She didn't tell me. I heard her telling your father, just before dinner. Why? Weren't you going to tell me?"

"Oh yes, of course. Of course I was! But there was so much to talk about, and all the others were there."

"Is he so terribly rich?"

"Doctor Dinsmore? Yes, he's rich."

"And what does he get out of all this?"

"I don't understand you." But of course she understood him, and she went on without further prompting. "He knew my mother, Gavin. Mother says she told you that I was adopted, that she and Dad didn't know anything about my people. He did; he recognized my voice, and he says I look like my mother."

"That wasn't all he had to go on!" Gavin opined shrewdly.

"Yes, it was. There was no other proof."

"Then he's your father himself!"

"No. I asked him that." Becky's manner was quiet, weary. Gavin abandoned the investigation, frowned thoughtfully as he rubbed out his cigarette on the soap dish that still embellished Becky's old washstand.

"So you're fixed, Beck?" he said.

"He called it 'a very modest little income,'" said Becky.

"Well, I hope to God you're going to settle down now and give me a chance to know my own kid," Gavin said. "There are an awful lot of darned nice little places in this town, and with what you've got we oughtn't to have any trouble. You've kept your folks guessing long enough, and I've felt like a fool when people asked me where you were! The Joe Ferattas have got a place out in the Bruce Salletts Park, and I'd like to be out that way. You've had your fling, Becky, and there's a lot of husbands would want to be pretty damned sure what it was all about! But I guess we can call it quits. Sue Varney was telling me the other day that before you got out you went in to talk to Judge Miller about a divorce. I told her it was the first I'd heard of it! I said, 'She hasn't got a leg to stand on, as far as divorce goes!'"

Becky was hardly listening as the stream went on and on.

Her thoughts flitted to Hillover, solid and splendid among its great bare trees, with the frozen water at the foot of the lawn and the soft lights indoors glinting on lines of books, on mellow old rugs, on the gracious curve of stairway.

She thought of Europe, of a scientist only too eager to share its marvels with a woman and a small boy. Paris with the trees green in June sunlight; the Villa d'Este with the lake rippling in opal magic to the edge of the terrace; glorious London with sunset light touching the crouching lions of Trafalgar Square.

She thought of New York's grimy streets, of her breathless triumph when she had thought that she could conquer them, of the dark apartment house in the Bronx, and Mae Devvins' small pale dirty babies squirming in a kitchen, and little Gibbs sneezing and coughing croupily among them, Rheingolder's, crowded and hot and scented with some sweet stifling disinfectant, and the mingled smells of dyed wool and wet mackintoshes and cheap perfume and unwashed, overpowdered women . . .

"So what are you going to do about it?" Gavin was demanding in triumphant conclusion. He had evidently been making a telling argument. "Your friend wouldn't be so pleased about that!" Gavin said.

She knew she shouldn't ask it, but it was asked. "About what?"

"About my suing him for alienation of my wife's affections!"

Becky laughed. "He wouldn't care at all."

"This business of giving a married woman an income—it don't look any too sweet, if you ask me!" Gavin's tone was mild, slightly injured, not that of a man who believes what he implies.

"I suppose I could refuse to touch the income?" Becky said idly.

"I thought you said it was because he had known your mother, loved her, maybe?"

"I did."

"Well, then why shouldn't you use the money?"

"I'm asking you."

Becky was not looking at him. She stood at the window, looking out at the silver moonlight that flooded the yard and dripped in shining fringes through the oaks. She spoke quietly, her face half turned, her tone not so much critical as bored and weary.

"So what are you going to do?" Gavin repeated his question after a moment of silence.

"I don't know, Gavin."

"How do you mean, you don't know? You're going to stay here, aren't you? After the way you've treated your father and mother, to say nothing of me! Honestly, Beck," Gavin said, changing suddenly to his winning, attractive voice, coming to stand behind her at the window, "that wasn't square. Honest it wasn't! It seems to me you ought to settle down here now and give them and the kid and me a break."

"I don't know what I'm going to do."

"Well, I'm going to stay on here," Gavin stated flatly, "and my kid stays with me. If you're going to keep running away you haven't a leg to stand on! I want a home and I want Gibbs. I know I've kind of thrown you down, different times, but that's past. There's no use hauling up the past."

He walked to the crib, looked down at the sleeping child. Gibbs was lying on his back, his exquisite small face flushed with sleep, his silky dark hair loose on the pillow. Becky held rigidly to modern theories of keeping toys and sleeping hours at wide distances, but her mother had put Gibbs to bed tonight, reveling in the half-forgotten luxury of having a baby boy in the house again, and tightly with one small square hand Gibbs clasped his velvet elephant.

"I'm crazy about him," Gavin said.

Becky said nothing. She had turned back to the moonlight and the tall trees that were silvered by it and the dim high line of the mountains, furry and misty and floating far beyond.

"I will lift up mine eyes to the hills whence cometh my strength," she thought. "God, help me!"

"So now you know where I stand!" Gavin said, his tone faintly threatening, faintly indicative of a desire for peace. "What did you say?" he asked at the door.

"I didn't say anything."

"Well," he said, lingering, "I just wanted you to know how I stand. It doesn't help me a bit here in town to have my wife and kid wandering all over the country making all kinds of friends! I don't say it wasn't a decent thing for this doctor to do, but you don't know but what he took this money away from your mother years ago and really owes it to her. He might have. I don't mean stealing, but investments or something like that. Maybe he sold a piece of property for her and couldn't find her to hand over the money. Anyway it's fishy, giving you money because he liked your mother! But I don't care. It 'll help us get a start here, and, Becky, once we're started we're going places, believe you me! I've got a lot of friends in this town—I handled a loan for your father a while back . . ."

And again her thoughts came back from far places to hear his half-warning, half-anxious query:

"So what do you think you'll do? The sooner you make up your mind the easier for everyone."

And again Becky answered mildly, speaking over her shoulder:

"I don't know."

"Good night!" he said. He came across the floor and kissed the back of her neck. Then he was gone; she heard the door close behind him.

Becky went and stood looking down at Gibbs. Her face was expressionless. She was conscious of no particular emotion, only of being very tired. She began slowly to undress.

In her wrapper and slippers, with all the lights out, she went to the window again. The moon was wheeling low in the sky; far overhead there was a spread of cold flashing stars. Against them the silhouette of the mountains rose black and solid and protecting.

She sank to her knees, her arms crossed on the window sill, her tired forehead pressed against the cold glass.

"I don't know what I'm going to do," she said aloud. And almost automatically the words followed: "God, help me. Help us all! Show me what to do and I'll do it, no matter how hard it is! Don't let me make any more mistakes!"

CHAPTER XXXVIII

ON ONE of the wildest winter days that Rebecca Gibson Flood had ever seen she looked from the kitchen window to see a station taxi valiantly battling with wind and storm on its way to the ranch-house door.

Sleety rain was sweeping over the world, shutting out the mountains, bending and cracking the high branches of the oaks and maples in the yard, beating the churned black puddles of the corral into deeper blackness and treacherousness, smiting the ranch-house roof with white whirlwinds of water that dripped and gurgled in the leads and spouted in gutters.

But the kitchen was warm and bright. Becky, suspecting that it was Gavin who chose to arrive in this fashion rather than walk the two miles from town, flung open the door and called out a welcome.

"Come in! Isn't this terrible? Look out for dripping on my floor."

"I'll have practically to undress out here unless I'm to ruin everything!" the newcomer gasped, shedding a great raincoat and flinging aside his hat as he came to the doorway. Becky took one look at him, clutched at him, her own breath gone.

"Steve—Doctor Dinsmore!" she whispered, her face suddenly flying April colors.

"Becky!" he said, laughing, his cold cheek against her own for a second, his arm about her. "Let me come in! How cozy you are!"

"But you—*you!*" Becky was incoherent with amazement

312

and joy. "To come in out of this—this hurricane!" she said. "You're soaked!"

"No; not a bit. Not a bit wet, really. It was just outside— I stepped right from the train into the taxi. Well, Becky, Becky, Becky, let me look at you! And this is Gibbs!"

They three were the only occupants of the kitchen. Becky put Stephen into her father's old chair and drew Gibbs to his knee.

"Isn't he lovely? Isn't he brown?"

"My dear, I can't look at anything but you. You're lovely and brown too! Lord, what smells so wonderful? I don't believe I had any lunch."

"Doctor, why no lunch?"

"I was busy. I operated at the Stanford in San Francisco this morning."

"And that's what brought you out!"

She had forgotten how utterly charming he was, tall and lean, with his plain, keen, eyeglassed face—or was it handsome? She never had decided; it didn't matter. The hands were as keen, as fine and clever as the eyes; the voice was like no other in the world. Becky could not feast her happy eyes enough on the sight of him.

"No, that isn't what brought me out at all," he said, not looking at her. He was looking at Gibbs, whose small square shoulders he was fingering with the doctor's experienced hands. "He's in great shape," he said. "So you've got a railway, have you?" he asked.

"It's Andy's," Gibbs answered seriously.

"My brother," Becky said. "Oh, Doctor, how good it is to see you!"

"I thought you called me 'Steve' when I came in?"

"I did, but I didn't think you heard me! Tell me, tell me, how is everything and everybody, and how are you? You're staying? We've a spare room now that Bob and Spin are off at college."

"Not overnight. But I'd stay for dinner."

"I'll telephone Mother; she's at the club, and she'll stop at the Exchange and bring home artichokes and steaks, and you'll eat three times too much! Oh, Steve, to have you here in our kitchen! And Hatsy's fine, and Europe was fine, and Barbara's going to be married?" She could not get his news fast enough. "Not to Larry, is it?" Her face sobered at his nod. "Not really?" she asked.

"I think so. She really loves him, Becky, and she's played about a good deal without finding anyone she likes half as much. He and I had a talk about it. Duane is quite blind now, poor fellow, and won't ever do any work again. They plan to live outside of Paris somewhere, and she'll have enough money to let Laurence do it the way he wants to—picturesquely and decently. Harriet's reconciled to it. Barbara's twenty-six now; it isn't as if she were eighteen. And Barbara," Stephen added with a little smile, "may surprise him more than he does her. She knows her own mind. There'll be no nonsense about it! He'll have to fight to be something more than Mrs Moulton's handsome artist husband."

Becky laughed joyfully as she put food before him. The man began heartily on the cold turkey, the sizzling hot potato cake, the smoking cup of coffee.

"Becky, you're a magician! Tell me about you. Has it been hard?"

"When you've made the supreme sacrifice," Becky said, sitting down opposite him, "nothing is hard. When you've given up the one and only thing you want, then all the little things flock out and begin to show how wonderful they are. Sunsets, I mean, and spring, and just having a clean warm bed at night and a good book. I've everything—except what I want. And I suppose what I want is me—the inside, essential me—and that, not having it, I'm dead, and enjoying all the privileges of a disembodied spirit."

Stephen gazed at her for a long time in silence.

"Your husband?" he finally asked.

She looked up from a contemplation of her linked fingers.

"Is here, and well and busy," she answered composedly. Volumes were unspoken behind the words. The doctor frowned.

"Working, eh? In one of your three letters—you realize I have had only three in a year?—you said he was not working."

"He works off and on. As a matter of fact he and Harry Grace are all agog about some mining discovery they've made up in the mountains. There never will be anything in it, but Gavin talks as if it were a matter of millions, and it gives them an excuse," Becky finished tolerantly, "to go up there continually and camp. He's going again tomorrow."

"You've grown up, Becky," Steve said.

"Have I? I hope so. I have bad times," Becky confessed. "But most of the time I'm happy—way deep down inside me. My feet are on the ground; no matter whether things go right or wrong I'm always sure of that. I'm where I belong!

"You know—I wrote you?—that my father died last March," she said. "It was very sudden. He simply dropped in the store, and never moved or spoke again. Then Mother needed me, and as Gavin was away almost the whole summer it worked very well. He was off on trips with Harry, and we were here. Everything's settled now, and Mother has enough, and she's very happy with Gibbs. So that saved me the decision of moving to a separate place with Gavin."

The doctor studied her with a faintly knitted brow.

"How much of a wife are you to him, Becky?" he asked.

Her color flamed up; she looked at him courageously, answered gravely.

"I am his wife."

"It had to be that way, I suppose?"

"It had to be that way. He was jealous, wretched, argumentative. Just before my father's death he had a talk with me—Dad did, I mean. Gavin wanted Gibbs and me to go up to the mountains for a camping trip; and I made up my mind then to—to stop fussing, to be as generous as I could."

She stopped on a note of timidity, her beautiful eyes questioning. Stephen cleared his throat.

"You were right, of course. And there's been—there's been some happiness in all this, Becky?" he asked hesitantly.

"Oh yes!" she answered soberly. "When your heart is dead you're saved so much pain," she added after thought. "They've all been so happy; we've had so many good times together, picnics and camping and Mother so content! And it was a joy that my father was so happy. When we came back from our camping trip he could see that things were all right between us. We took two of my brothers with us, and they had a glorious time. I knew then—I knew that what I had done was right."

"D'you love him, Becky?"

"No," she said simply, "but many a woman is being a good wife to a man she doesn't love. Oh, I know," Becky went on with the wise smile that he found new and infinitely touching in her twenty-six years, "I know there are lots of women who say very smugly that they couldn't live with a man they didn't love—not as his wife. Well, I'm different. I can. I can give him my full—my full life as a wife, since it means harmony and happiness here. I think there's a lot of nonsense," she added evenly, "about this whole thing. I think a lot of women haven't any code about it at all, haven't common decency about it. Anyway . . .

"Anyway," she added on a different note as Stephen sat watching her and did not speak, "I live for a dream. Beyond all this that I'm doing now there's the dream of an old brick house, painted white and standing up on terraces, snowy terraces, above the water. And inside there's a dream of big fires in old fireplaces and crystal candlesticks and books and

a fire screen with spaniels embroidered on it and a real dog
on a hearth rug, waiting for the doctor to get home. And
when I'm blue, Steve, I simply withdraw into my brick house,
I walk through all the rooms, trailing a velvet gown. I sit
there and talk in the firelight about London and Paris with all
the leaves green, and the Villa D'Este."

"It's all there waiting, Becky," Stephen said, clearing his
throat again.

"I know it," she said in a low voice. "It keeps me happy to
know it." And then, laughing: "Ah, here's Mother!"

Sarah came in, breathless, rosy, packages under her arm.
At long last she faced the man who had searched for so many
years to find out what she could tell him of a frightened
woman in a big city, a woman facing a supreme ordeal alone
and straining all her wits to protect the future of the unborn
child she carried.

They talked and talked, eager to end the long silence.
Becky moved about the kitchen, lighted lamps, introduced the
cold, red-cheeked younger brothers as they came in. And it
seemed to her like a dream.

CHAPTER XXXIX

THREE DAYS LATER, coming out of the Exchange, with Gibbs beside her and with her arms full of bundles, at three o'clock on Saturday afternoon, she was surprised to see Gavin waiting at the wheel of her parked car.

"Gavin, I thought you'd gone up to the camp yesterday!"

"Nope," he said. "Harry's up there. But I stayed overnight at Joe Martin's."

"Oh? You didn't telephone."

"Nope. Going home?"

"On my way." She bestowed her parcels in the back seat, which was already packed with boxes and bundles. "You've put some things in here?" she asked.

"Things Harry wanted." Gavin's hand in its heavy driving glove was playing with the gas feed, but he did not start the car. "I hear What's-his-name's coming back?" he asked.

"Doctor Dinsmore? Coming tonight. And he flies East tomorrow," Becky answered. "He had to go back to San Francisco to see his patient, but she's out of the woods now and he's coming up for dinner."

"On the bus?"

"No; he's rented a car. The driver will sleep at the hotel."

"I see." Gavin stressed the first word as if there were something difficult to understand in the statement.

"Are you coming home for dinner, Gavin?"

"Nope. Once was enough." He was speaking with deliberate rudeness, with a deliberate lack of sympathy. He had joined the family for dinner on the occasion of Stephen's first visit; had been civil, his manner just on the edge of boredom through the meal. Afterward he had said that he must go uptown and had vanished, leaving a much relieved atmosphere behind him. Since then Becky had scrupulously refrained from mentioning Stephen in his presence, had been careful not to ask him how he liked the visitor.

"He's in love with you, isn't he?" he said now.

"Who? Stephen? He—why, no. What would make you think that?" Becky stammered uncomfortably. "He likes me."

"I wonder!" Gavin said dryly. "I thought he was an old doctor with a beard," he went on with apparent irrelevance.

"He's fifty-one—about."

"And a lot more than that!"

"No; that's all. His sister told me in reference to something else."

"How d'you mean, 'in reference to something else'?"

"Well, I mean that she didn't think I was especially interested; she didn't say it just for my benefit."

"But you *were* especially interested, eh?"

"I don't know that I was."

Gavin said, "I see," again, and appeared to ruminate.

"Mother wants these things, Gavin; she's making upside-down cake and everything."

"All right, we'll get started. I suppose she's having a regular party for him? She thought he was just about tops, didn't she?"

"She likes him," Becky agreed simply. Least said, soonest mended when Gavin was like this.

"I've got to go by Sadlers'," he said, "and leave a message."

"Well, I don't want Gibbs out too late in this weather. It feels as if it was going to rain again."

They drove southeast, passing the straggling outskirts of the town.

"So he can afford to bring a car and a man all the way up from the city, can he?"

"Apparently." Gibbs comfortable and quiet in her lap, Becky looked at the cold winter landscape. The little houses seemed to have withdrawn into themselves, shriveled somehow. Bare little yards, garbage barrels with their covers half on, children's red and green wheeled toys abandoned among the frosted toppled chrysanthemums and shrunk rosebushes in the driveways. "How white the mountains are!" said Becky. And then, in sudden suspicion and surprise: "Where are we going? You've passed the Sadler place!"

"I thought we'd go up to the cabin," Gavin said with an unconvincing air of easiness. "Harry's short of bacon and matches."

"Up to the cabin! You mean up at the lake? Gavin, it's sixty miles! We'd never get back for dinner!"

"Then we can have dinner up there," Gavin said, not turning.

Becky was silent a second, choosing her tone. He was joking, of course.

"What do you mean?" she demanded in an unalarmed voice.

"I mean that I have to go up there to get this stuff to Harry. I should have gone yesterday," Gavin said, "and I thought it would be nice to have you and the kid along."

"But, Gavin . . . Mother . . . and Doctor Dinsmore's coming to dinner!" Becky exclaimed confusedly. "I've got to get home by five. Mother wanted to make a celery-root salad——"

"I telephoned your mother and said we'd be back for lunch tomorrow."

"When did you telephone Mother?"

"Before you came out of the Exchange. I was waiting in the car awhile, and then I went in and told Belle Rossiter to telephone your mother in about twenty minutes that we'd gone up to the cabin."

"But, Gavin, you knew Doctor Dinsmore was coming to dinner! He's coming all the way from the city. It isn't fair to leave it all to Mother!"

"She seemed to have plenty to say to him the other night."

Becky laughed nervously, trying for good humor.

"But this is simply *childish*," she said. "Don't be so silly, Gavin! If you had some friend who was coming to dinner do you suppose I'd be so—so simple as to kidnap you and carry you off so you couldn't speak to her?"

"There's no reason why a man and his wife shouldn't go up to their country cabin overnight," Gavin said stubbornly.

"Well, of course there isn't! But without any warning . . . no nightgown for Gibbs . . . and on the night that company's coming for dinner—it's so silly! Turn the car around now, Gavin, and be sensible!"

"You're in love with him!"

"Gavin, that's a foolish way to talk. I like him tremendously. I've every reason to. But he goes back to New York tomorrow, and I'll not see him again! Do be sensible about this."

"No," he said, somewhat shaken by her tone of coaxing, but still driving steadily toward the white-capped dark line of the eastern mountains, "I've got to get up to Harry. I promised to be there yesterday, and then like a fool I got into a game out at Martin's. I slept today until noon, and by that time Harry was telephoning about every five minutes to know where his tobacco was. I've got to get up there. I'll tell you— I'll bring you back after supper."

"Gibbs out after dark, a night like this! It feels as if it was going to pour!"

"There's only a few miles of it that's bad. And Harry had no matches and no tobacco. He was crazy. His car isn't working, and I came down Wednesday and said I'd be right back."

"You didn't have to take me," Becky thought of saying. "I'll get even with you for this piece of nonsense! Robbing me of my last time with Stephen!"

Such remarks, as she had reason to know, would have no effect whatsoever upon Gavin, unless indeed they settled him still more stubbornly in his course.

"I think you're behaving very childishly," she said aloud presently. "But there's no use quarreling about it. If you choose to drive on and on I can't very well jump out of the car with Gibbs in my arms. I'd have been delighted to go up to the cabin with you any time you wanted to go. I love the mountains and I've never been up there in winter. But this is just—*silly*. And someday when you very much want me to do something for you—lend you thirty-five dollars to hand over to Joe Martin for a poker debt—I'll remember it!"

For some time Gavin, watching the rising road carefully, opposed to this only the unanswerable argument of silence. After a while he said sulkily: "I'll be damned if I like to see my wife so crazy about another man! 'Oh, Doctor, do you remember . . . ?' and 'I'll never be able to thank you for . . . !'

"All that *gush*," he went on sourly as Becky was silent. "He's supporting you, that's what it amounts to!"

"More than you ever did!" she thought. Aloud she said: "He knew my mother."

"I'll bet he did!" Gavin agreed in a tone of little-boy defiance.

"You're a poor unfortunate creature, Gavin," Becky said in her heart. "Your mother divorced your father when you were four, and put you with an aunt who whipped you. You never knew your father until he reappeared without a job, having served a term for misappropriation of funds. Your mother married a man from whom she was divorced after he'd spent every penny she had and mortgaged her home, and you had to go into court when you were sixteen and testify that your stepfather struck your mother! Everything you learned was smarty and show-off and superficial . . ."

"It's snowing!" she interrupted her thoughts to say suddenly. "Look, Gibbs, that's snow! Do you remember snow in New York?"

"She sure is coming down," Gavin said. "What do you know about that!"

"And we're not halfway, Gavin," Becky said with a touch of anxiety in her voice.

"Oh yes; we've only about sixteen miles now. I took the new cut. Notice how wide it is?"

"I didn't know it was open. I've never been up this way before."

"It's not finished, but you can get through."

The car left clean soft tracks in the powdery softness of the snow. Nothing else seemed to be moving on the roads. Gavin came to a full stop with an exclamation of disgust.

"God," he said, "I got through here Wednesday!"

Just ahead of them in the snowy dusk the new road ended abruptly with a line of planks and barrels and a dim red lantern beyond which was a welter of newly cut churned earth filled with ruts that were frozen stiff. The whole was rapidly whitening under the fluffy, steady fall of the snow.

On the right rose the steep pine-clad bank. There was old snow thick on the trees; now and then a great lump of it slid down with a puff of white, leaving a piny branch bare. On the left the tops of the trees descended steeply to a gorge far below. Everywhere was whiteness, stillness, chill in the thickening dusk.

"We'd better go back!" Gavin said seriously. Becky's heart gave a little twist at the tone of his voice.

"Round up past the Basin to the cabin?" she asked.

"Nope. I think I'd better get you and the kid back to Salletts. She's blizzarding."

"It *is* a regular blizzard," Becky agreed, impressed.

The snow, which had been falling in gentle straight lines that turned and twisted in the gray air, had now begun to drive, and drive fast and thick in one direction. When Gavin got out of the car to get his bearings it plastered his face instantly with white; his cheeks were wet and fresh as he got in again and began to maneuver the car slowly about in a circle.

CHAPTER XL

BECKY'S HEART was singing. They were going straight home. She looked at the switchboard clock: five minutes past five. They would be home at seven, perhaps a little earlier, if they got out of the snow into clearer going; they would come in into warmth and safety and welcome and be given a late supper and explain and laugh and she would see Stephen's eyes watching her again. The bliss of it, the richness of it, shelter and food and love!

"Just keep an eye on the bank there and give me hickey," Gavin said.

"It is hard to see it." She looked carefully. Sometimes little tips of partly submerged pines, showing above the snow, gave her a line; sometimes there was only whirling whiteness over unimaginable space. "Go slow, Gavin."

"I was a fool to try this cut. But I got through here just this week all right!" Gavin muttered.

"It feels bumpy," Becky said warningly. "Heavens, what a smother even a baby blizzard is!"

The scrapers on the windshield squeaked busily. Darkness was deepening, somewhere behind the storm. The headlights threw pink disks upon the blown, slanting lines of the falling snow. Wind was shrieking overhead, high and thin, or perhaps, Becky thought, it was only the gale against the movement of the car. On the engine the wet whiteness fell only to slide and melt away, but the guards and window casing were already powdered deep.

"The snow had begun in the gloaming," Becky said cheerfully.

"I remember that in schoolbooks," Gavin observed between his teeth.

"Gavin, this is merely a suggestion: but we could, you know, we could wait until this lets up a little. We might get off the road, going on this way," Becky said, troubled by his manner.

"We *are* off the road," he answered almost absently, as if his anxieties had long left the initial disaster behind. "We missed it somewhere. She wedged against a stump or something a minute back."

"We're off the road!" Becky's tone was alert, unfrightened.

"I think so. I think we're against a stump. Damn it!" Gavin said the last word under his breath. He got out of the car into the soft driving smother. "My God, you can't see anything!" he shouted, coming to the window to call back to her.

"Get in, Gavin. You'll only get yourself drenched when that melts!"

"It's the damnedest thing I ever saw!" he said. He re-established himself at the wheel, snapped up the switchboard light and turned off the ignition and the headlights. They sat in a little oasis of light and shelter in the midst of the snowy shadows and silences of the great Sierras.

"I suppose we'd better wait. It's the only thing we can do," Gavin said.

"Well." Becky's tone was resigned. The vision of the warm home kitchen, the warm home welcome, vanished.

"Mum, I'm hungry," Gibbs said conversationally.

"Are you, darling? Well, you'll have to wait—— No, I don't see why he should wait!" Becky said. "I've bread here and canned milk. Oh, but we haven't a can opener!"

"I've got a lot of stuff for Harry, but it's mostly canned. Crackers, though, and cheese."

"Well, have you your knife? Could we punch holes in a can of milk for Gibbsy?"

"I'll see what's in the toolbox." They had something to do now. Becky got into the back seat and fussed with grocery packages. Gibbs knelt on the front seat, looking back at his mother's activities. Gavin found a screwdriver and punched holes in a can. Gibbs had the smooth tin top of a one-pound coffee tin for a plate, and ate bread soaked in canned milk and snow. Becky and Gavin took turns drinking canned tomatoes from a triangular jag cut in the can and ate crackers and yellow cheese.

"Keep that tomato can, Gavin. I'm going to see how much of the top I can punch off. I could heat his milk in it for breakfast."

"Breakfast!" Gavin echoed. "This is going to break. We'll be on our way in bright moonlight in an hour or so."

"I hope so. But if we *should* be here for breakfast . . ."

"I wish we had a couple of blankets," he said with an anxious glance in the dim car light at the boy.

"Thank heaven we have one! I'll roll him up very comfortably back here. I think I'll take his shoes off. Gibbsy, isn't this fun?"

"Is this a picnic?" Gibbs asked suspiciously.

"Not exactly. A sort of snow picnic. What time have you there, Gavin?"

"My God, you'd think we'd just moved into a new house!" Gavin said with a reluctant laugh. Becky laughed too. She wrapped up the bread in its oiled paper bag, stored the eatables neatly on the floor. Afterward, when Gibbs was tucked up warmly in the doubled blanket, she crawled over to sit next to Gavin again.

"Any sign of its breaking?"

He flashed up the lights. They showed, as they had showed for two hours, only the steadily driving slant of the snow. Gavin snapped them off again. At his left the window was opened a grudging half inch; even through this the air whistled eagerly and icy cold.

"I believe it would be better to open a window on this side, Gavin. Much quieter. Could we be gassed or anything if we shut it all up tight?"

"Not with the ignition off. Becky," Gavin said, "you certainly are a sport! I let you in for this."

"Well, we'll always remember it!" she said cheerfully. She twisted about sideways in the seat to face him, one elbow over the back of the seat. "Gavin, what do you *think* will happen?" she asked.

"I'm damned if I know." He was smoking a cigarette. "Not much can!" he said. "When the snow stops I'll see where we are. If we're not much off the road we could back up. If we're stuck I can hike over to the nearest pole line and get some sort of a telegraph message through."

"How on earth could you tell them where we are, Gavin?"

"Well, we aren't more than two or three miles back from where they've shut off the new cut, and the telegraph poles are all numbered. They'll find us all right. They'll get a wrecking car in here. Has that kid gone off to sleep?"

"Like a lamb." Becky glanced back at him. "I'd crawl in there with him, but then I'm afraid neither one of us would sleep," she said.

"He's a good kid," Gavin said half aloud. "How long would this food last, Becky?"

"We sound like explorers! Oh—days. It would be monotonous, but we could live. Fifty pounds of potatoes, only no butter and no salt. But matches; we have matches. If the snow stops tomorrow we could start a smoke fire maybe, if we could find some wood that isn't soaked. And you know they'll be after us immediately, Gavin, with planes and guns and everything! That is unless we just tamely back her up tomorrow and get home about eight. This is just as good as a little house; just like being in a little cabin."

On the side on which she had opened the window the air

was warm and still. The snow piling up on the opposite side of the car acted as an actual shield. Becky thought longingly that if she only had a great fur blanket she could have curled down comfortably enough for sleep. She felt chilly and weary, and before nine o'clock was drowsily resting against Gavin's shoulder. Gavin braced himself against the closed door of the car. They dozed uneasily, awakened to shudder in the cold, settled themselves again.

Gibbs slept heavily until midnight, then awakened, crying and alarmed. Becky climbed back to join him, changed the position of everything and settled herself and Gibbs under the blanket on the floor of the car. Gavin joined them and somehow between twisting and napping and awakening they wore away the dark hours and found that the clock's hands stood gratifyingly at seven and that the snow had stopped.

Gavin was out in the drift immediately and Gibbs and Becky scrambled down to join him, to breathe the intoxicatingly pure sweet air and look about them.

The car had indeed left the road, gliding smoothly down over a low bank into a small mountain meadow, cupped between glittering peaks and fenced with pines. Across its level snowy stretches the sunrise of a winter day was sending clean pale orange streaks. The sky was paling rapidly from the opal beauty of dawn into palest blue-white; the sun came over the southeastern range and laid clear blue shadows upon the snow. The top of the car was three inches deep in ermine, the wheels almost buried.

"Gavin, any chance of a fire?"

"Not with everything so wet."

"We could put gasoline on it to get it started."

"Ha!" he said, struck.

"Then I could make coffee and toast. No butter!" Becky lamented.

"What could you make coffee in?"

"The coffee tin. I've just been thinking it out. I could put the rest of the coffee into a bag. We've milk. And we've bacon! Do let's try for a fire!"

They floundered through the drifts to a short slope where young pines grew so dense that the snow had been kept out. Here Becky snapped twigs and Gavin struggled with live branches; they scraped a space of ground clear and put twisted paper bags beneath the branches and soaked the pyre with gasoline. Presently a wild whirl of smoke and flame went up; Becky approached with her coffee tin and the delicious odor of broiling bacon penetrated into the fresh pure air.

"No sugar, no butter," Becky said as they enjoyed the meal.

"You'd picnic in a jail!" Gavin observed admiringly. His cup was a small evaporated milk tin from which the top had been patiently removed with sixty confluent punches; Becky drank from the three-cornered gash in the tomato tin. Gibbs had a great deal of toast and bacon, and drinks of weak coffee.

"As long as we can flounder around in it, this is kind of fun. Gavin, is our best bet to wait until they see our fire?"

"Look here, Beck. See that rock up there? That's right above the rangers' camp."

"Ah well, but it's three miles up!"

"About two. Then down the other side about two, and we strike a telephone and everything!"

"I'd be afraid, Gavin. There'd be drifts over our heads. Or there might be draws or canyons we couldn't get over."

"I wasn't thinking of you. I was thinking that at worst it'd take me two hours to get to the top, two hours down. That's only a mile an hour—— Lord, I ought to make that! Think you could keep up this fire?"

"Well, of course. But it seems kind of silly. They're bound to come up here today anyway!"

"Here's the thing: they mightn't think we'd come up this way. There's a big sign saying that this road is closed. But I got through on Wednesday and I was sure we could squeeze through somehow yesterday. They must have been working on it this week; I thought they'd stopped work on it. But anyway, nobody's going to suppose we ran past that sign, and unless they do, they're apt to think we went off the road somewhere up on the Basin side. They might waste a couple of days scouting around over there."

"A couple of days!" Becky glanced at Gibbs. "He'll get along all right, but this isn't the right food for him," she murmured, "and if he should catch cold . . . I didn't get much sleep last night and I don't want to get too sleepy, for fear he'd wander away and fall in a drift or something."

"Well, I think I ought to do something to get us out of it."

"I know. But suppose you fell and broke your leg?"

"I won't fall and break my leg! I can always get back. Look, it's nine o'clock now. Say I get to the ridge at eleven, I'm down there by two at latest, and we get going!"

"But suppose you get to the top, Gavin, and don't see the rangers' camp?"

"But I will. See that big scar against that rock? Boggs cut that himself when they were surveying last year. There's a fire trail right over the summit and down to the camp."

Becky, ankle deep in soft snow, face grimed and hands sooty and greasy from primitive breakfast preparations, stood staring up at the face of the great spur that rose to meet the whitening sky toward the east.

"I don't see any fire trail."

"It's there all right. And I can't hang around here all day, Beck, cooped inside the car. It's bad for the kid, too. We're in a mess, and the sooner we get out of it the happier I'll be."

"There's no wind," Becky said, reasoning it out.

"Not a breath. But that means it 'll be much colder here tonight."

"I could clear this snow away from the car maybe."

"With what?"

"Well, with my hands. Mother's old driving gloves are in one of the pockets; I could use them."

"I wouldn't move that snow. It kind of insulates the car. You like it, don't you?" Gavin said to Gibbs, who was plunging about happily enough, his face marked with soot and bacon, his wet cheeks blazing red.

"Gavin, shall I give you some bread and cheese to carry in your pocket?"

"I ought to be there by lunchtime. However, do that. That's a good idea. Keep this fire going, Beck. I'll see the smoke even if I miss the car."

"Well, here!" She plunged her feet bravely into the high-piled snow on the running board, cleared the top of the car with great flail-like sweeps of her arms. "There, you can see that square of black all the way!" she said, brushing snow from herself vigorously. "And I'll honk. And don't worry, now. If there's any delay—telephone wires down or something—don't worry. I've got potatoes in the ashes there for his lunch—— I wish we had salt. I don't wonder sheep come down from the mountains for salt licks."

They stood beside the car in the streaming cold sunshine. Their breathing poured like white smoke into the crisp clear air. For a moment an odd sense of the community of interests, of thoughts, of flesh and blood, that is marriage caught at Becky's spirit; her fears went out to protect this man as if he and she had been indeed one body. Lean and worried and needing a shave, buttoning up his thick old coat and turning the collar up to meet his cap, Gavin was oddly, in this second of accentuated sensibility, her husband. She was touched and troubled and a little afraid.

"I don't think—perhaps—you ought to do this!"

He kissed her by way of only answer, picked up Gibbs and touched his face to the cold, rosy little face.

"As long as you think you can get along until maybe this afternoon without me."

"I'm going with Dad!" Gibbs stated, struggling in his father's hold. Becky saw that Gavin was pleased.

"You couldn't, Scout. Look where I'm going to walk!" Gavin said.

The tone was one he had rarely used of late, never to Gibbs. Becky thought that it had more of gentleness, more of fatherly kindness in it than she had ever heard from Gavin before.

"You and I'll wait," she said. They stood together, mother and son, as Gavin started up the hill. But it was cold, standing still, and Becky had gone back to the fire and was wiping pine cones on her skirt to feed the drowsy little flame when she heard Gavin shout. He was perhaps a quarter of a mile away up the hill, but his voice came clearly down to her.

"I think I've struck the fire trail!"

"Oh, goody!" Becky called back, waving her arms.

She and Gibbs were tired and chilly and yawning now, and presently got back into the car, took off their wet shoes, rolled themselves in the blanket and sat talking, Becky sick for sleep but afraid to drop off for fear that the child might slip away from her and get into danger. The switchboard was a danger; the deep snow was a danger; the fire was a third danger. She told Gibbs stories until her head was sunk against his in utter weariness. Presently she struggled out again, shivering and shaking in the cold, and dragged their potatoes from the ashes. She broiled more bacon, mixed more milk and coffee. It was only eleven o'clock but they were both ready to sleep.

She looked up at the sheer rise of the snowy hill. For three or four hundred feet Gavin's path showed flattened and broken through the snow. After that it disappeared between bowed white junipers and she lost it until it emerged, half a mile away, trailing diagonally across a stretch of open, with granite rocks rising in dark islands against the powder that lay like sugar over all the world.

When lunch was over—and between the paucity of utensils, the awkwardness of dealing with snow and wetness and soot and flame, the inconvenience of twigs for broilers and punched tins for cups, it took more than an hour to prepare it—she settled Gibbs flat on the back seat, covered him warmly with the blanket and sat down herself on the grocery box padded with one of the leather seats from the front of the car. She tucked her coat about her as well as she could, leaned her body against the child's body and fell into a heavy uncomfortable sleep.

Now and then she stirred and sighed deeply, readjusting herself from one uneasy position to another. As long as Gibbs slept she must get what rest she could, for she must be on watch during his every waking moment.

CHAPTER XLI

IT WAS DUSK when they fully awakened and Becky, frightened and stiff and cold, thought at first that they had slept into the night. The clock said three; all the world outside the car was whirling grayness again. Three o'clock at night?

No; it couldn't be. She got to her feet in the cramped space. There was but a tiny crack of window open; all the glass was opaque with rime. She felt dizzy and ill but she managed to climb into the front seat and open the right-hand door, the only one not blocked deep with snow.

It was snowing again, harder and swifter than ever. The sweet cold flying flakes caught at her hair and melted wet against her cheeks. Snowing again! But Gavin . . . but Gavin . . . !

Her stupid thoughts cleared, righted themselves. Gavin had crossed the mountain long ago if it was really three o'clock. He would be at the rangers' camp long before this. Perhaps even now the great patient snowplow was coughing its way up the grade.

And her fire would be out, of course. Not that it mattered, for he could not see smoke in this heavy snowfall though the whole mountainside were on fire. Suddenly smitten with panic, she honked the horn madly, three times, four times, stopped when she saw Gibbs's frightened face. Awakened, the small boy burst into tears.

He was uncomfortable, perspiring and prickly from sleep, yet cold already from the air admitted by the opened door. Becky got in again and took him in her lap, comforting him, and they sat for a long while wrapped in the blanket, Gibbs drowsy against her breast, she thinking, thinking.

She must count her provisions carefully now. Two small unopened cans of milk, a loaf of bread and the fraction of a loaf, coffee, potatoes, three cans of beans in tomato sauce, a few crackers, a little cheese, one can of tomatoes, a package of cornstarch, baking powder, matches, about a third of a pound of bacon, a bag of dried apricots.

When the milk was gone Gibbs would have to live on potatoes and beans. That is if the weather cleared and Becky could get the fire going again. Gavin had drained off a little gasoline into the tomato tin; she had cleaned it afterward to use as a coffee cup but she could use it again. This was danger now; her heart beat hard and fast as her spirit rose to face it. Danger! Of course it was. Every spring the rangers brought in the news of travelers lost in the Sierra storms, campers and prospectors who had found a long grave in the snows. Why should she be any luckier than they? But she had the car, she had food and matches.

Suppose when Gavin arrived he had found the rangers' telephone out of order? That might easily be, for the night before there had been that terrible wind. Then whoever was there—there were usually two of them—would have to wait until this snow ended to get down the road to Esterhazy's old place, which was the nearest ranch. Old Mrs Esterhazy must have a telephone; she was a great hulk of a woman, mustached and with a voice like a man's, but she would surely have a telephone as a protection, for she had lived there all alone since May had married and the old man died. He had died in the snow, old Kit Esterhazy; he had gone out hunting for a Hereford bull who had come safely swinging home before his old master had made his first half mile.

Becky's thoughts wandered. She thought of the home ranch in the spring with apple blossoms white and pink against a pure blue sky, with the air warmer—warmer every hour—

and the larks whirling up with their delirious notes pouring
back like scent and sweetness and song and color combined on
a vagrant breeze; she thought of spring when the calves
bawled and butted their angry little heads into buckets of
bran, and when the frogs sounded so clear in the warm
nights—languid, slow-stepping spring over the orchards;
Mission bells and trembling scarlet columbine starring the
wet, scented loam of the deep woods.

And the dear security of home! Why did anyone ever leave
it?

"Mother, I'd like something to eat," Gibbs said politely, his
little mouth close to her ear. "And can we go home?"

"Not until Daddy gets back, my darling. But I'll fix you
some more of that snow ice cream. Would you like that?"

"It would be cold," Gibbs observed with a sigh, and re-
lapsed into silence. She wondered what he was thinking,
what the mind of a four-year-old was making of this situation. Her gallant, glorious little companion of so many adventures had been betrayed into a terrible one now.

"But no worse," Becky's thoughts ran anxiously, "then
taking him into a Bronx flat in a house that smelled all summer long of bad plumbing, and giving him food that was the
cheapest in the city; no worse than those hot weeks when we
used to go up on the roof with the Devvinses and the Fealys.
We've got this car to shelter us; that's more than these travelers who get lost have had! We've got some food. I suppose
we could live for a week on this food.

"They're not coming for us today," she thought as darkness shut down again and the storm's low whispering voice
rose into a whine far above her head. "That's wind blowing
way up in the trees, but I'm glad of it! Wind may blow the
snow away."

Was it only this morning that she and Gibbs and Gavin had
been laughing over a gipsy breakfast in the clear winter sunlight? That he had started up across the mountain with his

confident long strides, turning to wave and shout at her that he had found the trail? It seemed aeons removed from this sober twilight of lonesomeness and fear.

The clock had stopped. She had only the fading dim light to guide her, and when it was gone the endless dark hours seemed to last forever. Now and then she gave Gibbs bread spread with cold beans. At first he did not like it and merely nibbled a cracker and a little cheese. But at some later period, when she started up from light sleep to find him wakeful in his blanket, he ate the despised bread hungrily, and she and he had quite a talk in the black dark that the feeble car light seemed to accentuate rather than lessen.

"Tomorrow, if the snow stops, we'll start another fire and cook some potatoes. I know just where the trees are where Daddy started it, but while the snow was blowing around so fast I was afraid I'd lose my way."

"Tell me about Little Sambo and the Tiger Kitten," Gibbs responded. Becky told him that and other stories, and after a while they both went to sleep again to the moaning and whistling of the winds outside in the dark, and the whisper of snow against the glass of the windows.

They wakened in the dark and ate again and slept again and Becky dreamed dreams of summertime, of hot noon shadows in great woods, of swimming parties to the lake on dry bright moon-washed July nights. Through all her dreams snow fluttered down softly and wind moaned and she said to the girls in Rheingolder's that it was too cold to be drinking so much iced tea—glasses and glasses of iced tea in the dirty dressing room at Rheingolder's, while heat shimmered over the city, and the papers said "no relief in sight."

She would start up and see the dim interior of the car and the sleeping child, and shudder and draw an end of the blanket about her as she changed her position for a little more sleep.

Then it was day; the dark was gone. She could see pearl-gray snow still racing down softly, still curtaining away everything else but its inexhaustible self. Morning had no other evidence than the dull light; no sunshine, no warmth, no glimpse of trees or mountain or sky.

The trees where they had built the fire were only sixty or seventy feet from the car, but she dared not try to reach them through the blinding whirls of wet cold whiteness. If she once lost her way it might be impossible to get back to the car again. The thought made her shudder and she wondered if Gavin had lost his way. But it was not likely! He had had but four miles to walk, a two hours affair ordinarily, and even counting on the steepness of the fire trail and the delay caused by drifts not likely to take him more than twice that. And the snow had not recommenced until late in the afternoon.

She calculated and surmised until her head felt giddy and stupid with thought, dozed, tried to coax Gibbs to eat. The hours went on and on and she came to be only half conscious of them, and of the fall of the snow. Her dreams grew as real as reality itself and it was only when she must prepare food for the child that she fully roused herself. He was very good; he was touchingly, heartbreakingly good. He played with strings, looped them and pulled on them; he climbed up and down on the seats. Now and then he asked her politely if they could go to Grandma's house. "I could walk there with you, I think," he said.

Darkness. Semidarkness. The pearly gloom of the encasement of the storm. Becky's head ached heavily; she slept by snatches, awakened, laid her hot feverish face against the little boy's cool fresh cheek, dozed again. It went on and on; there was no end to it.

"You mustn't get out of the car, Gibbs. Not until Daddy comes. If Mother falls asleep you won't get out of the car, will you?"

Stale bread, and only a little of it. Beans sticky and disgusting in the mutilated tin. A few crackers soft and crumbly. Raw potatoes. The last can of tomatoes gone.

And then, suddenly, at some hour unknown, except that it was day, there was glorious light again! The snow had stopped. The sun had risen and was flashing opals and diamonds from a white world.

Becky stumbled out, Gibbs with her, and stood blinking and breathing deep. "Resurrection!" she said aloud, not knowing that she spoke. "Oh, God, how beautiful the sunlight is!"

She could make her way to the pines now, and tear the snow away and find the ashes of the fire still mysteriously, faintly warm, and on their edges the two or three potatoes that had been baking under the fleecy covers for days and nights. She could drag a light dead tree in from the wood and shake it free of its coating of powdered sugar and drench it with gasoline.

"Look, darling, little bird tracks in the snow! And look, Gibbs, that's a bigger animal, a rabbit or a squirrel!"

Smoke curled and fumed upward, rich gray against a dazzle of marble white. Bacon again and coffee again, and Gibbs tumbling and laughing in clean drift.

"Oh, we'll get through now!" Becky shouted to him. They ate; they drank from the cans that steamed in the fresh pure air. And it was while she was discussing her hot baked potato, her bacon strips and coffee that Becky, electrified into a sudden certainty of hope, sprang to her feet and waved at the plane that circled above them in the bright light, that dropped a bundle, another bundle.

They were too far away for her to find; they fell into the woods, and she was afraid to go seek them. Nothing dangerous must happen further! She hugged Gibbs, and laughed and waited, eyes and ears alert.

CHAPTER XLII

OF THE ACTUAL RESCUE she remembered little, for at the sight of the plow above her on the slope, flinging great fans of loose dry white powder right and left where the road was, at the sound of warm eager human voices shouting reassurance at her through the honking of horns, at the touch of strong hands and the feel of warm blankets, Becky collapsed into something like a half-conscious faint. She could smile, she could cry, she could cling tight to friendly fingers, but she was unable to speak.

When she saw the green ambulance from the Pennoyer Memorial Hospital she laughed feebly. She was not a hospital case!

"My own room and Mother, Steve," she said as he bent over her on the ride home.

"Your own room, dear."

"You didn't go East?" she whispered. He shook his head. Becky laughed brokenly again when they got home, for her brothers, Andy and Gary, had been riding on the running board of the ambulance and yelling triumphantly at old friends in passing. And then in the hot noonday kitchen, she was crying bitterly, inexhaustibly, in her mother's embrace.

Her white bed; her fresh pajamas; a hot-water bottle at her feet. It all spelled peace, infinite, blessed. She could close her eyes and smile as she heard Gibbs's little bicycle squeak as he rode violently up and down in the yard. There was no snow here; there had been rains and the grass was sweet and green; birds were vociferous in the garden.

"What day is it, Mother?"

"Thursday, darling."

341

"And what day did they get me?"

"Yesterday."

"Only yesterday!"

"How's the head?"

"All clear. And no more nausea and no aches. But I feel so horribly tired all the time."

"You'll get rested. After all, you were lost from Saturday afternoon to Wednesday at noon, Beck. That was a terribly long time."

Becky's beautiful topaz eyes were wide open; they watched her mother from a white face.

"Steve?" she asked.

"He went away this morning, Beck. He's flying East. He looked in at you, but you were asleep. He left you this note."

"They found Gavin, didn't they?" Becky asked after a long silence.

"Who told you?"

"Gary. He didn't mean to. But he acted so queerly when he brought up my breakfast that I knew. So I asked him and he kind of blurted it out. Were they blowing the whistles in town last night for that?"

"I guess they were. There were a hundred fellows hunting for him. He was only about a quarter of a mile from the rangers' camp. But they think he might have taken the wrong spur first and got caught in the snow, and gone round and round in circles the way you do."

Again there was a silence. Becky lay thoughtful, her eyes narrowed, her brow faintly wrinkled.

"He would have lived if he'd stayed with us in the car," she said.

"That's what the paper said this morning. Said it was real heroic to risk his life for his wife and child; and so it was, too," Sarah said. "Poor fellow! Old Mrs Esterhazy came into town last night to talk about it. She was the one who saw your fire first, Beck, and phoned down. They all thought he was with you then. She said that he mightn't have been much of a business success, but she didn't believe Gavin Flood had an enemy in this town."

"I don't know that he did," Becky said dreamily. "Unless it was himself," she added.

"I don't like to hear anyone say anything against him," Sarah said firmly. "I'm going in to see him; he's at Flinn's."

"Funeral tomorrow?"

"At ten. Doctor Jenkins is going to pay the last tribute. Millie Scott phoned me awhile back that there wasn't one of the men she asked to be pallbearers that didn't say yes right off. Joe Feratta and all. She asked me last night if I'd like her to 'tend to it."

"I'll go down with you today. I'll get up now. You've been doing everything."

"I've Millie helping me nights. But she goes to the store mornings. I don't know as you're up to it today, Becky. You've had an awful shock, and there 're reporters and photographers from the city here in town, and they had it in the Oakland paper on the front page."

"About Gavin?"

"No, about you and Gibbs living in a stalled car for four days and nights! They got your high school picture and they'll try to get another. Millie and I thought Gibbs ought to go to the funeral maybe. But she phoned the Exchange and they didn't have a thing in black for little boys; all blue, with stars and flags on 'em, and anchors. You've got your good black, and Millie's got two hats for you to try on, and I got you and myself veils. The one I've been wearing is kind of worn . . ."

It went on, the homely comfortable talk, the practical plans. Gibbs came up panting from lunch, his kiss scented with ginger cooky and orange jelly, and went off for his nap. The racket of the boys' luncheon sounded downstairs; a pleasant buttery smell of frying percolated through the house.

Becky lay still, in fresh sheets, soft pillows, warm blankets, steeped in utter peace. She would not begin to think: there were avenues of thought along which she dared not go. There was Steve's good-by note under her pillow. She had read it once, she would read it many times. It was simple and short; it said no word of tenderness according to any common standard. Yet the lines, in his firm swift hand, told her what she wanted to know, and to Becky they blazed and glowed with love. Stephen had written,

MY DEAR, *this is good-by until April. Then I'm coming back and we can talk. It was a wonderful world with your beautiful mother in it, Becky, all those long years ago; it's a more wonderful world today.*

Yours always,
STEPHEN

In the touch of it, in the subdued medley of midday sounds and scents in the house, scents and sounds that mingled themselves with the spring fragrances and bird songs from out of doors, the squawk of a scandalized hen, the creaking of a gate, the hoarse little protest of a motherless calf, there lay the elements of an infinite content.

"I shouldn't wonder if I never had anything to run away from again," Becky said half aloud.